REALM OF SECRETS

A NOVEL OF THE RIANDORI REALMS

Stephanie Briarton

For information contact :

http://www.StephanieBriarton.com

Stephanie.Briarton@gmail.com

Cover design by MarcoLax DZ

Edited by Corinne Nicholson

Map designs by Stephanie Briarton (through Inkarnate.com)

ISBN: 978-1-0878-7823-2

First Edition: June 2020

10 9 8 7 6 5 4 3 2 1

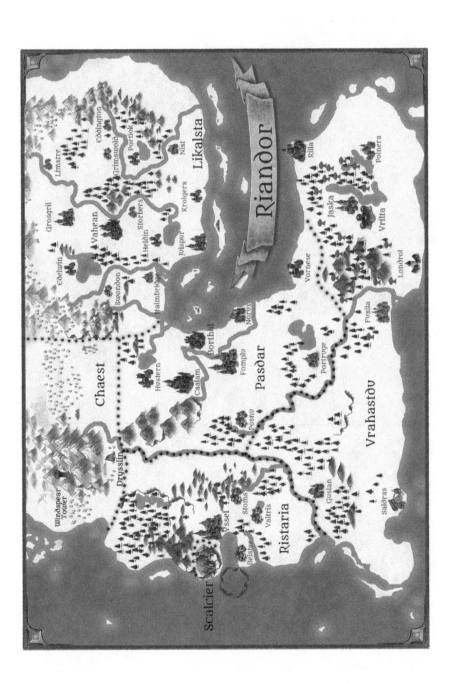

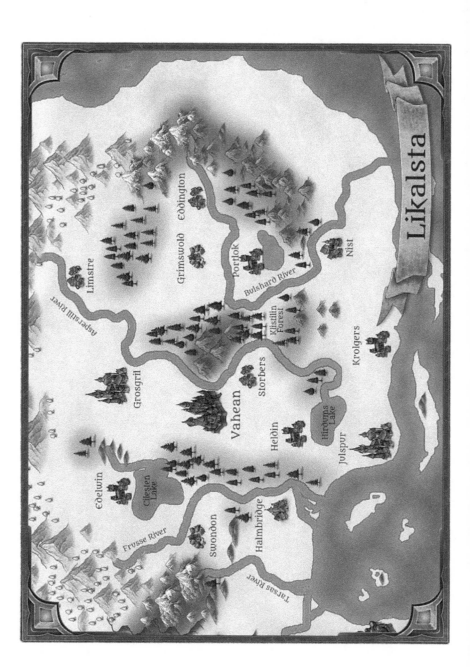

PROLOGUE

D aalok hugged the crying newborn to his chest as he dodged the lord marshal's sword. The blade sliced through the side of his jerkin, barely missing flesh.

His eyes darted around the storeroom for an escape. The lord marshal had him pinned at the back of the room, while the king blocked the only door with his sword drawn. The baby's mother, Cristar, was off to the side, wobbling back to her feet, and Eselle . . .

Daalok's breath caught when Eselle sprinted across the storeroom to their rescue, a dagger in hand.

She charged the lord marshal from behind. He ducked and spun around, then kicked Eselle in the stomach. The blow hurled her sideways, sending her crashing into Cristar. Both women toppled to the hard stone floor. The dagger flew from Eselle's hand and skittered away.

"Give me the baby!" King Vorgal demanded as he watched his lord marshal harrying Daalok and the two women.

"No!" Cristar wailed. She and Eselle scrambled free of each other. "Get my son out of here!"

Daalok gripped the boy securely and glanced at his friends. Cristar, exhausted after just giving birth and defending her newborn, gasped as she leaned against the wall. Beside her, Eselle swayed while struggling to her feet. Daalok had no combat skills, save for a minimal understanding of magic he couldn't reliably use. He edged along the wall, seeking a way around Lord Marshal Silst.

"What now, little mage?" the lord marshal taunted. He made a display of swinging the sword before Daalok, then thrust forward. Daalok leaped sideways and slid farther along the wall. "You can't even save yourself, let alone that little screamer."

Daalok tightened his hold on the wailing baby and rushed to the side. Before he cleared the lord marshal, the sword swept upward inches from his face. He jerked backward, penned in once again.

"You have *nowhere* to run," Silst snarled. "Give me the baby!" His jaw muscles quivered, and the veins in his neck protruded.

"Stop playing around, Silst," King Vorgal ordered. "Kill him and bring me the whelp."

The mage locked gazes with the lord marshal. Daalok shivered at those fierce brown eyes, and a bead of sweat ran down his back. He finally understood what he needed to do, but he was horrible at it. Had accidentally killed Millie's cat and a poor stag while trying to figure it out. But he was out of options.

If he tried, they could die. If he didn't, they *would* die.

Daalok harnessed his fear and focused his energy. With soft whispers, he started his incantation.

"What are you doing?" Silst's eyes grew wider, brighter for a moment before his jaw clenched, and he raised his sword high. *"You can't escape the past, little mage!"*

Daalok cringed and faltered, but he blocked out the lord marshal. From the edge of his awareness, he saw Eselle once again rush Silst. The mage pushed her from his mind, blocked out everything around him—focused only on the pressure building within his chest, the tingling along his skin.

The lord marshal took a mighty swing at both Daalok and the boy.

Daalok released his energy.

Protector, guide me.

The fledgling mage expelled his breath. The open space beside him wavered, transformed into a silvery, rippling pool of soft light as tall as he was.

Holding the newborn tight, Daalok sprinted through what he hoped was a viable portal . . . but not before the lord marshal's blade came down.

***

One Hour Old

Pain shot through his knees and up his thighs when he hit the ground. He thrust a hand against the cool brown grass to keep from crushing the infant. Dew coated his fingers, and he took heavy breaths of crisp, earth-scented air.

"Thank you, Protector, for keeping us safe."

The baby's shrill cries jarred his nerves, but he couldn't fault the boy. He wanted to cry too. Instead, he pushed himself upright and surveyed their surroundings. Tall trees spread across the horizon. They had lost most of their leaves for the season and would soon be bare. Nestled before them sat his home, the small town of Nist. The sight calmed his racing heart and warmed his strained muscles against the cold.

They were safe, but his friends remained in the clutches of murderous men. Once he found a secure place to leave the newborn, he would return for Cristar and Eselle.

He absently put a consoling hand on the baby's chest. The fussing eased, though didn't stop.

Sunlight streamed low over the forest, illuminating the cottages at the outskirts of Nist. A few people moved about in the early hour, but he was too far away to recognize anyone. It was strange what time did to one's memories. He hadn't been home for nearly half a year. The town seemed brighter and smaller than he remembered. Fresh thatch covered Holstin's house, and Lorstal's had a new fence around it.

He rocked the child as he soaked in the sight. "Don't worry, little one. My father won't be happy to see me, but he won't turn us away either."

Only crying answered him. He looked down.

Something red lay smeared across his hands and sleeve, and across the boy. His breath faltered. He snatched the cloth away from the tiny body, trying to figure out whose blood it was, where it came from.

CHAPTER ONE

Eselle gave the man her coin, smiled, and walked away. "Come again, miss," the proprietor called out from behind his worn counter.

Instead of answering, she waved goodbye and left the store, certain she would never see him again. She'd only come into town to purchase new fishing line and get a good night's rest. Though accustomed to sleeping outside, she preferred a bed when one was available.

Halfway to the town's inn, a low, rhythmic thumping came from across the square. A few townsfolk scuttled out of a nearby lane. A bad feeling settled into Eselle's gut. Perhaps leaving town would be better, after all.

Two mounted soldiers burst from the lane behind the locals. They turned toward the townsfolk. Another pair of soldiers rode into the square from a block farther down.

Eselle gave a silent gasp and rushed around the nearest corner. She nearly collided with a wall of sleek black warhorse.

Long legs rose above her as it reared, nostrils flaring angrily. Her blood pounded in her ears as she stared up at the courser's hooves about to crush her skull. She staggered backward. The stallion's forelegs slammed to the ground before her. It stomped and snorted while its rider twisted around to grab for her. Eselle ducked low and darted between the building and horse. Once clear, she sprinted down the street, not daring to take the time to see if the soldier followed her.

Someone behind her barked orders. "Those over there, round them up!"

Eselle rushed through the streets, keeping alert for more soldiers. She needed to get out of Grimswold before it was too late.

After running through an empty alley, Eselle slowed when she approached the edge of a candlemaker's shop. A glance around the corner revealed a pair of soldiers walking toward her. Swords drawn, they scanned both sides of the street. She pulled back, ducking behind a dozen or so crates stacked beside a nearby wagon.

At the sounds of scuffling, she flattened herself against the crates.

"Stop, all of you!" a man yelled.

Eselle held her breath. More commotion sounded farther off. She risked a peek.

A trio of townsfolk had been unfortunate enough to enter the lane with the two armsmen. One of the soldiers grabbed a man by the back of his jerkin, pulling him up short. The man struggled to escape, but the soldier hauled him around and pressed a dagger against his stomach. Eselle gritted her teeth, her hand on her own dagger. With the soldier standing with his back to her, it would be easy to slip in behind him and help the man.

But how many more would be saved if I can make it out of town?

Pursing her lips, she yanked her hand away from her blade to keep from pulling it. The captive lifted his hands, his features drooping, and followed the soldier's directions. While they walked toward the center of town, the remaining armsman chased more townsfolk around a far corner.

The odds of helping anyone were slim, and the risk of capture too great. More importantly, she needed to get information to her brother. If she didn't relay the news in the next week or so, Tavith could find himself in a precarious position, waiting for support which was no longer coming.

Once the street was clear, Eselle sprinted to the next building, a bakery if the smell was any indication. She stayed close to the wall while watching for more soldiers.

Their presence was commonplace among towns closer to the capital. This far out though, they only appeared every few months when the regional commander made his regular rounds. Eselle and her brother's allies had tracked the troops' routines in an effort to avoid them. Since this was the farthest east she'd ever traveled, she hadn't tracked this region herself. Their ally who had, hadn't expected the troops in Grimswold for nearly two months.

What had changed? This particular region was known to strictly adhere to its schedule, but this was the second time they'd caught her by surprise.

Do they know I'm traveling through this area? Or at least someone working for Tavith is?

When she reached the edge of town, neither soldiers nor townsfolk were in sight. The surrounding woods stood twenty paces away, across a grassy field. Eselle grabbed the straps of her pack and ran for the treeline.

Halfway through the field, a gruff voice thundered behind her. "Stop right there!"

Eselle skidded to a halt in the tall grass, grumbling under her breath. "Of all the . . ."

She took a deep breath. Panic would only complicate matters, so she pushed it down deep. With one last look at the thick forest, Eselle donned an innocent expression, raised her hands, and turned.

A young armsman with a crossbow stood before her. He didn't look much beyond a recruit, late teens at most, but he held the weapon with confidence. Though his uniform of red and silver was well kept, it appeared somewhat baggy for his slender frame.

"Where are you going?" He eyed the length of her.

"I was heading home."

His gaze lingered on some areas of her body more than others, the curves of her hips in her tapered trousers, the slope of her breasts, though her straight-lined tunic didn't allow for much shape. Eselle wished she had drawn her dagger before running. It wouldn't be much use against his crossbow, but it would have been something.

"You were running away from town," the soldier said. "Everyone was ordered to the town center."

"I don't actually live in Grimswold. I was only here picking up supplies. Since the request probably doesn't apply to me, I should get out of everyone's way." She pointed over her shoulder as she stepped backward toward the trees.

"It wasn't a request." He lifted the crossbow higher, his gaze steady. Eselle froze. "The commander ordered everyone to the town center." He nodded toward the dagger on her hip. "Toss that over here."

Eselle let out a faint huff, then pulled the dagger out and tossed it at his feet.

The soldier tucked it haphazardly into his belt, opposite his own, then motioned with the crossbow. "Back this way."

She peered toward the town. Raised voices came from somewhere within it, along with an occasional metallic clang and neigh of a horse. Burying her fears, she pointed behind her again. "But my home is that way." It was difficult to keep her hand from shaking.

"And I said this way," he countered with a stern voice. "No one leaves town until the commander says so."

The odds of escaping the armsman were slim, at least not without an arrow lodged in her back. Until another option presented itself, she could at least gather information. "I didn't think you were supposed to be here for a couple months. Why are you early?"

"Get moving." He gave a scowl and another jerk of the crossbow.

With a sigh, Eselle adjusted her pack on her shoulders, walked around him, and headed back to town.

"What are you doing here?" she tried again as they walked. She glanced backward several times, hoping he would move alongside her. If she could gain control of the crossbow, she might stand a chance.

"We always come through here."

Eselle wanted to roll her eyes or huff, but she restrained herself. "Yes, but not usually so soon. You're not due for a couple of months."

The armsman's slender face scrunched up in thought, she presumed calculating the date. "We always come through here," he repeated, then took a few quick steps closer to her.

She shook her head. Even if she couldn't get anything useful from him, he was now within reach.

Another soldier walked around the first building, only steps ahead of them. Eselle's hope of escape evaporated. Or, at least, became complicated.

"What do you have here?" The newcomer was stockier than his fellow armsman, maybe a couple years older.

"I found her running from town."

"Need help bringing her in?" He eyed her as the lanky soldier had, but his perusal seemed more analytical than lecherous.

"Not if that means I have to share her."

Eselle's stomach lurched. Though things like this were commonplace in these outlying regions, she had no intention of being part of it.

The newcomer chuckled. "You don't really think the commander will let you have her, do you?"

"Why wouldn't he?"

"You've been with us long enough. You know how he can be sometimes."

The lanky soldier only shrugged as they escorted her into town.

Grimswold's town square consisted of several simple, one- and two-story wooden structures built around a large open space, with communal cooking stations and a well off to one side. Currently, the most notable thing about it was the nearly two dozen soldiers—a relatively standard size for a regional commander's personal contingent. More soldiers were leading their own captives when Eselle and the two armsmen reached the center of town. A small group of young men, including the man she'd seen captured earlier, stood in front of a dilapidated church. Half a dozen armsmen surrounded them with drawn swords. Dust, kicked up from the road, lingered in the air.

The lanky soldier gripped Eselle's tunic by the shoulder and pushed her ahead of him.

"What's this?" a rough voice called out above the din.

Eselle turned to find another soldier striding toward them. In addition to the standard red arming doublet with silver trim, he wore the chainmail hauberk and leather armor—spaulders, vambraces, and greaves—of the higher ranks.

His dark eyes locked onto her, and she worried he recognized her. While her known description was not always accurate after all these years, or widespread for that matter, the intensity of his gaze made her fidget. When his expression eased, she still felt the urge to back away. Though he might not recognize her now, that didn't mean he wouldn't eventually discover her identity.

Though not the tallest man in his contingent, he still rose above most of them. His distinct lines and strong jaw drew her in, as did his clear brown eyes. Even the wrinkle between his brows, the one she suspected was more from frequent scowling than anything else, only added character to his features.

As he approached, she considered the best way to handle him. Would the innocent act work with him? Or would he respond better to something different?

Then she noticed the insignia on his collar as he drew closer. The circle with two diagonal slashes inside identified him as a commander in King Vorgal's army. Speaking on the king's behalf, he ruled this region. He was the law, for this town and dozens more.

Eselle recalled what she knew of Vorgal's staff, trying to discern which of the six regional commanders he might be. Unfortunately, she hadn't studied the military nearly as well as she had the nobility. Since he only appeared to be in his late twenties, yet had advanced so high, she suspected he was one of the three lower commanders rather than one of the three ranked ones.

He said nothing when he reached them, only glared at the two soldiers who had captured her. She was grateful that glare wasn't aimed at her but worried it might soon be.

The lanky armsman stood at attention. "Sir, I caught her running from town."

The commander remained silent, his eyes moving steadily between the pair.

Straightening, the other soldier chimed in. "So, we brought her back, sir."

"And she looks like a strong male of conscription age to both of you?"

The armsmen glanced at each other. The lanky one who had apprehended Eselle spoke. "No, sir, but—"

"And does she look pregnant to you?"

The soldier took a sideways peek at her. The side of his mouth turned up in a poorly concealed smile. "Not yet."

The commander struck fast. He grabbed the soldier by the front of his doublet and yanked him close. The crossbow hit the ground. Eselle flinched at the suddenness of everything.

Muscles clenched in the commander's jaw as he spoke through gritted teeth. "Does she look like the woman we heard about who is eight months pregnant?"

"I wouldn't know, sir." The armsman's voice quavered. He didn't seem to know what to do with his hands as they twitched at his sides. "I don't know much about pregnant women."

The commander thrust him away, making the young soldier stumble backward several steps. The armsman snatched up his weapon, then resumed his position, keeping his eyes somewhere around his superior's boots.

The commander stepped over to the other soldier. "Do you have anything to add?" The soldier shook his head and wouldn't lift his eyes above the commander's mailed chest. "Then why is she standing here interrupting my day?"

"I figured she had to be running away for a reason," the lanky soldier said. He sounded steadier but kept his eyes downcast. "I thought you might want to question her and find out why."

"If I had to question everyone who ran from my troops, I'd never do anything else." The dark-eyed commander looked at Eselle, scrutinizing her features again. "What's your name?"

"Tarania."

"Why did you run?"

"I was afraid of all the soldiers in town." Eselle added a little quiver to her voice. "I was afraid what they might do to me."

He watched her a moment longer, then nodded and looked back and forth at the men flanking her. "There's your reason. You idiots scared her." He nodded to the dagger awkwardly tucked into the lanky soldier's sword belt. "Is that hers?"

The soldier pulled the dagger out and handed it over. "Yes, sir."

Taking hold of Eselle's elbow, the commander glared at his armsmen. "Get back to rounding up conscripts. And find me the right woman. She'll be the one so large you won't doubt she's pregnant. Now move! We have enough work without you two wasting time pawing at pretty women."

Both armsmen nodded and scuttled away without a word. The commander peered beyond them and gave a firm, more distinct, upward nod. Eselle followed his gaze to a blond, armored soldier across the square. He seemed to be coordinating prisoners but stopped long enough to return his superior's gesture.

Before Eselle got a better look, the commander turned and led her away from the commotion of the town center. His profile was as solid as his grip on her arm. Though she had been hopeful about escaping the lanky armsman if she could get the crossbow, she felt confident she had little chance of escaping the man beside her—even with a crossbow.

Since she hadn't been in Grimswold long, she didn't know where they were headed. A series of two-story buildings stood along one side of the lane, while several squat ones lined the other. The identifying sign above one of the doors—Jail—made her yank back on the commander's grip.

"I'm not locking you up." He didn't look at her, but his voice had softened, lost the sternness he had used with the soldiers. "I just want to talk."

"About what?" She remembered how he'd scrutinized her features. As the jail grew closer, her pulse began a slow, steady rise.

"The real reason you ran from town."

"I told you, I was afraid—"

"Yes, I heard." He finally peered down at her. "That doesn't mean I believe you."

CHAPTER TWO

Eselle gripped her pack with her free hand as the jail loomed closer. Despite the commander's assurance that he didn't intend to lock her up, she bit her lip as they reached the building. He bypassed the dreaded door, his grip tight on her arm, and guided her to the business at the corner of the building. Muscles she hadn't realized she'd clenched suddenly loosened. At least she wasn't being imprisoned. Yet.

They walked through the doorway and into an office. Nothing connected it to the neighboring jail—no door, no archway, or even a pass-through window—which eased more of Eselle's tension. There was only the single door, with a pair of large, dirty windows on either side. Another set of windows hung along the outer sidewall, and a faint mustiness permeated the room. Two well-worn desks sat up front. Various bins and paperwork covered one of them. Three uniformed men sat around the other, which held a pile of money and some drinks.

One of the soldiers rolled a pair of dice. He smiled when they settled, while the other two men grumbled.

Beside her, the commander gave a single huff of amusement. "You two should know never to play against Holker. He cheats."

"I don't cheat," Holker said, then paused. "Often." He broke out in a grin as he gathered up the dice. "I don't even have to against these two. They're horrible players."

"I know, Commander," another soldier said, scratching his thick red beard. "I'm trying to figure out how he does it."

"Give it up, Lew." Holker beamed as he shook the dice. "You'll never outplay me."

Before they could start again, the commander ordered, "Out."

Holker stopped shaking his hand and glanced over his shoulder, seeing Eselle for the first time. The brief leer he gave turned petulant when he turned to her captor. "You said we were done for the day."

"And you are. But be done somewhere else. I need the room."

The winner's petulance returned to a leer. "Of course, Commander." He pocketed his dice and pile of coins.

As the soldiers left, Lew argued with Holker, demanding to know his secret, while the last soldier only muttered about his losses, seeming grateful their game was over.

Eselle peeked sidelong at the man next to her. While he appeared calm, her heartbeat hadn't quite settled yet. He escorted her to a chair at the nearest desk, pulled the pack off her shoulders with one hand, and set it on the floor.

"Now, the truth." With a firm grip on her shoulder, he pushed her down onto the seat, then took a step back and peered at her.

"I already told you the truth."

"You're not from here, are you?"

He still held her dagger. With a grip on the blade, he spun it in slow circles between his fingers, over and over. He paid it no attention. Did he even realize he was doing it? Shifting in her seat, she placed her feet securely in a position to bolt if she needed to. What would be the best way to alleviate his concerns or redirect his interest?

"No, I'm not from here."

"Where are you from?"

"Florial." The village was fictitious, one she had created after she'd been caught in one lie too many.

"Where's Florial?"

"West of here."

"Considering we're nearly at the eastern edge of the realm, everything is west of here." There was a small upturn to the right corner of his mouth as he spoke. He finally stopped twirling her dagger and tucked it into his sword belt, alongside his own sheathed dagger. "Be more specific."

"Um." Usually, saying the name and west made people lose interest. She stumbled over possibilities, then named the first town she thought of which was nowhere near his region. "It's near Halmbridge, but farther down the river."

"How far down?"

"Perhaps a couple of days ride. Three, if you walk."

"What's the population?"

"Around fifty or so, maybe a little more. I haven't really counted." She began to find her rhythm.

"That is, indeed, conveniently small." He clasped his hands behind his back and tilted his head as he watched her. "The problem is, I've traveled that area extensively, and I've never heard of Florial. Why?"

She could have kicked herself for picking Halmbridge. How was she to know his previous travels? It was too late to back down, so she continued to weave her tale.

"We don't have much to offer there, so we don't get many visitors. We're also pretty self-sufficient and keep to ourselves."

"But you left?"

"Yes."

"Why?"

"I wanted to see more of the world, be part of something bigger than Florial."

"You traveled nearly the entire length of Likalsta in search of something bigger?"

She shrugged. "There's a lot to see out there."

"And have you found what you're looking for?"

"Not yet," she answered, with more honesty than he knew.

The commander stared down at her. Uncomfortable with his continued scrutiny, she rose, forcing him to step back to make room.

If he wouldn't believe her, there was another tactic she could try. While it wouldn't make him lose interest, it could at least deflect him from her identity. And if he didn't fall for it, he might become so disgruntled he would cease questioning her.

She wasn't particularly skilled at seduction, only having used it sparingly with more easily manipulated underlings. Thus far, she'd never needed to take things beyond a few kisses or touches, a few suggestive glances. She'd never dared try with anyone of real authority. Not that she usually crossed paths with the higher ranks.

A commander at her disposal could be valuable. If she played things right, he could provide the most useful information they had ever gathered, as well as more tactical favors.

"You seem determined not to believe me, so I won't waste time trying to convince you. I do, however, want to thank you."

His eyes narrowed. "For what?"

"For getting me away from those soldiers. I worried about what they would do to me."

"Really?" He sounded unconvinced.

"You heard what the one said . . ." Eselle dropped her eyes briefly and swallowed pointedly, ". . . about me not being pregnant yet."

"But you're not worried about what I could do to you?" He stepped forward, removing any space between them. "Especially for lying to me? I could arrest you for running from town when I ordered everyone to the town center."

She fought the urge to step back. After all, this was what she'd hoped for. She studied him, tried to read his nearly black eyes and that enticing little corner of his mouth. "I didn't lie. And, yes, you could arrest me," she said. He was well within his authority to lock her in the neighboring cells. "I don't think you will, though."

"Why not?"

Slowly, she raised her hands to grasp the front of his sword belt. "You don't seem overly concerned with a single woman running off when more important things are occurring in town."

"What makes you think that?"

"Because we're in this office instead of the jail, and you're here alone with me instead of having an underling interrogate me." When he didn't reply, she added, "You said it yourself, if you had to question everyone who ran from your troops, you'd never get anything done."

His smile turned devilish. "You are clever."

The sight sent a pleasant tingle down her spine. It was impossible not to return his grin.

Eselle leaned closer. If he wasn't wearing the chainmail, she could play with his clothing. With only the sleeves accessible, her options were limited. Teasingly tugging at his sword belt could work though, so she did. "If you're not going to arrest me, am I'm free to leave?"

The commander glanced down at her hands as they fondled the leather. "That depends."

"On what?" She leaned a little closer while peering up at him.

His gaze returned to hers. "On whether you're telling me the truth." He was harder to distract than any of the soldiers she had previously tried to seduce.

"Do you really think I'm lying?" She ran her hand up his chest, along the cool rings of his chainmail, to the back of his neck, then slid her fingers through his thick, dark hair.

"Yes." His brows drew together slightly. "I'm not certain about what, though."

"Who do you think I am?" She leaned into him. There was a hint of apple mixed with the smell of leather and iron.

He scrutinized each of her features as he had the first time. What did he expect to find? Was he on to her?

"Doesn't matter," he finally said.

Before she could speak, he bent his head and kissed her. She was delightfully surprised by his sudden intensity. He clearly knew what he wanted, and as his tongue wrapped around hers, so did she. Under normal circumstances, Eselle would have pushed a target away by this point, only acted the tease to get information or favors. But it had been a long time since she had been intimate with a man. And the commander was an appealing one to consider.

A few more kisses wouldn't matter, a few more to strengthen her position.

He backed her against the desk and hauled her onto it. Without planning to, she wrapped her legs around his hips as he pressed against her. She wanted to touch him. She pawed at his chainmail, which prevented her from getting to him.

With a grumble at the barrier, she pulled her mouth away. "Why do you have to be wearing this?"

"You're creative enough to switch tactics and try seducing me. I'm sure you're creative enough to get around a little armor." Eselle froze, and he chuckled deeply. "I don't mind. And I certainly won't stop you."

Before she processed his words, he had her tunic unlaced and open. He pulled her shirt from her trousers, slid his warm, rough hand inside and cupped her breast. His tongue licked across her upper lip, and it was all the encouragement she needed.

She tried working her way through his layers. First, the sword belt. She didn't even feel bad when it slipped from her fingers and crashed to the floor with loud clanks. She tried to push the chainmail up and away from him. It proved too cumbersome. His spaulders would prevent her from removing it anyway. They had to go first.

Damn. Why was he wearing all this?

With a smile against her lips, the commander kneaded her breast. "There are easier things to remove if you're so inclined."

That both startled and excited her. Eselle reached under his chainmail and doublet, pulled his shirt clear, and slid her hands across his tight stomach. He was warm and hard, smooth and enticing, and she roamed over every part of him she could reach. His hands slid around and down her back. They slipped into her trousers and grabbed hold of her bottom, pulling her against him. She quivered with the need to touch more of him.

Lost in the feel of strong, warm, masculine hands on her, Eselle sighed and leaned into him.

The door burst open.

Two red-uniformed soldiers rushed in.

"Commander, we're—" one said and then clamped his mouth shut.

Eselle jerked straight in the arms wrapped around her. The soldiers came to an abrupt halt, staring at the couple at the desk. One man stood only halfway in the doorway. After a quick smile from each, they diverted their eyes. Luckily, between her tunic and the commander's body, the soldiers had no view of what was happening.

"We're, uh, ready for you in the hall."

She tried to scramble out of the commander's embrace and off the desk. One of his arms slid around her waist before she could, holding her securely. The other slid enticingly along her side and back to her breast, rubbing a thumb back and forth across her nipple. Without thinking, she leaned into his hand. Mortified at her response with the soldiers present, her eyes darted between the soldiers, the commander, and the door. She didn't know where to look.

"I'll be there shortly." The commander kept fondling her, his steady gaze never leaving her face.

The soldiers glanced once more at the pair before exiting.

The moment she tried to move off the desk, the commander tightened his arm around her.

"Let go," she ordered, her voice soft but firm. She could no longer meet his eyes. Instead, she stared at the insignia at his collar, a visual reminder this might not have been her best idea.

"Is that truly what you want? Because my men have seen worse than this." His arm slid down to her hips, pulling her closer against him as he pressed into her.

"I'm sure they have." The feel of his hand nearly made her sigh. "They also need you." *And I need to get my head straight.*

"They can wait."

"So can this." Eselle looked up at him, then realized her hands were still under his clothes, one splayed across his chest and the other on the small of his back. Startled, she pulled her hands back around, but not out of his clothing. Instead, she ran her fingers across his sculpted stomach. "It would also let us move things to somewhere more comfortable." Though her body approved of the multitude of sensations, the interruption allowed her brain to regain control. She needed to leave before the commander decided to detain her for less personal and more treasonous reasons. The soldiers' interruption was the perfect opportunity to slip away while he was occupied.

The commander gave a husky chuckle before he pinched her nipple. Eselle jumped with an involuntary giggle. He slid his hand from beneath her clothes. His reluctance was evident, but there was also amusement in his eyes, along with that upturned corner of his mouth. Instead of kissing that upturn as she wanted to, she slid off the desk. After tucking her linen shirt back into her trousers, she started retying her tunic.

It dawned on her that she still didn't know his name. Eselle opened her mouth to ask, but he was intently studying her features again. She wished she knew what he sought. "What . . . that is . . ." She brushed a stray strand of her light brown hair behind her ear. "We . . . I should probably be going," she said instead, giving her clothes one final adjustment.

"Not yet." The commander finished with his own attire and retrieved the blades from the floor. "I need to handle a few things. It shouldn't take long. Then we're picking this up from exactly where we left off." When she shifted her feet, he moved in to back her against the desk for another deep kiss. Before her head cleared, he ordered, "Stay here," and was gone.

As the door closed behind him, Eselle savored the lingering sensations. Why couldn't he have been an ordinary resident, one she could risk waiting for?

Gathering her wits, she rushed to the window.

The commander stood on the edge of the porch, calling over two soldiers. He secured his sword belt while they spoke. Eselle grumbled, seeing him tuck her dagger into it. After a moment, he pointed over his shoulder toward the office. Did he just put a guard on the place?

Eselle snatched up her pack, opened one of the side windows—cringed when it creaked—hopped through, and rushed for the trees. With any luck, she would be leagues away before he returned for her.

CHAPTER THREE

Eselle ran for the first quarter league after leaving Grimswold, then dropped to a brisk walk, catching her breath. A few hours later, well after her legs wore out and her lungs burned, she broke for the day.

It seemed unlikely the commander would send anyone after her. From what she could tell, he hadn't figured out her real identity, and she hadn't actually done anything illegal—that he knew of—so sending soldiers would be a waste of resources. To be safe, she made her campsite far back into the woods, well out of sight from the road. A cluster of oaks provided a good canopy where she curled up in her cloak and blanket. Despite the cozy campsite and her fatigue, sleep eluded her. The soothing sounds the regular forest inhabitants surrounded her—squawking, croaking, and chirping—but she couldn't help but listen for anything unusual.

Lack of sleep made traveling the next day arduous, but she managed a decent pace.

A few days later, Eselle reached her destination, the small town of Eddington. The first buildings came into view after she rounded a bend in the road. A broad stream swept past the edge of town, then snaked through a few evergreen trees before disappearing into a thicker part of the forest. With luck, the waters would be teeming with fish so she could replenish her food stores before leaving.

Eselle found most of her food in the wild, and her gear was comfortably broken in, sturdy and well-maintained, so she rarely needed to replace anything. There were other items, however, she needed to purchase—such as a new dagger. She made her first stop the general store.

From what she knew of Eddington, it was the farthest town to the east before reaching the Punstol Mountains. A few small settlements had been established in the mountains, but little else. Unless someone had business there, few people ventured past Eddington. The town had the only market for several leagues, and judging by the number of people milling around, it maintained decent business from surrounding villages and farmsteads.

After leaving the store, Eselle headed for the nearest inn. The proprietor didn't recognize her contact's description, just shook his head and apologized. She thanked him and sought out the next inn, the only other in town. It proved equally unsuccessful. She wasn't surprised she had beaten Jinsle to Eddington, so she rented a room and prepared to wait out his arrival.

Eselle dropped her pack in her room, then settled at a corner table in the main hall. The inn had a handful of patrons scattered throughout the dozen or so tables. A short hallway off to the right led to boarding rooms, and a staircase ascended to more, hers included. On the opposite side of the room, a long, well-worn bar kept patrons out of the kitchen behind it. The back wall held an unlit, over-sized fireplace that gave off a lingering smoky scent.

As she finished her meal, she waved a hand to hail the proprietor.

"Excuse me. Do you know when the regional commander is due? I have some business to discuss with him."

The proprietor was a small man, older in years and with a slight hunch to his shoulders. He seemed pleasant enough, though she rarely saw him speak outside of taking orders and collecting money. That was fine with her. She disliked innkeepers getting too friendly when she wanted to be discreet.

The man took a moment to think before he answered. "I don't believe he's due for another month or more. You may have a long wait, miss."

"It appears so. Thank you." Eselle gave an inward sigh of relief. If the last schedule change had been a fluke, and the commander and his contingent kept to their previous route, she wouldn't have to worry about running into them before she left. She could take the southern road and never see them again. If they'd changed more than their timing . . . well, she'd have to manage.

Eselle studied the growing crowd of townsfolk seeking food and company. With no other business in town, she didn't know what to do with herself until Jinsle arrived. An early start in the morning might help, maybe checking the stream outside of town for fish.

Another idea struck her, and she smiled. *In what devilish ways could Grimswold's commander help me pass the time, if only he was here?*

***

The next morning, Eselle took an indirect route to the stream, wanting to see more of Eddington. She didn't plan to fish until right before leaving, but it never hurt to take a look, find the best holes and see what kind of fish were present.

Well-maintained shops and homes lined the streets, several with signs of recent repairs. Most of the residents she passed wore straight-lined, woolen garments of subdued colors, but she occasionally saw women with a splash of color. The regional maps and reports didn't do this place justice. It was quainter than she had imagined. From her limited knowledge about these outlying areas, she had expected a rough and barren land with dilapidated structures and dirt-covered inhabitants. The truth exceeded her expectation.

A huge garden sat beside the last house on the lane, surrounded by a picket fence. Kneeling in a thick section of greenery, a woman tended vegetables. She brushed her unruly brunette curls away from her face where they'd escaped her loose braid, yet she wore a contented expression as she harvested what appeared to be leeks. Once done, the woman gathered her tools and vegetables, and pressed a hand against the ground to rise. As she did, the woman's stomach came into view, having previously been obscured by the lush vegetation. The sharply curving plumpness suggested the woman was nearing the end of her pregnancy.

A smile tugged at Eselle's cheeks as she walked by.

The woman held the underside of her stomach with the hand clutching the vegetables, while her other gripped her tools. A slight waddle showed in her steps as she emerged from the garden and headed toward the house. Eselle envied the woman's life of tending her garden and caring for her family, whether this was her first child or her fifth. Though, the woman didn't appear old enough to have many children. Eselle guessed her to be around twenty, a few years younger than herself. She wondered if the woman's husband was waiting for her inside, if he would sit on the porch with her before they headed to bed. While Eselle sometimes dreamed of that life, she enjoyed her freedom; plus, she had other responsibilities to consider to her family, her brother, their people.

Halfway to the house, the woman gasped and lurched forward. She dropped everything to grab her stomach. Eselle jolted at the sight and released her own gasp. She rushed through the gate, reaching the woman as she began to rise, and put a hand under the woman's arm to steady her.

"Are you all right?"

The woman studied her for a moment before donning a soft smile. "I'm fine. Thank you."

"Are you sure? You almost fell over."

"Yes. This happens all the time. It's nothing." The young woman shook out the skirts of her sky-blue dress, then began to bend down for her tools.

"Let me help you." Eselle gathered up the woman's gloves and trowel, as well as the dropped vegetables. She was pleased to find they were, in fact, leeks.

"Thank you," the pregnant woman answered, taking her belongings. "I'm Cristar."

"Eselle."

Why had she given her real name? It had left her lips before she realized it. Even a well-meaning stranger could reveal her to the wrong people and get her hanged.

The young woman scrutinized Eselle's features. "You're not from here, are you?"

"No. I'm passing through." It wasn't surprising the woman recognized her as a stranger. That was typical in remote towns; everyone knew everyone.

"Oh. So, you're staying at one of the inns? Are you at the Broken Spoke or the Old Goat?"

"The Old Goat," Eselle replied, for some reason unable to lie to the woman. Maybe it was because Cristar was vulnerable from her recent . . . whatever had made her nearly fall over. Or maybe it was her soft, pleasant smile. Eselle couldn't figure it out, but she needed to stop tossing out the truth.

"I've heard it's nice," Cristar said.

Eselle gave a noncommittal smile.

"Would you like to come up to the house for a drink? I have some freshly brewed tea, and I was about to make myself a cup. You can join me if you'd like."

Eselle hesitated.

"The leaves are from my garden."

Eselle glanced at the impressive assortment of vegetables and herbs. Some she suspected were for cooking, while others appeared medicinal. There was too much for the woman's family alone.

"I'd like that," Eselle said. "I could use a nice warm drink. Thank you."

"Have a seat on the porch, and I'll bring it out."

As they walked to the house, Eselle couldn't help looking at the woman's belly. "What happened back there? You said it happens all the time."

Cristar caressed her stomach with one of her loaded hands. "He kicked me."

"He what?" Eselle had never spent much time around a pregnant woman, being that she was either traveling or living on a farm with a bunch of men.

"He kicked me," Cristar repeated, then shook her head. "I don't really know if it's a boy, but he's been kicking a lot. I figure a girl would be politer and at least kick gently if she really had to. This guy's tough, though. He lets me know he's there and ready to come out and roughhouse." Some faint color rose to her cheeks. "It's silly, I know. I just think it sounds better than calling him 'it.' Anyway, this time he caught me off guard with a real wallop. He's going to be a handful, I can tell."

"How much longer until he arrives?"

"About two months. I can't believe he's almost here." Cristar smiled down at her stomach.

Eselle waited in one of the wooden chairs on Cristar's porch and examined the small, well-maintained house. The porch, over-sized for the house, appeared to be a newer addition with fresh wooden planks. She wondered if Cristar's husband built it. Facing west, it undoubtedly allowed for spectacular views of the sunset. She could easily imagine the baby playing out here while his parents watched.

Cristar stepped out of the house with a teapot and two cups balanced in her hands. "Here's the tea."

Eselle jumped up to help. After taking the items, she arranged them on the small table. Cristar strategically settled herself into a chair while Eselle poured the drinks.

"Thank you," Cristar said, taking the full cup from Eselle.

"You're welcome." Eselle raised the warm tea to her lips and enjoyed the fresh floral aroma that wafted up. "Mm, that's wonderful."

"I worried about the crop this year because of all the rain. Luckily, it turned out pretty well."

"Do you and your husband grow all this for yourselves, or do you sell some? I wouldn't mind buying some fresh supplies from you. Your crops look better than any I've seen in a long time."

Cristar sat silently and stared off into her garden. She blinked several times and swallowed before she looked back. Eselle recognized the change in the woman. While she'd never been married, she'd once had a significantly larger family.

"My husband died a few months ago," Cristar said. "It's just me here. The garden's mine, it always has been. Klaasen never had much of a green thumb. The first time he killed one of my plants,

I banned him from my garden on pain of . . ." Cristar looked down at her drink.

Eselle remained respectfully silent, running her fingers along the perfectly smooth wooden arm of her chair.

After wiping her eyes on the back of her hand, Cristar lifted her head. "Well, I told him I'd handle the garden. He worked miracles with wood though. He built the back room of our house, added the porch, built me a garden shed and himself a workshop out back. Plus, he's helped nearly every neighbor in town at one point or another on some project. That's how he did so much to our house; he traded his labor for materials and such."

Eselle felt a twinge in the back of her throat as she listened to the woman reminisce. "He sounds wonderful."

"He was." Cristar's voice had softened. She took a sip of her drink, then sniffled once before raising her head again. "Yes. I sell some of the crops to the general store and others directly to townsfolk. If you'd like to buy anything, it's for sale."

They finished their tea while discussing the various produce Eselle wanted to examine.

Once she had rearranged her supplies to accommodate her purchases, Eselle waved goodbye and headed down the road. After three steps, she stopped and gazed at the stream ahead of her.

Jinsle might still be a couple of days since she'd arrived early, seeing as she'd nixed her stay in Grimswold and hustled away. She glanced over at the garden, at the vegetables ready for harvest. Growing up, she and Tavith had run through similar, though much larger, rows of crops. It had been so difficult for Cristar to move about in the short time they'd spent together, even to simply get out of the chair.

Eselle turned and found Cristar watching her.

"I might be here for a couple of days. Or maybe more." Eselle took a few steps back toward the house. "Would you by any chance need help around here? I'm probably not as good as you with a garden like this, but I grew up on a farm, so I know a few things about plants."

"Oh, thank you, I couldn't afford to—"

"No." Eselle took another step forward. "I don't want you to pay me. I'm waiting for a friend, but he's late, and I'm bored. I thought this might be something to keep me busy. Plus, that's a big boy you're hauling around there, so you could probably use some assistance."

Cristar gave her a soft smile. "I'd like that. Yes, I'd appreciate the help."

"Great." Eselle examined the garden as she adjusted her pack. "Where can I start?"

CHAPTER FOUR

It had been three days, and her brother's courier still hadn't arrived. If not for enjoying her time with Cristar, Eselle would have cursed Jinsle Porlin's name.

Working the garden simultaneously invigorated and exhausted Eselle, and she found that cooking on more than a campfire had its merits. After months of traveling, it felt good to spend time with someone again, to help where she could. Cristar was easy to be around, easy to talk to, and seemed to delight in sharing her knowledge of plants and the ailments they could treat. Eselle hated the idea of leaving Cristar alone once she completed her assignment. The townsfolk would undoubtedly help Cristar, but Eselle worried anyway. Managing both the house and garden this far along in her pregnancy was taxing on the woman, and neighbors couldn't always be there for her.

Eselle dumped the scraps, from both dinner and harvesting, into the sty. "At least you'll feed her well this winter." The 200-pound hog nosed around in the mess, spreading it out, then started munching.

A distant pounding caught Eselle's attention. She stood still and listened. The noise grew steadily louder. She wrapped her borrowed shawl tighter around her shoulders and walked out from behind Cristar's house. The sound morphed into the stomping of hooves against hard-packed earth. Eselle eased to the side of the house and peeked around the corner, toward the center of town.

Huffing and grunting of horses mingled with voices calling about. Eselle's stomach clenched. What were the odds someone other than the regional commander had enough mounted men in the area to create that level of noise?

Between the waning daylight and the neighboring house blocking part of her view, it was difficult to make out what was happening—until several mounted soldiers rode by the end of the lane.

She pulled back and leaned against the house, gritting her teeth. Her luck with the military had taken a horrible turn for the worse. This was the third time she'd unexpectedly encountered a group of soldiers. Hopefully, by some miracle, it wasn't the regional commander and his troops from Grimswold. Though, his were likely the only soldiers this far east. Of all the regions in Likalsta, this one was the largest, but also the most rural and wild.

If not for the information she carried, she would consider another hasty getaway. Tavith needed to know their strongest ally, Earl Holgood, had rescinded his support. King Vorgal had long ago instilled fear in his nobles, so to have one stand by them at such personal risk had been a boon. Now it was gone.

Before anyone noticed her, Eselle slipped around the far side of Cristar's house and went in through the back door.

Cristar sat at the table in the center of the main room, grinding herbs from her garden. She'd been grinding a lot of them lately.

Eselle started to get the tub ready for cleaning dishes. Her mind wouldn't leave the troops, and halfway through set up, she walked to the window. She pulled back the curtain enough to peer out yet not be seen. The angle was even worse than her spot earlier. All she could make out were brief glimpses of horses and soldiers as they walked by.

"What's happening?" Cristar set her pestle down and rose from the table.

"Troops just arrived." Eselle stepped back from the window, and Cristar took up the position and peered out. "Do you know what they're doing here?"

Cristar dropped the curtain. "It's probably the regional commander making his rounds." She returned to her seat and grinding.

The herb gave off a faint minty scent. Eselle found it soothing, though not enough to completely alleviate her concerns.

Once she gave her information to Jinsle, it would warrant tracking the troops again. If this was the commander from Grimswold, then according to her information, they should be traveling north out of Grimswold, not east. Meaning both their route and timing had changed. Was this to prevent anyone from predicting their movements? Or had something happened?

"The regional commander?" Eselle asked, playing dumb. She washed the remaining dishes in the tub, more for the distraction than anything else.

"Yes," Cristar replied. "Though I didn't think he was due for a while yet."

"Does he usually arrive early?"

Cristar glanced up. "Not that I remember. He's pretty punctual, never arrives more than a couple of days either early or late."

"Could someone have called him here ahead of schedule? Maybe something came up that requires his attention or authority?" *Did he recognize me after all?*

"It's possible, but I haven't heard of any reason to. There haven't been any unusual crimes, or disasters, or anything we couldn't handle ourselves. It's probably nothing."

Eselle nodded, uneasy as she scrubbed a plate. What if Jinsle was late because he ran into the regional commander? It might be best to keep out of sight until after she relayed her information.

"I'm heading to the store tomorrow for some supplies." Cristar checked the texture of the herbs, then resumed grinding. "I'll find out what's happening while I'm there."

Eselle nodded, but she needed more information. "Who's the regional commander for this area?"

"Commander Silst."

The name made Eselle's back straighten. She focused and dried the dish in her hands. "Commander Silst?"

"Yes. Kyr Silst."

"The name sounds familiar." Eselle tried to sound casual, but her voice quavered. Thankfully, Cristar seemed too immersed in her work to notice.

Eselle had indeed heard the name, but she knew almost nothing of the man. Only that, of the six regional commanders, he was the senior ranking among them. He was the high commander—as opposed to the field, rear, or three lower commanders.

She glanced up at the little statue Cristar kept on her windowsill. The rough carving only partially completed, cut but not yet sanded and polished. She wondered if Klaasen had been working on it before he died. She didn't have the heart to ask. The entire piece was about the length of her hand, showing the Protector's Sword standing upright in front of His Shield.

Have I asked too much? To slip in and out unnoticed? Is it really too much considering it's Your people I'm trying to help?

"What does he look like?" Eselle asked, keeping her voice casual.

Cristar paused in her work. "I've never actually met him, only seen him from a distance. He's tall, has dark hair, a good build. The women in town are fascinated by his dark eyes. Though I'm not sure why. We have our share of dark-eyed men around here. That's about all I know. From a distance, he seems handsome enough, but I've not gotten a good look myself."

Eselle's pulse quickened as Cristar spoke. Eddington's regional commander sounded an awful lot like the one she'd encountered in Grimswold. Granted, the description was vague, but what were the odds there were two with matching features in the area? They rarely entered each other's territories.

The more she thought about their encounter, the more confident she became about her safety. While she worried how he would take her running away, he had seemed playful enough he might be entertained by it. Possibly.

Eselle put the last plate away on the shelf before tossing her rag beside the tub. "What kind of commander is he? Good? Bad?" She was leery of asking but hoped for the best.

For this question, Cristar was quicker to answer. "He's your typical commander, I suppose. Tough, but fair in judicial matters, disciplined, expects his soldiers to follow orders without question."

"So, he's a dictator," Eselle said, somewhat disappointed, but not surprised. From what she knew of the regional commanders, she expected most were like that. The frisky nature of Grimswold's commander had lured her in. She needed to make certain it didn't again. To distract herself, she bent down in front of the gray stone fireplace and stoked the dying flames.

"I think it's a little more complicated than that," Cristar said. "From what I've heard, he'll always side with King Vorgal's wishes, no matter the situation. He's completely loyal to the king. His troops commandeer our stores, and sometimes belongings, always take more taxes than should be due. They conscript our young men, and they certainly enjoy our women. He keeps them pretty well in-check though. From the rumors I've heard of other regions, we could have a lot worse than him watching over us. He's certainly better than our last commander."

"It's still horrible," Eselle bemoaned, adding another log to the fire. She should have known better. Since he'd saved her from his soldiers back in Grimswold, she'd thought he might be different, might keep his men from the worst of the crimes against their people. True, he'd seduced her—or she'd tried seducing him if she was honest—but that had been consensual. She'd hoped there was a chance he could be, if not good, less horrible. No matter how attractive he was or how well he kissed, he was Vorgal's high commander. That should tell her something, something she needed to make more of an effort to remember.

Cristar dumped the ground sage into a bowl, then put a fresh batch of the dried, pale leaves into the mortar and resumed grinding.

"The troops shouldn't treat their people so horribly." Eselle poked at the logs harder than she'd intended, sending sparks into the air. It was difficult to keep her anger from edging her voice. "They should protect them, not steal from them. And I don't only mean steal money and supplies, but young men and women's virtues."

"I agree, but we're not equipped to stop them. Other regions have it much worse. Their regional commanders let their troops ravage and brutalize their territories."

"It's barbaric." Eselle sat at the table across from Cristar, fuming as she rubbed her finger back and forth along a nick in the table.

Cristar put down her pestle. "As I said, I agree. But there's nothing we can do. King Vorgal gives his troops free rein, and they enjoy it at our expense."

It disturbed Eselle to hear the young woman speak so casually of the matter. "Just because he's king doesn't mean it's right." Her region had similar treatment. They were lucky enough that her brother's allies often warned them before the worst occurred. It also helped that their commander kept to his schedule, making it easier for people to predict his movements, to know when to hide both their valuables and themselves.

"I wish it was different, too," Cristar said, "that the troops didn't terrorize as they do. I've heard stories things were once peaceful before Vorgal became king. I can't even imagine it though."

"You mean when Folstaff Enstrin was king?" Eselle was careful to keep her voice steady.

"Yes. They don't mention him in schools anymore, but I've heard stories. They didn't even have a regular army back then. Or regions."

From what Eselle knew, Vorgal hadn't only created his own standing army, but stripped the nobility of their authority and had the mages assassinated. All that suffering and death simply to keep anyone from defying him.

Eselle's chest constricted. "I remember. My family used to live in Vahean."

"Really?" Cristar perked up.

A nod was all Eselle could manage.

"Did you ever see the king? Or queen?"

Eselle nodded again while trying to hold her features together. It never got easier, talking about her past. "Yes, I did. I left the capital not long after Vorgal slaughtered the Enstrin family and took the throne for himself."

Cristar's face fell into a sad, wistful expression. "I was four at the time, so I don't remember anything about it. I've always wondered what it must have been like, living under a noble king during peaceful times."

Eselle didn't want Cristar going into town as long as the soldiers remained. The woman had enough problems being as pregnant as she was. She didn't need to deal with handsy soldiers.

"Why don't you work in your garden tomorrow?" Eselle said. "I'll get the supplies on my way here in the morning."

"Are you sure?" Cristar's face relaxed, and the corner of her mouth ticked upward, just shy of a smile.

Eselle returned it. "I'm sure."

What are the odds I can get the supplies and to Cristar's house tomorrow morning without running into the commander?

CHAPTER FIVE

Eselle entered the store not long after the proprietor opened.

As she headed to the back, two armsmen entered behind her. Both appeared around her age, so not recruits. According to their insignia, neither had yet reached corporal, so they likely never would. Advancement in Vorgal's army was a cutthroat endeavor.

Both soldiers walked between the stocked tables and along the walls of shelves grabbing various items, from food to shoe brushes. The proprietor scowled but said nothing as they loaded their arms.

Trying to ignore them, Eselle collected her groceries. Cristar planned to harvest melons later, and Eselle worried she would do too much. The woman didn't know how to slow down. Eselle wanted to purchase the supplies, hustle to Cristar's house, and order her friend to plant her own little melon in a chair while she did the heavy lifting.

"Hey," one of the soldiers said to his comrade with a nod to one of the back tables, "grab those gloves for me, would you?"

The other man turned around and spotted the pale-green wool mittens on the table beside Eselle. He ignored her and snatched them up. "Got 'em. Anything else?"

"No. I think that's it."

"Then let's get back. I heard there might be an inspection later, and I need time to polish my boots."

The shopkeeper followed their every movement until they walked out the door. His scowl never faltered.

Shaking her head, Eselle returned to her shopping. How much money had the proprietor lost over the years to King Vorgal's soldiers? Incidents like this strengthened her belief that Tavith's plan was necessary. Vorgal's reign must end.

Eselle tucked her final item, a sack of flour, under her arm and turned around.

She jumped at the sight of chainmail. Her gaze darted upward, locking onto eyes so dark they looked nearly black. A burst of energy raced through her, and her entire body became alert. She hadn't even heard him approach. This morning he wore a red military cloak with silver trim. It was of finer quality than the ones the soldiers from earlier wore, as befitted the higher ranks. The sides had been folded back across his shoulders so they draped behind him. Regardless of how the next few moments went, he was a tantalizing sight to start her morning.

Standing between the loaded tables, he blocked her exit. "I had hoped you'd run off in this direction."

She gauged his expression before she replied, seeking any sign of recognition or anger. The smile on his lips, though subtle, reflected in his eyes. She couldn't help but return it.

Even so, it concerned her that, once again, he was ahead of schedule and in the wrong town. "Are you following me?"

"No. I wasn't. I have business in Eddington, but I had hoped we were traveling the same road. When I saw you enter the store a moment ago, it brightened my day considerably."

"Because you're happy to see me or happy to arrest me?"

His brows drew together. "Arrest you?"

"For running from Grimswold when you told me to stay put and ordered everyone else to the town hall." Eselle noticed her dagger still tucked in his leather belt beside his own, the hilts equally worn. It felt odd, and strangely satisfying, knowing a piece of her had been with him this last week.

"Ah, yes. Well, I'll overlook that for now, as long as you promise not to run again."

"And if I can't make that promise?"

The corner of his mouth turned up. "A good chase can be a powerful thing." He took the flour from her arms. "But what would it gain you? As we've seen, I'd only find you again."

"It didn't take you long to catch up." She watched as he casually confiscated more of her groceries. Each item he took made her pulse beat a little faster.

"No, it didn't. And imagine if I'd been trying." Despite their dark color, his eyes were bright when they met hers. "You should remember that if you decide to run again."

"What do you want from me?" He wasn't what she had expected of a regional commander.

His smile softened, turned nearly affectionate, and that only confused her more. A hardened soldier of his rank should not look at a woman with that degree of warmth. In her experience, the two didn't go together. Vorgal's soldiers got what they wanted from women, and the commanders more than most. It was never with affection, only lust and often ruthlessness.

Eselle shifted her stance and pretended to adjust the few remaining items she carried.

"What makes you think I want anything?" he asked.

"You're here, standing before me, taking my groceries, and blocking my path."

He gave a soft, knowing smirk. "Just being polite. Saying hello to an acquaintance and assisting a captivating woman with her groceries." With that, he stepped aside and swept his arm for her to proceed to the counter.

"Commander Silst," the proprietor said with a nod of greeting. The commander nodded in return.

Eselle's pulse quickened at confirmation of the commander's identity.

She kept her face blank while she placed her groceries on the counter. High Commander Silst deposited the items he'd carried for her, then stepped back and watched. She tapped her forefinger on the counter as she waited for the proprietor to tally her purchases. It was difficult to ignore the imposing presence behind her.

The commander stepped up, put his hands on her hips, and leaned down to her ear. "How long will you be in town?"

"I'm not sure," Eselle admitted. Her skin tingled at the memory of his hands gliding along her. "I might leave this afternoon." It wasn't a lie since it depended on when Jinsle arrived.

Eselle had enjoyed her time with the commander in Grimswold, seducing him for the advantages of his rank. It had become apparent though that he might be too dangerous to toy with. He wasn't like the lower soldiers she'd previously manipulated, but rather had a boldness only someone of power could wield. The high commander could be more hazardous than useful to her brother's cause and was one potential asset best left alone.

"How can I entice you to stay?" he murmured.

Eselle didn't tell him that his warm breath across her ear on the chilly morning was a good start.

The proprietor remained silent while he calculated his total and put her items into Cristar's grocery sack. But his eyes occasionally dropped to the commander's hands at her waist.

Caught between the counter and the large man behind her, Eselle suddenly felt trapped. She turned around to gain space, forcing Silst to take a step back, and peered up at him. "I wish I could, but I have family waiting for me. I should probably get back on the road."

"You never mentioned family before."

"Well, I didn't know you."

"So, are you looking for something better than a small town, as you claimed in Grimswold, or visiting family?"

"Both."

A hint of a smirk appeared. "Where do they live? The only thing farther down the road is the mountains. And you don't strike me as someone related to a mountain dweller."

"Oh? You know the mountain folk, do you?"

"I do." He watched her closely. "My region includes the mountains."

She met his gaze firmly, willing herself not to look away. "Well, then perhaps we'll meet again."

"Which settlement?"

The challenge was evident in his eyes as they crinkled at the edges. He wanted to see how far she would take the ruse.

"Doesn't matter," she said. "Perhaps I'll stay a little longer after all." Though she'd said it to throw him off, hearing the words aloud gave them a certain appeal. She still didn't know if he had discovered her identity, but he hadn't arrested her. Perhaps she was simply paranoid.

"You just said you might leave this afternoon."

"I'm reconsidering. There are things here I should take care of."

His rakish smile sent a shudder through her—not an unpleasant one.

The proprietor called out her total, and she spun around, grateful for the interruption. She had better self-control under normal circumstances, rarely letting anyone rile her. The commander unnerved her in the most interesting of ways.

Eselle handed over her money and gave a quick nod to the men. Snatching up the groceries, she hurried toward the door.

A deep chuckle rumbled behind her. "Tarania."

The name startled her. She stopped in the doorway and turned toward him. Being so out of sorts, she'd forgotten he only knew her by her alias. "Commander Silst?"

With an amused grin, he walked toward her and pulled her dagger from his belt. Holding it by the blade, he offered it to her. When her fingers grasped the hilt, he spoke. "I'll see you soon."

She nodded goodbye and hustled out the door.

Reaching the end of the lane, she tossed a backward glance. The commander stood outside the store, watching her.

Despite everything that suggested he could be dangerous, the thought of becoming entwined with him again made her smile.

***

Though Tarania turned her head quickly, Kyr saw the soft smile that graced her face before she walked down one of the nearby lanes. He watched a moment longer. The way she shifted back and forth between nervous and confident intrigued him. Just when he thought she was out of her element, she proved him wrong.

"Isn't that the woman who slipped away from you in Grimswold?" Josah Ilkin, his captain, walked up from down the road.

"Yes, it is." Kyr pulled his cloak back around his shoulders. It would be a couple of hours before it grew warm enough to discard it.

"Curious that we'd run into her again. Would you like me to have her brought in for questioning?"

Kyr glanced back to where Tarania had disappeared. He considered it for a moment, remembered the sparkle in her big, blue eyes when she challenged him, dared lying to him. She was a temptation he could easily get caught up in. "No," he finally said, "she's harmless."

"I doubt it."

"What makes you say that?"

Josah shook his head and chuckled. "Do you even know who's the cat and who's the mouse in this game you're playing?"

"Your faith is overwhelming."

"Only watching out for you," Josah said with a shrug. "You said she lied about where she's from. What else is she lying about?" Kyr wondered that himself. "With very little effort, she already has you believing she's harmless. And we both know that if that were true, she wouldn't have captured your attention so thoroughly."

"You think I'm being careless?" Kyr already knew the answer, but also knew he needed to hear it. With everything about to happen, this was not the time to get distracted.

"I'm just saying, be careful." Josah paused a moment, a thoughtful expression on his rugged face. "I can see the appeal though; she's pretty."

A smile tugged at Kyr's lips. "Now who needs to be careful? Remember, you're spoken for, and I just might tell Maksin on you."

"Yes, well," Josah sighed with his own fond smile, "doesn't mean I can't appreciate beauty when I see it. And I know him well enough to know he'd look twice too."

After one last glance at the lane, Kyr stepped into the street and headed toward the town hall. He needed to focus on more important matters. "What did you find out?"

Captain Ilkin strode beside him. "There are three women and five men. We can have them rounded up by lunchtime."

"Not yet."

After a pause, Josah said, "Yes, sir."

Kyr looked sidelong at his captain. "What's wrong?"

"Nothing." Josah kept his ice-blue gaze forward.

"You only 'sir' me when there are others around, or you want to say something you think I'll disapprove of."

Josah snorted. "I'll have to remember that."

"Out with it."

The street was quiet this early in the morning, but a few townsfolk roamed about on their errands. A couple of doors down, the tanner had gotten an early start and greeted two men who entered his shop.

Josah lowered his voice. "I'm wondering why we haven't collected from Eddington yet. For the last two months, we've collected from every town and village we passed through, but not Eddington. And we were here a month ago. What's different about this place?"

Kyr stopped and put a hand on his captain's armored shoulder. "You'll have to trust me."

"Always," Josah said, his expression steadfast. "But that doesn't mean I won't worry."

Kyr tapped the captain's leather spaulder as he released Josah's shoulder. "Noted. But don't. We'll collect everyone right before we leave. No reason to cause a stir before then." He resumed their walk down the center of the street.

"When will that be?"

"I'm not sure. No more than a few days, a week at most."

Josah nodded. "Do you still want to leave the prisoners outside of town? Or should I have them brought into the jail?"

"I don't want to alert anyone. Have the drivers and guards settle in where they are. We'll pick them up on our way out."

CHAPTER SIX

The tie on Eselle's tunic slipped from her trembling fingers. Closing her eyes, she sat on the edge of her bed and tried to slow her breathing. If she could get her day started, she could put the nightmare behind her. She clenched her hands into fists, then shook them out and tried again. Things would be better, they always were. She just needed to secure that last tie.

A warm breakfast with Cristar would surely help.

When they'd made their arrangement, Eselle had insisted the company and something to keep her busy were enough. Cristar, however, suggested paying by way of food. After a couple of meals of seasoned fish, spiced cabbage, lentils, and fresh bread, Eselle stopped resisting and gladly accepted payment. Cristar's cooking was considerably more delicious than the inn's pottage.

Once calmer, Eselle managed the tie, collected her pack and cloak, and left the inn.

Fresh air and soft morning sunlight eased some of her tension. She concentrated on the day ahead, on working in the garden.

How long had it been since she'd dug in dirt and tended crops? It felt good to nurture something again.

A young man rolled a barrel across her path. "Excuse me, ma'am."

A slightly older man followed with a second barrel.

Eselle stopped to let them pass, watching as they rolled the barrels toward the center of town. A curious thing considering the space consisted of only the well and a large open area. A few other people milled around, carrying sacks and lanterns, and . . .

Krithaefyst

Cristar mentioned its approach the other day, but Eselle had quickly forgotten it. In recent years, she often forgot about holidays. They seemed less important when she didn't have anyone to celebrate with, which was often the case due to her frequent traveling. She couldn't remember the last one she and Tavith had spent together. Depending on when Jinsle arrived, she very well might be present for this holiday.

Her mood brightened at seeing people preparing the square. The more she walked, the more the nightmare's remnants dissipated, replaced by images of Krithaefyst celebrations with Tavith. Her thoughts drifted further back, to holidays spent with their parents, their siblings.

Before those memories took hold, before they morphed back into nightmares, Eselle grasped onto the first thing that came to mind—Cristar's garden. She focused on the layout, tried to imagine the rows of vegetables and herbs, what grew beside what and why. Not long after, her thoughts cleared, and she closed the door to her past once more.

After rounding the final corner to Cristar's home, Eselle stopped short, pulling back behind the butcher's shop and flattening herself against the wall. Staring at the ground, she tried to calm her racing heartbeat.

Careful not to be seen, she peered around the building. High Commander Silst and another soldier stood deep in discussion halfway between her and her destination.

She wasn't prepared for the commander yet. Each encounter with him had thrown her off balance. She needed time to figure things out before she faced him.

The soldiers stood well out of range, making it impossible to hear their conversation. The commander glanced toward Cristar's house, the garden in particular. Eselle peeked farther around the corner. Cristar was out, walking the rows while she examined her crops. They had harvested many over the past couple days, and Cristar mentioned picking beets today.

Her eyes darted between Silst, the garden, and Cristar. Of all the places in town, why was he here? On this lane? At this moment?

Has he figured out I've been spending time with Cristar?

There were only two inns in the small town, so locating her sleeping accommodations wouldn't be difficult. But she wasn't comfortable with him knowing her daily whereabouts. Then again, he could just be admiring the garden's impressive variety.

Eselle decided to find a back route to Cristar's. Entering from the other direction wouldn't completely block her from the commander's view, but if she timed it right, she might manage it while he wasn't looking.

The lanes she took through the eastern side of Eddington were new to her. They seemed much the same as the rest of the town— except for an actual, presumably functioning, church. The building needed fresh paint, and the roof could use some attention, but the structure seemed solid. There were several new planks around its exterior. Their fresh clean appearance contrasted with the chipped paint on the older boards. Beside the church, set back a ways, stood several headstones. A couple could be described as ornate. Most were little more than a small boulder with carved words or images, a few given shape by some minor chiseling.

At the front edge of the cemetery, a man squatted down, pulling a vine from around one of the headstones. It gave him a struggle, but he finally won out and freed the marker. Vine in hand, he spotted Eselle as he rose. He broke into a grin and held up his free hand in greeting.

"Hello." As he walked toward her, he tossed the vine onto a pile of other eradicated weeds. Though he was easily the tallest person she had ever met—nearly two heads taller than her—he was also skinnier than most everyone she knew. His simple, white cassock had fresh dirt on it, and a hint of older stains suggested this was not the first time he'd tended the cemetery in it. The garment appeared cared for though. Stitched at the side of his chest was a silver Sword over a golden Shield. The man was a warder.

There weren't many actual priests around these days.

Most towns with functioning churches had a local who tended it. Since the massacre eighteen years ago, when over half of Likalsta's mages were slaughtered, few people wanted to be associated with the church in any official capacity. Even the majority of mages who had survived preferred fleeing to neighboring lands rather than risk execution. Now, instead of mages serving as the Protector's warders for His people, the posts were held by anyone willing.

"Hello, Warder."

"I don't believe we've met." His blond hair, a little shaggy at the edges, shone bright in the sunlight. "I'm Nossen Hilbert."

"Tarania Gilfer," Eselle said, with a nod of greeting.

She hated it when she had to lie to a warder. Thankfully, it didn't happen often. Since the lies shielded more than herself, hopefully the Protector understood. Though, since He had let her run into troops three times, perhaps He didn't.

"It's a pleasure to meet you, Tarania." His pleasant nature made it difficult not to return his smile. "What brings you to Eddington?" He wiped his sleeve across his brow.

"I'm only passing through on my way to see family."

"Oh, lovely. Do they live nearby?"

"No, I'm afraid not. I'll be on the road for some time."

"Well, may the Protector watch over you in your travels."

She wished He would. "Thank you, Warder Hilbert."

"I do hope, though, that you'll stay long enough for Krithaefyst. It's only a couple of days away."

Not knowing when Jinsle would arrive, Eselle hated to commit to anything. It had already been five days, so she expected him soon.

Eselle gave a noncommittal grin. "I'm not sure when I'm leaving." His features sagged a bit. "But if I'm still around, I would love to."

"Lovely. It would be a pleasure to have you with us. The usual activities will be held in town, but I'll also be holding services that morning. You're more than welcome to attend."

"I'll consider it." The services, she was all but certain she would miss. She preferred the holiday's community events as people prepared for winter. It had been a long time though since she'd heard a service, and clearly, she and the Protector had some things to discuss. Perhaps she actually would consider it.

She nodded toward the small, partially restored church. "Did you repair this yourself? I noticed some new boards."

"Some." Warder Hilbert followed her gaze. "The townsfolk help when they can. It's slow going, and there's still a good bit to do, but it's getting there. One of the families from outside of town has extra materials and four strapping boys, so they've offered to replace the roof for us during Krithaefyst. After the service, of course."

"That's kind of them. How long have you been working on it?"

"Oh," he said, turning back with a thoughtful expression, "I suppose about a year now, maybe a little more."

"Is that when you moved here?"

"No, I was born here. It's when the regional commander changed. The old one wouldn't let us have a church—let the poor thing nearly collapse from neglect. The new one said he didn't care what we did with it, that we could either rebuild it or burn it to the ground. I chose to rebuild it." He peered back at his church with a smile.

Eselle gazed at the half-patched building with him. "It's beautiful."

***

The morning of Krithaefyst, a trio of lads loaded Cristar's herbs and vegetables onto a cart for her.

"Thank you, gentlemen," Eselle said with a grin and a bow.

The oldest, only a few years into his teens, bowed back, then turned a broad grin toward Cristar. "If there's anything else I can do for you, Miss Maesret, just say it."

"I will, Graan. Thank you." Cristar waved goodbye before he and the other boys hauled the cart away.

Eselle chuckled. "I believe that young man has a crush on you."

Cristar's features bunched briefly, then turned amused. "Graan was only being polite."

With a shrug, Eselle picked up the large, thick coat from where she'd laid it over the fence. Cristar had decided to donate Klaasen's coat for Krithaefyst, knowing a neighbor could benefit from it this winter. Not surprisingly, she wasn't yet willing to part with the rest of his belongings. It had only been a couple of months since his death, after all.

"Ready?" Eselle asked. They could already hear the cacophony from the town center.

Cristar wrapped her shawl snugly around her. With her large, empty basket in hand, she nodded.

The square was overrun with more people than Eselle realized lived in the area. Everyone, it seemed, had come in from the outlying farmsteads.

An array of stations stood throughout the square. Some managed clothing donations, repaired small household and farm equipment, or were making large batches of medicinal items, including tinctures and salves. Smoke-laced floral scents drifted from the cooking stations.

An assortment of livestock being brought in for slaughter added to the commotion, from chickens past their laying years to fattened pigs, including Cristar's. A station down one of the side streets was well underway with butchering and smoking.

More activities covered the far side of the square, but too many people blocked Eselle's view. Eventually, she would work her way through them. For now, she was assigned to basket-filling duty. Graan and the other two boys worked on unloading the cart of melons, beets, and several other vegetables she and Cristar had harvested for Krithaefyst.

The assortment of donated crops covered a space the size of a house, with a few more carts lined up to unload. It was significantly more than Eselle's own town managed, where most residents could barely feed themselves through winter, let alone have extra food to share and trade.

"Tarania, I'm glad you could make it." Warder Hilbert gave her a beaming smile and waved her over. He was knee-deep in turnips.

She glanced at Cristar, who was already getting set up for her duties. Thankfully, she didn't appear to have heard the warder. Eselle hadn't yet figured out how to tell her friend other people thought her name was Tarania. The truth wasn't an option, but everything else sounded almost as bad. What would Cristar think if Eselle admitted to hiding her identity from the authorities, or lying to a warder? Working different stations might buy her another day, but her luck wouldn't last forever.

Jinsle, where are you?

Warder Hilbert's cassock sleeves were rolled up to his elbows. "You can help me fill these baskets over here."

They spent the next couple of hours doling out food, from different types of squashes to slightly-past-ripe berries.

Cristar sat several stations down with a couple of other women, darning neighbors' clothing as it was brought to them. Each time Cristar handed someone their repaired item, her eyes grew brighter.

Eselle eventually needed a break. Warder Hilbert joined her.

"Thank you for helping us today," he said, as they sat on some nearby crates. "It's very kind of you."

She kneaded some lower muscles in her back. "You're welcome. I'm glad I was here for it."

The warder spent the next several minutes telling Eselle about the church's new roof being built, the town's history and its people, of how proud he was at the day's turnout. She nodded along, not knowing any of the townsfolk he pointed out. When he lifted his hand and gave a nod off to the side, Eselle followed his gaze.

Standing in front of the smithy, Commander Silst surveyed the townsfolk as they worked and socialized. His expression was solemn, his arms crossed over his chest as he spoke to a blond soldier wearing similar armor. The commander watched the warder for a moment, then glanced at Eselle beside him. He gave them a curt nod before returning his attention to his conversation.

Not since their first meeting—well, the beginning of their first meeting—had Eselle seen him so serious. After all his bold flirtations and devilish smiles, it felt odd to be so coldly regarded.

"You know Commander Silst?" Hilbert asked.

Eselle blinked as she turned back to the warder. "What? Oh, no, not really. You?"

"No. I've only spoken to him twice now, once when I asked about the church and then this morning when he stopped by the service."

"He went to your service? But the troops are prohibited from associating with the church."

The warder chuckled. "Oh, he wasn't there to attend, I'm sure. He just stood in back with his arms crossed and that same inscrutable expression he has now. Undoubtedly making sure I didn't say anything too treasonous about the king or the Protector."

She quirked a brow. "And did you? Say anything treasonous?"

With a shrug, the warder's eyes gleamed. "One could argue that the Protector himself is treasonous."

Eselle returned her attention to Silst.

The soldier with him took in the celebration, his face cheerier than his commander's. He soon said something, nodded, and walked off. The commander's eyes continued to roam over the crowd. Eselle couldn't tell if he was pleased with the gathering, only tolerant of it, or was considering shutting it down. Not for the first time, she wished she could read him better.

She wondered what he was looking at, or for, when he studied the crowd. Searching the square herself, it dawned on her there was not a single soldier present. In fact, she hadn't seen one all day, not until the commander and the man with him. Was that intentional or coincidence?

Warder Hilbert spoke beside her, resuming his stories. Eselle tried to pay attention but kept glancing toward the commander. Perusing the celebration, his steady, wandering gaze eventually returned to her.

The commander didn't nod this time, but he didn't turn away either. Eselle locked on those dark eyes. For the briefest moment, one corner of his mouth twitched upward. The breath Eselle released came out as a partial laugh.

Silst turned away and headed toward the nearest lane. The relief that had been brewing inside Eselle shifted back to disappointment as she watched his departing back. He passed some apple crates, plucked one off the top, and walked away from Krithaefyst.

CHAPTER SEVEN

A week after Eselle arrived in Eddington, Jinsle still hadn't shown. The number of excuses she could fathom—that didn't involve injury, imprisonment, or death—were dwindling

To distract herself, Eselle focused on helping Cristar. She had thought she knew a good bit about gardening, but Cristar proved her wrong. Though the basics were the same, the quantities and varieties of vegetation required a different skill set, one she enjoyed learning.

Commander Silst had been busy with town business, so she had only spotted him a few times on her trips to and from Cristar's. Thus far, she'd seen him first and been able to avoid an encounter. Each day without speaking to him made it harder to remember how dangerous tangling with him might be.

Eddington was not nearly as bad off as other towns she'd visited. True, she'd seen some minor skirmishes between the soldiers and townsfolk, and there was at least one young, unwed woman she suspected was pregnant because of passing troops, but the town's spirit remained intact. In other regions, hers included, the commanders allowed their troops to run roughshod without repercussions. What caused the difference?

Cristar had spent the last couple days working with townsfolk to prepare various medicines with the leftover supplies from Krithyafest. Having never been good at medicinal arts, Eselle didn't want to get in the way. Instead of joining in, she planned to meet Cristar at her home afterward. Eselle had spent the last couple of mornings at the inn establishing plans to add an herb garden and some other crops to Tavith's farm. Even if the plans never came to fruition, it kept her occupied.

Just short of lunchtime, the door to the inn's main hall opened, letting in a swath of bright light that obscured the figure in the doorway. She squinted, then recognized Jinsle Porlin as he stepped into The Old Goat. Eselle perked up and stood as she waved him over.

It had been over two years since she'd seen him, since they'd begun working for her brother and taken off into different parts of Likalsta. Jinsle's face brightened when he saw her. He worked his way through the tables that were gradually filling with patrons. She'd chosen the table in the back corner of the room, for both a semblance of privacy and to afford a view of the door should he arrive.

Eselle gave her friend a quick hug. Best to keep things brief and not draw attention. There was likely nothing to worry about in such a remote town, but with a few soldiers eating their warm meals across the room, she didn't want to take a chance.

"Sorry I'm late," Jinsle said, tossing a stray lock of his dark hair away from his face. His fair cheeks stood flushed from the chilly day.

"I was beginning to think you were dead."

He took the chair beside her instead of across the table, allowing for his own view of the room. The noise steadily grew as patrons filed in for lunch. Speaking in her room would be more private.

Before she could suggest the change, Commander Silst stepped inside with two soldiers. She recognized one of his companions as the blond man she had seen him speaking with at Krithyafest. He wore the same chainmail and leather armor as his commander, while the other soldier had only the standard red arming doublet. The commander didn't see her before the soldiers already present called them over. As the two parties converged, Eselle watched the commander and other armored man scan the room.

The moment Silst saw her, his eyes stopped, holding her gaze. Despite Eselle's mixed feelings, her stomach fluttered.

While the armsman joined the already entrenched group, the commander spoke with the blond man. They took a seat closer to the bar, across the room from both Eselle's table and that of the other soldiers. Once settled, they spoke with the innkeeper, then fell deep into conversation.

"I think we should find somewhere else to speak," Jinsle said.

Eselle contemplated the two tables of soldiers. "No. That might be more suspicious. With all this other noise, they can't hear us if we keep our voices low."

"You certain?"

The distance made it difficult to see the blond man's insignia, but only the lord marshal, commanders, and captains wore both the chainmail hauberk and leather armor. He wasn't the lord marshal; she'd seen the lord marshal once, and he looked nothing like this man. No other commander would be this deep into the region, so she assumed he was a captain. Likely not a city captain, ruling as the commanders ruled the regions, but rather the regional commander's second. He was part of Silst's personal contingent that accompanied him to be deployed at his whim. The man appeared to be in his mid-twenties, his features a stark contrast to his commander. In addition to the blond hair, his eyes were so light Eselle could see them from across the room. What the men did share, however, was a ruggedness that would make anyone question crossing them.

"It'll be fine," Eselle said. "They're caught up in their food and conversation. Relax, and no one will suspect anything."

Jinsle pursed his lips and folded his arms across the table. "Fine. But what dumb luck to be here at the same time they are."

"Everyone's gotta eat."

Though the inn's cook wasn't terribly skilled and kept to pottage, using whatever was on hand, today's meal smelled particularly pleasant. The sweet, hearty aroma coming from the kitchen made Eselle's stomach growl.

"I don't mean eating; I mean their being in this town at all. They should be at least a hundred leagues northwest of here."

"Do you know why they aren't?" She glanced at the table of soldiers. None paid them any attention.

Jinsle shook his head. "I got held up at Baron Winstrom's and came straight here. We need to track these new patterns and get word to others to do the same in their regions. It could be nothing, but we should make sure."

Eselle nodded. "Have you heard anything about the other regions altering their patterns?"

"No. You?"

"No. It bothers me."

"It could be a precaution on their part," Jinsle said. "I've heard they're searching for something or someone. They're snatching women from some of the towns."

"They usually do."

"Not for their own perverse pleasures. They're arresting these women and transporting them to the castle."

That made Eselle's skin crawl. "Do you think they're hunting for me again?"

Jinsle gave a hesitant, thoughtful shake of the head. "Not this time. They're taking all sorts of women. I saw two being hauled out of a town a couple of weeks back: a tall blonde and an average-sized brunette. Their appearances were nothing alike, though the brunette had your basic size and coloring. As much as the king would love to get his hands on you, I don't think this is about you this time."

Hopefully not.

Eselle peeked over at the commander and his companion and forgot what she was about to say. With effort, she refocused and ignored the dark eyes watching her from across the room.

"Is the baron still with us?" she asked.

"Of course. Why?"

"Because Earl Holgood isn't."

"What?" Jinsle asked sharply. After a quick glance around the room, he leaned back in his seat and assumed a casual posture. "He was so devoted, the first noble to pledge himself."

With a sigh, Eselle sat straighter. "He wouldn't give his reasons exactly, something about keeping his family safe. He vowed he won't reveal our plan, but he's not with us anymore."

"I wouldn't blame him, except that keeping Vorgal in power is more dangerous than removing him." Jinsle pursed his lips, frowning at the center of the table.

Eselle had to agree. "Regardless, we have to let Tavith know. He was counting on the earl. He'll need time to readjust."

Jinsle nodded. "I should get this to him immediately. I'll head out this afternoon."

"I hate to put you right back on the road," she said, reaching to give his hand a grateful squeeze, "but I hoped you'd say that. Have some lunch first and then rest up in my room a bit before you leave. I won't need it until tonight anyway."

"Thanks. You should come with me. Your brother's close to moving, and I know he'd like you there alongside him."

She wished she could help Tavith. "No. Right now, he needs warriors and military strategists, and that's certainly not me. I'd only be in the way. I'll stay here and track these new movements, see if I can discover what's happening."

"You sure?"

"Yeah." She could do more good out in the realm, gleaning information, than she ever could at the farm.

A glance toward the commander revealed Silst eyeing her while his companion spoke. They had bowls before them. The commander didn't seem interested in his, as he only held his spoon and listened.

Jinsle followed her gaze. Instead of commenting, he waved to the innkeeper for a couple of bowls of pottage.

The meal proved more unnerving than speaking about their plan in the same room as six soldiers. When the commander got lost in conversation with his captain, Eselle found herself studying him. The moment his attention drifted her way, she turned to Jinsle and asked the first thing that popped into her head. How were so-and-so and what's-his-name the last time you saw them? Really? Great.

Her arguments about steering clear of a dangerous man slowly eroded under that dark-eyed gaze.

"What's going on here?" Jinsle finally asked as he finished his bowl.

"What?"

"You and the commander keep ogling each other. Are you working him?"

Eselle peered down into her half-eaten bowl. The pottage had ended up smelling better than it tasted. "No, but I considered it."

"Perhaps you should consider it again."

She peered up to see if he was joking but found him straight-faced as he regarded her.

"I know it's distasteful—and incredibly dangerous if you get caught—but he's obviously interested. Think of the information you could get from someone like him." Giving a discrete nod at the commander's table, he asked, "That's Silst, right?"

"Yes." She glanced up to find the commander focused on his companion.

"Who better than the third most powerful man in the realm to give you information about the most powerful man in the realm?"

"The second most powerful?" Eselle said, quirking a brow.

"Well, yes." Jinsle nodded with a shrug. "But I'd steer clear of the lord marshal if I were you. He's twice your age, extremely unpleasant from what I hear, and thoroughly entrenched in Vistralou. And the castle isn't the safest place for you."

Eselle wondered if she could do it, succeed in manipulating information from Silst without getting killed. As limited as her seduction skills were, it was safer not to attempt it, but Jinsle had a point. The commander definitely seemed interested. It would be easier to track his movements if she developed a relationship with him, possibly traveled *with* him rather than followed him. But it went far beyond her comfort level.

"I'll consider it," she said, stirring her pottage absently.

"Judging by the looks he's giving you, I'd say you could do it in your sleep, but I don't think much sleeping would be involved."

Eselle glared at her friend, her cheeks growing warm. She snuck a peek at the commander. He and his captain appeared deep in conversation, so hopefully he hadn't noticed.

"You're terrible." Eselle chuckled lightly, jabbing Jinsle's arm.

"And tired. Now that I'm full," he said as he patted his belly, "I'll take you up on that offer of your room. After a quick nap, I'll head out. Is there anything you want me to relay to Tavith?"

"Just that I'm proud of him. And good luck."

With a nod, Jinsle smiled. "Good luck here."

Eselle gave him directions to her room, then watched him head up the stairs.

The moment Jinsle disappeared, Eselle peeked back at the commander and his captain. As they spoke, the commander nibbled his food. She wondered what they were discussing.

Eventually, she succeeded in dismissing him from her mind while she returned to her list and garden designs. Once the ideas began to flow, she blocked out the entire room and finished drawing the layout for the herbs.

A scraping thump sounded when the chair beside Eselle slid from the table. She jerked her head up and found Commander Silst. He took the seat beside her, the same Jinsle had chosen. Instead of speaking, he pushed Jinsle's bowl aside, studying her silently.

Eselle folded her paper and put it in a pocket. "How was your pottage?"

"The same as yours, so I'm sure you already know." His gaze was steady, his features calm.

She swallowed thickly. "Then it must have been pretty good. Mine was."

He reached over to her bowl and tilted it to look inside. "Doesn't seem like it. You barely touched it."

"It looked like you barely touched your own."

"That's because I wanted to be touching something else."

The memory of wrapping her legs around him, pressing against him, made her shift in her chair and glance away. She swallowed and surveyed the room full of patrons. The soldiers from earlier had left, along with the captain, but five more had entered and were receiving their meals. At least a dozen more townsfolk and travelers sat throughout the tables and bar. Everyone was caught up in either food or conversation, so no one noticed her heated cheeks. Only the commander. She'd never blushed this much in her life. She didn't dare look to see if he wore that devilish half-smile she adored.

"Since I can't touch what I want at the moment, why don't we continue our discussion of your hometown and traveling plans."

Keeping her curses in her head, she turned back to him while mentally reviewed their previous conversations to ensure she didn't contradict herself.

Eselle scooted her chair back from the table a little. "I'm surprised you waited this long."

"I've been busy with town business, but you now have my undivided attention."

She saw the challenge in his eyes, the playfulness that caressed her as sensuously as if his hands were on her. Her skin tingled at the anticipation. She feigned interest in setting the bowls aside. "What do you want to know?"

"Where are you really from?"

How far would he push these questions? Enough to make her stumble over them and catch her in the lies? She sat back in her chair. "Is it more important where I'm from or where I'm going?"

"That depends. Where are you going?"

"I haven't decided yet." She needed to track his movements, and she also worried about Cristar being alone near the end of her pregnancy. For the last couple of days, she'd considered staying longer, helping Cristar instead of leaving her to the townsfolk who had their own lives to worry about.

"Is there anything I can do to help you decide?" His unwavering gaze held her enraptured.

There are several things.

His determination was evident, so she decided to chance it. Eselle leaned forward on crossed arms and appreciated his strong features—the sharp jawline and straight nose, the upturn at the corners of his mouth—before she settled on his eyes. If he wanted her story, she would give him one.

"My name is Tarania Gilfer, and I *am* from Florial. If you haven't heard of it, then perhaps you're not as well traveled as you thought you were. My parents died when I was young, so my aunt and uncle raised me, alongside their own daughter, a snotty little brat who liked to cut my hair in the middle of the night. While I watched my cousin marry the simplest man in the village, I realized my life would remain the same drudgery as it always had been. I would find another simple man—though there wasn't much of a selection of available men in Florial—I would get married, have babies, and then die, all without having any say in how my life turned out. No, thank you. I packed food, an extra set of clothes, a few other supplies I stole from my aunt and uncle while they were sleeping, and then slipped away."

He listened intently, appearing pleased she revealed so much, but she couldn't tell if he believed her or not. If he was smart, he wouldn't. None of it was true. She figured the most believable stories were often the most boring, so she'd invented the most boring thing she could imagine. The less there was to question, the easier it would be to maintain the lie.

"I've been traveling ever since," she continued, "searching for a decent place to settle down or an adventure to have. Once I decide where I'm heading, I'll let you know."

The commander leaned over, his voice a little deeper than usual. "Why didn't you tell me this before?"

"I was afraid of what you'd do to me. Traveling alone can be dangerous, especially for a woman."

With their faces close as they both leaned on the table, Eselle couldn't help but appreciate his features, the depth of those dark eyes, and his full lips. If she leaned a little closer, she could taste them again. She reached out to lightly grasp his chin and run her thumb along his bottom lip. It was as silky soft as she remembered.

Eselle's eyes rose back to his. She had no warning.

He sprang from his seat, grabbed her by her arms and hoisted her up. Her chair toppled over with a hard smack against the floor as the commander backed her into the hallway behind them.

CHAPTER EIGHT

Eselle couldn't catch her bearings, not until after the commander had her behind the hallway curtain. Loosely tied across the entrance, the faded brown drape only somewhat obscured them from view. He pressed her against the wall and kissed her.

The swiftness of his actions had kept her from thinking clearly. Instead of pushing him away, she gripped his chainmail and pulled him closer. Metal clinked when she tried to dig her fingers into the cool rings of his hauberk. His hands slid along her waist and gripped her hips tight against him. Eselle zealously met his delving tongue. Unconcerned with modesty, she lifted a leg and wrapped it around one of his. A deep moan rumbled out of him, setting her flesh ablaze as he trailed kisses along her neck.

Movement off to the side caught Eselle's attention. The innkeeper set her chair upright and looked sidelong down the hall at them. He picked up the bowls before walking off with a frown.

She tore her mouth free. "Commander, wait."

His lips grazed her skin as he spoke. "Don't call me commander when you're wrapped around me like this." His warm breath tickled the hairs on her neck. When he nibbled her ear, she giggled and couldn't even remember her own name, let alone his. "It's Kyr, not commander."

With her breathing coming deeper, she tried to collect her thoughts. A difficult thing to do with his enticing tongue licking across her jaw, sending tantalizing shivers all the way to her toes. "Kyr, wait."

"I don't want to wait again."

His hips pushed into her, and Eselle forgot her argument. With a gasp, she yielded to her need. She reached her arms up over his shoulders and tried to hold him tight, but those damn spaulders were in her way. She really hated his armor.

Grabbing her by the thighs, Kyr lifted her up onto him.

She clamped her legs around his waist.

Remembering why she'd wanted his attention, Eselle pushed back against his shoulder. "Wait. Kyr, hold on." He nipped her lip, and she jumped, her pulse quickening at the thrill. She struggled not to lose herself in him. "Someone will see us." When he only tried to kiss her again, she pulled back. "Your soldiers may have seen a lot, but I don't want to show them more." She faltered when he pressed her back against the wall and tugged open the bottom laces of her tunic, then moved upward for the next. "I'm serious," she murmured, tilting her head to let his sinful mouth continue exploring her.

"Where's your room?" His tongue traced the outline of her jaw.

She released a ragged breath. "Upstairs, second door."

"Too far," he muttered against her skin. His teeth grazed her earlobe.

"Where's yours?" There was a quiver to her voice. Her legs tightened around him, and she dug her fingers into his soft, thick hair.

"Mayor's house."

"Too far," she said.

Kyr shifted her along the wall but didn't pull up from her neck. A faint click sounded. Unconcerned with their destination, she allowed him to carry her through the doorway beside them. Only when they dropped onto a cushioned surface did she realize he'd taken her into one of the inn's guest rooms.

The thought of stopping him barely crossed her mind. It didn't matter that someone could walk in, or that she hardly knew the man lying on top of her. After so many solitary months on this assignment, she yearned to satisfy her own needs. And the commander was certainly interested in helping her with them.

As incredible as he felt pressed against her, Eselle craved more. She wanted to get past his armor to the man beneath. While she worked on his many ties, he fervently helped her. His leather armor dropped to the wooden floor in a series of thuds, quickly followed by the chainmail. A few layers later and Kyr pulled his shirt over his head.

Eselle sat up and kissed his sculpted chest, with its light, even speckling of dark hair. She ran her fingers along the bottom of his ribs, gently enough to make him shiver. He gave a sigh before pressing her down against the bed. In one smooth maneuver, he slid her trousers off and flung them away.

Before she could utter a playful comment, Kyr pushed her shirt up and kissed her stomach. Heat pooled everywhere he licked, stroked, and nibbled as he slowly worked his way up to her breasts. He flicked his tongue across her nipple before taking her completely in his mouth. Eselle pulled at his shoulders, needing him against her. His hungry kisses drove upward, claiming her lips, and she wrapped her legs around him.

She had freed Kyr of his armor, his sword, his shirt, but she had not undone his trousers. He didn't seem inclined to rush, but she ached. She tried to entice him with her body, pressed her breasts against him, ground her pelvis into his; he only slid a hand along her hip, her bottom, the backside of her thigh as he pulled her leg close.

The teasing became too much. Eselle reached between them and began undoing the laces of his trousers.

Feeling his lips curl up in a smile against hers, she jabbed him lightly in the ribs. "You were waiting for me to do this, weren't you? To undo your trousers myself."

He chuckled, leaning in to kiss the tender space beneath her earlobe, making her breath catch. Her hips instinctively pressed into him.

"And if I hadn't made the move?" Her voice had grown breathy.

"I knew you would."

"Do you play this game with everyone?"

He kissed along her chin and around the other side of her neck. "If I did, would it matter?"

"Definitely not." She resumed untying his trousers. Shoving them halfway down his hips, she turned toward his kisses and coaxed his mouth back to hers.

The moment she felt his tip press against her, he thrust.

Eselle shuddered at the feel of him filling her so completely. Moaned and writhed as he ravaged. Dug her fingers into his pounding hips as they met her own. Cried out as her body clenched in orgasm at the same moment he erupted inside her.

Lying beside Kyr sometime later, feeling his hard, warm body pressed against her back, Eselle felt more relaxed than she had in months. She tried to pretend she was just another townsfolk capable of having a normal life, as she had always wanted. But that could be years from happing, if she ever found it. If she did, she would miss traveling, but more and more she found herself envious of women like Cristar. Eselle didn't need everything—the husband, kids, house, town that still enjoyed celebrating holidays together—but something more than scheming with her brother would be nice. She missed having a large family around her.

Reality rushed back when Kyr's arm wrapped tighter around her, holding her close. She had never forgotten it exactly, but tried to ignore it for a short while, pretend it wasn't important. Unfortunately, the man she'd chosen to spend time with ranked higher than was safe. But then, he was also high enough to prove a valuable resource, whether he knew it or not.

Eselle stroked his forearm. The soft, dark hair seemed sparse enough to go unnoticed unless one was close. Gliding her fingertips through it had a soothing effect. "How long will you be in Eddington?" she asked.

"I asked you first."

"True, but I already answered. I don't know."

"Well, neither do I."

Eselle couldn't tell if he was playing or not, but decided to try again later, when they were less comfortably satiated.

"I should get going." She had plans to meet up with Cristar soon.

Before she could escape, Kyr rolled her onto her back beneath him. He leaned above her with a lazy, satisfied smile. "What's the rush?"

"Other than having errands," she mused playfully, "there's the matter of someone walking in on us. This isn't my room, and I assume it's not a second one of yours."

"No."

"It's someone's." Eselle pointed across the room. In a corner sat two packs and a traveling chest. Other various personal items lay scattered about. Despite the awkwardness of using another patron's room, at least her own had been quickly dismissed. Jinsle was likely still using it, and she really didn't want to explain a sleeping man in her room. "They could return anytime. We're lucky they didn't while we were . . . busy."

Kyr chuckled low and deep, vibrating her chest where he lay against her. "Let them." He ran his fingers along the side of her face, studying her. "We'll tell them to come back later."

She tingled at the feel of his fingers caressing her jaw, then down her neck. Her argument melted away as he explored her, taking everything in. His dark eyes changed when they reached her necklace. The simple silver chain had slid from beneath her shirt. Six knots lay along it, one for each member of her family.

His brow furrowed as he studied it. He lifted the chain from her skin and ran his thumb along the knots. "What's this?"

With a quick kiss, she pulled the necklace from his fingers, then attempted to roll out of bed. The moment she moved, he wrapped one leg around hers and held her in place halfway beneath him.

"It's a necklace," Eselle answered. She tried to ignore the warmth of him pressed against her, but it was a challenge.

"Why is it knotted?" His voice came soft, casual, but she felt uncomfortable with his continued interest.

"Because I don't take care of it, and I'm horrible at untangling it." The necklace was a personal matter, and she didn't know him well enough to share the truth. "We should get dressed. I'm sure you have lots to do today, what with governing the region. Plus, the patron actually renting this room might walk in. You wouldn't want them to see what you have to offer, would you?" She playfully leered down the length of him and smirked; he still hung impressively out of his trousers. "Or maybe you would."

His eyes remained on the necklace as it lay against her throat. Once again, she could no longer read him. She was about to ask what was wrong when he finally met her gaze. His hand slid firmly beneath her bottom and pulled her against him. Leaning down, he kissed her.

Instead of the fevered passion from earlier, things became slower, deeper, more arousing. They needed to leave, but Kyr felt too comfortably familiar, fit too perfectly against her.

Eselle shoved him aside, rolled him onto his back, and mounted him. The smile he gave turned to a moan when she reached down and grabbed hold of him. She slid down onto him, taking him deep inside, claiming every last inch. Her hips moved in slow, deliberate circles. He grazed his hands along her thighs, then up her stomach and under her shirt as he sat up. His hands slid up her breasts, and she raised her arms to let him pull her shirt over her head and toss it aside.

She continued grinding against him as he kissed her breasts, licked and kneaded. When she slid her fingers through the hair at his neckline, it was damp from their previous exertions. She held him to her and buried her face in his hair, smelling sweat and leather, and mountain springs. It brought memories of the springs near her home.

A needy whimper broke free. Eselle gripped his shoulders and pushed him down onto his back. His eyes shone bright once again as he caressed her thighs, lying there watching her.

From her position straddling his hips, she got her first good look at Kyr. They'd been in a flurry of motion before, but sitting there, fingering the contours of his stomach, she appreciated his strapping, masculine form. In addition to a few hairline scars scattered about him, he had a long, fairly smooth scar running diagonally across his entire left shoulder, dipping downward toward the front as it met his bicep. It appeared old and precise, as though done by a sharp blade. The only other significant scarring he bore were angry-looking burns around his right elbow and halfway up this arm, and a few smaller ones halfway up the same side of his torso. Again, they seemed old, but extensive. She couldn't help but reach out and slide her fingers along the puckered flesh.

As she studied them, he wrapped his arm around her and pulled her down to him. Instead of catching herself, she slammed down against his chest and wantonly kissed him, driving her tongue into his warm, wet mouth.

Eselle thrust her hips faster, surrendered to the pleasure building inside her. His hands moved feverishly along her body, hers dug into his hair as she rode hard.

Shudders started as she neared. Pulling away from Kyr's mouth, she leaned upright, moving frantically against him. He grasped her hips and pulled her tight against him, pushing in deeper. Their moans mingled; their cries entwined. They locked up together and ground against each other in ecstasy.

Later, after finding her breath, still lying atop Kyr, Eselle traced a bead of sweat along his throat with her finger. His hand ran slowly through her loose hair, grazing her back with each stroke. It was too easy to consider staying like this with him. With an inward sigh, she reminded herself she still had things to tend to today.

The moment she tried to roll off Kyr, he cinched his arms around her. "Wait . . . Do me one favor."

"What?"

He clasped the back of her head, holding her close as he spoke against her hair. "Remember this."

She wasn't likely to forget. The experience had been both fierce and gentle, and she wasn't certain which she enjoyed more: when he took what he wanted, or when he savored every moment. Her body warmed at the memories. "We really should be going."

After sliding off him, she found her shirt amid the boots, garments, and armor splayed haphazardly across the floor. She pulled it over her head, then tucked her necklace back inside. Kyr rolled to his side and watched her put herself back together but made no effort to do the same. He was absent all but a sheen of sweat, which made his rugged body glisten in the light coming through the window.

When he lifted himself off the bed, she appreciated the way his muscles moved, even the scarred ones. He approached while she tucked her shirt into her trousers. Lifting a hand to cup her face, he ran his thumb along her jaw and studied her features.

Eselle shifted her stance but stood in place. While she enjoyed looking at him, she was unaccustomed to people looking too closely at her. She'd always tried to avoid notice, made certain few people remembered her after she left a place. Between her work and heritage, it was safer. Perhaps this situation was different, and she should be flattered he cared to look at all. From what she'd heard, most soldiers taking advantage of women didn't want to get to know their conquests, but rather took what they wanted and moved on. But then, as much as she had participated in the seduction, she'd taken advantage of him too.

"I suppose you're right. We should be going," Kyr said, sounding oddly resigned. After one last lingering kiss, he dropped his hand with a backward step, and still made no effort to redress himself. His eyes dipped to her neckline briefly. "I have something important to do today . . . And so do you."

He watched Eselle as she donned her tunic, adjusted the last of her clothes, and retied her braid. She stood there for a moment, unsure how to say goodbye after everything they'd done. Finally, she stepped forward, pulled him down to her, and kissed his cheek.

Eselle didn't allow herself to look back as she hurried out the door. She had plans, so she forced her legs to keep walking, when all she really wanted to do was climb Kyr again.

***

After Eselle completed a couple errands, she headed to Cristar's house. Seeing several soldiers along the way barge into various houses, she moved to the town's outskirts. The long route might be better.

Vorgal's ruthlessness well underway. But then, I just came from the bed of the man allowing it, so what does that say about me? She frowned at the thought.

Should she investigate? Or, with her information relayed and Jinsle already gone, should she leave? She could return home and assist Tavith in the next phase of his plan. But Cristar shouldn't be alone at a time like this. The thought of leaving another person behind disturbed Eselle. She just couldn't leave before knowing her friend was all right.

Eselle picked up the pace. Entering Cristar's home from the forest side would be the safest. If anyone tried to detain or arrest her, perhaps seducing the commander would prove its worth already.

The moment she turned the final corner, Eselle glimpsed a soldier walking through Cristar's front door. Her chest grew heavy as she hustled through the rear garden gate. Before she moved past the bare tomato plants, she saw the young woman kneeling in her garden. Eselle gave a relieved sigh and made her way through the vegetation.

"Cristar, we have to go," Eselle whispered.

"Go where?" Cristar pulled off her gloves. Her apron was covered in dirt from where she'd been preparing a section of garden for the upcoming winter.

"The troops are breaking into people's homes. I saw one enter yours a moment ago. We need to leave."

Cristar seemed unconcerned but tried to stand. To achieve it, she rocked a few times. In the end, Eselle grabbed hold of one arm and helped lift her.

"The troops do that sometimes," Cristar said, brushing the loose soil from her apron. "They're looking for anything illegal or otherwise valuable or useful they can steal. Trust me, I keep the truly valuable things well hidden. You don't live in Likalsta without learning a trick or two."

Eselle tried to relax, but something felt wrong. The fact that Kyr and his contingent arrived early bothered her. The fact there'd been relatively little commotion from them, but they now burst into people's homes bothered her. It hit her more deeply than she could explain. "Still, I'd feel better if we went into the woods until this is over."

The soldier—the blond captain she'd seen at the inn earlier— emerged from the back door, spotting them immediately. "Stay where you are."

Eselle felt the instinctive need to bolt, but she couldn't leave Cristar. Instead, she stood beside her friend. This could be a standard raid. No reason to believe anyone had discovered her true identity. But why send a captain? Usually the lower ranks ransacked homes. Maybe they knew something after all.

The captain went for Cristar and grasped her arm. "Come with me," he said, then pulled Cristar toward the fence.

Eselle gaped. "What are you doing?"

"We're under orders to bring in all pregnant women." The captain didn't look anywhere but ahead of himself.

Eselle followed them from the garden and onto the road. "That's insane. I'm going to talk to Commander Silst and get this all—"

"The high commander gave the order, told me himself to come get this one."

Eselle stood frozen, then rushed ahead to block the soldier's path. "When did he give this order?"

"Half hour ago."

Shortly after I left him at the inn.

"I didn't do anything." Cristar's voice held a shrill edge. She tried to pull her arm free.

"You're pregnant," the captain said. "That's enough." He stepped around Eselle and resumed escorting his prisoner.

"But being pregnant isn't a crime," Cristar said.

"It is now."

CHAPTER NINE

Five Years Old

When he stepped into the small, dimly lit bedroom, the lad looked noticeably better. The fever had broken earlier in the night, and the boy slept easier now. He sat down on the side of the bed and lightly brushed the boy's hair from his face. Illness was rough on the young. He was thankful to the Protector for helping the boy get through the worst of it.

"Are you watching me sleep again?" The boy's rich brown eyes opened.

The man chuckled. "Yes, I am."

After he'd lost his home years ago, the man had never expected to have children. The day he found himself alone with the boy, he hadn't been prepared, especially for the array of emotions that went with raising a child. Whether he worried about how to feed a newborn or proudly watched the boy climb massive trees out back, the child kept his heart pumping. Thankfully, the youngster was a nimble one and conquered anything he decided to climb up, over, or through.

"I can't sleep. Can you tell me a story?"

The boy was young enough that any story would do; his favorites revolved around the lost dragons of Windspear. The time had come though, to begin telling the most important story of the lad's young life. It was one he hoped the boy would grow to appreciate over the years.

"Okay. I have a new one for you tonight."

The boy's smile was weaker than usual, but it reached his eyes as he rolled onto his side to get comfortable, tucking his hand beneath his head.

Before the man started, he pulled up the thick wool blanket to cover the lad's arm. "Far away, there was a king named Vorgal. Now, he wasn't a nice, wise, or handsome king, like in the fairytales. No, he was a cruel man. He hurt his people."

"Why?"

The man froze midthought. "Oh, um. Well, I guess . . . maybe he was sad and wanted other people to be sad too. Or maybe someone had hurt him, so he wanted others to hurt. Or maybe he was just mean. I'm not really sure."

"How did he hurt them?"

"Well, he made them pay lots and lots of taxes, and—"

"What's taxes?"

"Oh, um, taxes are when you give money to the place where you live to keep it working right." The boy's face scrunched up. "It's not important. But people sometimes didn't have enough money left to buy food. And he had the former king and the mages executed. When—"

"What's executed?"

"Killed."

The boy gasped.

How had he drifted into the darker portions of this story? He definitely needed to save the more complicated and gruesome details for when the boy was older.

"Anyway, trust me, he was a bad king. He was so bad, so mean, that one day a seer used her ability to curse him by telling him when he would die."

"What's a seer? And how did she know when he would die?"

The man leaned in to rub his thumb along the boy's pale cheek. "I love your questions, little one." Now that the fever had broken, he worried the boy felt too cold. He pulled the blankets up higher, all the way to the boy's neck, and tucked them in.

"A seer is someone who can foresee the future. She told the king that a baby would be born in his thirty-sixth year, one who would kill him. The king was still young, so he didn't worry for many years. He thought he had plenty of time. But when the baby's birth drew closer, he got scared. He sent his soldiers out to find the baby.

"Eventually, one of them did. Before King Vorgal could hurt the child, the boy's mother had one of her friends take him to safety."

The boy laid wide-eyed, staring up at him. "Where did they go?"

"No one knows, but one day he'll return." The man adjusted the boy's blankets around him. They were already snug and perfectly placed, but he felt the need to make certain.

"The baby was a boy?"

With a fond smile, he replied, "Yes, lad. It's said he was the most beautiful baby ever born."

"What's his name?"

"His mother hadn't named him before her friend took him away, so only her friend knows."

The boy yawned. "Is King Vorgal real?"

"Vorgal is very real."

"Is he our king?"

The man pushed a stray lock back from the boy's cheek. "No, he's not. Vorgal is far away, with other things to worry about right now. We have a good king. A just king."

"Will King Vorgal come here?"

The man thought about that before answering. "I wish I could say no, but I don't want to ever lie to you. What I can tell you is that you won't have to worry about Vorgal for a long time."

"Do you really think the baby will stop him?" The boy's eyes drooped, the story and late night having done their work.

"Yes. When the time is right, he will."

"Why can't someone else stop King Vorgal?"

The man shrugged. "The seer's vision showed the baby, no one else. Now, get some sleep."

"But I'm not tired," the boy said, despite losing the battle to keep his eyes open. "I want to hear more about the baby."

"I already told you about him. The mother's friend took him to safety, and no one saw him again. Not his mother, not her best friend, not—"

"You said her friend took him away." The boy rubbed his eyes.

"Well, yes, one of her friends did. The mother had another friend though, Eselle. She was a courageous woman, a loyal friend when the mother needed one. Eselle saved the young mother and their other friend several times while they traveled together and protected the baby before he was born."

"How?"

Even though the boy needed sleep, the man figured it wouldn't hurt to tell a little more. The boy's latest yawn threatened to dislocate his jaw, so he'd likely fall asleep well before the story ended.

"How did she save them?" the man mused. To tell this tale right, he should start with the beginning. "Well, first, Eselle was the bravest person to ever live."

CHAPTER TEN

W hat's happening?" Eselle stormed alongside the captain and Cristar. "Why is she being arrested?"

Eselle had enough training from allies that she might be able to overcome a single—albeit lesser trained—soldier, but not this man. He exuded a confidence similar to his commander, stood several inches taller than her, and moved with a grace only achieved through years of training. Rescuing Cristar by brute force would not be an option.

The soldier continued without looking at either woman. "All pregnant women are being rounded up."

"Why?" Cristar asked. She cradled her stomach with her free hand, while the soldier had a firm grip on her other arm.

"It's not my place to say. Commander Silst will give an announcement shortly."

There had to be more happening. Jinsle mentioned women being taken to Vistralou. He hadn't said whether they were pregnant, but the troops sought a pregnant woman in Grimswold.

Eselle hustled ahead of the captain, getting in front of him. "But this doesn't make sense."

He brushed her out of his way, but she kept blocking his path, determined to get answers.

"Look," he snapped, coming to a halt, his voice rumbling the more agitated he became, "do I have to arrest you too?"

He glared at Eselle. She stood straight and glared back. His ice-blue eyes sent a chill through her, but she wouldn't back down where Cristar was concerned. Before either looked away, another voice came from behind her.

"Good work, Captain."

Eselle turned to find Kyr and another soldier approaching from one of the adjoining lanes. They had a woman between them. Though her stomach was significantly smaller than Cristar's, she was far enough along Eselle was certain she was pregnant.

"Take these two to the wagon," the commander told his soldiers. They both nodded and escorted their charges down the road.

"What's happening?" Eselle asked.

Kyr eyed the departing group for a moment before answering. "We're heading out, back to Vistralou."

"I don't mean that. Why are you rounding up pregnant women?"

"King's orders."

Eselle watched as her friend was taken away. Her hands clenched with the need to do something. "Why?"

Kyr shrugged. "It's not my job to interpret the king's decisions, only to make certain they're adhered to."

"She's my friend. Is there anything you can do?" Eselle couldn't bear the thought of what might happen to Cristar, couldn't fathom what the king had in store for these women.

"Do? What would I do?" He seemed almost impassive.

"Release her." Eselle stepped closer. "As a favor to me."

"Why would I do that? The king's orders are to bring in all pregnant women." He was cold, businesslike, and she didn't know how to reach this version of him.

Eselle didn't try masking her pleading. "She's my friend."

"So you've said."

"She didn't do anything."

"She became pregnant."

When Eselle opened her mouth to protest, he gripped her arms and looked calmly at her. The warm strength of his hands soothed her nerves.

His voice softened the slightest bit. "I'm sure none of these women have actually done anything to deserve being arrested, but it doesn't matter. If the king declares pregnancy is a crime, then it's a crime. End of discussion."

"But . . ." Eselle glanced once more after Cristar. The soldiers and women rounded a corner, and she lost sight of her friend. "Why would he want them arrested?"

Before speaking, Kyr released her, and his voice grew firm again. "Instead of arguing with me or questioning the king's desires, you should be grateful I'm not taking you in for observation. We both know there's a possibility I might return for you in a couple of months. It could be easier to collect you now, especially considering you're a known runner."

Eselle stepped back, her mouth hanging open. With her concern for Cristar, she hadn't considered herself. If she did end up pregnant, would he really arrest her? Even if the child was his? It was too much to consider. She needed to focus on Cristar since she was in more immediate danger.

Kyr raised a questioning brow, then sauntered off after the rest of the group. Eselle followed at a reluctant distance. She needed to see where they'd taken Cristar.

Two wagons with open metal cages on the back sat at the edge of town. One wagon held a few young men—Eselle assumed conscripts—while a woman sat in the other. Each wagon offered little room but allowed the prisoners to be unbound for the journey.

The captain who had arrested Cristar stood off to the side, coordinating troops for their departure. Two armsmen stood with Cristar and the other pregnant woman behind the wagons. Several townsfolk had gathered nearby, demanding answers, while a handful of soldiers held them back. Among the crowd was Warder Hilbert.

"Commander Silst, may I speak with you," the warder called out above the noise. He pushed his way to the front.

Kyr glanced over at him, gave a brief frown, then stepped toward the gathering as he called for attention.

Eselle watched the proceedings at the wagon, only listening when Kyr spoke.

"The king has decreed that until further notice, no woman is legally allowed to become pregnant. Anyone already pregnant must be reported and brought to Vistralou Castle. Anyone who becomes pregnant from this moment forward will be subject to imprisonment and possible execution."

The entire crowd gasped. Eselle gaped at him, feeling like he'd kicked her in the chest.

Kyr scanned his audience shrewdly. "Anyone caught harboring or failing to report a pregnant woman will be subject to execution."

The majority of the people stared with varying degrees of uncertainty. After nearly two decades of seeing their young men forcibly carted off for conscription, the townsfolk appeared sadly resigned to losing more of their own. Only the warder and a few others stood with gritted teeth and scowls. Eselle silently cursed Vorgal Grox for this new cruelty. No decent king could have an excuse for this.

"Inform everyone of this news," the commander ordered. "I'll collect anyone else you find the next time we pass through."

Most of the crowd gazed in anguish at their fellow townsfolk in the wagons. Some turned toward others for consolation. A few clenched their fists and sneered at the soldiers, mostly Kyr. Eselle suspected more than one woman would soon find a sudden need to be somewhere else.

With a huff, she returned her attention to the women at the wagon. One of the armsmen pulled out a set of keys and unlocked the cage. He stepped back as he opened the door, sliding the keys into his pouch.

She fidgeted, trying to think of an argument that would convince Kyr her friend should be an exception. Granted, she didn't know Cristar well, but she'd grown close to the woman. She'd heard stories of Cristar's family and husband, relayed stories of her own, some of which were true. Cristar had shared her garden, something she rarely did with anyone, even her husband. She didn't deserve this. None of the women did, especially for something that was a natural part of life.

"Sir, may I speak with you?" Warder Hilbert pushed through the lingering townsfolk and stepped up to the commander.

Eselle shimmied through the crowd, wanting to get closer to hear what the warder had to say. From what she'd seen, he was a voice of reason and compassion. Perhaps he could talk some sense into Kyr, convince him the king's order should not be upheld.

"I'm busy at the moment, Warder." The commander didn't look at Hilbert, but instead oversaw the women being loaded. "Next time I'm in town, I'll make sure to visit."

"This can't wait." The warder stepped in front of Kyr, demanding attention.

"This *will* wait." The commander nonchalantly motioned to a couple of his armsmen.

The soldiers stepped over and took Hilbert's arms.

"What are you doing?" the warder asked.

"I already know your arguments and have no interest in hearing them." Kyr looked to the armsmen. "Escort the warder back to his church, then catch up with us." The soldiers nodded.

"You can't do this, Commander. These women have done nothing. Nothing!"

The hope that had brewed in Eselle when the warder interceded died as they dragged Nossen Hilbert away.

There had to be something that would save these women, and the conscripts. She looked at the men just as the last one was loaded. An armsman closed the door behind him. The click of the latch rang like a death sentence. In a few months, these men would likely be dead on a battlefield far from home, just to gain a few leagues for the realm.

After the second woman climbed into the cage, one of the armsmen grabbed Cristar's arm. "You're next." He jerked her forward, making her stumble.

Eselle's breath caught, and she lunged forward. She was too far.

Before Cristar hit the ground, Kyr reached out and grasped her arm, catching her with his other and keeping her upright. Concern was evident in his features as he studied her, holding her steady. Cristar met his gaze for a long moment with an uncertain one of her own. Her face soon transformed into a determined scowl Eselle was proud of. Kyr's expression turned stern, and he released her.

The same hand that had caught Cristar flew backward, striking the soldier across the face. The armsman stumbled and fell on his butt. The high commander reached down and hauled the man up by the front of his arming doublet. He punched the soldier in the face, breaking the man's nose and bloodying his own knuckles. The soldier went slack in his superior's grip. Eselle sucked in a breath while staring at Kyr's clenched jaw, startled by the raw fury that rolled off him.

He raised his fist again but held still as he glared into the soldier's bleeding face. "*Gently.* She's pregnant and they're not to be harmed. Do that again, and I'll gut you and leave you for the carrion birds to feast upon."

The soldier nodded with a slight wobble. The commander, his features no less strained, shoved the armsman away. The man stumbled and fell back to the ground.

Eselle saw her opportunity. She moved in to help the soldier to his feet, grabbing him under one arm.

Careful to keep Kyr's attention upward, looking at her face, she threw all her anger into her voice. "What's wrong with you?"

He didn't respond, only met her glower with his own. She forced herself to hold back a smirk when the right side of his jaw clenched.

The armsman brushed her hands away the moment he regained his balance and stomped off.

So did she, before Kyr decided to detain—or arrest—her.

She made her way back to the dwindling crowd. Most of the townsfolk had returned to their lives, but several remained.

While the wagons rolled out, the soldiers mounted their horses and followed. The high commander, atop his large black courser, inspected his contingent as it filed past. Once the last soldier rode by, Kyr regarded Eselle with an unreadable expression, then rode off. She stood there a moment longer as he nudged his stallion into a canter that took him to the front of the line.

Kyr had a job to do, a duty to his king, but Eselle had her own duty to consider.

She rushed back to the inn, with the soldier's keys tucked securely in her pocket.

CHAPTER ELEVEN

Eselle threw open the door to her room at The Old Goat and dashed in.

"Damn it, Jinsle."

Though late to arrive, he had been quick to leave. The room stood empty.

She would have been more upset if getting the information to Tavith wasn't so important. Still, she could have used Jinsle right now. While she didn't exactly have a plan yet, an extra set of hands could have come in handy.

Eselle shoved her few belongings into her pack and hurried back out.

Halfway to the edge of town, she stopped. Cristar couldn't return home, at least not anytime soon. Kyr hadn't mentioned what would happen to the pregnant women, whether the arrest was permanent, or they would be released at any point, possibly after giving birth. She surveyed the town around her, then turned down the lane on her left.

Once at Cristar's house, Eselle rummaged around until she found another pack. She tossed in everything the woman would need, including some of Klaasen's old clothes so Cristar would have trousers instead of dresses. She filled both packs with as much food as would fit. They could find plenty to eat in nature, but additional food stores never hurt when a pregnant woman was involved. She hurried through the house, not wanting the contingent to get too far ahead.

For the first league, Eselle's heart pounded as much from fear of losing Cristar as from running. She stopped when her lungs burned near to bursting and forced herself to sit against a tree to catch her breath. Speed would do no good if she reached Cristar too winded for a rescue. The wagons would slow the soldiers down, so she had time. If nothing else, she could catch them when they stopped for the night.

A few more leagues and Eselle saw the rear guards ahead. She ducked into the trees for the remainder of the journey. The red doublets and cloaks clashed with the greenery of the woods, letting her stay farther back without losing sight of them.

Three additional wagons traveled with the soldiers, bringing the count to five. Two contained what she assumed were conscripts but may also have been criminals. The third wagon contained five more women.

Where did they come from?

Eselle recognized Cristar and the other Eddington women, but was too far away to see anything more. She pursed her lips and moved between wide trunks and heavy brush. Each time leaves crackled or branches snapped beneath her feet, she froze. Most of the ground cover was old, the cooler season only just starting, so thankfully it didn't produce much noise. Another few weeks and it would be covered with dried leaves.

Shy of a couple hours later, the caravan stopped. Letting her fears get the better of her, Eselle considered a rescue attempt, but there were too many soldiers to risk it. The high commander had his full contingent with him, a little over twenty armed men.

Eselle found a spot amid thick brush that allowed her to get a little closer.

The armsman Eselle had pick-pocketed earlier walked to the back of the wagon holding Cristar's group. His nose had taken on a bright red, bulbous quality, which extended beneath his eyes, making them look puffy. He checked his pouch, then a couple of pockets. He patted himself down. Other soldiers gathered around him, Eselle presumed for guard duty.

"Open the cage," one of them said.

"I'm, uh . . ." The armsman who had lost the keys continued patting himself, checking places he'd already checked.

"Why aren't the prisoners out of the cage yet?" Kyr pushed aside soldiers as he approached. "We have a schedule to keep, armsman."

The soldier stood straight, his arms to his sides. "I know, sir. I, um, I . . . I seem to have misplaced my keys."

The commander stared at the man for a long tense moment. Even from back in the trees, Eselle saw his features tightening while the armsman paled.

"What do you mean, you *misplaced* them?"

"I . . . can't find them." The soldier's voice dropped—Eselle barely heard him—and none of the others made a sound.

The commander grabbed the man with both hands by his arming doublet, spun him around, and slammed him against the wagon.

All three women jumped back in the cage. Eselle held her breath.

"I know what misplaced means," Kyr said through gritted teeth. "I want to know how you propose we open this cage if you've lost the key."

An odd part of Eselle felt bad for getting the soldier in trouble, but then she remembered he had also manhandled Cristar and made her stumble.

The armsman's jaw moved, but no words came out. His mouth finally clamped shut. From the new angle, Eselle couldn't see Kyr's face, but she suspected she wouldn't want to.

Kyr yanked the armsman away from the cage and tossed him to the ground. Pulling out another set of keys from a pouch on his belt, he held them up for the armsman to see, then threw them with enough force they bounced off the man's padded chest.

"If you lose those keys, I'll lose you at the bottom of the nearest lake." The commander stormed off.

The soldiers standing around began shifting. A few chuckled as the reprimanded armsman stood on shaky legs.

He fidgeted with the keys, examining each one. "Shut up. You wouldn't have fared any better." The remaining soldiers broke out in laughter.

Eselle settled in where she was while the guards released the women long enough to relieve themselves. As she waited, she thought about what she had seen. Kyr's temper was more formidable than she had realized. She couldn't reconcile the two men in her mind, the one who'd passionately though gently caressed her, and the one who'd beaten his soldier back in Eddington and threatened him moments ago.

The contingent continued on for several more hours, taking occasional short breaks. Though Eselle was accustomed to long days of travel, she never walked this far at this pace, trying to keep up with people on horseback. Eventually, she had to slow down, let the soldiers get a little ahead and hope they didn't venture off the main road.

Shortly after they stopped for the night, she caught up with them.

Eselle crept around to the side of the encampment, keeping to the woods as she debated how long to wait after everyone went to sleep. A guard would be posted, and she would have to move eight pregnant women without noticed; after all, she couldn't rescue one and not the others. The men from the cages, however, she decided to leave. She didn't know if they were conscripts or criminals, and she wouldn't risk finding out after it was too late. If Tavith succeeded, they would be free before they saw any battle.

The women were removed from the wagons, allowed another break, and given food. Some of them, like Cristar, showed their anger and discontent openly, while others appeared more resigned. Eselle wondered how long ago those women had been arrested. After the meal, the women were crammed into a tent too small for their numbers.

Seems I didn't need to steal the keys after all.

A guard stood before the tent, while another patrolled the camp perimeter. The moon hung high in the sky, shining bright enough Eselle had little difficulty studying the patrolman's patterns. The downside, of course, was that the soldiers would have just as little difficulty spotting escaping women.

The longer Eselle waited, the more she fidgeted. She sat behind a tree and gathered up some pine needles, picking them apart to keep her hands busy. She wanted to get started, get the women to safety.

What if in trying to rescue them, she somehow made things worse? There was also the issue of getting caught herself. If the commander arrested her and returned her to Vistralou . . . if the king got his hands on her . . .

With a shake of her head, she pushed the thought aside. Cristar needed her. As she waited, Eselle pulled her hood up and wrapped her cloak around herself against the cool night.

An hour after Kyr and most of the soldiers went into their tents, she moved. Hopefully, they were deep asleep by now. After the guard passed, she crept closer, behind a tree twenty paces from the women's tent. She stowed the two packs beside it and waited for the patrol to make another loop.

After he passed, she snuck behind the tent with her dagger and slowly slit the back of it open, keeping as quiet as possible. She sheathed her dagger, ready to slip into the tent.

A familiar voice sounded from around the front side. "Armsman Fruise, how are the prisoners?"

Eselle froze.

"They're quiet, Commander."

Eselle imagined the soldier snapping to attention as she silently grumbled at her bad luck.

"Good. I want them up and ready to travel first thing in the morning."

"Yes, sir. They'll be ready."

"Good man," the commander said. "How long have you been in the army now, armsman?"

"Going on six years, sir. Five in the infantry in Heldin and one with you."

Eselle rolled her eyes. How long did they plan to talk? She had expected Kyr to be asleep by this time. If she'd known he was awake and moving about, she would have waited for him to retire. Now she stood exposed with the patrolman due back shortly. She couldn't leave though, not without knowing which direction the soldiers faced. As they reminisced about old adventures, she slipped into the tent.

One of the women jerked upright with a gasp, but Eselle put a finger to her lips. The woman clamped a hand over her mouth. Everyone lay huddled together on the ground under blankets. Cristar sat up with a relieved smile. The tightness in Eselle's chest eased. She motioned toward the front of the tent and repeated her silencing gesture. As the men spoke outside, the women nodded. Eselle pointed to the back of the tent and waved them forward. Several women frowned. A couple slid their blankets and skirts aside to show where they'd been shackled together at the ankles.

Eselle grimaced. She had not accounted for that.

The keys.

She'd expected to use them on the cages, but they might be useful here. They jingled when Eselle dug them from her pocket, and she flinched. A sudden burst of laughter erupted outside the tent, making a couple women jump. Holding the keys as securely as possible, Eselle tried one on the nearest shackle. It didn't fit. She tried another. All the women watched, some with focused expressions and others with evident fear. Her hands began to sweat, and her cloak and tunic suddenly felt too hot. Five keys later, the lock clicked. Eselle moved steadily through the women, cringing with every clink of metal. It would have been a lot less nerve-wracking if the two soldiers weren't right outside. There was only a piece of material between the women and the men with big swords and anger issues.

Eselle sat at the back of the tent, listening for the patrol to pass again. After he did, she climbed out of the tent and risked a peek around the edge. It would be pointless to run if anyone faced their direction. Both the commander and armsman stood with their backs to the tent as they laughed about an incident with a hog a year back. Only hours ago, Eselle would have appreciated Kyr's deep throaty laugh. After what she'd seen earlier that day, she never suspected he was capable of such merriment. The rumbling quality of it reminded her of other throaty noises she'd heard from him recently. Despite the immediacy of the situation, a pleasant tingle ran through her at the memory.

Eselle stuck her hand into the tent with the signal, and the women filed out. They moved as swiftly and silently as possible.

Once in the shadows of the trees, Eselle studied the camp, making certain no one realized the women were missing. Things looked clear. She motioned everyone farther into the forest as she collected the packs and followed.

The moment they had the slightest semblance of distance and cover, one of the women spoke. "Thanks," she said and started to walk off.

"Wait," Eselle whispered, handing Cristar her pack.

As Eselle approached her, the woman stopped and peered back, rubbing absent circles on her faintly rounded stomach. Like the rest, she appeared considerably less along in her pregnancy than Cristar.

"You can't leave on your own," Eselle said. "Plus, that's the direction they're heading."

"I have to get back to my family. They'll be worried." Another woman mumbled similar sentiments, but the rest remained silent, hopefully understanding the situation. Though that didn't make them look any readier for what lay ahead.

Eselle nodded. "I understand, but . . . what's your name?"

"Fresta."

"I understand, Fresta," Eselle said. "But we need to stick together and head that way." She pointed deeper into the woods. According to the maps she'd studied, the forest only lasted a short while before they'd find civilization again. At that time, they could find supplies for the women.

Fresta peered toward the woods for only a moment. "My children need me." Her voice held an edge of desperation.

"It's too dangerous. We're still too close to the soldiers as it is. We need to keep moving, as far from them as possible before they realize you're gone."

"If we split up," Fresta said, "they can't come after all of us. Some of us might make it back home."

"There are more of them than there are of us. So, yes, they can come after all of us. And they know where you live. Going back there would only put your family in danger. Please, we have to move."

"But if we—"

Loud voices and rustling brush came from behind them, growing louder.

"They're coming," Eselle whispered. "This way." With a wave of her hand, she took off deeper into the forest.

Within moments, a shrill yell echoed through the trees. Eselle's heart slammed against her ribs. She stopped and turned. Only Cristar followed her, though she was farther back than Eselle had realized. She waited for her friend to catch up.

Two of the women had already been recaptured. They both screamed and struggled as soldiers hauled them back to camp. More soldiers chased down the remaining women as they scattered in every direction. One armsman started after Eselle and Cristar. Before he took three steps, Kyr grabbed the back of the man's doublet and hauled him around.

"Go secure the camp," he said, his voice gruff. He was absent his armor, and his doublet was only half laced, but his sword was strapped securely to his side.

"But—"

"GO!"

The soldier flinched and ran back to camp.

Cristar hadn't stopped running, and Eselle waved her forward. She wanted Cristar in front.

When Kyr turned back to them, his face was devoid of any merriment Eselle heard from him earlier. The only thing remaining was a scary determination. Little more than fifty paces away, he sprinted straight after them.

Eselle gasped.

Cristar finally reached her.

Eselle pulled Cristar by the hand to haul the woman ahead of her. "Don't look back, just run."

As the commander's longer legs ate up the distance, Eselle studied the areas ahead, seeking something to help them escape. Cristar was simply too pregnant to run fast enough and too cumbersome for any crafty maneuvers that might help them hide. If they couldn't gain distance, Eselle needed to buy her friend time.

She'd lost too many people, and Cristar and her baby would not be added to that list.

Cristar struggled with the terrain and her uncertain balance, occasionally wobbling or slowing down to tackle rough patches. Despite her troubles, she ran faster than Eselle had expected. It wasn't fast enough. The commander quickly closed to within twenty paces. He would be on them in no time.

Eselle panted frantically, but her blood surged through her. She tried to keep Cristar well ahead of herself so Kyr would have to deal with her first, but stay far enough ahead of him that she wouldn't have to deal with him any sooner than necessary.

At the speed they moved, it was impossible for anyone to keep quiet, so she heard his pounding footsteps when he drew close. She wasn't certain if he would try to tackle her, grab for her, or simply stab her in the back. From the little she knew of him, she suspected he would try a takedown first.

The moment his fingers grazed the back of her pack, Eselle ducked and swerved to the side. His momentum carried him beyond her. She'd hoped he would have landed on his face. Instead, he took a couple of jolting steps and slid to a halt, stopping quicker and more gracefully than she had expected.

His breathing was steadier than hers, but his chest heaved with each one.

He definitely had the size and training advantage, but she'd done some training of her own. Some of her brother's allies had been soldiers, both before and after Vorgal seized power. They'd taught her what they could, considering her chosen duty. Her training hadn't been tested yet, only used to keep some frisky men at bay. She hoped it was enough for her first real challenge.

Eselle's breaths came easier, and she trembled with anticipation.

"You certainly are a slippery one," he said. "Always running away from me."

She raised a taunting brow and braced herself for an attack. "That should tell you something."

One corner of his mouth quirked upward. "Perhaps it should. But then, I'm not really interested in you."

The moment he spun and darted after Cristar, Eselle's stomach dropped. In evading him, she'd placed him between her and her defenseless friend. And he'd more than proven to be the fastest runner.

Eselle bolted. The harder she pushed herself, the farther ahead he got. The more the distance increased, the more her throat tightened around her whimpers. Memories of her family surfaced, of running through the halls while they were dying nearby but being unable to get to them, unable to fight off the attackers, unable to save even herself. If not for Tavith, she would have died alongside their family. She wished her brother was with her tonight.

The commander slowed for a moment to adjust his position for an embankment. Eselle blessed any little bit of gained ground. She reached the top of the slope and found him in a controlled slide, stabilizing himself with a hand behind him.

Cristar ran ahead through slender beams of moonlight as they broke through the canopy. She'd lost ground and headed into a denser part of the forest. Once the commander was down, he would catch her in minutes. Seeing him descend nimbly, Eselle started after him. Her fingers dug into the cool dirt behind her, rocks and twigs biting at her hand.

When Kyr reached the bottom, Eselle's desperation got the better of her. She launched herself at his back and slammed into his shoulders. She hit a little off center and sent him stumbling forward. He kept upright with several unsteady steps, while Eselle struggled to hang on. As he righted himself, he reached up, grabbed her arm, and hauled her around his shoulder.

Eselle grabbed onto his doublet as she fell and yanked while kicking into his legs, sending him tumbling face-first down beside her. She spun around and rolled up onto her feet as he reached for her. His fingers only grazed her boot.

Scrambling sounded behind her. The commander had already regained his feet.

Cristar had increased her lead, but not nearly enough. Buying time wasn't sufficient. Eselle needed to prevent the commander from following.

A sturdy-looking branch lay ahead. Eselle rushed toward it. She pretended to stumble, hitting the ground harder than she would have liked. Reaching up for the branch, she pulled it close. Sweat ran into her eyes, but there was no time to wipe it away.

As she hoped, the commander reached down for her. Eselle whipped around and swung for his head. The dry branch broke in two. He dropped to the ground sideways and hit with a thud.

Eselle snatched his sword from his scabbard and stepped back, waiting for him to rise. Kyr remained motionless on the ground. Had she injured him more than she'd intended? She wanted to check, but worried about getting too close. Then she saw the rise and fall of his chest, faint but steady. With a sigh of relief, she ran after Cristar.

After a dozen or so paces, she threw the commander's sword into a bush.

Have fun fishing that out.

CHAPTER TWELVE

If Eselle remembered the maps correctly, the buildings she saw in the distance should be Portlok. The unexpected arrest and subsequent escape a few days back had gotten her a little turned around.

While there'd been no sign of pursuit, Eselle breathed easier knowing they were well out of Commander Silst's region. Though, she did find herself worrying about him. She'd left him breathing, but that didn't mean he woke up or anyone found him. She'd never injured anyone like that, knocked anyone unconscious. Thus far, she'd only dropped an ally on his butt during practice. What if Kyr had been hurt more than she realized?

She couldn't dwell on it, not when she had Cristar to take care of.

"What do you say we get a room for the night?" Eselle asked. She slowed her pace, giving them time to consider options before getting too close to the town.

Cristar put her hands to her stomach. "You remember I'm pregnant, right?"

"I thought we could pad you up and make you look less pregnant, just heavy. We could stuff our spare clothes into the ones you're wearing. You have plenty of room, after all." The clothes Eselle had found for Cristar had been Klaasen's, who apparently had been much larger than his petite wife.

"What if it doesn't work? And shouldn't we get back into the trees? We're almost close enough someone might see us."

"I know, but I also know this has been hard on you, especially sleeping on the ground. One night in a real bed would do you some good."

Cristar perked up at the mention of a bed. Eselle had given the woman her bedroll, but even with that she tossed and turned trying to get comfortable. Hopefully, they could purchase a second one at a store in Portlok.

With a slow shake of her head, Cristar rubbed her stomach. "I don't know."

The street wound between two of the outer buildings, the width suggesting it was a main thoroughfare into Portlok. At one corner of the entrance, two stakes with rounded tops protruded upright from the ground.

Eselle opened her mouth to speak but closed it when a shriek emanated from the town. Looking toward it, she realized what the stakes held. Her breath caught, and she thrust her arm in front of Cristar to stop her.

A woman ran through the street ahead of a pair of soldiers. A third soldier cut her off when he stepped out from around the corner of a building. He grabbed hold of her and carried her off out of sight. The other two hustled after them. Eselle glanced over at Cristar, worried more than anything about her friend's safety. If she tried to help the woman, the soldiers would outnumber her, and Cristar would be left alone.

Tavith's plan couldn't begin soon enough. The Likalstan people needed to be saved from Vorgal and his troops.

Two townsfolk dashed past a side street ahead, followed by more than a handful of soldiers. Eselle took Cristar's arm and pulled her back. Cristar wrapped her cloak around her stomach and retreated without question.

"Perhaps the woods would be better after all," Eselle said, trying not to sound alarmed. "It seems the regional commander is in town."

"I think you're right."

Before she turned away, Eselle swallowed and clamped her mouth shut to stop her jaw from quivering. Looking at the stakes—more precisely, the heads topping them—she whispered, "May the Protector embrace you."

They walked for nearly an hour before either of them spoke.

"Why is this happening?" Cristar said.

Eselle glanced over her shoulder at her. "What?"

"Outlawing pregnancy."

No logical answer came to mind. "I don't know."

"How long do you think it will last?" Cristar's brow furrowed, and her lips pursed.

Eselle wished she had answers, but there was no understanding Vorgal; she refused to call him king.

She began to make out signs of a structure ahead. After pointing it out to Cristar, they crept forward, careful to keep to the thickest brush for cover.

A small log house sat in a large opening among the trees. It needed minor repairs but appeared sturdy. Though it was already near dark, the farmhouse remained unlit. Perhaps the residents were away, and she could find a comfortable bed for Cristar after all.

"Stay here," Eselle said. "Let me look around first."

"No. You take that way," Cristar said, pulling the dagger Eselle had given her, the one she'd purchased in Eddington. "I'll take this way. We'll meet on the other side."

Cristar was right. It would go faster if they both combed the area, and without knowing where anyone might be, it could be just as dangerous to leave her here as let her search the grounds. With a nod, Eselle headed out around the north side of the house, while Cristar took the south.

Before they got too far apart, Eselle peeked back as Cristar disappeared around a tree trunk. Eselle sighed. Cristar would be fine.

Eselle worked her way along the edge of the trees, dagger in hand. Ground cover gave the occasional rustle beneath her feet, but she heard no other sounds. The back of the house proved uneventful. She continued. There were no windows on the north side, but rather a large stone chimney that showed no signs of smoke. Moving around to what seemed like the front of the house, Eselle studied the property. A rough dirt lane disappeared through the woods, a stream flowed beyond it, an old barn stood at the opposite side of the clearing, and a well sat in the middle of it all.

After they met up, Cristar relayed that she had found nothing of significance along the south side, only a struggling garden and haphazard wood pile.

Eselle cautiously stepped onto the porch, rapped on the door, and called out a greeting. No one answered. She tried again a little louder. It remained silent, so she lifted the latch and cracked the door.

A putrid odor slapped Eselle in the face. Stepping back, she tried unsuccessfully to wave the smell away. Her nose twitched. Cristar had moved back too, stepping down off the porch. After a few deep, fresh breaths, Eselle held her breath and peered inside.

The sun had nearly set. The curtains were open and let in enough light to reveal the house's interior. She kept her hand over her mouth and pinched her nose closed as she entered. Cristar started to follow, but Eselle motioned her to stay outside. With a frown, Cristar stepped back.

The single room house had a small kitchen area on one side with a fireplace for cooking, and a table with three chairs. The house seemed cozy, with several rugs and some nicely carved chests. She imagined it would be rather toasty with a fire lit. A double bed with rumpled, though decent looking, blankets sat against the far wall.

Stepping closer, she saw feet beyond the bed. The instinctive deep breath she took was a mistake. She clamped her hand harder over her mouth, willing her stomach back down. Her pulse quickened, and her grip tightened on her dagger.

Eselle eased around the bed. A gray-haired man lay sprawled on the floor, with what she suspected was a knife wound in his back. Her throat tightened, and she turned away to leave the house.

"What is it?" Cristar asked when she emerged. The woman had sheathed her dagger and held her cloak tightly around herself.

"Well, the place is available," Eselle said solemnly. "But it looks like the previous owner was murdered."

"What? How do you know?" Cristar's voice rose a little as she spoke.

"There's a dead man in there, looks like he was stabbed in the back. Probably robbed."

"Do you think it was the soldiers in town?"

With a shake of her head, Eselle answered, "I don't think so. At least, not on this trip. It looks like he's been dead for a while, maybe as long as a month."

"Poor man. May the Protector embrace him." Cristar studied the house, her eyes sad. "Was anyone else in there?"

"Not that I saw. It's a pretty small house, one room, easy to see everything. I didn't notice anyone else, dead or alive."

"We should bury him."

Eselle nodded. "It's getting dark. For tonight, let's sleep in the barn. We'll bury him tomorrow."

Cristar only nodded agreement.

"I want to check out the house," Eselle said. "Why don't you get us set up? I'll meet you there."

"All right."

Due to the foul stench, Eselle made the search of the house quick. She confirmed the man was indeed alone. She found a lantern and some blankets that would not only keep them warmer, but help Cristar sleep a little more comfortably.

Once they settled in, Eselle relayed her plan. "We should clean up the house and stay here until the baby's born."

"Stay?" Cristar tucked a blanket around her legs. The nights had become downright chilly, but the days were thankfully still pleasant.

"Since no one's found him yet, this place should be pretty safe. If anyone does come along, we'll come up with something. Maybe say we're the man's nieces or other relatives of some sort. If not, what better place could we find? There's shelter, a well, all the basic comforts of a home. Not to mention a bed for you. It's perfect."

Cristar wore a thoughtful expression. "What about your family? Your brother? Don't you need to get home?"

"Yes," Eselle admitted. "But not right away. The man I met in Eddington was for family business, but I managed that. So, Tavith doesn't need me right now. You do."

"Are you sure? You've already done so much for us."

"I'm sure."

The woman still seemed hesitant. "Normally, I would say I couldn't ask you to do anything more, to continue risking yourself. For my baby's sake though, thank you; the company and assistance would be greatly appreciated."

Eselle smiled. "I've thought about taking you to Swondan with me, but it might not be wise for you to travel. With this house, we should be pretty well hidden until you're able to."

Cristar's eyes glistened above her gentle smile. "The Protector has blessed us with finding this place. It's perfect."

CHAPTER THIRTEEN

Kyr gave his men their final orders and walked across the bailey, intending to head straight for High Mage Klaskil's office. He needed to speak with the old man and hoped to do so and be back in the field before the lord marshal discovered he'd returned.

Lord Marshal Huln was a formidable leader, but he was an ass. Between their history and Huln knowing Kyr actively sought to steal his position, some animosity was to be expected. The lord marshal didn't hide that he wanted Kyr removed from service, and Kyr delighted in aggravating the man at every opportunity.

As Kyr passed the training yard, he witnessed the king strangling an armsman, his brawny arm wrapped securely around the man's throat.

Swords lay on the ground nearby, so the sword practice had likely somehow turned into a brawl. Since the onlookers cheered, Kyr didn't concern himself further. No doubt the young armsman losing consciousness wasn't doing so because he let the king win, but because Vorgal had actually beaten him. The king was a dangerous opponent. Kyr had never known him to miss his practice sessions, though suspected it was as much to take his frustrations out on the soldiers as to keep his skills honed.

Once the armsman's eyes closed and his arms went limp, the king tossed him to the ground and ignored the applause. The armsman would never hear the end of it when he regained consciousness, but he would have a story to tell.

"Commander Silst," the king called out before Kyr could get away.

The high commander stopped obediently and sighed. He didn't have time for the king right now. Kyr put on a humoring smile and turned around.

The king stalked toward him as he stalked toward everything these days. Vorgal had once taken great pride in his appearance, but the last couple of months he'd stopped concerning himself with such things. Though still robust, he seemed slimmer. His face was haggard, and his shoulder-length black hair was a mess, not just from the recent bout. He'd always been difficult to serve and had become more so recently. The servants feared him, the nobles avoided him, and the military stayed out in the field as long as they justifiably could. Those trapped into service at the castle diligently obeyed and turned a corner when they found themselves in the same room or hallway as the king.

Unfortunately, there were things in Vistralou Castle that Kyr needed, people he needed.

Prince Tryllen followed behind his father, eventually hustling up alongside him. At seventeen, the young man was the spitting image of his father. For several years, Vorgal had been grooming his son for leadership, occasionally even doting, but recently the prince had been as neglected at Vorgal's grooming habits.

The king frowned when he noticed Tryllen and waved the young man away.

"But, I—" the prince started.

The king's wave became more animated. His frown turned into a sneer.

The prince's face twisted into a scowl as he glanced between his father and Kyr. After an exaggerated huff, the prince trudged back to the training grounds. Being related to Vorgal couldn't be easy, but Kyr only had so much sympathy for the lad. There were times he was too much like his father.

"Your Majesty," Kyr said, bowing his head when the king reached him.

"Have you brought me more women?" King Vorgal eyed the side of Kyr's head but said nothing. Unless overly displeased with something, the king never commented on a subordinate's appearance, whether on their attire or a deep bruise that covered a good portion of their right temple.

"Yes, sire. Seven. They're being taken to the dungeon."

The king nodded and waved for Kyr to walk with him. Kyr gritted his teeth. How long would the king delay him?

"Is anything unusual about them? Anything that might suggest one carries the baby I seek?"

"No, Your Majesty. Nothing to indicate the women have unusual pregnancies or carry anything but an ordinary child."

"What of others born recently? Have you heard mention in the realm about special births? Something we might have missed?" The king unrolled the sleeves of his sweat dampened shirt as they approached the keep.

"No. Nothing about babies born without our knowledge or assessment." Kyr forced his jaw to unclench. They entered the great hall and headed to the stairs at the back. Even Kyr avoided too much time with King Vorgal and only lingered long enough to maintain the monarch's favor. Unfortunately, no matter how far out in the field you traveled, the king's orders still reached you, especially those you loathed the most.

For the last couple of months, Vorgal repeated this round of questioning whenever they saw each other. He insisted on being present at each birth, to examine the child personally to ensure he knew the moment the prophesied baby was born.

Kyr slaved away to keep the king happy, but he had no affinity for the monarch, despised the man even. Despised him and despised this hunt that led to so much needless death. Killing a man in battle was one thing, but killing innocent babies was something he couldn't stomach.

The mothers were worse, though. He'd rather listen for an entire night to the terrorized pleas from the prisoners in The Crypt than an hour of the wails of the women who'd lost their children. All because Vorgal killed their babies when they were born before they could kill him.

King Vorgal nodded in approval, a grimace marring his sharp features. "Keep me posted. And find me that baby," he snapped as they started up the stairwell.

"Of course, Your Majesty."

"What of rumors I've heard about a living Enstrin?"

"I've heard no such rumor." Kyr kept his voice under tight control. If the king had heard of an Enstrin, things could change dramatically. It was long known the former ruling house had been massacred at Vorgal's order, every last one.

"You're my high commander, you should know about these things before I do," the king said without any actual heat behind it.

"Of course, sire. But if I may, what is the rumor?"

King Vorgal Grox gave an aggrieved sigh. "I've heard there is an Enstrin living in the west somewhere."

Kyr nodded. "Do they know which one?"

"No. Bodies were found for all but one of the children. I don't recall which. A daughter I think."

Kyr remained silent when they reached the top floor and headed down the hall to the king's chambers.

"The lord marshal is tasked with checking into it. I want you to keep an ear out though. Let me know immediately if you hear anything. Anything at all. The last thing I need is a living Enstrin."

"Of course, sire"

Kyr was ready to leave his monarch behind when they reached the doors to the king's chambers. He needed to speak with the high mage. The king, however, motioned for him to follow. Kyr kept the sigh to himself this time and entered.

The room was mildly ornate, but Kyr had seen finer furnishings in an earl's estate at Heldin. The sitting room held a few couches and chairs, an enormous fireplace, and a couple tables for the king to spread out whatever his current interest happened to be. At the moment, the tables were covered in books and scrolls.

Between distance and angles, Kyr couldn't tell the subject matter. One title started with "Prognosti . . ." He couldn't make out the rest on the worn cover.

"What do you know of the prophecy?" King Vorgal stepped over to a table at the side of the room. He picked up a deck of cards and waved Kyr over.

"That you seek a child destined to destroy you. And that the child will be born in your thirty-sixth year."

"Which began not long ago." The king laid the cards down and spread them around.

Kyr had seen the king use these previously. Vorgal had often laughed with the prince over them, but recently, the cards only upset him.

King Vorgal concentrated on the cards, slid them around the table, and gathered them up again. After straightening the deck, he laid five cards face-down one at a time, taking his time to position each carefully.

"Did you know I was illegitimate when I was born?"

"No, Your Majesty. I didn't." Kyr had actually known for many years and wondered why the king mentioned it. Though he favored Kyr, and Kyr had fought hard to make it that way, he rarely opened up with anything of value. Kyr wouldn't interrupt him now.

"I was." The king turned over a card. It held the image of a man sitting on a throne with a staff in his hand.

Kyr didn't know what it meant, but certainly the image represented the king.

"I was born to a woman who'd spent a single night in my father's bed shortly after his wife died." As the king turned over another card, his movements slow and precise, he uncovered an image of a hideous horned creature.

Kyr was at a loss for its meaning. It couldn't be good though.

"He'd already had a son by his dead wife, so he didn't have interest in me, left me with my mother. Until, that is, his beloved son died, and he needed an heir. Then I suddenly had value."

The story sounded similar to Vorgal and his own son, though without the dead wife and first born.

The next card showed several swords in the back of a man who lay face down on the ground. There had to be at least ten of them skewering the poor fellow. Did it mean a betrayal, or that something bad was about to happen?

"Do you know what my father did?" the king asked.

"No." Kyr was caught up in the cards. What did they mean? He wouldn't interrupt the king to ask, not when the king was revealing things which might be useful.

"He came to our house, grabbed hold of me, and dragged me away as my mother begged him to release me. She offered him everything she could think of, but he refused it all."

Another card revealed a knight on horseback, brandishing a sword. That had to be a good card, something that would make the king happy. The king scowled, and the right side of his mouth turned up in a snarl.

King Vorgal took a moment, his features slowly calming, before he continued. "Did you know she was a seer?"

"No." *Yes.* In all his investigations of the king, Kyr had discovered extremely little about Vorgal's mother, so he listened intently.

"She didn't need cards to see things, but enjoyed reading them all the same. I never inherited her seer's gift, but she taught me the cards, before my father snatched me away when I was eight. I didn't learn much, but I learned enough. Enough to know my fate hasn't yet changed since the day my mother cursed me."

No explanation was needed when the king turned over the last card. Staring up at King Vorgal Grox was the face of death itself.

"Enough to know my killer is still coming."

The king stared at the cards for a long time, and Kyr waited until he was ready.

King Vorgal finally looked up. He seemed ill, but put on a steady face. "I'm certain even you can understand the general meaning of these cards. No matter how many times I try them, they're always the same. Always. Never different by even a card."

Kyr didn't know what to say, so he remained silent as the king perused the cards one final time.

The king sounded steadier, stronger than he appeared, despite the edge of desperation. "I need you to find that baby, Commander. Now."

CHAPTER FOURTEEN

Kyr took the most expedient route through the keep on his way to Nikos' study. If the old man was in residence—and hadn't been sent on another inane assignment—he would be studying or teaching his apprentices at this time of day.

The plain wooden door opened moments before he reached it. One of the high mage's apprentices, Agrath, rushed out with an armload of tomes. The man stopped, squeaked, and stood straighter when he noticed the high commander. Despite not serving under Kyr, having to answer only to the king and high mage, the apprentice truckled to anyone of even minimal rank. Nikos swore Agrath held incredible talent, but that talent would be wasted if the apprentice didn't grow a backbone. Perhaps further instruction under Nikos could remedy that. From what he'd seen, both apprentices were in awe of their master.

"High Commander Silst," Agrath blurted out as he dipped his head. His eyes darted back and forth across Kyr's chest and insignia.

Kyr gave a snort. "Is the high mage in?"

"He's in the workshop, sir."

"Doing what?"

"Teaching us hy . . . hyr . . . no that's not right." Agrath's face scrunched up. "Hydro . . . Hydo—"

"Hydrokinesis?"

The apprentice's eyes darted to Kyr's face for a second, then immediately back down. "Yes, sir. Hyrdokensa . . ."

"And can you do it?" Kyr asked, unable to listen to him butcher the word again.

"Can I do what, sir?"

Kyr rolled his eyes, not that the apprentice noticed anything except Kyr's chainmail. Was there anyone he would look at straight? "Can you control water?"

"Oh, no, sir, not yet. But the high mage thinks we're ready to start learning."

"I'll walk with you."

"Sir?"

"To the workshop."

It was a wonder Agrath hadn't irritated King Vorgal enough to have him executed and demand the high mage get a replacement. Finding mages was difficult though. Few remained in Likalsta, and with the threat of execution, those few were understandably reluctant to reveal themselves. Once another mage surfaced, the man would need to protect himself, prove his worth rather than his ability to grovel or wet himself every time someone of the smallest authority entered the room.

Walking down the hallway toward the workshop, Agrath twitched, opening his mouth several times before shutting it again.

Kyr grumbled. "What is it? What do you want to say?"

The apprentice flinched. "It's nothing, sir. It's just, well, I wanted to ask, but I didn't think I should, at least not the high mage, I wondered, that is, well—"

Kyr stopped beside the fellow and glared.

The mage stumbled as he halted, miraculously not dropping any books.

"Spit it out. What do you want to know?"

After a few gulps, Agrath licked his lips, keeping his eyes to Kyr's chest. "You fought with Master Klaskil at the Battle of Julspur, didn't you, sir?" Though he managed to get the words out coherently, his voice shook.

"Yes, I did."

"Is it true that when the Julsperan troops had ours outnumbered and trapped against the ocean, it was High Mage Klaskil who bombarded them with a firestorm?"

"Yes, it's true," Kyr said, his irritation waning as Agrath's fears visibly gave way to enthusiasm. "If he hadn't arrived when he did, we all would have been lost." The memory still bothered him, reminded him of when he'd received his own burns. He absently rubbed his scarred arm. He forced his hand down and focused on the man's questions.

"You were among the trapped troops?" The mage's voice rose when he spoke, his eyes grew wider. "You saw Master Klaskil win the battle?"

"Yes. We'd split our forces, planned to attack from multiple sides, but the Julsperans were prepared. They trapped us between them and the ocean. They'd also called in their allies from Krolgers, so we were vastly outnumbered. Even after eliminating half their forces, while losing only a quarter of ours, we were still trapped. The high mage arrived just in time, galloped in brandishing his sword and pulling down fire. He incinerated the Julsperans and their allies."

Kyr had never seen anyone in such awe. Caught up in the story, Agrath finally met his eyes, though he probably didn't realize it.

"They say he's one of the strongest mages in history," Agrath said. "That after he apprenticed for the previous high mage for a few years, he wanted to take over, so he squeezed his master to death. Didn't touch him, just squeezed him until he popped. Very messy."

"Well, I don't know about that," Kyr said, and he was pretty certain the previous high mage had died of consumption, "but I know he's the most powerful mage I've ever heard of. I wouldn't make him angry if I were you."

"Are you two done yet?" snapped a sharp voice from down the hall.

Nikos stood in the workshop doorway. Instead of his usual black cassock, or even his brown doublet, the high mage wore a simple, blue linen shirt. The sleeves were rolled up above the elbows. His stitched leather mask, made of various-sized pieces in an array of browns, covered everything above his mouth except his blue eyes and short-cropped brown hair. As always, with so much hidden, it was difficult to decipher his emotions. From what little Kyr could see, the high mage didn't look pleased.

"Inside. Now," Nikos said in a clipped tone, waving the apprentice toward the workshop.

Agrath gave a quick nod to Kyr. "Thank you, High Commander." He kept his eyes downcast and hustled inside.

Nikos closed the door and glared at Kyr. "What do you think you're doing, filling my apprentice's head with ridiculous stories about fire from the sky?"

Kyr stepped forward, laughing. "Sorry. But you must admit, you did save us that day. And you did throw fire at the troops."

"Yes," Nikos said, sounding a bit exasperated, "but I only grabbed the existing fire and redirected it. You make it sound like I made it rain fire, make it sound more spectacular than it was.

Now his head is filled with grand ideas of what he could do one day."

"Well, maybe it didn't actually come from the sky. But to see that wall of fire crash over the Julsperans like a wave? Even I thought it was the most incredible thing I'd ever witnessed. I've certainly never seen anything like it since."

"Thank the Protector."

"And what does it matter if he has grand ideas? I'm sure he can't do anything remotely that complex yet and probably never will. Until then, he'll be afraid of you and pay attention when you speak."

"True." Nikos nodded to the bruise that had taken over Kyr's temple. "What happened? Are you all right?"

"It looks worse than it is." Kyr waved the concern away. "We need to talk, privately."

Nikos motioned for Kyr to follow. He rolled his sleeves down over his slender arms while they walked back down the hall to his office.

A well-used lounging area sat before the cold fireplace. The only other furniture was a cabinet on the back wall and a desk off to one side. Books took up nearly every surface—some in stacks, others thrown open, their covers worn from long use. Beside the cabinet, a door led to the mage's bedchamber. On the opposite side of the room, a balcony offered a pleasant view of Vahean and the surrounding countryside.

Nikos glanced once more at the bruise while he closed the door. Kyr took a breath. "I found her."

Nikos' eyes grew wider behind the eye holes of his mask. "You're certain?"

"I wouldn't have said anything if I wasn't."

"You can hold that sass for someone else." The mage's ire was short-lived. He pulled the chair from his desk and sat. His voice softened. "How did she look?"

"Exactly as described. Though, you could have warned me."

"About what?"

The commander studied the high mage's blue eyes, tried to decipher the expression under the horrific mask. Kyr finally shook his head. "Never mind."

"So, the women are together then?"

"Yes. Exactly as you predicted."

Nikos gave an amused smile and motioned to Kyr's temple. "Is that where you got that bruise of yours?"

Kyr frowned and gingerly touched the side of his head. "An underestimation, admittedly. It won't happen again."

"Good. And they're on the run?" Nikos was earnest once again.

"Yes. I scared them sufficiently that they'll run right where we want them."

"Good work."

"It won't be easy to keep them out there. I still think we should bring her in."

"No. We've discussed this. It's too soon. If you bring them to the castle now, it could ruin everything. The baby isn't due for over a month."

"This kind of traveling can't be easy while pregnant, especially as it gets colder," Kyr argued, not for the first time. "Are you sure?"

"She'll be fine, and the baby will be fine. Trust the Protector. Trust our plan," Nikos said. "Keep them safe and moving in this direction. But don't let anyone know what you're up to. Above all, keep everyone else off their trail. It's vital you're the one to bring her in, that no one else knows about her. Not the lord marshal, and especially not the king."

Kyr stepped in front of Nikos and stared down. "How am I supposed to manage all that?"

"That's your job!" The mage stood, meeting Kyr's glare. "You know this territory, know your soldiers. Figure it out!"

Kyr gritted his teeth, finally stepping away. "I want this over." The weight of years pressed down on him. He didn't want to fight with the mage, but everything came pouring out. "When will it end? When will everything I've done be enough?"

"We're almost there."

"I've heard that before. For years, I've literally fought my way to the top, made certain I was stationed in exactly the right places. Well, it's time. This needs to end."

"Stop whining," Nikos said, matching the heat of Kyr's words. "Nothing happens without my approval or before its time. The baby isn't ready. You can't rush these things. Keep them safe, keep them moving, and keep everyone off their trail."

Kyr remained silent and glanced away. Nikos stared at him until he finally turned back. It was unnerving to look into the mage's stitched leather mask, like peering into one of Kyr's nightmares. Most people couldn't do it, but he had seen what lay beneath the mask. It no longer disturbed him, but even so, he didn't like looking too closely or for too long.

"We're almost there," the old man said again, his voice softer. "But you have to be patient a little longer. Don't bring her in before everything is ready and don't rush to the end. If you do, you might find that end isn't where you thought it was."

Kyr knew he was right, but that didn't alleviate his anxiety over all the variables ahead. Finally, he took a deep breath and nodded. "You're right."

"Be patient. While you handle the women, I'll work on ridding us of Huln. Once you take his place, we'll be fully prepared."

"His high mage and his lord marshal," Kyr mused.

"Indeed."

CHAPTER FIFTEEN

Kyr would have preferred to catch up with a few more contacts before leaving Vahean, but time was short. He would have to trust his captain to manage things for him.

"I want to come with you," Josah said. A light drizzle had started when they entered the bailey.

Roughly a dozen wagons sat in a line, from the southeast corner of the keep, along the edge of the training ring, past the barracks, and along part of the outer wall. Damp shivering women filled them to capacity. Some wore rags, others fine dresses befitting wealthy merchants' wives, and all wore piteous expressions. One wagon had already been unloaded, and now drove back toward the gate. Two armsman and a constable discharged the next, passing the women off to castle guards.

Thankfully, Kyr's own rural region had contained relatively few pregnant women, and even fewer in their later months that his men could locate. When riled properly, rustic folk could spread news faster than the king's messengers.

Commander Helitt walked along the remaining wagons, examining each as he went. Next in line for a rank, Helitt ruled his region strictly, often brutally, and only occasionally fairly. His proud, cheery smile made Kyr consider detouring to remove it. Loyalty and a job well done were admirable, but no one should take pride in this particular duty.

"I appreciate that, Josah," Kyr said, forcing his attention away from the prisoners. "But I need you to handle things while I'm gone."

"Where are you going? Why the change in plans?"

"It's not a change," Kyr admitted, adjusting the saddlebags over his shoulder. "Just something I never told you about." His second gave a disgruntled expression. "This part doesn't concern you. Manage the region, but make certain you're back in time, and everyone is prepared. I'll need you here for Springtime."

The captain replied with a reluctant nod. "We'll be ready."

They entered the stable and found Maksin, one of the stablemen, standing outside Sherwyn's stall, feeding the horse carrots. The man's golden-brown curls would have made him look younger than his years, but the ragged scar that ran from his hairline above his left temple and down across his cheekbone countered it.

"No wonder he never wants to leave here," Kyr said, raising his voice.

The burly stableman scanned the area, his one good ear trying to locate the sound. His face lit up when he saw the men approaching.

"You spoil him," Kyr admonished with a laugh.

"Someone has to. He tells me you skimp on the treats."

"He's lying." Kyr reached the stall and stroked Sherwyn's sleek neck. "He gets plenty. I even stocked up on parsnips before we leave."

Maksin's eyes darted to the saddlebags, then back and forth between the soldiers before finally settling on Josah. "You're leaving already? You just got home."

Josah put a hand on Maksin's arm. "No. Not right away, at least."

"I have something to take care of," Kyr said, "but Josah and the rest of the contingent are staying behind."

Josah gave Maksin's sleeve a reassuring tug. "I'll still be here for a couple of days."

The stableman scowled briefly at both soldiers, the scar adding an intensity difficult to achieve otherwise. "You could have told me that from the beginning. Or better yet, when you returned a couple of hours ago."

"It's my fault," Kyr said. "I only told him about this moments ago."

Maksin's features loosened, more so when he looked at Josah. He finally gave a snorting chuckle. "Why couldn't you have been a blacksmith or stone mason? Or something else that stays put?"

Josah shrugged with a smirk. "Because this way you appreciate me more when I'm around."

Maksin's lips twitched, as though trying to scowl, but a smile crept through. He turned to the stallion and retrieved the halter beside the stall door. "I'll get him ready for you, Commander."

"Thank you."

"Figures I'd find you with them." The snide voice came from behind Kyr and Josah.

Kyr shook his head, turning. Maksin tensed, already facing the approaching lord marshal. Josah's features grew tight, and his fists clenched as he turned.

Drus Huln, the king's lord marshal, strode down the center of the stable, sneering at all three men. He wore the same uniform as Kyr and Josah, and though average height, the broadness of his shoulders made him seem taller than he was.

Kyr glanced over his shoulder at Maksin. "Prepare my horse." He handed the saddlebags to Josah. "Captain, make certain he has everything as I like it."

Josah glared at the lord marshal a moment longer before finally turning toward Kyr and gave a sharp nod. "Yes, sir." Dropping his voice, he added, "Be careful out there."

"Be careful in here," Kyr said. His second nodded and headed off with Maksin and Sherwyn.

The usually stoic Huln held his sneer while watching the men leave. "Smart, sending your little pets away. If it were up to me, they'd both learn the limits of corporal punishment."

Kyr stepped in front of Huln, blocking his view of the departing men. "What do you want?"

The lord marshal's features twisted as he stared at his high commander. "I believe there should have been a 'sir' in there."

"Probably."

Huln's nostrils flared, and he adjusted his stance, stood straighter. He was still a few inches shorter than Kyr, who took delight in looking down at his superior. It was because of Huln, on his order, that Maksin had been jumped by half a dozen soldiers two years back. By the time Kyr stumbled upon the assault, the damage had already been done, leaving Maksin scarred and deaf in one ear.

Despite the horrors, two good things had come from the attack—Kyr had gained allies, and Maksin and Josah had stopped dancing around each other and actually talked. Kyr envied the couple's closeness, their dedication to each other. It was a large part of why he requested Josah Ilkin for his contingent shortly following the incident.

Nikos was right. They needed to be rid of Huln.

Kyr's fingers itched to draw a dagger. He could tell by the man's squinted eyes that he was up to something.

"My men told me disturbing news when they returned." Lord Marshal Huln turned deceptively casual, clasped his hands behind his back, and walked slowly around the aisle.

Kyr waited to hear the man's latest issue with him.

A hint of a smile pulled at the corner of Huln's mouth. "They informed me one of the women escaped you." When Kyr didn't respond, only watched him negligently, Huln continued. "Apparently, you let a woman sneak into camp and release all the women. My men said the prisoners nearly escaped, and that the one you chased actually did, along with the woman who freed them."

He circled around Kyr as he walked, forcing Kyr to turn with him or risk having the lord marshal at his back.

Huln nodded toward the bruised temple. "You're supposed to be this great fighter, won more fights in Skogsmead's ring than anyone, but it seems you can't even best a woman. Why are you my high commander, again?"

"Because the king likes me more than he likes you," Kyr taunted. It might be childish, but he loved to irritate the lord marshal, and his answer was the truth. His rise to high commander had nothing to do with Huln and everything to do with impressing the king. Years ago, even before the attack on Maksin, he and Huln had gotten off to a horrible start, so he'd put his efforts into other avenues for advancement.

Kyr kept his expression calm while he considered who among his soldiers reported to Huln. "But, why did *my* men tell you all this?"

Huln stepped closer, within inches of Kyr, the glare returning. "Every man in this military works for *me*. Remember that when you spout your lies to the king. I know you're angling for my position, cozying up to the king. But what you need to remember is that I can have you strung up by dinner."

"Do you really think the king would let you have me killed?" Kyr asked, his gaze unwavering.

Huln ground his teeth. "Perhaps having one of *my* soldiers shove a knife in your back while you're asleep would be a better ending for you. Either way, your days are numbered. After I tell the king you let one of the pregnant women escape and lied about it to him, you'll be closer to the grave than my position."

He's right about that. He'd hoped Huln wouldn't have realized the ammunition he held with that bit of information.

"What do you want?" Kyr asked.

"Want? Me? I want you gone from here. I want you dropped into The Crypt to be forgotten as you rot for eternity. I want to walk through this castle without worrying what pesky plot you've cooked up."

"Well, I doubt you'll be that lucky."

"Oh, yes, I will. Once I tell King Vorgal that you've—"

"That I what? That I lost a couple of women in the woods and was too embarrassed to tell my beloved king that my overconfidence got the better of me?"

"You think it's that easy?"

It was never that easy. Not with Vorgal. But Kyr needed to leave the castle, so it was time to bluff. He donned his cockiest expression and took another step closer to the lord marshal, who now stood between him and where Maksin was readying Sherwyn.

"I know it's that easy. You know as well as I do that the king will pitch a fit, he'll stomp and yell, and then tell me he needs me to get back out there and bring him the woman. So that's what I'll do. While you stay behind and whine about the king eventually realizing I'm a better leader, I'll be out there doing my job. So, move. Now!"

The longer Kyr spoke, the tighter Huln's face grew, until he fumed. The lord marshal stood his ground.

With a silent chuckle, Kyr stepped around him. "That's fine," he said. "I understand. I'll see you in a couple of days when I return with the woman."

"Commander!"

Kyr stopped, but didn't turn around. "Yes, Lord Marshal?"

"Where are you going without your contingent?"

Kyr forced his jaw to relax as he smoothly turned around. "The contingent will meet me in Limstre in a few days while I retrieve the woman. I don't need them for this."

"Judging by that bruise on your temple, I'd say you need all the help you can get." Huln smirked. "You might want to take a few real men along in case there's a fight."

With a humoring smile, Kyr turned and went to retrieve his horse. Hopefully, the lord marshal wouldn't throw any obstacles in his path before he got through the gate. He worried what problems Huln could cause while he was gone, but trusted Nikos could handle it.

He breathed easier when he finally reached the castle's outer gate and passed beneath the raised portcullis. Whatever the lord marshal had planned, he apparently didn't intend to prevent Kyr from leaving the premises. Things weren't necessarily in the clear, but it was a good sign, and Kyr would accept as many good signs as came his way.

"Commander Silst, sir. Wait for us."

As he halted Sherwyn, Kyr closed his eyes and wondered what the lord marshal had done.

CHAPTER SIXTEEN

Just before lunch, Eselle looked through the window. Overhead, the sky remained a light gray, but closer to the mountains it grew ominously darker. Occasional flashes of lightning and frequent deep rumbles drew ever closer. How long until the storm reached them? How long would they be stranded inside for once it did? Perhaps she should bring in more firewood, just in case.

Upon stepping outside, she found Cristar on her knees at the edge of the trees.

Eselle rushed over. "What's wrong?"

Cristar turned with a smile. "Nothing. Look what I found."

Slowing, Eselle watched her friend pull long, pointed leaves from a limp bush. "Isn't this used for rashes?" she asked.

"Yes. And swelling, blisters, and a few other things." Cristar had collected a small pile of them on the ground. "It's a bit late in the season, but it should do well enough. Since we couldn't pack any of my herbs or medicines before we left, these might come in handy."

Eselle studied the threatening skies. "Let me help." She knelt across from Cristar. "How much do you want?"

"All of it. The plant's about to die back for the winter, so it won't do anyone any good. I can prepare the leaves for drying while we wait out the rain."

"Okay then." Eselle began plucking.

Halfway through harvesting, Cristar jerked, put her hand to her stomach, and took a couple of deep breaths. Earlier in their travels, Eselle would have worried, but she'd grown accustomed to Cristar's baby unexpectedly knocking the wind out of her. It seemed to happen more when the young mother bent down. She imagined the baby protested his cramped quarters.

"Another big one?" Eselle asked.

"Definitely. My tough little guy here has been moving a lot lately." Cristar wore a pleased expression.

They gathered the leaves in time to make it back inside right as a drizzle began. Soon after, the heavier rains settled in. Eselle was grateful they'd found the house for shelter and hadn't been caught outdoors during a storm like this. Though small, the place suited their needs. Cristar's home was slightly larger, but only because her husband had been a carpenter and added on to it. In recent years, Eselle had grown accustomed to living outdoors, so she gladly conceded the bed to Cristar and her overgrown belly.

Deep into evening, Eselle enjoyed her warm tea while staring into the fire. Cristar laid on the bed, propped on her side, absently rubbing her stomach.

"I noticed we're running low on spices," Eselle said. "I'm debating running into Portlok to pick some up."

"What about the soldiers?"

Eselle turned away from the fire. "It's been two weeks; the regional commander would have moved on. It should be safe as long as I don't linger or call attention to myself."

"I don't like it."

"It's either that or no seasoning. I'm fine without, but I know you like more flavor. I'm happy to go."

"No." Cristar gave a firm head shake. "I have a bad feeling about Portlok. I'd rather have *you* here, than dill weed or basil. I'll be fine without."

Cristar make an odd noise and looked at her stomach.

Eselle sat straighter. "You okay?"

"Yeah. It's nothing."

"Did he kick again?"

"No, just moved. I think he's trying to find a comfortable position."

Moved? Eselle sat forward on her chair. "Does he do that often?"

"Sometimes. Come here." Cristar tossed the blanket back so Eselle could sit on the edge of the bed. She pressed Eselle's hand against her stomach and waited. Nothing happened. "Hold on. He'll move again." Cristar gently pressed the side of her belly, then shifted Eselle's hand along the opposite side. "He's over here. Well, his feet are. I just felt him flutter them."

It must be amazing to be so connected to another, like Cristar was with her child. The closest Eselle came to that was her brother, but she doubted it was quite the same.

She jumped when something slid under the surface of Cristar's stomach. "What was that?"

The pressure was stronger than she'd expected. It soon returned, pressing against her hand. She didn't know whether to enjoy it while it lasted or pull back in horror.

Cristar pushed her shirt back from her stomach. Eselle saw the faint outline of a tiny foot pressed against the woman's stomach. As soon as she saw it, it vanished. Cristar chuckled, her voice rich with joy. Eselle's eyes remained where the tiny foot had been. Until that moment, he'd been more of an idea. She'd been focused on protecting her friend more than the baby. That tiny foot changed things.

"He doesn't do that often," Cristar said, "but it's amazing when he does."

"Does it hurt?"

"No. It's just strange to feel your insides shifting, to know there's a little person in there. The first time he moved, I didn't know what to think, but some women in town told me it was normal. Now, I enjoy it. It lets me know he's okay in there."

As Cristar rubbed her stomach, Eselle saw a few more ripples as the baby shifted. Soon he slowed down, then eventually quit, either having found a comfortable position or growing tired from all the exercise.

"I wish Klaasen could have felt his child before . . ." Cristar trailed off as she pulled her shirt back down.

"I'm sure he would have loved that." Eselle didn't actually know, but supposed most fathers would have. "What was he like?"

Cristar slid up the bed to sit against the wall. "He was sweet," she said with a fond smile. "He was kind, funny. As you know, he was good at building things. He was handsome," she mused. "And he was tall, had dark hair that curled when it got too long, and beautiful brown eyes. I loved gazing into those eyes before we went to sleep." She stopped for a moment, a faint smile on her lips as she stared at the fire. "When he hugged me, he nearly swallowed me. I loved that. I felt so safe with his arms wrapped around me."

Eselle tucked her legs up beneath her as she listened.

"He would have been a wonderful father," Cristar said, her voice sure and strong. "He was so playful at times. I miss that. Miss how he made me laugh, made me feel special. He would have made our child feel the same."

"He sounds perfect."

Cristar chuckled, then snorted. "I love the man, but he wasn't perfect." Eselle raised an intrigued brow. "I already told you how he killed my plants. And he wasn't much better when he helped me cook. Then there was his temper. He didn't get mad often, but when he did, he was fierce. Once, he got into it with a neighbor, and they both ended up bloodied."

"Really?"

"Oh, yes." Cristar's features softened again. "But he didn't anger often. And never with me or his family. It was usually with whatever project he was working on. In the end, he was gentle. I miss him."

Eselle reached out and hugged her, blinking away her own tears as Cristar did the same.

***

Most everyone in the room jumped when the door burst open, including the high mage, Nikos Klaskil.

Every soldier, the lord marshal included, put hands to swords upon seeing the wide-eyed, red-faced Baron Dorlin in the doorway.

The man's intensity made Nikos' back straighten. This wouldn't end well.

"I need to speak with you." The baron's eyes bored into the king for only a moment before dropping, his features softening. "Your Majesty."

King Vorgal stood statuesque beside the table, his features tight. Nikos willed the baron to leave and forget his grief. Confronting the king, especially in front of his staff, was foolish at best.

Baron Dorlin stepped forward. "Your Majesty, I must speak with you."

The king turned back to the map laid out before him. "What do you want, Dorlin?"

After perusing the pair of nobles at the table, the high mage, and lord marshal, the baron ignored them. "Sire, my daughter was arrested this morning."

"I know."

"But, sire, she's my daughter." The baron's voice rose, his eyes growing wide again.

"And you told one of your friends that she's pregnant."

The baron's lips showed the slightest quiver. He took another step forward. "Your Majesty, I've served you faithfully from the very beginning. You can't arrest my daughter."

"I can arrest anyone. That's a privilege of being king."

"You can't do this!" Baron Dorlin fumed, twitching as he shifted his feet.

Nikos understood the baron's pain, knew he would not stop. Getting between the king and the baron though, was not something he could risk. Sacrifices had to be made.

Baron Dorlin strode forward and slammed his fist down on the table. "I demand you release her immediately!" The king finally glanced up. "She's done nothing to you, and I've done everything you've asked. You will give me this!"

The guards had already surrounded the man, penned him in at the end of the table. One nod from the king and two of them grabbed the baron's arms. King Vorgal remained apathetic.

"The only thing I'll give you is a cell in The Crypt."

Dorlin blanched.

Nikos' stomach dropped. He'd known from the beginning the king wouldn't yield, but he'd never suspected he would go this far.

King Vorgal's dungeon was notorious for its hideous conditions, deprivations, and cruel guards. Few people left the dungeon alive. Yet it paled to The Crypt.

The hideous combination of dungeon and torture chamber was where Vorgal sent those he particularly despised or who dared oppose him. The atrocities were horrific and uninhibited, from the flaying to the dismemberment, each done in pieces over long agonizing periods, just shy of death so they could be repeated over and over, year after year.

The Crypt was eternal agony.

"Your Majesty," one of the other nobles said, "I know Dorlin offended the realm with his insolence, but surely . . ." The man dropped his head when the king turned his fiery gaze upon him.

Vorgal studied each face around the table. "You're only here out of my good graces. Anyone who wants to claim otherwise can join Dorlin right now." Every eye in the room turned away.

After another royal nod, the guards pulled the baron from the room. His cries, both pleas and profanities, echoed even after the doors closed.

"How are we looking?" King Vorgal asked the lord marshal as though nothing had occurred.

"The troops will be ready in time, sire." Lord Marshal Huln appeared equally unphased. "We should be able to complete the march and take the lands before the winter weather sets in."

"Excellent." King Vorgal ran his finger along the route the troops would take. "How much longer before they're ready to march?"

"The last troops should reach the staging area within a month."

"Your Majesty," Nikos said, keeping his voice respectful. "I understand the need for western expansion, but before we commit our troops, are you certain you want to take Pasdar by force and not at least attempt negotiation?"

The king fixed his high mage with a glare. "People respect strength more than words, Klaskil. Are you questioning my judgment?"

"Never, Your Majesty. I would not presume to question your decisions. I only wish to remind His Majesty that shortly after our troops march, the Pasdarans will call in their allies, the Ristarians."

"Of course they will." Vorgal waved his hand, dismissing the statement. "But the Ristarians are as impotent as the Pasdarans."

The high mage stepped closer to the table. "Sire, the Ristarians—"

"Are weak and pathetic. For centuries, they outnumbered their enemy and still lost their war. I won't waste time worrying about them."

Nikos nodded in deference, not mentioning that the war ended with a peace treaty rather than a defeat. "Understandable, sire. The part I'm concerned about, however, is that the Ristarians will undoubtedly bring Jalat soldiers with them."

Vorgal Grox froze, his eyes darting to the western coastline. Huln stood a little straighter, puffing his chest out a bit. The two nobles gazed at each other but remained silent.

"You're certain?" King Vorgal didn't take his eyes off the map.

"I have not foreseen it, sire. However, sources tell me that since their war ended, the two armies are training together, the people reconciling. Many Jalat returned to various trades, but they still hold a substantial army. If the Ristarians march, the Jalat will join them."

"How many would you estimate?" Vorgal glanced back and forth between his lord marshal and his high mage.

Huln's brows drew together as he considered it. Nikos had already thought through this argument extensively.

"I have no definitive answers, but I roughly estimate the Pasdarans will send around twenty thousand troops, the Ristarians probably another ten thousand, and the Jalat two thousand."

Stepping around the table, still examining the map, the king asked, "How many troops would be necessary to defeat the Jalat?"

"If reports of the Jalat-Ristarian war are accurate, considering our troops are mostly conscripted soldiers with only standard training, and the Jalat were born to war . . . ten thousand."

The king's brows rose, but he showed no other response. His gaze intensified along the map's western coast. "And are your reports accurate?"

"I believe so, Your Majesty."

"Sire," Huln's voice sounded subdued, "Long ago, I met two Jalat soldiers, traded training tips. I've seen how they fight."

The king gazed at his lord marshal. "And?"

Huln frowned. "They're dangerous."

"How dangerous?"

"I'm embarrassed to say how quickly they beat me."

"Not surprising, two on one."

With a shake of his head, Huln spoke solemnly. "No. Each. I'm afraid the mage's estimates may be accurate."

Vorgal returned his attention to the map, tapping a finger at the edge of the table. "Klaskil? Can you destroy them? As you did with the Julsperans?"

Nikos laid his hands along the edge of the table. "It will depend on how many mages the other armies bring with them. The Ristarians and Jalat aren't known to have many, and none in their militaries, but the Pasdarans have at least five that I know of. The apprentices and I will need to counter them if our troops are to have a chance."

With pursed lips, the king stared at the map for a long moment. When he raised his head, he rapped his knuckles on the wooden table. "If I have to throw ten thousand troops to their deaths, so be it. I want that land."

***

After the meeting with Vorgal, Nikos fled before anyone could stall him. Soldiers died every day, whether at war or training or tripping down the stairs. That didn't make being complicit in sending more to early graves any easier. If expansion wasn't so vital to the king, he would advise against it, but the king's mind was set.

Without intending to, Nikos found himself approaching the old chapel. He often did when things bothered him. Though the king had never expressly forbidden his high mage from using it, he had made it known he was displeased with the mage's continued faith. All it had taken was a reminder from Nikos that the Protector had given the mages their abilities, so He could take them away just as easily—leaving King Vorgal without one of his most powerful weapons.

The large wooden doors creaked when he opened them, the hinges having long been ignored by the castle's staff. That the chapel remained still amazed Nikos. Despite his warning to the king, he had expected Vorgal to at least strip the room of its contents—especially since no one but Nikos seemed to use the place.

The pews held over a decade's worth of dust. The windows, though washed clean by the rain on the outside, were coated in grime and cobwebs on the inside. More webs decorated the rest of the room. The only clean parts were the alter and the Protector's Sword and Shield. On every visit, Nikos wiped them down with rags he kept in one of the desecrated reliquaries. Per his ritual, he cared for them again.

Only afterward, and after he'd brushed the residual dust off his black cassock, did he step up to the Sword and Shield. He placed a reverential hand against them where their tips met at the bottom point, at the same height on the wall as his head. He closed his eyes, breathing deep. If only he could breathe in the Protector's guidance. Once he felt a measure of peace, he opened his eyes.

"Protector, I've tried to serve as I thought would please You. I confess that in these last few years, when I have come to You for guidance, I have felt less and less certain of my path."

Nikos peered up the length of the Protector's tools. Polished clean, the silver blade reflected a warped image of Nikos back to himself. A soft ripple began in his chest, spreading outward, easing his tension. "Now I see that I was wrong to doubt. The time approaches. You have led me true, and I thank You for that, for everything You have given me. Given those of us who have served."

A moment of apprehension seized him, and he lowered his eyes to where his hand rested on the Sword tip. "I must ask for one more favor, great Protector. It's selfish, I know, but only You can grant this." Nikos dropped his voice to a whisper. "Protect my son, guide him. Above all else, please, bring him back to me."

"What was that?"

Nikos jumped and whirled around at the voice behind him. Prince Tryllen stood so close, Nikos nearly hit the young man when he turned about.

"Did you say you have a son?" The prince's amber eyes flashed with amusement.

"It's rude to eavesdrop, Your Highness." Nikos stepped around the prince, intent on leaving. When Tryllen grabbed his arm, he stopped but didn't turn around.

"How is it I've never heard of this son?"

Nikos concentrated on keeping his breathing steady, his reactions to a minimum. Though others received it worse from the prince, he hated times like these when Tryllen managed to corner him. If only the Protector would look away for a moment so he could deal with the prince how he wanted to. It would be so easy to work a little magic to make the man's life miserable—an irritating rash here, an inconvenient wart there . . . so many possibilities sprang to mind.

Luckily, Tryllen was not a complete idiot and knew not to thoroughly enrage a mage, especially the high mage. Still, he loved to walk the line.

"Well, mage? Answer your prince."

Keeping his eyes forward, watching the open doors, Nikos kept all emotion from his voice. "My son is not something I like to discuss."

"I order you to."

A slow, dangerous smile crept onto Nikos' face as he slowly turned his head. "Only your father can give me orders, young man." The smile dropped away as he glared down at the prince's hand on his arm, then back up into Tryllen's widening eyes. "I suggest you release me."

Prince Tryllen's features dropped. He let go and took a couple steps back. His hands couldn't seem to decide where they needed to be, but finally settled as he crossed his arms over his chest. "Does my father know you have a kid?"

"I have no idea. It's never come up in conversation. And I suggest it never does."

"Why?"

Nikos was surprised to see what appeared to be genuine curiosity in the young man's face.

Without intending to, Nikos answered. "My son and I went our separate ways over a decade ago, when he was sixteen, not much younger than you."

"Why?" The prince's voice was firm. Nikos suspected he was trying to sound like his father.

"That is between my son and I." Nikos walked away from the prince.

"I demand you answer me, mage!"

Halfway to the doors, Nikos whispered under his breath.

"Mage . . . I . . ."

Rustling sounded behind Nikos. A stomping foot and scuffling, cursing and the sound of a boot hitting the floor. More cursing.

As he passed through the doorway, the high mage smiled. Only once he was safely in the hall did he speak. "It was weak of me, I know, Protector. But I can't say I'm sorry."

CHAPTER SEVENTEEN

Kyr rode into another town in a long line of them.

A cheery voice boomed from a side street. "Kyr!" Commander Skogsmead ambled down the lane with his arm around a young, pretty brunette. Holding his hand high to catch Kyr's attention, he gave a broad smile that showed all of his yellowed teeth. Fresh stains spotted the front of his arming doublet. Judging by the man's slight sway, Kyr guessed they were ale. While the field commander wore his red uniform cloak against the chilly weather, he was absent his armor. Apparently, he had given himself the night off and, knowing the aged soldier, was likely coming from a tavern.

Skogsmead jerked his hand down and stood relatively straight. "I mean, High Commander Silst. It's good to have you visit us here in ..." The man surveyed the town surrounding them, his brows furrowed. "Well, damn. Where are we?"

Kyr laughed and dismounted Sherwyn. "I've forgotten myself, old friend." With the reins in one hand, he clasped Skogsmead's hand with the other. "It's good to see you again. I heard you'd been promoted to this territory. Congratulations."

"Ah, thank you. I'm still trying to get back ahead of you though. You certainly don't make it easy." The smell of ale filled the air around the old soldier.

Kyr grinned. "Well, don't try too hard. You might hurt yourself."

Skogsmead stared at him for a moment and then guffawed. The young woman at his side peered sidelong at him, her gaze uneasy, but she didn't pull out of his grasp. The field commander finally noticed the three saddled soldiers behind Kyr. With a nod in their direction, he asked, "Anyone important?"

"Not at all." Kyr gave a lazy glance and roll of his eyes. "Just lackeys Huln assigned to spy on me."

With that, Skogsmead ignored them. "Can you believe I trained this whelp? Can you?" he asked his companion. "When he first showed up at the castle . . . what? Twenty years ago? He was one of my lowly recruits, and now I have to salute him!"

"It was only twelve years ago. But before you start with your tall tales, where's a good place to settle for tonight?"

"This way. I'm in the mayor's house as usual. He has an extensive wine cellar and a couple of lovely servants we can enjoy." He pulled the young woman closer as he smiled. "Plus Ula here. She's my favorite in this town. I keep her with me whenever we visit."

The woman walked timidly alongside the field commander, never complaining or trying to prevent anything Skogsmead did. Like most favorites of the regional commanders, she seemed to understand it was better to have one man regularly climb on top of her with every visit, than several one after the other. Not every favorite was opposed to the idea, since the commanders inevitably gave them gifts, from dresses to make them prettier to extra food for their families to make them compliant.

Considering the girl's gaunt face, Kyr assumed extra food wasn't one of the gifts Skogsmead offered, if the old miser gave her anything but more of himself.

Kyr had never seen the benefits from any of it, favorites or gifts alike. When the mood struck, he preferred someone who actually wanted to be there. Not only were they eager, but quite often enticingly creative.

After leaving Sherwyn with the mayor's stable hand, they entered the commandeered residence. Skogsmead dropped his red cloak on a side table and walked off, calling for refreshments. Kyr tossed his own on a nearby chair.

Off to the side, Ula worked on the tie to her cloak. Her fingers held a faint tremble, but she managed, if slowly. Kyr stepped toward her. Her gaze darted up, and she started to step back, but stopped mid-stride. Skogsmead apparently had her trained. Likely, she would let Kyr do anything he wanted to her. He only reached around her and pulled the cloak from her shoulders, then laid it in the chair beside his own.

She remained still as a statue when he walked off to find Skogsmead.

Despite the warm fire and comfortable furniture, Kyr couldn't relax after the long ride. He didn't concern himself with where the other soldiers would sleep. They could sleep under their horses for all he cared.

"How long has it been?" Skogsmead asked after they'd all adjourned in the salon. He settled Ula on his lap, lifting her skirts enough so he could run his hand absently up and down her thigh.

"Too long. I'd guess three years."

As they talked, a blonde serving girl entered the room and poured their drinks. Once done, she stepped to the side and stood against the wall.

Skogsmead drank half his glass. "Ah, too long indeed. But I see you've held up well. Not too many bruises fighting your way up to high commander."

"No." Kyr rubbed his temple where his latest bruise was barely noticeable anymore. "Not too many." Simply the ones only he knew about.

"Well, I'm proud of you, proud of how far you've come." Skogsmead held up his glass to Kyr. "To you, my friend."

Kyr held up the glass out of convention, but set it down without drinking.

He wanted to return to the road and find the women again. His entire plan with Nikos hinged on keeping them close, which they were since he should reach Portlok by the following night. That they weren't actually in sight yet had him bristling with nervous energy.

The primary concern was the soldiers Huln sent with him. If he simply lost them, they would return to the castle, and the lord marshal would send more troops to this area, which would make it impossible to keep the women hidden. Bribing the soldiers wouldn't work, because Huln wouldn't send anyone he thought might be bought or persuaded to join his enemies. He would make sure they were loyal to him alone.

There was only one viable option then. When the time was right, the soldiers needed to have accidents. He could work with that. He was good with accidents. Until then, he could use them for some legwork.

"Kyr!" Skogsmead's voice reverberated in the large room.

Kyr jerked his attention back to his host. "Sorry. What?"

"Where have you been? I've been rambling for five full minutes, and you've been drifting off, thinking about who knows what. She better have been pretty, with big tits and a tight—"

"It wasn't that," Kyr said, waving away the thought. "I'm chasing some fugitives, and I was planning my route for tomorrow."

"Well, that's boring." Shifting Ula in his lap, Skogsmead motioned to the blonde serving girl. "Entertain my guest."

The woman glanced down at Kyr, sitting across from the field commander. Her smile faltered when she walked over, but she pulled up her skirts enough so she could climb onto Kyr's lap. She was slender, blonde, and exceptionally pretty. Before she could straddle him, Kyr took her hand and gently pushed her away with a shake of his head.

The most important thing now was to find the fugitive women. Until he could, he was wound too tight to relax. There were few ways better for forgetting your troubles than with a beautiful woman, but not like this and not with her. This wasn't the woman he wanted on his lap. Unfortunately, with his current assignment, the chances of that woman doing anything with him again had been lost.

The blonde servant glanced questioningly at Skogsmead, who motioned her to try again. Kyr quickly stood up, ending the issue. He couldn't explain it to them, but there was only one woman he wanted touching him, and she wasn't blonde.

"That's not necessary, really. I'm too tired for that sort of entertainment tonight."

"Then lay back and enjoy yourself while she does all the work. Or, hell, she has a mouth and can—"

"I've had a long day." Kyr held up a hand to cut the man off. "I'll have an even longer one tomorrow. I just want to relax for tonight."

"That's what she's here for." The field commander studied Kyr as though he'd lost his mind.

"Not that kind of relaxation," Kyr said. "The sleeping kind. Alone," he added when he saw Skogsmead begin to speak. The blonde servant appeared uncertain about what to do, so Kyr waved her off before the field commander intervened. She rushed from the room, a genuine smile tugging at her lips.

"It's been years since we've seen each other," Skogsmead said. "We have to do something to celebrate."

"We can do something the next time I pass through." It was difficult to refuse the man since Skogsmead had been the first one in Vorgal's army to appreciate and encourage him, to give Kyr a fighting chance, literally. He was like an uncle to many of the younger soldiers: a crazy, often drunk, but brilliant uncle.

"It's taken this long for us to be in the same town at the same time, and chances are I'll have moved on when you come back through here. So, no. We're doing something." He suddenly thrust his hand up in the air. "Wait, I know. We can go watch the games. Like in the old days."

"The games?" Kyr retook his seat, skeptical of what he heard. "You still do that?"

"Of course. They were always a great hit among the troops, and they're an even bigger hit now with the locals."

"The locals? What do they fight for?"

"Recently, I've had them fight for extra rations for their families. With the food shortages in this region, it's a tremendous incentive. We have more of the local men fighting than we have time to watch while we're here. They actually fight for a chance to fight. It's amazing." The field commander chortled.

With the women close and his goal quickly approaching, tonight was not the night to indulge in Skogsmead's usual debauchery. "That sounds fun. But again, I'll pass. I really just want to get some sleep for tomorrow."

"Oh, come on. The fights were always one of your favorite things. I couldn't keep you away from them."

"That's because I was in them." Kyr tried to keep the irritation from his voice. "I was the defending champion, so it was difficult not to show up."

Skogsmead laughed and turned to Ula. "You should have seen it, my dear. When he trained under me, I had them all fight 'til submission or knock out for unit leader. He got beaten the first few times he tried, but eventually he won. After that, no one beat him for . . . what? Two years?"

Kyr looked into the fire, following the flames. "About that. And no one ever did. I was reassigned."

"That's right, no one ever did. They tried though, even transferred in to have a go at you." Skogsmead slapped Ula's thigh in amusement. "Oh, those were good times. I remember that one fight, the big one. You remember the one I'm talking about. What was the boy's name?"

Kyr tugged lightly at a stray thread on the arm of the chair. "Haynewith."

"Yes, that's it. He put up quite a fight, that one. Several times I thought he'd actually take you. It got close more than once. But you held on."

Kyr only nodded, struggling not to mentally relive the bout.

Ula actively stared at the front of Skogsmead's shirt while the man grew more animated in his storytelling.

"You should have seen it. They must have fought for close to an hour."

It hadn't been nearly that long, but the man liked to tell his tales, so Kyr let him.

"They fought all over the training grounds, injured more than a few bystanders and broke two of our practice swords, several bows, and practically everything else in their path. I thought they'd kill each other. But Kyr here is too good. In the end, just when I thought that boy had him beat, had him pinned and was ready to bash his skull with the pommel of his dagger, Kyr turned the tables and used the dagger himself." Skogsmead's smile lit his entire face. "Cracked that boy's skull like a melon. A pretty impressive feat since the boy had already broken all your ribs."

"Only two of them," Kyr said, his voice somber. He reached for the glass he'd set down and took a long pull.

"Well, I imagine they're still cleaning that boy's brains off the field."

Kyr downed the drink. Skogsmead had always loved his fights—his games as he called them—and assumed everyone else did as well. After all, why would they come and participate if they didn't love them? He had apparently never considered that the prize was sometimes too good to pass up. For someone who wanted to advance in the military, being the reigning champion of such a spectacle was a way to garner attention from more powerful people. And it had. After word had spread about the youngster who'd won Skogsmead's fights for so long, others came to watch. Eventually, someone above Skogsmead had requested Kyr's reassignment. From there, he'd soared through the ranks. And he only had one rank remaining before he reached his goal.

He sometimes wondered if it was all worth it, the fighting and the death. Though the fights had helped his career, he'd never forgotten Haynewith. He still woke in a cold sweat, remembering the feel of the boy's skull cracking beneath his hands.

A shiver ran through Kyr. He shook it off before speaking, trying to sound cheerful. "As much as I would enjoy attending the games again, I think—"

The field commander abruptly pushed Ula off his lap, making her nearly fall to the floor. He rose swiftly and crossed over to Kyr.

"Whatever excuse you're about to give, shove it. We're going." Before Kyr could protest, Skogsmead took his arm, led him to the door, and grabbed their matching red cloaks. While shoving Kyr through the door, he called out back through the house. "Ladies, keep our beds warm 'til we return."

***

More than a little frustrated that he'd gotten such a late start the next morning, Kyr reluctantly grabbed Huln's soldiers before he rode out.

He had known better than to let Skogsmead lure him to the fights, but it had always been difficult denying the man for long. In the end though, Skogsmead was right. Kyr had been so tense lately it was good to indulge in a few vices. Between reminiscing with Skogsmead and the ale, he'd actually relaxed. At least, until he had woken up late the following morning and couldn't make the next town by nightfall.

The delay wasn't the end of the world, only one more irritant. The soldiers with him were another. He frequently wondered if it was too early for them to have one of their accidents.

There were several farmsteads around Portlok he needed to search, but he didn't want to drag three unknowns along with him. Aside from spying on him, he didn't know what other orders Huln might have given his lackeys. Until they outlived their usefulness, he sought reasons to split up or leave them behind in Portlok. By the fifth time, they grew wise to his excuses. Apparently, Huln had ordered them to stay with him at all times, so the few times he'd managed to separate from them had been a miracle.

When the last farmstead proved fruitless, occupied only by a large family of potato farmers, he grumbled all the way back to town.

Where were they?

At the town's crossroads, Kyr ordered each soldier to take one of the main streets and ask about the women at the various businesses. With any luck, someone had seen them or knew of other farmsteads Kyr had missed.

"Lord Marshal Huln said not to separate," one of the soldiers needlessly reminded Kyr.

"I don't care." Kyr's jaw grew tight. "This isn't the lord marshal's assignment, so he doesn't get a say. Now move it."

"But—"

Without warning, Kyr jabbed the man in the throat. He'd had enough. The soldier stumbled backward. He choked and sputtered as he grabbed his neck and gasped for breath. One of the others checked on his comrade, while the third watched Kyr cautiously.

"I don't want to hear about what the lord marshal wants," Kyr said, his voice rumbling with anger. "You'll each take a street and ask around. Once you're done, meet here."

They all watched him now. The battered soldier rubbed his throat, his eyes watering.

"Any questions?" He looked at each of them in turn.

They all shook their heads.

"Anyone want to tell me again what the lord marshal ordered?"

The head shakes became more vigorous.

"Then move out."

Once the lackeys dispersed, Kyr tackled the remaining street. Based on Nikos' information, he knew the women were near Portlok, but he didn't know where exactly.

It had been over two weeks since he had last seen them. As much as he disliked the idea, it was time for another good scare to get them moving again.

An hour later, after Kyr had asked at the smithy, a dusty fellow wearing mismatched attire approached him. Between the tight, faded blue trousers with more patches than pants, and the mud-stained orange jacket that ballooned on his slender frame, Kyr didn't know where the odor came from. The man definitely needed a good bath, or dunking in the local stream.

"I heard you're looking for some women," the man said.

"Yes. Have you seen them?"

"I saw something, but what are you offering? Is there a reward?" Though the man tried for a certain nonchalance, Kyr saw his eagerness for a big payout.

"The reward is the continued use of your hands, if you know anything." Kyr let the man stew a bit.

The emotions that flickered across his face amused Kyr tremendously. First, the vagabond appeared confused, then startled as he reconsidered his position. He seemed ready to dash away, but then took a quick look at the town layout, Kyr's proximity, and hesitated.

Finally, as the man began to panic, Kyr figured he'd made his point. "But I might have a few coins to spare for someone who can actually lead me to them."

Somewhat settled, the man gave a careful nod. "Two women?"

"Yes."

"One of 'em's pregnant?"

"Yes."

The man shifted back and forth on his feet. "I might have seen 'em a couple days back?"

"Might or did? Because the reward is vastly different for each."

"Did. I did see 'em," the dusty man said.

"Good. Can you show me where they are?"

"I can tell you. It's not far."

"Does anyone else know their location?" Kyr eyed the man closely.

"No."

"You're certain? You didn't tell anyone else?"

"No."

"What about the other soldiers who arrived with me?"

"No. You're the only one I've spoken to."

Kyr considered the situation. If he left immediately, he could be out of town before the lackeys realized he was gone. He'd have to leave Sherwyn at the stable though. No time to get his horse without risking them seeing and wanting to tag along.

"Have you heard anyone else mention them or otherwise indicate they know where the women are?"

"No, just me. No one else knows where they're at." The man's smile twitched, and his eyes turned bright. Kyr saw his eagerness to keep any reward for himself.

Now Kyr needed to get to the women before anyone else did.

"Directions won't be good enough. I need you to take me to them."

CHAPTER EIGHTEEN

After organizing her wood stack, Eselle brought several pieces inside. She set the ax by the doorway and started a fire in the fireplace. While a pot of water warmed, she pulled out a knife and prepared dinner. First, she cut up some potatoes, and then some onions they'd salvaged from the previous owner's garden. Though a little soft, the onions appeared decent enough to eat.

Before she finished chopping, scuffling sounded from outside. The door flew open and Cristar burst inside, her eyes bulging.

The hairs on the back of Eselle's neck rose. "What's wrong?"

"He's coming." Cristar's every movement jittered.

"Who?" Eselle rushed to the window and peeked out, tightening her grip on the knife. A quick scan of the yard showed no one. She looked farther up the haphazard trail which led to the road.

"Commander Silst!" Cristar whispered.

Just as the woman said it, Eselle saw him sauntering down the trail toward them, still far enough off that he couldn't hear them if Cristar had spoken normally. Eselle wouldn't let him arrest her friend again.

As tense as seeing the commander made her, she also felt relieved he was all right, that he'd survived her clubbing him in the head.

"Did he see you?" Eselle asked. His line of sight would have allowed it, and Cristar had obviously seen him.

"I don't know. I was focused on my sewing." Cristar held up the baby outfit she'd been creating from scrap materials they'd found. "When I looked up, he was walking toward the house, so I ran inside."

He was significantly closer now, his pace unchanged, and he appeared to have someone walking behind him. With the angle, Eselle couldn't make out who, but she suspected it was one of his soldiers. She closed the curtain and pulled away from the window.

Eselle put the knife on the counter and grabbed the ax from beside the doorway. "He'll be here any minute. We have to go."

"Where?" Cristar's voice sounded higher than usual.

"Out the back before he gets here."

"It's too late to run, ladies," Commander Silst called from outside. He was nearly at the front porch from the sound of it.

Eselle slipped on her pack, prepared ahead of time for this type of emergency. She handed Cristar her own and pulled her toward the back door.

"You're outnumbered, and my men have the place surrounded," the commander yelled. His voice was calm despite the volume.

Eselle froze and fumed. She should never have allowed them to get trapped. Cristar shoved the half-sewn baby outfit into her pack, then fumbled it on.

"There's nowhere to run, so you might as well come nicely, prevent this from escalating and risking someone—say, a certain overly pregnant young woman—from getting hurt. How far do you think a pregnant woman can run anyway? You know she wouldn't get far."

Eselle rushed through the room, keeping low, and closed all the curtains. Once done, she snuck back to the window and peeked out again. Kyr stood in front of the house and appeared as patient as she had ever seen him. It almost seemed he was having a friendly conversation with them. A man stood behind and to one side, but Eselle didn't know him. He wasn't a soldier, but rather looked like a dusty vagabond, wearing a baggy jacket and tight blue pants. The moment she snuck her look, Kyr noticed and smiled at her. His eerily friendly expression sent a shiver right down her spine.

Eselle pulled away from the window while considering their options. She didn't know how many soldiers he had with him, or where they were positioned. If he'd brought his entire contingent, there could be twenty men out there. She didn't see anyone when she peered out each of the windows, but between the trees, barn, boulders, well, and woodpile, they could be anywhere.

"What do we do?" Cristar kept low despite the curtains being drawn.

"I don't know," Eselle said. Her fears mounted as she ran through scenarios, but found nothing that would work. Without knowing where the commander had positioned his men, she didn't know which direction to run in, other than not through the front door where Kyr himself was positioned. She might be able to handle one of his soldiers, but she was pretty certain she wouldn't stand a chance against Kyr.

"We have to get out of here." Cristar pressed a protective hand to her stomach as she reached for the knife Eselle had used earlier. The sight made Eselle smile. She knew where the woman's unborn child got its toughness.

"We have to know where to run first."

"Come on, ladies," the commander called out. "It's time to surrender."

Eselle looked discreetly out the back of the house again. As she scanned the area, she didn't see anyone.

"You have two minutes before I send my men in to get you."

"We have to run for it," Cristar said. "Take our chances." The desperation in her voice grew steadily stronger as she rubbed her belly.

Eselle watched out the rear window for a moment longer, minutely studying the area. "I think he's bluffing."

"What?" Cristar gingerly pulled back the other side of the curtain to look for herself.

"I've studied the whole area and I don't see anything. His soldiers may be good, but not that good. One of them should have shifted by now and revealed himself, even for a second. I think he's bluffing. I think he's the only one here. Him and whoever that is with him."

"So, we run for it out the back while he's out front yelling ultimatums," Cristar said, shining with ferocity.

"We run," Eselle agreed. "I'll go out first to make sure we're safe, then you rush for the trees. I'll come up behind you with the ax and cover us. Whatever you do, don't stop until you're certain you're safe. I should be right behind you, but if I get held up, I'll catch up with you as soon as I can. Okay?"

Cristar grabbed each strap of her pack and stepped to the edge of the door. "Okay."

"Ready?" Eselle asked, her hand on the door as they prepared to leave the small house that had sheltered them.

"Ready," Cristar said resolutely.

Eselle yanked the door open and took half a step out. She stopped when a muscular fist punched her wrist from around the edge of the doorway. The impact made her drop the ax. Another hand snatched it from the air. Commander Silst stepped in front of her, gripped her wrist, and yanked her from the house. She stumbled forward and landed on her knees. Spiking pain shot through her legs and hips.

Cristar charged with her knife. The commander sidestepped and grabbed the woman's wrist. He twisted it around her and forced her to turn with the arm or risk breaking it. She dropped the knife, and he released her, sending her shambling down the single step into the yard.

With Silst distracted, Eselle regained her feet and launched herself at him. She plowed into his stomach. He grunted when they hit the ground. The ax flew from his hand and landed several feet away.

Though the commander's body cushioned her fall, Eselle felt a jolt. She immediately straddled him and punched. He tried to knock her arm away, but she landed the blow across his cheekbone. Pain splintered through her hand at the contact.

·Kyr rolled them over and climbed on top of her, pinning her arms by her sides as he sat on her chest. She swung a leg up and around, catching her ankle beneath his chin. Using her leverage, she pulled back on his head, hauling him off her.

As the commander rolled up to his feet, Eselle did the same. Cristar moved in with her retrieved knife, but Eselle waved her off.

Turning back to her opponent, Eselle doubled over when a kick landed against her stomach. She staggered back, remaining bent over while waiting for him to step closer. The moment he did, she thrust the heel of her hand up into his chin. His teeth clacked, and he grunted.

Eselle gave two swift jabs to his ribs. Unfortunately, unaccustomed to fighting armored opponents, she hadn't considered the commander's riveted chainmail. It chewed up her knuckles, and she staggered back, shaking out her injured hand. She would have stopped after the first jab, but she had been so focused she was moving in for the second one before even registering the stinging pain of the first.

Silst chuckled. "Care to try that again?"

"No," she said snidely. "Thanks anyway. I think I'll stick to punching your face."

"You can try."

She did. Taking a swing at his head, she was disappointed when he blocked it. But she already had an uppercut in motion, hoping to catch him by surprise. She didn't. He blocked that too, then countered with his own punch. Eselle ducked it and thrust a foot into his shin. He sidestepped and swung his own leg out to sweep hers. She jumped up to avoid it, but he spun with a backward elbow jab.

Pain exploded through her face, her eyes watered, and she stumbled backward to fall on her rump. Eselle grabbed her bleeding nose and tried to clear her watery vision, even while scrambling to her feet, knowing he would be on her again soon.

The commander stood still while he watched her. She wiped the blood that had dripped down from her nose, tasted it as she gasped to regain her breath. Her previous training hadn't prepared her for this degree of fighting. What else could she do to get them free?

"We don't have time for this." Silst walked to where the dusty stranger stood over Cristar.

The vagabond had somehow taken Cristar's knife away and stood guard over her. She sat on the ground with her legs tucked beneath her, but didn't appear injured, only subdued as she watched the combatants. The commander held out his hand to the pregnant woman. She looked at it, then glanced up at him, her brows drawing together.

Eselle's breath was already labored from the recent bout, but seeing her friend in danger, it faltered. The commander's gesture couldn't be as gentlemanly as it appeared.

And she was right. The moment her friend was on her feet, he pulled Cristar around the front of him. He drew the dagger at his hip, then held it beside him. The young woman only reached his shoulders and seemed so small and helpless in his arms.

"Please," Eselle said breathlessly. "Don't hurt her." She hated herself for failing Cristar and her child.

Silst watched her, the right side of his jaw clenched as he spoke. "I want both of you to behave while I get you secured."

"I won't let you hurt my baby," Cristar said, her voice a near hiss.

"I have no intention of hurting your baby." He motioned Eselle back into the house, then nudged Cristar to follow. "But if you do anything stupid or try to prevent me from bringing either of you in, I'll do what I must."

CHAPTER NINETEEN

The vagabond kept watch outside while the others went inside the farmhouse.

Eselle grabbed a rag from the table to press to her bleeding nose. The blood had dripped down onto her tunic and hands.

Both women dropped their packs by the table where Silst indicated.

"What do you want from us?" Eselle's voice sounded muffled behind the rag.

The commander motioned Cristar to sit on the bed. "You're fugitives. She's wanted for being pregnant, and you're wanted for breaking her out of my custody." He pulled a chair away from the table and moved it to the end of the bed. "Sit," he ordered Eselle.

"Why is being pregnant suddenly a crime?" Cristar's voice shook with anger as she held her stomach.

Eselle studied the commander for any distraction. Undoubtedly knowing she was the bigger threat, he watched her just as closely.

"The king ordered all pregnant women be rounded up," Silst said. "And that no new pregnancies occur until he allows it."

"Why?" Eselle asked.

"Because a seer told him a baby born this year would one day kill him."

"And you think it's my baby?" Cristar said.

The commander shrugged and stepped backward to where they had dropped their packs. Holding his dagger in one hand, he hauled Eselle's pack onto the table. While he rummaged through it, he kept an eye on them as he spoke.

"The seer wasn't specific beyond saying the baby would be born in King Vorgal's thirty-sixth year, which began a little over two months ago. So, this baby could have been born last month or might not yet be conceived for another few weeks."

"What will he do with my baby?" The anger in Cristar's voice slowly transformed into fear.

Kyr peered up at the young mother; his eyes softened for the briefest moment before he looked away. Regaining his tough exterior, he tossed Eselle's belongings onto the table.

"How can he tell when the baby is born?" Cristar asked.

He pulled Eselle's rope from her pack. "There it is," he said with a smile. "I knew you'd have some. After all, what decent adventurer doesn't carry rope? Though, to have it all the way at the bottom seems a bit inefficient."

Motioning at them with the dagger, the commander grew stern. "If either of you try anything, this will get very ugly."

Eselle knew their pitiful odds of escape. She wouldn't risk Cristar's safety. With a scowl, she stayed put when he sheathed his dagger and stepped behind her.

"The baby," Eselle said.

"What about the baby?" Silst held her wrists together as he started to tie them to the back of the chair.

"How can the king tell when the baby is born? When will Cristar's child be safe?" As Kyr's strong, calloused hands worked the ropes around her wrists, Eselle remembered them gliding along her body. The memory was both welcome and disturbing considering the current circumstances.

"From what I know, there's no way to identify the baby King Vorgal seeks."

"What about a birthmark?"

"Nope."

"A sixth finger on its right hand?" she asked.

"Not that I've heard."

"Is it possible there's something you haven't heard?" Eselle asked, desperate for anything that could help them and save the realm's babies.

"Anything is possible, but it's unlikely. I have plans that hinge on this matter, so I've researched it extensively." With a final tug at the ropes, he stood and stepped back around her. "There's nothing to identify this destined child."

"What about the seer who made the prophecy?" Cristar asked. "Can't someone go back and ask about that?"

"Again, no." He started digging through Cristar's pack. The first thing he pulled out was Cristar's sewing, half formed into a tiny outfit for her unborn child. Kyr held it up, silently examining it before shaking his head and placing it on the table.

"Why not?" Cristar asked.

"Because she's dead. Vorgal killed her for making the prophecy."

Eselle frowned. "Why? I would think he'd want to keep the person with the information alive."

"One would think. But it wasn't revealed out of kindness, or even assistance. It was a curse, his mother's revenge to look into his future and tell him how he would die. So, in a fit of anger, the king killed her. He's lived with this knowledge for seventeen years, knowing it would happen, but being unable to do anything until the time finally arrived."

He pulled Cristar's sheathed dagger out of her pack. "You really should keep this on you, you know." His voice sounded surprisingly sincere. "For occasions like this. While I disarmed your one hand, you could have struck me with this."

"Thanks for the lesson." Eselle released her pent-up sarcasm.

"Why would his mother do such a thing?" Cristar shifted on the bed, settling into a more comfortable position.

There was a sad edge to her question, but Eselle couldn't relate to it. The fact that the man's mother recognized the evil in him was enough to bolster her belief he needed to be stopped.

The commander glanced up from searching the pack, a curious expression on his face. "Do you really want to know?"

Cristar met his eyes intently. "Do you know?"

"As I said, I've researched it extensively."

After a hesitant moment, Cristar nodded.

"It doesn't matter," Eselle interrupted. "He's despicable, and no one should feel sorry for him."

With a shrug, the commander answered Cristar's question anyway. "Regardless, about a year before he seized the throne, Vorgal killed his father. From what I gather, the man was never satisfied with Vorgal, always made it known he preferred his legitimate heir. That son, however, died several years prior from some illness. Eventually, Vorgal stabbed his father after dinner one night when his anger overcame him. He blamed a servant for it and let the man hang. That's how Vorgal became a baron.

"A year later, baron wasn't enough. He gathered allies—mostly through bribery, threats, or blackmail from what I can tell—and had the ruling family assassinated. Knowing the mages would pose a threat, both during and after the murders, he arranged to have as many killed as possible on the same night. Another year after that, his mother learned about Vorgal's patricide. From the reports I've read, the argument was extreme and covered a wide range of Vorgal's crimes. That's when his mother told him about his upcoming death."

"So, he killed her?" Cristar's voice trembled softly.

Silst took a moment before nodding and returning to his search.

"Can't they find another seer?" Eselle asked. "Get more information that will save the other children being born?"

"They've tried. But mages aren't forthcoming about their abilities, what with the king trying to exterminate them. The only one with any reliable information is the king's high mage, but he can't tell the king anything more than he already knows."

"So, all these babies will die? To save one man? One horrible man?"

The commander nodded. "Apparently. The king believes the loss of one year's worth of children is worth his continued existence."

"Well, he's wrong," Cristar said fiercely. "My child is worth so much more than he ever will be."

Kyr regarded the young woman with a thoughtful expression. "Let's hope so."

It must be horrible knowing when you would die, but that doesn't justify killing others. Eselle prayed the tyrant's mother was right, and this mysterious baby would one day slit his throat. Disturbed by her thoughts, she remained silent.

After Cristar's pack proved unsuccessful, the commander checked in cabinets and chests, anything that might contain something to use as a restraint.

Watching him rummage through the house, Eselle tried to see him for who he really was. She'd been seduced by Kyr's charm and playful nature, but when it came down to it, he was Vorgal's man. How had she let herself get involved with him?

After most of her family had been killed, Eselle had grown up on a farm full of men who didn't seem to realize she was a girl. They'd taught her everything from living off the land to fighting, anything they thought might help her. Things that certainly weren't considered ladylike. They'd spoken openly and treated her as one of them. She was accustomed to abrupt men. Did Kyr remind her of the friends she'd left back home? As he tied up Cristar, she figured now wasn't the time to examine this unexplainable interest.

"What do you plan to do with us?" Eselle asked once she and Cristar were secured.

While the commander had used Eselle's rope on her, he'd been unable to find anymore. Ultimately, he had pulled the sheets off the bed and began tearing. He bound Cristar's wrists with the bedsheets and tied her hands to the bedpost.

"Now that you're both secured, I need to head back to town and pick up those men I told you were surrounding the house."

Eselle snorted. "I knew you were bluffing." Why hadn't she acted on that belief earlier? If they had rushed out the door immediately, maybe they could have escaped.

"Dear, sweet Eselle," he said with a faint smile as he gazed into her angry features. "You always were a smart one."

Eselle froze.

She had never told him her real name.

Other than Cristar, she hadn't mentioned it to anyone since before giving the commander her alias. She kept her face under control and said nothing, waiting to see what he did next. But she saw it in his taunting eyes. He knew. And he wanted her to know he knew.

"Why are you leaving us here tied up and alone?" Eselle asked instead. "Someone could come along and do who knows what to us?"

"True," the commander said, ignoring the obvious subject change. "Someone might harm the two fugitives I apprehended and who are probably destined for the gallows anyway. Whatever am I thinking?" His amusement unnerved her. "I don't feel like keeping you two in line the entire way back to town, so it'll be easier to go back, get my men, and then return for you."

After he checked Cristar's bonds once more, he knelt in front of Eselle and rested his hands on her thighs. "I know you'll miss me terribly, but I won't be gone long. I promise."

Eselle scoffed and turned away, giving a tug at her bonds. To her surprise, they gave a little. It wasn't enough to come free, but enough she might be able to escape before he returned. She stopped struggling and let him think she had given up.

The commander headed to the door. "Get in here."

Eselle examined the stranger when he entered. He was rumpled and dusty, and held the ax as he examined the room. Seeing the women, he smiled. There was no warmth in his features.

"Did you see anything out there?" Silst asked. "Anyone or anything of concern?"

"No. Can I get paid?"

"Certainly. But first, you're sure no one else knows the women are here?"

"Positive."

"Good. While I get your money together, go back outside and continue keeping watch."

"Why?"

"Because I said so. And because you want to get paid."

The vagabond shrugged and turned to leave. Before he made it two steps, the commander stepped in behind him and snapped the man's neck. The motion sent the vagabond spinning around. Silst caught him as he fell, then rose with the man securely over his shoulder.

He bowed his head to the women. "Goodbye, ladies. I'll return as soon as I can. Until then, stay put and be safe."

CHAPTER TWENTY

Ten Years Old

He worried when he saw the lad enter the room. Behind the boy's fatigued features was a fire that hadn't been there before.

They had both known what needed to be done, had begun training for it. But they'd been comfortable, safely tucked away in their little corner of the world. They'd taken that peace for granted and forgotten their purpose. Until the new king sent his troops to remind them.

They hadn't expected Vorgal's soldiers to reach this far north. It was the edge of civilization, after all. No one chose to live here except a few crazy hunters and trappers. But King Vorgal hungered for control. Yesterday, his soldiers had tried to take everything their settlement had saved for the harsh northern winter.

The troops hadn't counted on the level of commitment their little community had to protecting itself and its families. The fight had been gruesome, with too many dying on both sides.

Among them were the boy's only friends. Though neither he nor the boy had grown particularly close to anyone in town, those two young lads had been the exception. There weren't many youngsters in the area, so to have three boys relatively close in age was lucky. They'd bonded over childish issues and adventures. Now, the remains of two of them were set for burial later that day.

The memory of their little bodies shook his faith. When he had found himself raising the boy years ago, he had thanked the Protector for the opportunity they'd been given. This reminder of what else the Protector allowed to happen made him doubt everything.

Looking at the lad across the table, he silently thanked the Protector his boy had been spared in the massacre.

He pushed a plate of food toward the boy. "It's just bread and cheese, but after yesterday you should eat. I'll make a better lunch, but I wanted something ready for when you woke."

"I'm not hungry." The boy gingerly adjusted the sling around his injured arm. He used his good hand to push the plate back to the center of the table.

They sat there in silence for several long moments. Neither knew how to express what they felt.

Finally, the boy raised his head. "Why did He let it happen?"

"What do you mean?" The man worried about what the lad was truly asking.

"If He's supposed to protect us, why did He let everyone die?"

With a deep breath, the man nodded. "I know it's difficult to understand. I've questioned Him at times myself, but we need to have faith He's guiding us to do the right thing."

"But . . . my friends and . . ." The boy took a shaky breath.

"I know. Believe me, I know. He can't be everywhere all the time. That's why He gave some people the ability to help Him."

"Mages." The boy's voice was soft, empty.

"Yes, most of whom became warders."

"And who He let be killed." Those young eyes grew fierce.

It pained the man to see the boy broken. "I can't answer to that. If He protected us from everything though, we would never learn how to protect ourselves, or protect others. Or even learn the compassion needed to want to protect others."

The boy stared at the center of the table with a dour expression, his features drawn tight. The man reached out a hand to take the boy's good one.

After a moment, the boy's face turned resolute. "I want to start training again."

Those were words the man had both prayed for and dreaded. Nothing in life had turned out how he'd expected. Even with all his knowledge, all he had been through, he was at a loss as to where to go next. While he knew what he *needed* to do, he wasn't sure about what he *wanted* to do. But there was more to consider than himself or the young lad with the pained eyes who sat across from him.

"All right," he finally said, releasing the boy's hand. "We can resume practicing once your arm is better. But I've already taught you what I know, and that's not much. We need to find you a better teacher."

"But you've always trained me," the boy said, looking hesitant.

"Yes, but I'm not a fighter. That was never my strong suit. If you're to be trained properly, as you should be, we need someone with real skill who knows more than the basics. We need to find a true warrior to teach you. That means leaving here and heading to a larger town or city."

The boy wore a concerned expression. "Why can't someone here teach me?"

"Because they're not skilled fighters either. They can hold their own against those conscripted troops Vorgal sent, but his real troops, the properly trained ones, would have killed everyone here in short order. Anyone who can stand up to soldiers like that won't be wasting away in a mountain settlement. We need to go find them."

The boy's reluctance showed in his tight eyes. He'd lived here most of his short ten years and had known little else. But he'd been sheltered long enough.

"Don't worry, lad. I'll be there with you. I'll teach you all sorts of other things you'll need to know. And, if we're to do this right, I should probably do some training myself." He grabbed the boy's good forearm lightly. "Don't worry. This will be an adventure. We'll go out and see the world, meet new people. And you'll learn how to fight, how to handle yourself."

"Could Eselle fight?" the boy asked, startling the man with mention of her name. It had been a long time since they'd discussed those stories. Perhaps it was time to reveal more of them.

"She could," he said. "She wasn't half bad. Though she tried to avoid it when possible. She preferred to sneak past or around any potential threats and go unnoticed. But when she had to, she could go up against the toughest of them."

"Could she go up against me?"

He smiled at the youthful ego. "She'd struggle with it some," he chuckled, glad the boy had taken to the stories. "But if she tried really hard, yes, I believe she could." The boy seemed to consider it for a moment. "Did I ever tell you how she first rescued Cristar?"

CHAPTER TWENTY-ONE

The rope had felt loose earlier, but now that Eselle was ready to escape, the knot seemed to have fused into one solid piece.

"What do we do now?" Cristar asked.

"Well, we certainly don't wait for Commander Silst to return." Eselle yanked on her bindings.

"How long do you think he'll be gone?"

"Heading into town and back? Maybe an hour. Not as long as I'd like. "

Cristar worked on her own bonds, conveniently tied in front of her. For being ruthless, the commander strangely respected the comfort of a pregnant woman.

The rope shifted around Eselle's wrists. Wriggling her hands some more, she managed to loosen the knot, and the rope dropped to the floor. She rolled her shoulders, working the kinks out, before assisting Cristar.

Once they were both free, Eselle grabbed their packs from the corner where the commander had tossed them. After reloading their supplies, she peeked out the windows. A quick check showed no sign of anyone out the front or back of the house.

"I think we're clear," she said. "Let's get out of here before he returns."

Eselle found the ax and knife they'd used earlier at the edge of the trees out back.

Instead of taking the lead, she relayed directions to Cristar and kept watch for anyone following them. If the commander had spoken truthfully, and he really left for his troops, it would still be awhile before he returned. If he had lied, there was no telling who or what might be behind them.

Each time Eselle saw a branch sway, her pulse quickened. Every time a shadow shifted in the dimming sunlight, she tensed.

They stuck to the trees while skirting around a nearby lake. Only when the growing darkness forced them to, did they stop for the night. By then, Eselle's legs shook too much to continue anyway. She sat against a boulder to catch her breath. Cristar appeared in no better condition. The woman had a sheen of sweat across her brow and breathed heavily. They took a long moment before they unpacked any supplies.

Once situated, Cristar checked Eselle's bruised face and scraped knuckles. While her hands weren't too bad, Eselle couldn't help but squirm when Cristar examined her nose. Though the commander's elbow hadn't broken it, she had bruises around her eyes and significant swelling. Cristar bandaged her knuckles, adding the salve she'd made from the comfrey leaves they'd harvested at the farmhouse.

The women wrapped themselves in their blankets and huddled together for warmth against the large boulder. Eselle decided against a fire, worried it might reveal their location if Silst guessed their direction. She figured that in a couple days, they should be safe and would certainly need the warmth during the chilly nights. For now, the risk wasn't worth taking.

"I've been thinking about where to go," Cristar said. "My sister-in-law and her family live a few villages north of Eddington, in Vorhest. They'll help us if we can get there."

"It's too dangerous. We need to head west."

"Why west?"

Eselle's first instinct was to lie. She'd grown accustomed to it because it was safer—for her, her brother, and the people who counted on them. It seemed wrong now to continue keeping things from Cristar. They had been through too much together.

"West is where Swondan is. My home. My brother's there, with others who can protect us."

"My family can protect us, too. I know it's dangerous, but they could keep us hidden, safe."

Eselle shook her head. "Not like my brother can. Plus, we would be putting your family in danger. Commander Silst knows where you're from, so he can question the people in Eddington to learn about the rest of your family. Once he finds out about them, he could have Vorhest searched so thoroughly nowhere would be safe. I don't believe he knows enough about me though to know about Swondan or my brother. We'll be safe there. And even if he does know or finds out, my brother has the resources to protect us. Trust me."

Cristar frowned while staring at the ground before her. Eselle knew her friend worried about delivering her baby on the road, away from family. She couldn't blame the woman.

"I've trusted you this far," Cristar said, looking back at Eselle, "and you haven't let me down. I guess a little longer won't hurt. But why did Commander Silst come after us?"

Eselle shrugged. "The king's afraid of some baby that's coming."

"I know, but that's not what I mean. The commander seemed determined to bring us in."

"Those are his orders."

"Yes, but he could have sent his soldiers after us. Why do it personally?" Cristar asked. "Do you think I might actually be carrying this baby the king wants? And maybe he and Commander Silst know it?"

Eselle thought for a moment, worried that might be true, but then shook her head. "No. If that were the case, they would send the entire army after you. Since it only seems to be Commander Silst, I'd guess it's more personal for some reason." Recalling their time at the inn, she wondered if that might have anything to do with it. She immediately dismissed the idea. "Maybe he's upset you escaped, that I helped you, and wants to handle it personally." Eselle shrugged. "Frankly, I can't figure him out, how he can go from gentle to violent so quickly. There are times I think he's a little unhinged, that he might just be crazy."

Cristar pulled her blanket farther up over her shoulders. "You may be right. There's something off about that man's eyes. I can't put my finger on it, but they bother me."

Adjusting her own blanket, Eselle decided Cristar deserved the truth. She had the right to leave Eselle's company if she wanted, especially if she thought it was safer for her unborn child.

"There's one other reason he might be after us," Eselle said. Cristar peered over at her curiously. "He could be after me."

"You? Why?"

"Because my birth name is Joeselleen Enstrin. My father was King Folstaff Enstrin." She let that news soak in before she continued.

Cristar's eyes grew wider as she sat straighter. "Your father was the king?"

"Yes. When I was eight, Vorgal coordinated a mass slaughter at the castle and took over. Only my brother and I escaped."

"I remember hearing about that when I was younger. Not the actual event, I was only a few years old when it happened, but other people talked about it when I was a little older. They said things like, 'That never happened when Folstaff was king,' and 'I remember when King Folstaff would . . . something or other.' I never really thought about it being real."

"Well, it was very real. I still have nightmares about that night." Eselle stared at her boots where they peeked out from beneath the blanket.

"Is that what wakes you sometimes?"

Eselle nodded. Cristar had asked her about the nightmares before, but she'd brushed off the woman's concerns, pretended it was nothing.

"How did you escape?"

"My brother saved me."

While Cristar watched her in the dim moonlight, Eselle reluctantly described what she remembered.

"My younger sister, Lissil, and I were heading to bed. We'd just gotten to our room when we heard a commotion from the hallway. We couldn't tell what it was, so we went to look. At first, we didn't hear anything again, didn't know where the noise had come from, so we gave up and headed back. Then we heard it again, a strange metallic sound. Lissil thought it was someone banging dishes.

"When it sounded again, we realized it was swords clashing. They grew louder. Then we heard sounds of fighting and moaning. We didn't know what to do, so we turned around to find an adult. I was terrified that whoever had made those noises would find us. We ran through the halls. I was too afraid to call out for fear the wrong person would hear us.

"Then we turned a corner and ran into five armed men who wore bloodied house armor. I thought . . ." She stared down at her wrapped knees and took a couple of breaths before she continued. "I thought we were saved. The man closest gave the worst smile I've ever seen. Right before he drove his sword straight through my sister's stomach." Eselle took a stuttering breath, then pulled the blanket up tighter around herself. The memories never faded, no matter how many times she examined them.

Was there something I could have done differently to save Lissil?

"What happened then?" Cristar asked, her voice soft. She reached her arm around Eselle and hugged her close.

"I ran," Eselle said, still ashamed of herself. In that moment, she realized she'd needed to say these things aloud for a while. Though only a child at the time, afraid and defenseless, outnumbered and untrained even if she'd had a weapon, she still felt strangled with guilt about leaving her dying sister behind for fear of her own life.

"I ran," Eselle repeated. "They chased me, yelled that they would kill me like they had my sister. I was terrified and ran blindly. Every time I saw a corner to another hallway, I took it. I prayed it would throw the attackers off, that they would fail to see me take a turn and keep running in the wrong direction. Nothing worked. Finally, I turned a corner and saw three more guards." She heard Cristar give a sharp, faint inhale, but she didn't look over. If she saw her friend's expression, she would lose control. She had cried enough tears years ago and promised herself she was done with them.

"I froze, terrified, just as the false guards ran up behind me. I thought I was dead, especially when one of the men in front of me grabbed me by the arm and yanked me toward him. I screamed, but he tossed me behind him, so I was between him and the two with him. Then he and the others fought the traitors, always keeping me behind or between them. That's when I knew these were the real house guard. But the pretenders were better fighters.

"They killed the first guard quickly, and the other two made a wall of themselves before me. Then another guard fell." She could still hear the gurgle as blood flooded the guard's throat. "The last guard kept fighting, kept pushing me farther behind him down the hallway as the attackers advanced. I knew we were about to die."

Eselle had to blink away tears before she could continue.

"While the last guard fought, my brother, Tavith, arrived. He grabbed my hand and pulled me after him. While we ran through the halls, I told him about Lissil, and he told me our mother and other sister, Avassa, were dead. We arrived at the council chambers, where our father and brother, Brassil—who would have been the next king—waited for us, to find they were both dead already." She stared out at the dark trees. "They were so covered in blood I'm not even sure how they died, which wound was the fatal one."

With a sniff, Eselle wiped her eyes once more and pulled her knees up tighter. "Now Tavith is the rightful heir."

"Tavith is the brother living in Swondan?"

"Yes."

"How did you two escape?"

"Vistralou Castle has secret passages. Being part of the royal family, we were told of a few should we need to escape situations like that one. Tavith and I headed to one when we encountered another band of invaders. By that time, most of the castle guards were dead, and we were on our own. Tavith had done some sword training, so he bought us some time. But he was only a boy in his early lessons. Truthfully, I think the attackers were amused by his attempt and only toyed with him, planned to draw it out before they killed us. Again, I thought we were about to die. One of the invaders hit me and knocked me down, so I didn't see much after that, but I know a few of our guards came in. They eventually subdued or killed the attackers, but not before only one guard remained. He was too badly injured to flee with us, but he saw us safely to the passage and covered our escape."

"I had no idea the attack was that brutal," Cristar said. "I heard the stories, but they didn't do it justice, just said the former ruling family was killed."

"Even the word brutal doesn't fully encompass what I saw that night."

Cristar hugged her closer, reminding Eselle of how her mother had held her similarly when she was little.

Once Eselle felt calmer, she pulled away, staring silently into the thick trees around them.

"The stories say everyone died." Cristar peered at her, but Eselle couldn't meet her eyes yet.

"I think they mistook one of the serving boys for Tavith. There was a boy in the castle around his age who resembled him. They know I escaped though since they were short one body."

"Have they been looking for you this whole time?"

"They were for a while, but over the years the searches have become less exhaustive. Plus, enough time has passed, they're not entirely certain what I look like anymore. That helps."

"But you think Commander Silst knows who you are?"

"Yes."

"How would he though?"

"Did you tell anyone about me, mention my name to them? Maybe Warder Hilbert or a neighbor?" It was difficult to see Cristar's expression in the darkness.

"No. I spoke to some neighbors while you were in town, but not about you. Only plans for the baby, how their family was doing, and such."

"Then I have no idea how he knows, but he does. Back at the farmhouse, he called me by my name, which I never told him. He looked directly at me when he said it, and I could see in his eyes he said it purposefully." Eselle turned toward Cristar. "As much as I enjoy having you with me, and how much I want to protect you and the baby, if he is chasing me," Eselle said reluctantly, "you might be safer by yourself. I don't want to endanger either of you."

Cristar glanced away for a moment, then pulled her arm from around Eselle. "And, if he is after you, it might be safer if you didn't have a pregnant woman slowing you down." They watched each other for a long, silent moment. "You said the first time he chased us he came after me. It's entirely possible he's after both of us and splitting up will make it easier for him to pick us off."

"True." That oddly made Eselle feel better since it was a valid reason for sticking together. "Where would you go, anyway?"

"I don't know, but I'd rather stay with you if you'll let me."

"I'd like that," Eselle said.

"Swondan?"

"Swondan."

Cristar pulled her legs up beneath her. "What kind of farm does your brother have? Anything I can help with?"

A wry smile took over Eselle's face. "It's not just a farm. We have crops. Lots of them, in fact. But it's an excuse for Tavith to have a large number of *farmhands* around. They're really my brother's allies."

"Allies for what?"

"They help him coordinate things." Eselle gave a deep sigh. If Cristar was to continue with her, she deserved the entire truth. "The farm is my brother's base of operations while he plans to retake the throne. The people who live there work to keep up appearances and bring in money to help pay for supplies, weapons and such, and feed everyone, but mainly they're devising a plan to remove Vorgal from power. If you continue with me, that's what you'll be getting involved with."

Cristar didn't look nearly as surprised as Eselle had expected, and she didn't hesitate in her response. "Okay, I can accept that."

Eselle smiled, relieved, but needed to make certain the woman considered things clearly. "Before you agree, I should tell you that my brother has worked out agreements between key people that will let him march on the castle soon." Cristar nodded in acceptance. "I don't know if we can reach Swondan before then, but if we do, and things don't work out for my brother, you'll be at a primary target for retaliation."

"Then your brother better win." Cristar placed her hand on her stomach. "We're staying with you."

CHAPTER TWENTY-TWO

Eselle examined the water before stepping onto the first log. The spray coming off the rocks suggested a strong current. She couldn't be certain, but she suspected the deepest point of the river would reach her waist, maybe a little higher. With the thirty or so pace width, she would have preferred to cross at a narrower gap. This was the best spot they'd found for a few days, and Eselle worried they might not find anything better. An abundance of logs had stacked up at a bend to form a makeshift dam, and branches had become entangled with them which could be used to assist with balance.

With their meager head start on Commander Silst, putting a river like the Bolshard between them was an advantage.

Eselle eased her feet along. The damp logs seemed solid enough, but she searched for slippery spots.

Cristar stepped onto the first log and reached for some anchoring branches. "I never did like swimming. I'd really hate to go now."

"Don't worry, we'll be across in no time." Eselle wasn't as confident as she tried to sound.

The women shimmied across several logs. The water battered the wood beneath them, jostling the haphazard structure just enough to make Eselle question her decision. It was too late to turn back though. She needed to keep them ahead of the commander.

After they reached the halfway point, Eselle breathed easier. Not much longer and they would be safely back on land. Nearing the far shore, she glanced behind her. Cristar had stopped to pull her foot out of a log.

"Are you all right?" Eselle asked, turning around, ready to head back.

Cristar didn't appear to have much trouble, but with a vastly pregnant woman crossing logs on a large swift river, one could never be too concerned.

"I'm fine. I just stepped into a rotten spot."

Eselle watched a moment longer to be certain. Confident Cristar was once again on track, she resumed her own journey.

With her first step, her foot slid out from beneath her. She fell sideways into the river.

The current yanked Eselle beneath the surface.

Water rushed into her lungs.

Which way was up?

She thrashed for what she hoped was the surface.

A memory flashed.

Let the water carry you upward.

Who had told her that?

Her hip slammed into something. She cried out instinctively, and a fresh deluge of water flooded into her mouth.

She flailed, fought for air . . . then tried to calm herself, force her muscles to relax. The best she could manage was a rigid stillness.

The river tugged at Eselle's cloak, pulling it against her throat. She worked her hands up to untie it. The cloak rushed away behind her. The current wrenched her pack, jolting her exhausted body. The gear weighed her down, especially the ax. She struggled out of the straps. The water caught her movements. Her shoulder finally wriggled free.

As her burden fell away, she forced the panic down and tried to control her gasping. She rode the current and prayed it took her upward. She only needed one gulp of air.

An eternity later, the water grew brighter. The surface approached.

Something crashed into Eselle's shoulder. She hurtled off into another direction, the river roaring in her ears. She struggled, fighting the instinct to correct her course.

Her head finally broke free. Eselle coughed up what water she could, even while more slapped her in the face. Floating on the surface, she focused on breathing. Eventually, she might try to work the river, but for now, she simply enjoyed having air again, even if every inhalation tore at her throat and burned her lungs.

Eselle couldn't stop coughing, but her breaths came easier with each one. She thanked the Protector, or anyone who listened, that she'd made it. Granted, she wasn't out of the river yet, but she had a chance. She floated on her back and looked up at the sky, at the soft blue sprinkled with puffy white clouds. It felt all the more serene after her near death.

She jerked to a halt. Water washed over her head. The current pounded against her as something held the back of her tunic.

A masculine voice came from behind.

"Gotcha."

Eselle instantly tried to yank free. She had no leverage, nowhere to place her feet, the river was too deep.

The hand tried to haul Eselle toward shore but made only minuscule progress against the thundering water. She reached around, tried to pry the fingers free, preferring to brave the river instead of being recaptured.

"Stop," the man pleaded. "I barely have you as it is. You have to help me."

The voice was softer than she expected, despite its urgency. Craning her head around, she realized it wasn't Kyr who gripped her tunic. He didn't look like a soldier either. At least, he wasn't in a uniform or anything that resembled one. He might still cause her trouble, but given that he was trying to rescue her, she decided to allow him. She was pummeled and winded and needed help. Besides, saving someone from a river seemed like a lot of work to rob or kill them.

The man gripped a downed tree near the edge of the river, anchoring himself. The water reached his chest. As he hauled Eselle closer, he angled her toward shore. She kicked against the current trying to reclaim her. When something grazed her side, she twisted and pushed off it. After a few tries, they maneuvered close enough to the bank that the man found better footing and helped Eselle to her feet.

She stumbled ashore, dropped to the ground, and rolled onto her back.

"Thank you," she croaked. She regretted it only for the slicing pain it caused her throat.

"Are you okay?" He sat beside her. "Is anything hurt? Broken? You don't seem to . . . Wow, you must have hit your face on something."

"Yeah. I hit it on someone's elbow. But that's another story. I'm fine, I think." She searched his features.

He appeared around Cristar's age, and his expressive, baby-blue eyes were large as they scanned her over. Short brown hair lay plastered against his thin face, and his well-worn clothes clung to his slender frame. His concerned expression seemed genuine as his gaze returned to her face.

"Your shoulder is bleeding," he said.

The sleeve of her tunic had a tear. It steadily grew darker as blood soaked into it. The young man eased the opening wide enough to examine the injury beneath.

"It's difficult to see, but it doesn't look too bad."

Rustling startled Eselle, and she jerked upright. Even her exhaustion couldn't prevent fear of discovery. Her luck seemed to hold, though, as Cristar crashed through the brush; one hand pushed branches aside while the other shielded her stomach.

"Thank the Protector," Cristar said, rushing over. Her heavy breathing and flushed face nearly matched Eselle's.

Eselle sighed in relief and laid back down while Cristar sat beside her. It had become harder for the poor woman to reach the ground in a timely fashion, which made Eselle doubly grateful for the stranger. She wouldn't be able to help Cristar up anytime soon.

"Are you okay?" Cristar asked. "Is anything hurt?"

"I'm fine. Just a little battered. And cold," she added when a shiver swept through her. Looking up at them turned disorienting, so she tried to rise.

Both Cristar and the young man helped her, but the moment she gained her feet, she swayed. More parts of her ached than didn't. She nodded toward some boulders. "There. Help me sit against one of those."

They escorted her over, and Cristar got her situated as the young man became a whirlwind of motion.

He rushed around the area, gathering wood and tossing it into a pile. "I'll get a fire together. We have to get you warmed up. I could use some warming too. And you might want to change out of those wet clothes. I'll turn away or go for a walk or something when you're ready. Let me know. I can make us some warm food too. I was getting ready to camp for the night anyway."

"Thank you," Cristar said as he stacked the wood. "If you hadn't helped my friend, I'm not sure what I would have done."

He peered over with a humble smile but didn't waver from his task. "My name is Daalok, by the way. Daalok Borwin."

"I'm Cristar Maesret. And this is my friend, Eselle."

They nodded greetings, then remained silent while Daalok started the fire. It didn't escape Eselle's notice that Cristar had omitted her last name. Luckily, Daalok didn't seem to realize.

Without her pack, Eselle borrowed Cristar's spare clothes. The only non-dress clothing she'd found at Cristar's house had been Klaasen's. Normally, they would have been large for Cristar, but with how pregnant she was, they fit pretty well around the stomach.

While Eselle changed, Daalok ventured off for more usable wood and to change his own wet clothes.

Eselle had expected to find several bruises, but the sight of her left thigh startled her.

Cristar gave a strangled sound. "Sit. Let me look at you." She took Eselle's good arm to help her down.

In addition to swelling, the bruise on Eselle's leg covered her entire outer thigh, from hip to knee, and stretched halfway around it. She also had a sizable bruise forming on her right shoulder around the gash they found earlier. It was bound to make most anything she tried challenging at best.

After her examination, Cristar felt certain there were no broken bones. She stitched and bandaged the gash, then helped Eselle dress.

"What should we do about Daalok?" Cristar asked once they'd managed to get Eselle into the trousers.

"I don't think we can really do anything tonight, only play along and accept his help. Tomorrow, though, we should make certain we head in opposite directions."

Cristar shook out the shirt. "You need to stay off that leg for at least a day, if not longer."

"We don't have that kind of time. Commander Silst could be here at any moment. We didn't have much of a lead to begin with."

"We don't even know for sure he's behind us, that he knows which direction we took. Or that he would suspect we crossed the river. You won't be able to walk tomorrow. Trust me."

"Why don't we wait and see how I am? If I can walk, we'll leave. If not, we'll figure it out." She didn't tell Cristar, but she had every intention of leaving in the morning, no matter how her leg was. She needed to keep Cristar and the baby safe, and wouldn't be the reason they were captured again.

"It might help to have Daalok along." Cristar held the shirt up for Eselle to put her head through. "At least until you're back on your feet."

Eselle considered that. Cristar could do less and less as her pregnancy advanced, and Eselle was now wounded.

"Plus," Cristar said, "Daalok might be able to help if anyone finds us, especially if he has any fighting skills." The young man didn't carry any visible weapons, so they didn't know his talents.

"He might." Eselle shoved her good arm through a sleeve. "There's also the matter of you being pregnant, and it being illegal."

"True, but he could expose us when he's either with us or after leaving us. There's nothing we can do about that."

When Eselle gave a shrug, she cringed as pain radiated through her shoulder. She tried to ignore it. "I'd hate to put him in danger though, especially after he saved my life. And we can't exactly tell him we're being chased by Likalsta's high commander."

Once they had Eselle dressed, Cristar stood back to look at her. The shirt and its sleeves hung to Eselle's thighs, and she had to hold up the trousers to keep them from falling. The legs pooled around her feet.

Eselle had never paid attention to how much Cristar rolled up the sleeves and legs of her husband's clothes, but apparently Klaasen had been a large man. She sighed. "My own clothes can't dry fast enough."

Cristar chuckled, then went to rummage in her pack. "So, what do we do?"

"Daalok might be helpful, but he's also a liability. I think we should leave him behind." Cristar nodded, but Eselle couldn't tell if it was because she agreed or deferred to Eselle's judgment.

Eselle propped herself back against the boulders, pulling the blanket Daalok had left them around herself. The warmth of the fire eased some of her sore muscles, but she didn't relish the idea of sleeping on the ground.

After Cristar called to Daalok that it was safe to return, he entered camp with an armload of branches.

While he worked on building up the fire, Cristar prepared a poultice. She held up some spare cloth. "I don't have enough to bandage both your shoulder and thigh." Her eyes moved between Eselle's injuries. "Your thigh needs the poultice more, so—"

"I probably have something," Daalok said, pulling his pack closer.

Not finding what he wanted near the top, he pushed aside his belongings and dug farther. Eselle noticed a piece of white material near the opening, but he bypassed it as he searched. Eventually, he produced enough cloth that Cristar could dress both Eselle's shoulder and thigh, as well as make a thin sling for her arm.

While Cristar cared for her patient, Daalok returned to the fire. He soon built it to a steady blaze. Cristar pulled out their remaining supplies and food while Daalok retrieved his own. Between them, they dined on cured meat, cheese, some flatbread Daalok had bartered for at a farm a few days back, as well as wild berries Cristar had found at the edge of a field the previous day.

"How are you, really?" Daalok asked while they ate.

"I'm fine," Eselle said. "Just some bruises and a few scrapes."

"But not . . ." he said, then gestured to his face where hers was bruised from the commander's elbow. The bruises around her eyes and nose had faded some, but still had a way to go.

"No. That's from picking a fight with someone bigger than me. But that's fine too. It barely hurts anymore." *Or maybe the other pain just overshadows it. It's hard to say.*

"Good." He took another bite of cheese. "Where are you two headed?"

The women exchanged a glance. "Cristar has family nearby," Eselle said. "So we're heading there until the baby arrives." She was curious to hear his response, how he felt about Cristar being pregnant, but he didn't flinch. Was it possible he didn't know about the new law?

"Yes," Cristar said. "Since my husband died, I thought it would be better to have family around."

He frowned. "They're making you travel in your condition? Why didn't they come stay with you?"

"Well," Cristar said slowly, "they have children, so we thought it best to let them stay in their own home."

Daalok nodded but looked unconvinced. "I guess that makes sense. It would still be better if one of them stayed with you, so *you'd* be in your own home, comfortable while you go through something so important."

The women glanced at each other again.

"Yes," Eselle said. "That may have been better, but . . . I was heading this way anyway, so I could help her. And it's really not that far, so . . . well, it's all decided, so there's nothing to be done, I suppose."

"Where do they live?"

Eselle dreaded answering. The last time she had picked a random town hadn't worked out well for her. If she at least knew which direction he planned to travel, it would help.

"Which way are you heading?" she asked instead.

"I'm not sure yet. Is it near here?"

"Polsiteer," Cristar said smoothly.

Daalok scrunched his brows, as did Eselle, and asked, "Where?"

Eselle knew this area well, from maps at least, and she'd never heard of the place. It was possible the maps weren't entirely complete, but she suspected Cristar had concocted the name.

"It's a small village. Tiny, really. Not far from here."

"Oh. Well, it's good you don't have far to go. In your condition, I mean. Perhaps I'll travel with you to make certain you get there safely."

Eselle waved him off nonchalantly. "Oh, you don't have to. I'll take care of her."

"But you're injured. You might need help too."

Cristar gave a stiff smile. "Really, you don't have to. I'm sure you have people waiting for you."

Daalok hesitated, glancing off at the fire briefly. "Not really. I'd planned to camp around here for a couple of days, do some fishing and foraging. After that, I'm not sure where I'm headed. I might as well be useful and help you ladies get to your family."

"What about your family? Shouldn't you get back to them?"

He shrugged. "I lost my family a while back. So, I'm looking for a new place. Who knows? I might stay in that village you're heading to."

Eselle nodded reluctantly. How could they get rid of Daalok without being overly rude? He'd saved her, after all. Perhaps that showed what sort of person he was, to risk his life for a stranger.

What would happen if Silst arrives and tries to arrest us? Or someone asks about us later, and Daalok tells them everything because he simply doesn't know any better? Or isn't the honest man he appears to be? Why did he hesitate when asked where he's going? Does he not know? Or is there more to his journey? Or more to his leaving home?

Eselle's questions only emphasized the problem. They didn't know him well enough to trust him.

Perhaps a good night's sleep would help her think of a polite way to tell him they didn't want his company tomorrow.

***

Daalok rolled over for the hundredth time in the last hour. He pulled his hood up to keep his ears warm as he stared into the dark forest.

Even five months after leaving Nist, he still didn't know where to go or what to do with himself. He didn't know if anyone back home had come after him. As a precaution, he avoided everyone on the road.

When he'd heard screams, then seen someone being swept down river toward him, he'd acted instinctively. He'd jumped in the water to snatch her when she rushed by.

They obviously didn't want him to travel with them, but with one pregnant and one injured, they needed help whether they admitted it or not.

Rolling over again, Daalok watched Eselle as she slept beyond the cold fire. With her battered face, he worried she might be running from an abusive relationship of one sort or another. *Did a husband or father do that?*

For the first time, Daalok felt he could actually do something important, help someone. Granted, anyone could help them, but he was here and willing.

I'll see you two safely to Polsiteer, wherever that is.

He hated to admit it, even to himself, but there was another benefit to helping the women. If anyone *had* followed him, they would be hunting for a man traveling alone. The women could be good camouflage, help him even if they didn't know it. No matter what excuses they conjured in the morning, he would outmaneuver them.

Daalok pulled the blanket higher, up over his hood for added warmth.

His attention turned to Cristar as she lay on her side. Her mouth hung open slightly, and she gave the faintest snore. *What are you really doing out here? Especially in your condition?*

Was her husband really dead? Or had that been a fib too? They had a good story, but something about it seemed off. They thought too much about their answers, consulted each other too frequently.

But who am I to judge? May the Protector forgive me, but I wasn't entirely honest myself.

If they knew who . . . what, I am, they'd definitely leave me behind.

And I couldn't blame them.

CHAPTER TWENTY-THREE

Eselle cried out as lighting shot through her thigh and her leg buckled.

Daalok caught her before she fell. Careful of her injured arm, he steadied her while she hobbled to regain her balance.

"Sit her down," Cristar said.

Eselle frowned as Daalok helped her back to the ground. "I hate to admit it, but you were right. I can barely stand, let alone walk."

"So we lose a day." Cristar looked to Daalok. "Can you make us something for breakfast while I take care of her?"

"Of course." He headed off to the other side of the fire where their packs were stowed.

Cristar sat beside Eselle. "That expression tells me where your thoughts are. But let's not worry until we know there's something to worry about." Eselle opened her mouth to speak, but Cristar overrode her. "We're not even certain Commander Silst found our trail."

Eselle picked up a rock and clawed the dirt with it. "I hate that I'm holding us up. We should be leagues downriver by now."

"We will be soon enough, but not if you don't rest that leg."

While Cristar applied fresh poultice to both Eselle's shoulder and thigh, Daalok brought them bowls of porridge.

Finishing off the wrap around Eselle's shoulder, Cristar said, "We may have to stay here for a couple of more days."

Eselle set her bowl in her lap untouched. "We can't lose that much time."

"Your leg needs rest."

"It's only bruised. You said there's nothing broken, so I'll be fine tomorrow. We can take frequent breaks along the way."

"No." Cristar sounded exasperated. "Protector help you, you're stubborn. Between the swelling and bruises, even you have to admit it's bad. You need to stay off it."

Eselle started to argue, but Cristar threw her a glare that made her shrivel instead. The woman's unborn child would stand no chance against that expression.

Daalok watched the exchange while eating his breakfast. When the women stared at each other in their silent argument, he set his bowl down and gathered up his pack. "I'm going to see about catching some fish. I'll be back."

The women ignored him as he left.

"Fine," Eselle said sharply. "We'll stay until we agree my leg is healed enough for light traveling. But," she threw a finger up, "we'll try our best each morning to head out. Perhaps we're being followed, perhaps not, but we can't stay in one place too long."

Cristar seemed to consider it. "All right. But," she said, holding up her own stern finger, "we must *both* agree to your traveling. You may be eager to leave, but I'm eager to see you properly healed."

They each nodded agreement, even while holding onto their frowns.

Hours later, Daalok sulked back into camp with nothing to show for his efforts.

"Where are the fish?" Eselle asked.

"I didn't catch anything."

"Why not?"

"You'd have to ask the fish. They weren't biting."

Eselle studied the river. Cristar had planned to cook the fish for supper that night and prepare the rest for traveling. "I would have thought you'd catch more than we needed. This river is loaded. How are they usually?"

"I don't know. I've never fished here before."

"Well, what kind of bait are you using?"

"Bait?"

"Oh, good grief." Eselle lifted her arm. "Help me up. I'll show you how to fish." Cristar rounded on her, but Eselle cut her off. "I'm not going far, and I'll sit the entire time." She nodded toward the sling. "I couldn't fish with this anyway. But I need someone to get me to the river, then I'll tell him what to do." Cristar glared. "If we want to eat decently tonight and have fish to take with us, this is the best option. Plus, it gives me something to do other than sitting around feeling useless."

"Fine." Cristar pointed to Daalok. "But keep her off that leg."

The young man put an arm around Eselle and hauled her up. Acting as her crutch, he showed her where he'd tried fishing.

"Well, no wonder they weren't biting. There aren't any fish here. You see how exposed the area is? No rocks or logs?"

"Isn't that a good thing? Plenty of room for them to swim around?"

"No. You'll find more fish closer to places where they can hide." She examined the riverbank for promising spots. "Let's try over there." She pointed to an area with several rocks that had caught some passing branches over time.

"How long have you been fishing?" Eselle asked as Daalok helped her along the river.

"Just the last couple of days."

"No. I mean how many years."

He turned his gaze toward the river. "The last couple of days."

"Oh. Well, that could have something to do with it too."

***

From his position atop the ridge, Kyr spied the women at their campsite inside the treeline—along with their new companion they'd picked up.

"There they are," one of the soldiers said. He spurred his horse to rush after the trio.

"Stop!" Kyr barked.

The soldier pulled back on the reins, sending the horse into an uncertain dance before he regained control. "But, sir, they're right there."

"I see that. I did not order you after them though. Did I?"

"Sir?"

Ignoring the soldier, Kyr considered options. He needed to keep things balanced awhile longer. "We'll follow them, make certain they continue in this direction and don't venture off into the mountains ahead."

"Sir?"

"If they do, we'll deal with it, steer them back on course. I want them to continue on this path. Understood?"

"No, sir. Our orders are to bring them in. The lord mar—"

"The lord marshal is not here," Kyr snapped. "Nor do I care what he wants. I remember a recent conversation about just that topic." One of the soldiers rubbed his throat while the others stared. "Until I order otherwise, we follow them."

"But we're supposed to bring in pregnant women." The soldier's voice was weaker than usual.

Kyr grumbled inwardly. "I don't have any experience with pregnant women," he said with feigned patience. "They're something I try very diligently to avoid, but my understanding is that they require a lot of attention. Would you like to care for a pregnant woman for the next, oh say, week until we can get her to the castle?"

The soldier blanched. "No, sir."

"Neither do I. Since they're halfway heading in the right direction anyway, we'll follow them, steer them when needed, and let those other two deal with her."

Kyr sent the soldiers off to set up camp while he continued to watch the group. He would have preferred to bring them to the castle, or somewhere else safe, but Nikos was right. Things needed to play out how the high mage had seen. With the nights getting colder, however, and Cristar getting further along in her pregnancy, he worried. Eselle's new limp was another concern. With her injured, it slowed the group even more, not to mention weakened them. If anything happened, and he couldn't reach them in time . . .

Sherwyn shifted beneath him and pawed the ground. Kyr reached down and rubbed the courser's neck.

"I know," he said. "I feel the same way." He gazed at the sky ahead, growing steadily darker with the fading sun. "Any help would be appreciated."

Only when the trio finally went to sleep did Kyr return to his own camp.

As the soldiers followed over the next couple of days, the women and their companion veered around Vahean. They were several days south of the capital, but they seemed to be skirting the southern end on their way to their destination. Kyr thought it risky and never would have taken the route himself in their circumstances. It did, however, keep them close enough to

Vistralou Castle that when the time was right, he could get them there reasonably quick. If pushed, Sherwyn could travel the distance in little more than a day. Walking, though, the trio would take considerably longer. Huln's lackeys might prove useful after all. If needed, he could commandeer their horses, especially once Cristar could no longer walk decently. Three accidents could yield him three horses to transport the group quickly.

Two days later, Kyr noticed the travelers veering closer to the mountains—and closer to dangerous terrain and wildlife. He ordered one of the soldiers out onto a rocky promontory that could be seen from the group's campsite. The armsman's orders were to be seen, but not look like he knew he was seen. It didn't take long for the group to move back into the safety of the forest. The king might only be interested in the baby, but Kyr couldn't risk losing any of the group. Doing so would cause him all kinds of problems.

A few more days, and he noticed Cristar waddled more than usual. She could no longer rise easily on her own from the ground, nor could she get down. Torn between reluctance and excitement, he knew it was time.

Watching the soldiers who'd been restrained more than they cared to be, he considered his best options to do this quietly. The soldiers might be eager for action, but none of the people at the campsite were particularly dangerous. Eselle could handle herself pretty well, but she was injured. Though her limp had improved considerably, he could still see it.

Waiting until the group was splintered would be best, until one or more wandered off for an errand.

***

"We'll certainly eat well tonight." Eselle eyed their half dozen catches.

Daalok grinned broadly. "Thanks for teaching me. I would have starved without you."

"Nonsense," Eselle said, patting his shoulder. "Some time on your own, and you would have figured it out."

After securing their supper in the net, they walked back. The moment they crested the hill beside their camp, they froze.

Cristar sat stiffly on the log Daalok had hauled over to the campfire for her. Beside her, Commander Silst knelt while stoking the fire with the stick Eselle had used earlier. He seemed either mesmerized by the fire or deep in thought. He had that concentrated vacancy to his eyes which could have been either. Three soldiers she didn't recognize stood against trees or sat on a boulder off to the side. All had their hands propped against their sword hilts.

Eselle dropped the fish beside her. Could she pull her dagger fast enough? Probably not. She'd never really practiced throwing it, so her aim was abysmal. And anything less than a direct hit could make things worse.

"They found me," Daalok said sharply.

Eselle's eyes darted toward him, but she had no time to wonder what he meant.

Silst looked up as though he'd expected them, as though Daalok's outburst hadn't occurred. His focused expression slowly shifted, and he gradually lost all visible emotion. After a moment, Eselle realized his gaze didn't rest on her, but Daalok.

"Who's this?" Silst's voice was as devoid of emotion as his expression. She'd never seen him so unreadable. He set the stick down and rose from his place beside Cristar.

Eselle glanced at Daalok, sorry he'd gotten caught in the middle of their troubles. She and Cristar had debated telling him about their woes, especially since he didn't seem to know about the pregnancy ban, but finally agreed on a truncated version—bad men chased them. He had seemed content with that explanation and wanted to remain with them. Now, Eselle felt guilty they hadn't told him more, told him the full extent of what he would get into.

"He's a traveler we met," Eselle said. "He was nice enough to share his supplies after I fell into the river and lost most of ours."

The commander studied each of them for a long moment. Eselle wished she could read his mind. There were at least twenty paces between her and Cristar, and one between Cristar and the commander. Eselle knew who would win that battle if he decided to hurt her friend or use her as leverage.

"Come sit," Silst finally said. His tone was strong, but not harsh.

Instead of complying, Eselle regarded Cristar. The woman's eyes were fierce. With a discrete twitch of her head, Cristar nodded toward the commander beside her, then the opposite way toward the forest. Eselle immediately dismissed the request to run. When she looked at Silst, he was watching her. The corner of his mouth slid upward the slightest bit.

"You can try, if you like," he said. "But we both know you won't." He took the only step between himself and Cristar, putting a hand on her shoulder. "You would never leave a friend behind."

Damn it. How did he find us?

Silst glanced at Daalok. Eselle didn't know Daalok well but worried he might try to run. When he only glanced back at her, he seemed to understand. They had no choice, not with Cristar so close to danger. They joined their friend and the fiend who held her.

The commander ordered one of the soldiers to retrieve any weapons Eselle and Daalok carried. After their daggers were confiscated, Silst sent an armsman to take the fish and prepare it for dinner, while the other two took care of their horses for the night.

Once everyone was settled around the fire, Commander Silst retrieved the fire stick and studied them in turn. The stick in his hand, its end charred and glowing orange, seemed more like a weapon than a tool. Whether it was his serious expression, the stick itself, or the way he brandished it, it had nearly the same effect as if he'd drawn his sword. Despite their larger number, now that Daalok had joined them, Eselle felt certain the commander could subdue them all by himself. All he needed to do was gain control of Cristar, and they would fall into place, which was likely why he'd positioned himself beside the pregnant woman.

"You," Silst said as he pointed the stick at Daalok. "You said we'd found you. What did you mean?"

Daalok sat speechless for a moment, then stammered, "I . . . I meant us. I meant, strange soldiers we don't know found us and might take our supplies, or kill us, or—"

"Enough," the commander said, his voice tight. Daalok snapped his mouth closed. "That's an odd slip. Is there something I should know about you? Something you'd like to tell me before I discover it myself and arrest you for whatever it is?"

Daalok wrung his hands in his lap, his eyes wide. "No, sir. There's nothing to tell. I slipped up is all."

Silst glared half-heartedly at him a moment longer, then nodded, his half-smile returning. Eselle could tell he didn't believe the young man, but he also didn't seem overly concerned about Daalok.

He's after me.

Or is it Cristar?

Perhaps Cristar was right, and he was after them both.

Instead of questioning them, Silst simply sat beside Cristar, keeping them in suspense regarding his intentions. Cristar shot him a sideways scowl.

"What now?" Eselle tucked her fingers beneath her to keep them still.

"Now," Silst said, "we wait for our meal, get a good night's sleep, and head to Vistralou in the morning."

"And our friend? You'll let him go after we leave?"

"No."

Though she'd hoped for a different answer, she wasn't surprised by it. "But he's not part of this."

"By being here, he's harboring a pregnant woman."

Eselle gave up the argument before she even tried. In her experience, once the commander decided something, he kept chasing what he wanted. Not long ago, she'd appreciated that.

Later that night, they had all gathered around the fire to sleep, though many of them laid awake. Only two of the armsmen slumbered. The third stood guard not far away.

Eselle couldn't sleep for the obvious reason, they'd been recaptured. She worried what would happen once they reached the castle, but also felt guilty getting Daalok caught up in their misadventures. They should have told him more. She also wondered about his odd outburst. Eselle presumed her friends couldn't sleep for the same reasons. As to why the commander remained awake, she could only guess.

As she considered him silently, she realized he was watching Cristar, whose bedroll was directly across the fire from him. At first, she'd thought he simply watched the fire, but his gaze was too focused, too precise. It didn't drift with the wavering flames.

Eselle glanced at Cristar, who tossed and turned as she sought any semblance of comfort. She wished she could help her friend, but with their limited resources, the only thing that would help would be the baby's birth. And that certainly couldn't happen right now. They didn't have the proper supplies and they were prisoners of people who wanted to harm him.

Looking back at the commander as he lay on his side and watched her friend, Eselle began to worry. She'd noticed him watching Cristar previously but hadn't thought anything of it. Now, it dawned on her that he gazed at the young woman rather often, more so than Eselle was comfortable with. His expression tended to soften slightly the longer he watched her.

When Cristar rolled over again, holding her stomach with both hands, Silst propped himself up. He grabbed the legs of the sleeping armsman above him, and shook them vigorously. The man bolted upright with a glazed expression.

"Give the woman your bedroll," Silst ordered before the armsman had gathered his senses.

"What?" the soldier asked, his eyes slowly focusing as he glanced at his commander.

"Give the woman your bedroll," Silst repeated. The armsman noticed the threat in his superior's eyes and scrambled from his blanket and wrapped cloak. "And wake the other lackey and have him do the same."

"That's not necessary," Cristar said, her features uncertain.

The armsman stopped and looked at his commander. The scowl he received got the soldier moving again. He pulled the bedroll up and shook his comrade awake.

Cristar hesitated when the men handed over their bedrolls. She stared at Silst, her brows tense and jaw tight, but he remained silent as he sternly returned the gaze.

Eselle wanted to intervene simply to reassure Cristar, but she agreed with their captor on this. Cristar could use the extra comfort. If she had a bedroll herself, she would donate it, but hers was currently on the bottom of the river. And poor Daalok had never had one to begin with. Now only Cristar and the commander would sleep with any degree of comfort.

After a tense moment, Cristar conceded and moved aside to add the bedrolls to hers. Once she was settled, the soldiers returned to their blankets, both looking grumpier for their loss. Silst settled back down as he regarded the young mother awhile longer.

With growing concern, Eselle watched him until he finally closed his eyes.

CHAPTER TWENTY-FOUR

The long day proved an ordeal for the simple reason of their new traveling companions. By the time they stopped for the evening, Eselle was ready for it to be over.

She and her friends gathered around the beginnings of a campfire. One of the soldiers stood guard nearby, while the others gathered more wood and prepared to cook dinner. Commander Silst stood off a ways tending his horse, instead of leaving it to an armsmen as he had the previous day.

Eselle watched him remove the saddle and set it to the side. He pulled something from one of the saddlebags. With his back to her, she couldn't see what it was, but he put it in a pouch on his belt. While he brushed the stallion, his features eased from the strained look he'd worn most of the day. He appeared much like when she'd first met him, at least after dealing with the armsmen who had apprehended her, then again in Eddington before he'd arrested Cristar.

Without planning to, she rose and walked to where he groomed the steed.

The commander glanced over when she drew close but didn't stop brushing. "What can I do for you?"

Eselle asked something that had bothered her since it happened. "Why did you kill that vagabond at the farmhouse, the one who told you where we were?"

"Because I didn't want him telling anyone else your location." He had finished brushing one side of the courser and worked his way around to the other. The horse nudged him as he passed, and the commander rubbed the stallion's muzzle.

"Who would he have told? Your soldiers so they could tell you?"

"It's complicated." His nonchalance irritated her.

"So, explain it."

He sighed. "These three idiots," he nodded toward the slowly evolving campsite, "are loyal to the lord marshal, not me. They're a slap in the face since the lord marshal and I despise each other. It wouldn't surprise me if they tried sneaking you out around me and bringing you in on the lord marshal's behalf. I'd rather get the credit for your apprehension."

"What does it matter who brings us in?"

"In King Vorgal's military, the only thing that matters is results. He who delivers them advances."

"And you only have the lord marshal in your way?"

He reached up to brush the horse's back. "Yes."

"To outdo the lord marshal, you snapped that man's neck?"

He turned his head to regard her for a silent, unwavering moment.

Eselle held his gaze. "You killed him without forethought or hesitation."

He didn't reply.

"You didn't give him a chance to fight back, to plead his case."

"Do you think he let the man who'd lived in that farmhouse plead his case when he killed and robbed him?"

"What?"

"Didn't know that part?" He shook his head. "That vagabond you're concerned about knew you were there because he'd killed the owner several weeks prior. Killed him and robbed him of some insignificant family heirlooms. Certainly nothing as valuable as the man's life. When he saw smoke from the house later, he investigated. Discovering it was only a couple of women with no discernible valuables, he decided it wasn't worth his time. Until he learned I was searching for you." The commander stopped brushing and turned toward her. "Then, he offered to sell your location to me. And if he would have sold it to me, he would have sold it to anyone he thought might pay. Still think he didn't deserve his fate?"

She wavered at his explanation. There was no way to know if he told the truth, but she had no reason to doubt him either. She'd never known the commander to be a liar. In fact, he usually answered more bluntly than she expected, or was sometimes comfortable with. But then, if he was simply a good liar, how would she know?

The courser turned his head to Silst. It nudged his chest, making him smile. He put a hand on the horse's head, rubbing it a moment before gently pushing it back. "Be patient."

Eselle fought the urge to smile at the pair. The matter of the vagabond still bothered her. "You didn't give a moment's consideration whether he deserved to die. You just killed him. Was it all to advance in your beloved military?"

He showed no sign of unease with her question, but he didn't answer.

"But you made your soldiers give their bedrolls to Cristar." Eselle nodded toward her friend, whose back was to them as she sat beside Daalok at the now lit campfire. The commander followed her gaze for a moment, then resumed his work without a word. "Why?"

"Because she's a pregnant woman in need of comfort."

"As easily as you killed that vagabond, I doubt a woman's comfort matters to you." There was a harsh edge to her voice, but even as she said it, she remembered how he'd taken her comfort into consideration at the inn.

"Perhaps. But she's a woman, she's incredibly pregnant, and even the worst of mankind have mothers. If my mother was out here in conditions like this, I hope someone would do the same. It might not get as much use as it once did, but I do have a heart."

Eselle stepped closer. "Are you sure?"

The commander stopped brushing, turning toward her as his features darkened.

She stood her ground. "Are you sure that's the reason and not something else?"

"What else could it be?"

"What most men are interested in where a woman is concerned."

She hated to say it, hated to put the thought in his head if it wasn't already there, but she needed to know why he watched Cristar.

At her words, his brows knit together in thought, then released in realization. His eyes darted to Cristar for a moment, then back to Eselle, his expression quickly under control again.

He stepped closer. The warhorse once again nudged him, but he gently pushed it away as he focused on Eselle. "What would you do if those are my intentions?"

"I'd demand you forget them." She stood straighter. "I don't like how you look at her, or how often."

"Would you rather I look at you?"

That caught Eselle off guard. She hadn't considered that. Could she work this to her advantage, distract him from Cristar while they worked on an escape? Remembering their encounter at the inn, the feel of him moving against her, with her, in her, she knew it wouldn't be a difficult sacrifice. But she wasn't certain she could manage it after everything that had changed.

Silst's eyes narrowed. "You really would do anything for her, wouldn't you?"

Eselle's cheeks warmed realizing he'd followed her thoughts. "She's my friend."

"Lots of people have friends they wouldn't risk much for."

"Then they're not really friends, are they?"

He put a hand on the stallion's neck, rubbing slowly. "Perhaps not. What makes her different? Worth all this trouble?"

Eselle would have bristled at such a question, but the softer tone of his voice threw her off. "She's a good person, with a generous heart. She would do the same for others."

"You sound certain of that."

"I am."

"Why?"

She didn't know how to explain it. "I feel it. Each time she shares a story about her husband, a dream for her child, teaches a neighbor how to use medicinal herbs, brews me a cup of tea at the end of a long day. I won't let anyone hurt her. Or her child."

The commander watched her for a moment, then cleared his throat and returned to brushing the horse.

"You didn't answer my questions, about your interest in my friend."

"That has never been an option with her."

"Why should I believe you?" She didn't want to provoke him, but Cristar had already suffered enough losing her husband and being forced on the run while pregnant. She didn't need to deal with anyone's bold flirtations. She should be in her home with her feet up while Eselle tended her garden and brought her tea.

"You have no reason to believe me, but I assure you, that is the farthest thing from my mind where she's concerned."

"Why do you watch her?"

"I didn't realize I was."

Eselle saw no flicker of dishonesty in his response, but nothing else either. She doubted it was that simple, but she also doubted he'd reveal his reasons.

"Then stop watching her."

Silst tossed the brush over by the saddlebags and stepped closer. "You didn't answer *my* question."

"What question?"

"Would you rather I look at you?"

The stallion dropped his head over the commander's shoulder. Silst reached a hand up and scratched the side of the horse's head.

"Is that what you want?" Eselle asked. "For me to be jealous and want your attention for myself?"

"We're not talking about what I want. But who wouldn't want the interest of a beautiful woman?" Stepping out from beneath the horse, Silst strode closer.

Eselle had to move backward. Within a couple steps, she reached the tree behind her.

His playful smile returned, the lopsided one she loved so much. She tingled at memories of the last time he'd stood this close.

His hands found her hips. Her fingers found the cool metal across his stomach. She didn't push him away, only met his dark gaze.

"No answer?" he asked.

Eselle started to say something but closed her mouth. She didn't actually know the answer.

A hand lifted to caress her cheek, fingers grazed along her jaw. "Then I'll have to decide for myself."

"Comman—"

Fingers covered her lips, and he gave a slow shake of his head. *Don't call me commander . . .*

It wasn't the high commander with her in that moment.

It was Kyr.

Her pulse quickened; her hands slipped around his sides. She'd missed him.

He leaned closer, leaned down. Soft lips grazed her temple, accentuated by the rasp of his late-day stubble. His mouth slid across her cheekbone.

Lifting her face—

Kyr whipped around, reaching for his sword. The courser jerked back from him. Kyr's hand froze on the hilt. The horse stomped and huffed loudly. As mount and rider stared at each other, both settled.

"Sherwyn, you damn glutton!" Despite the volume, Kyr laughed when he spoke, relaxing his stance and releasing his blade. "You ruined a perfectly good moment."

Eselle stood still, eyeing the pair. This was the man she had known, not the soldier who followed orders.

The warhorse stepped closer to his rider. The commander pulled a couple snapped parsnips from the pouch on his belt. "No patience, all stomach." He fed the horse, who ate eagerly, then peered back, his features slowly shifting from a smile to something more somber. "Though, perhaps that's for the best."

Perhaps it was.

They'd both lowered their guard, yet still remained on opposite sides. She had her purpose, and he had his.

But Kyr was still in there. Buried beneath all the duty, but there. The small fire burning deep inside her felt freshly stoked.

She pushed off the tree with a bittersweet smile. "I should get back."

He nodded with a resigned expression, holding out another parsnip for the horse.

The sound of crunching continued as Eselle walked back toward the camp.

CHAPTER TWENTY-FIVE

A couple hours after everyone bundled up in their blankets for sleep, Eselle remained wide awake. She envied the others as she watched the reason for her insomnia lying on his side across the dying fire from her. Plenty of moonlight shone down to make out his features as he slept. His sword lay beside him, and he'd stowed his armor for the night as usual. He seemed more relaxed than she'd ever seen him.

Eselle scanned the campsite. Her friends slept nearby, along with the commander and two of the soldiers. The third had wandered off, keeping watch. Unwilling to give away her plan yet, she discreetly rolled onto her back to locate the armsman.

His smug face loomed above her while his dagger pressed into her ribs. She sucked in a breath to yell out—a warning or plea for help, she didn't know—but his hand clamped down over her mouth. All she managed was a muffled sound.

"You should be asleep," he whispered. His breath smelled of the dried meat they'd eaten for dinner. "Keep quiet, and this will be over quickly."

Before he finished speaking, the two other armsmen opened their eyes and rose quietly. One remained at the side of the dwindling fire, the other pulled his dagger and crept around behind Kyr.

While the soldiers obviously had ill intentions for their high commander, Eselle didn't know their plans for everyone else. Just because one subdued instead of killed her didn't mean they wouldn't eventually. It could mean they planned to eliminate the most dangerous threat first.

As the soldier positioned his dagger between Kyr's shoulder blades, Eselle watched Kyr's peaceful features. She envisioned his contented smile as he lay naked beneath her.

Eselle thrust her hand up into her captor's jaw, making his teeth smack together.

At the same moment, the soldier behind Kyr attacked. Before his dagger struck, Kyr rolled over and drove his own dagger upward through the soldier's throat. The armsman froze, but Kyr didn't. He yanked the dagger free, then rolled the other way and threw it backhanded at the man beside Eselle. The blade whistled past her ear. It hit the soldier's neck, and he jerked backward. Blood spurted onto his chest as he tugged at the hilt. The man made pitiful, gurgling moans. Eselle scrambled away from the grisly scene and toward her friends.

"What did you do?" The last armsman stared back and forth between his fallen comrades. Instead of waiting for a response, he drew his sword and charged his commander.

Cristar and Daalok stood beside Eselle, watching in confusion. Eselle couldn't fathom what had caused the dissension, or why Kyr had been prepared for it. He'd mentioned the soldiers were loyal to the lord marshal, but they were still part of the same military.

Wouldn't that alone garner enough loyalty not to kill each other?

The commander deflected the armsman's blow. The weapons rang loudly against each other. Kyr countered, and the armsman blocked. He swung again and caught the man across the arm, keeping the armsman on the defensive. The young soldier finally found an opportunity and thrust. Kyr sidestepped, grabbed the armsman by his doublet and tossed him into a tree. The man cried out. Gripping his shoulder, he dropped to his knees.

The horses shifted nervously at the edge of camp. Kyr's black courser snorted and stomped, pulling on its lead.

How difficult would it be to get Cristar onto one of them? The fight will be over before we can saddle them. Can she ride bareback? If she fell . . .

It wasn't worth the risk. And with two soldiers down, and Kyr likely to take the last, Eselle's group would soon have the advantage of numbers. While everyone was distracted, she slipped away.

Kyr approached his armsman from behind. The young man pushed up from the ground, then turned. Kyr kicked him squarely in the chest. Falling back into the tree with a thud, the soldier dropped to his hands and knees; his sword slipped from his fingers.

Each time the dazed armsman regained his feet, the commander knocked him down again. Eventually, the man remained on the ground.

"Why did you attack me?" Kyr's voice sounded gruff.

The soldier swayed unsteadily. "You killed the others."

"I've killed a lot of soldiers, and for far less than mutiny. Answer the question."

The man hesitated, then slowly rose to his feet. "The lord marshal ordered us to kill you and bring the prisoners back to him."

Kyr nodded, his lips tight. "That's unfortunate for you." With a punch to the face, Kyr sent the man tumbling down.

Grabbing a thick, fallen branch, the soldier spun up off the ground, thrusting his makeshift weapon. The commander shifted out of the way, gripped the soldier's chin with one hand and brought his sword across the man's throat.

Cristar and Daalok gasped, turning away as the armsman crumpled.

Eselle had maneuvered around Kyr, gaining her position unnoticed. She smiled when he quickly glanced around the site, then jerked around to find her behind him. The surprise in his features dropped into a frown when he noticed the sword in her hand.

"Drop your weapon." Eselle held her blade toward his chest.

Kyr studied her before he finally tossed the sword. It landed at her feet with a thunk.

Daalok and Cristar approached but stopped well short of the commander.

Eselle nodded toward the fire. "Over there."

Instead of complying, Kyr openly assessed each of them. He looked first at Cristar, but only briefly, then over at Daalok a little longer, then finally at Eselle the longest. His brows furrowed for the slightest moment before he finally stepped backward and raised his hands.

"What now?" he asked.

"Now we tie you up."

After they reached the dwindling fire, Eselle sent Daalok to find rope in their packs. Kyr glanced at Cristar again. She stood with the bloodied dagger he had used to kill the first two soldiers. Seeing his glare, she fidgeted before looking away. Eselle could sympathize. She'd been the recipient of that glare, and it was difficult to face.

"I'll collect the weapons," Cristar said, then walked away.

Once the pregnant woman was out of range, Kyr attacked.

As quick as he was, she had been prepared. She knew he wouldn't surrender because they had the advantage. The man was a warrior.

Kyr's arm swept the sword up and away, but Eselle had already been moving. Instead of a stabbing motion his layered arming doublet may have protected him from, the blade swept up and across his chest and shoulder. It took a long slice through both cloth and flesh. His face tightened, and he groaned behind clenched teeth, but didn't slow. He twisted his arm around and snatched the sword from Eselle's hand.

She slammed her other hand into his chest and shoved. He retreated a step before he grabbed for her wrist. She spun and ducked to the side. He swept her leg from beneath her, sending her down onto her back. The air rushed from her lungs, but she rolled way while gasping for more. A hand dug into her hair when she reached her knees and hauled her to her feet. A cry escaped her. With a backward kick, she hoped to catch a shin. She only grazed his leg. He held her by the hair to face the others.

A flash of flame rushed from the campfire and up Kyr's arm.

Eselle flew forward as he shoved her out of the away. She landed on her hands and knees. Lunging back to her feet, she retreated. Kyr scrambled backward. He'd dropped the sword, and his eyes bulged as he tried to escape the flames.

The fire stirred fiercer than before, unexpectedly revived, but was once again contained within its boundaries. Daalok stood beyond it with one hand held toward the flames as he watched Kyr.

"Get away from her!" Daalok's voice shook a little, but it was strong.

Though his clothing hadn't ignited, Kyr put considerable distance between himself and the fire. The commander patted down his faintly smoking sleeve as he stared wide-eyed at the flames. Eselle remembered the burns on his arm—the same arm tonight's blaze tried to take a piece of—and understood his ill-concealed fear. Whatever had happened to him had maimed more than his arm.

Eselle regarded Daalok as he watched the commander. He still appeared the gentle young man they'd only recently come to know, but he held a stronger underlying current. Despite that newly revealed strength, he quivered the slightest bit. While he obviously knew some magic, he didn't appear comfortable with it.

As the three companions closed ranks on their captive, keeping him penned between them, Kyr turned away from the fire. Eselle held a sword, Cristar had retrieved the commander's sword, and Daalok stepped around the campfire with one hand held palm-out toward the flames.

Kyr's gaze settled on Daalok. His expression wasn't the threatening one he donned in situations like this. It wasn't fear, exactly. It wasn't respect. It was something she couldn't identify before it faded behind his returning self-control. He collected himself slower than usual, but soon glared at them all in turn.

Eselle raised the sword tip a little higher for emphasis. "Put your hands where we can see them. Toss your weapons over there." She indicated a spot several paces away at the edge of camp.

Kyr slowly raised his hands. His left arm stayed a little lower than the other. Was he about to try something?

Considering the amount of blood steadily darkening his doublet, it was also possible she cut him deeper than she realized.

With a silent chuckle, he reached down with his good arm and pulled a dagger from his belt, then the one from his boot. Obediently, he tossed them to the ground, then put the hand back up.

"*All* your weapons," she said.

"What else is there?"

"I know you carry at least one more dagger." She wasn't about to tell her companions how she knew that.

With a devilish grin, he reached behind himself. Eselle motioned to Daalok, signaling him to be ready. Kyr saw the motion and froze. He moved slower as he pulled another dagger from behind him and tossed it with the others.

Eselle's eyes narrowed as she watched him. "There's something else. I know there is."

He shrugged, then stood there looking bored.

"I'll pat him down," Daalok said.

"No." Eselle held up her hand to stop the mage. "You watch him. Roast him if he moves."

Kyr's eyes widened as he glanced at Daalok, but quickly returned to his otherwise tolerant expression. After the incident with the fire, Daalok was the only member of their group Kyr seemed to fear. Eselle worried about getting within reach of him, but until he knew what Daalok could do, his fear of fire prevented him from risking anything.

Blood coated Eselle's hands when she searched his torso. She wiped it off on his doublet, noticing him smirk. Ignoring it, she continued. Something hard at the back hem of his doublet proved to be two more knives, secured in specialized sheaths built into the lining. She tossed them with the others and found nothing else.

Once Eselle and Daalok had the commander bound with his hands behind his back, they secured him to a nearby tree. Cristar walked up with a collection of bandages, her poultice, and a few other items.

"What's that for?" Daalok asked.

"We need to check his shoulder, bandage him up."

"What?" Daalok put a hand up to stop her. "Why?"

"He's injured." Cristar watched the young man, her face slowly drawing together in concern.

Eselle studied Kyr across the campsite. He leaned against the tree, his head tossed backward, and his shoulder glistening in the moonlight from where it still bled.

"The man's a killer," Daalok said. "He was taking you to the king."

"She's right." Eselle stepped over to her friends. "We can't leave him here wounded."

Daalok glanced back and forth between the women. "We most certainly can. He'd do the same to us."

Eselle wondered about that. Daalok was probably right, but she'd never killed anyone. Worrying about Kyr when she'd clubbed him was enough to remind her she didn't want to start. They'd leave the commander alive, and she suspected he'd escape the ropes in short order, but the amount of blood worried her. "Regardless, he's tied up and we have the supplies. I'd feel better treating him before we leave."

"Me too," Cristar said. "We can't leave him to die."

"He won't die." Frustration edged Daalok's voice. "It's probably a flesh wound."

"A flesh wound doesn't soak half your torso," Eselle said.

Daalok frowned as he considered them both, then peered over at the commander. "You're right, but let's make this quick. And I'll do it. I don't want either of you near him. Tell me what to do."

Cristar stepped forward, but Eselle considered Daalok's words. She didn't want Cristar close to Kyr either. The commander had proven to be tricky.

"We can manage this," Eselle said, taking the supplies from her friend. "Why don't you go pack our things, get us ready to leave." She cut off Cristar when she started to protest. "Really. I know how to dress a wound, and this one should be easy enough. I can talk Daalok through it." Cristar frowned, but moved off to do as requested.

The young man kneeled and began to undo the commander's doublet.

Kyr's eyes narrowed. "What do you think you're doing?"

Daalok didn't glance up from his task as he sighed. "They said we have to patch you up before we leave."

The commander chuckled deeply, looking up at Eselle. "Of course, they did. Ever the kindhearted souls."

Eselle ignored him.

Once the doublet and shirt were pulled away from Kyr's shoulder, they found a lengthy slash. It ran diagonally across one side of his chest, just past the end of his collarbone, and stretched up along the top of his shoulder. It nearly touched the top of his existing scar.

A grin spread across Daalok's face. "Seems we're not the only ones to take a slice out of you."

"True." Kyr once again eyed the man undressing him. "But no one has lived long enough to strike twice." He gave Daalok a menacing glare that quickly had the mage focusing on his work.

The new injury wasn't as deep as Eselle feared, but it bled significantly and still needed to be closed. It seemed to be nearly stopped. The fresh wound was a stark contrast against the older scar. Looking closer, she realized that though the older wound had healed well, the scar ran deep into his muscles. She wondered what had happened, how extensive the damage had been at the time.

Eselle guided Daalok through cleaning, stitching, and dressing the commander's chest.

"Why would your men be ordered to kill you?" Eselle finally asked, unable to get the images out of her head.

"Because Lord Marshal Huln knows I'm trying to steal his position."

That was not an answer she had expected. Eselle took a moment as she gathered bloodied cloths. When Daalok tied off the bandage, she was grateful they could finally leave. The commander's cold-heartedness disturbed her, made it harder to remember the man she'd been with in Eddington.

"And that's worth killing for?" she asked. "Why not demote you? Assign you elsewhere?"

"He can't." After watching her for a second, he explained, "I have the king's favor. He would never allow Huln to do either. The lord marshal knows his time is short, and he's become desperate."

Daalok gathered the supplies he'd used and headed off toward their packs.

"Why do you even want his position?" Before Kyr answered, she held up a hand. "No, forget that. For the power, right?" He only raised an approving brow. Shaking her head, Eselle spoke more to herself than anyone present. "I'll never understand someone like you."

"Yes, you do," Kyr said. "You don't seek your own direct power, but rather, power for your brother, which to some degree is power for you."

"That's not true." It concerned her how much he knew.

"What's not true? That you seek to put your brother on Likalsta's throne?" The side of his mouth turned up with a taunting smile. "Or that Tarania is an alias and you're really Joeselleen Enstrin, second-born daughter to King Folstaff and Queen Dianesse Enstrin? If I'm correct, that would have made you fourth in line for the throne. Until, that is, Vorgal Grox decided he didn't want to take orders anymore and slaughtered your family to take the crown for himself."

Too startled to respond, Eselle only gawked. She rose, tossing the bloodied rags aside. Daalok stood nearby watching her. Cristar already knew about her past, but Daalok hadn't heard this story before. He appeared uncertain. She figured they were even. She had her own questions about what he had done earlier.

Before they left, Eselle needed to know her brother was safe from Vorgal's clutches. "How do you know all this?"

Kyr smirked. "Why would I ever reveal my sources?"

"How long have you known?"

"Since seeing that necklace of yours."

Unconsciously, Eselle felt for the necklace through her shirt, but immediately released it. She knelt again, though farther from the man than previously. He might be tied to the tree, but he was still dangerous.

"What else do you know about me?"

"I know you like being taken from behind just as much as you like being on top."

Eselle jabbed him in the shoulder before she realized it, right where she had sliced him earlier. The moment she connected, he doubled over as much as the ropes allowed, and a loud pained grunt escaped him.

"By the . . . " Instead of finishing, he stomped a foot and gave a loud roar through clenched jaws. It startled Eselle, but not as much as when he went suddenly still, then raised his head enough to glare at her as he spoke.

"I know who you are, that your brother, Tavith, the former spare, is alive, and you're working together and with others in a ridiculous attempt to retake Likalsta's throne. What specifics I know . . . well, you'll have to wait and see if I show up at your door someday. Someday soon."

Eselle only vaguely registered the fresh blood seeping through the bandage. Her punch seemed to have broken some stitches, but this time she wasn't as concerned.

The group swiftly gathered their belongings. Eselle and Daalok each grabbed a saddle. While Eselle approached a tall sorrel rouncey, Daalok went to saddle Kyr's black courser. The moment he stepped within arm's reach of the horse, the stallion reared and lunged toward the mage. Daalok scrambled backward as the horse stomped forward and snapped at him. Eselle rushed to Daalok's side. The horse stood in place, huffing and making the occasional stomp as it watched Daalok with wild, angry eyes.

A deep laugh spread throughout the campsite. Eselle pursed her lips and closed her eyes. It figured the horse would be as aggravating as his rider. After a deep breath, she motioned Daalok away from the unruly warhorse.

"Forget that one," Eselle said.

Daalok took one last look at the fiery steed, then moved to saddle the bay gelding. As he passed Eselle, he dropped his voice low. "Protector forgive me, but I really wanted to steal that man's horse."

CHAPTER TWENTY-SIX

No one spoke about what happened until the next evening, agreeing it was more important to put distance between them and the commander before tackling such a serious conversation. Shortly after dusk, they gathered around the fire for warmth. Clouds blocked the sky, so the only light came from the flames. Thick shadows spread through the trees, making them look fuller than their nearly bare limbs were.

Eselle began with the obvious. "You know magic."

"Yes." Daalok glanced up briefly before he stared back into the fire.

"Why didn't you tell us?"

"Why didn't you tell us you were a princess?" He sounded genuinely curious, but Eselle suspected he also wanted to deflect the question.

"Fair point. But Cristar knew already. I told her not long before you joined us. And honestly, it's not something you tell people you've just met."

His head turned halfway toward her, but his eyes wouldn't meet hers. "What did the commander mean about a necklace?"

Perhaps if she shared some details, he'd feel comfortable enough to share his own. His magic seemed a difficult topic for him. Eselle slid her cloak back enough to pull the necklace out of her shirt and held it up so Daalok could see. The silver chain with six knots glinted in the firelight.

"This is the necklace he was referring to. He saw it back in Eddington, but I have no idea how he could have recognized me from it. There are only a few people who have ever seen it."

Both Cristar and Daalok studied the necklace in the flickering firelight.

"Why is it knotted?" Cristar asked. She hadn't seen it either.

With the knots precisely placed, equally distant from each other, it was obvious she'd made them intentionally.

"They represent my family, my brother Tavith and the others Vorgal murdered eighteen years ago." Looking at each of the knots, she softly named them. "My father King Folstaff Enstrin; my mother Queen Dianesse; my older brother Brassil, who would have been the next king; my brother Tavith, the only one still alive; then my older sister Avassa and younger sister Lissil." Before she was halfway through, her throat began to tighten, but she pushed on. Enough years had passed that she had learned to control herself in public, but it still took some effort. Clearing her throat, she slipped the necklace beneath her shirt and wrapped her cloak around her.

"I'm sorry," Daalok said.

"Thanks. But what about you?" After offering more than she'd intended, she wouldn't let him deflect anymore. "Why didn't you tell us about your magic?"

"The same reason you didn't tell me about yourself. Most people are afraid of magic, and I didn't know how you'd react.

Also, once I found out you were being chased, I thought maybe I could help. I'm not the best fighter, but I wanted to do something." He shrugged. "I've been away from people too long, worried I'd be discovered. I can't keep doing that. It's lonely on the road, and I wanted to stay with you."

Eselle could relate to that. She thought she'd grown accustomed to being alone, but then she'd gone and tangled with the high commander. She should have known better. She *had* known better, but she had done it anyway. If she hadn't, he never would have seen the necklace, and they might not be in this predicament.

Cristar smiled warmly, but Eselle was still leery. For the most part, she trusted the young man, but she didn't like secrets. She certainly had her own, but other people's secrets could get you killed. Though, he had saved them by fighting off Kyr with his flames. That was useful.

"How long have you been able to do magic?" Eselle asked. The best way to alleviate her concerns was to learn about their newly revealed mage.

"I discovered it when I was twelve," he said softly. "I didn't do much at first. Everyone said magic was evil, and I knew they killed mages, so I kept it to myself. I was terrified someone would find out, so I didn't use it." He picked at a corner of his cloak, played with the hem while staring into the fire. "After a couple of years, I got curious. I didn't feel evil, so I figured it couldn't hurt to know what I was dealing with. Unfortunately, there wasn't anyone around to teach me, so it was a lot of trial and error. A lot more error than trial, really."

A memory flashed through Eselle's mind. "That white cloth in your pack? Was that a warder's cassock?"

Daalok looked down at the cloak hem. "Yes."

Cristar took a quick breath. "You're a priest?"

"I was."

"Isn't that dangerous," Eselle asked, "becoming a warder when you're also a mage?"

With a nod, Daalok shrugged and raised his head. "Perhaps. I thought it might also be the last place anyone would look for a mage. After all, most of the warder mages were killed years ago, so who would suspect a mage of becoming a warder now?"

He has a point.

Cristar's gaze was soft as she watched him. "I suppose we should be calling you Warder Borwin."

With a fervent head shake, he said, "Please, don't. That part of my life is over. Daalok is fine."

"What kind of magic can you do?" Eselle asked.

"I didn't learn much back then, and I can't do much now, but I have figured out how to move things. Without touching them, I mean," he added with a bashful expression.

Eselle sat straighter, studied the young man intently. "Is that what you did with the fire?"

"Yes."

"Can you create fire?"

"No," he said more confidently. "I can't create something out of nothing. But I heard from a gypsy once that some mages can build things from energy, or something like that. I'm not exactly sure what he meant. There aren't many resources for mages anymore. Not like under the old king." He paused as his face scrunched up for a moment. "Under your father, I guess. Anyway, the gypsy also mentioned portals to travel through. I thought that was fascinating, so I tried to figure it out. After what I thought was a couple of successes with things like rocks, I tried it with a cat, but that didn't work out so well, and I was exiled from my home."

"Exiled?" Cristar reached out and put a consoling hand on his shoulder.

Daalok studied his hands and blinked a couple of times. "Yes. I was courting a young woman, Millie, and I thought she would understand, so I showed her what I was working on. I sent her cat through what I thought was a portal that would move it several paces away from us." He dropped his head and picked at one of his fingernails. "But it never came out. She ran to her father, who rounded up a bunch of others, and they cast me out. I've been traveling ever since."

"How long ago was that?" Eselle recalled her previous suspicions about him hiding something. It pained her to realize what he'd hidden was his shame over something so natural. In their current world, that kind of power could mean a death sentence.

"I left home about five months ago."

"So you've been traveling through the countryside?"

"Yes. I've looked for a new home, but I want to get as far from my old one as possible. Mostly so I'm not tempted to return and beg forgiveness."

Now that the sun had set, the temperature dropped quickly. The fire had burned down considerably, so Eselle added some wood.

Cristar inched closer to the fire. "What else can you do?"

"Not much, unfortunately," Daalok said.

Eselle's heart went out to him. "Can you show us something?" She was uncertain if it was rude to ask but too curious to be overly concerned.

"I'm out of practice, and I was never really very good to begin with, but I'll try."

Daalok sat straighter and glanced around. He set his cup down on the ground in front of them. Staring at it, he appeared lost in thought. His hands were before him, low toward his knees, and occasionally moved, though in no pattern Eselle could discern.

She wondered if the movements meant anything or were to help him focus. His lips moved faintly, and he mumbled to himself. She wanted to ask but didn't want to break his concentration.

When she thought she should console him and let him know it was alright if he couldn't manage anything, the cup jolted. As she watched, it jolted again, then slowly rose from the ground. The height wasn't enough to get anything under the cup, but it had risen.

It crashed down with more force than it should have given its height. Water splashed over Eselle's legs.

"I'm sorry," Daalok blurted out. He grabbed the cup and tossed it aside, then brushed the water off her pant legs. "I'm sorry. I told you I wasn't any good."

"It's alright." Eselle grabbed his hands to stop them from frantically wiping at her. "Don't worry. I'm fine. I'm just a little wet."

His features turned forlorn. "I'm sorry. I can get better. I promise."

"That was amazing." Cristar wore a warm smile.

Daalok returned it, seeming to forget his embarrassment.

They talked more about Daalok's past, but soon the young man started yawning, so everyone curled up in their blankets for sleep.

Shortly after Daalok dozed off, Eselle noticed Cristar still awake. The young mother frowned as she laid on her side and rubbed her stomach.

Careful not to wake Daalok, Eselle whispered, "Is he kicking again?" Ever since she first felt the baby kick, she'd been fascinated by it.

Cristar's frown deepened. "No, unfortunately. He hasn't kicked in a few days."

Eselle sat up. "Is he still moving? Like when we saw his foot that one time?"

"A little, but not like that."

"When did you feel him last?"

"He moved this morning. But it was only a little shift. And before that, it was two days ago." Cristar turned sad eyes to Eselle. "I'm worried."

Eselle didn't have any advice for her. She didn't know about this sort of thing. "I'm sure he's fine," she said anyway. "He's probably running out of room in there. Or he could be incredibly comfortable, all snuggled into his mother's warm belly."

"I hope so. But what if something is wrong?" Cristar's eyes glistened in the low firelight.

"I don't know." It pained Eselle that she couldn't offer more. "All I can tell you is that whatever happens, I'll be there with you. And we'll do whatever we can to make certain he's okay."

"Thanks. I don't know what I'd do without you." Cristar's voice sounded a little throatier than usual.

"I expect you to name him after me, of course," Eselle said, trying to sound more jovial than she felt. "Though I suggest toughening the name up some. Maybe Manselle or Esellan. You have plenty of time to figure it out."

That put a bittersweet smile on the young mother's face.

CHAPTER TWENTY-SEVEN

Minutes after Kyr entered Vistralou Castle, Josah Ilkin intercepted him.

"I heard you were back," the captain said as he stepped in alongside Kyr.

"You have quick ears."

"And a good lookout." Josah studied both ends of hallway. They were alone for the moment. "We need two more trustworthy men to pull off everything smoothly."

"I'm sure you'll have no trouble finding them. I'm only here to get information, then I'm heading back out."

"Is that wise? We need you here to handle the final details."

Striding purposefully through the keep, Kyr frowned at the truth of those words. He lowered his voice in case of prying ears. "The last pieces aren't in place. I shouldn't take long."

"This is your plan, not mine, but need I remind you we're only days away?"

"I know," Kyr snapped. Things were getting too far out of his control, and he was running out of time.

"How important are these last pieces? Can we manage without them?"

How important?

Everything centered around them. And they'd slipped through his fingers.

Kyr stopped suddenly. "I know we're close. But *nothing* can happen until I have everything in place."

Josah nodded sharply. "Should we postpone?" Even though Josah didn't know the entire plan, he knew more than anyone except Kyr and Nikos.

Kyr took a deep breath. "It must be in three days. Until then, prepare everyone and keep to the plan. But hold until you hear from me."

They paused as two servants carrying cleaning supplies passed through the hallway.

"We could use you here," Josah said once they were alone.

"I'm needed more out there. You know what needs to be done, and I trust you to handle it."

"You should at least take more men this time. We completed your rounds, so they might be useful, and it'll keep them out of trouble."

"They might also get in my way," Kyr said. Josah shrugged. "But you're probably right. I'll be outnumbered otherwise. Prepare half the contingent and have them meet me at the gate."

Josah nodded. "You should be quick about it. Because the other matter you had me look into, I've heard rumors the Enstrin heir has recruited the Heldin city captain."

"Then it's good we recruited our own city captain. Speaking of, will he have Vahean's troops ready for us?"

"Yes. I've spoken with him personally, and he's prepared. But the Enstrin's troops are secretly massing. They could march at any time. Once they do, he'll have eight thousand soldiers tearing through Vahean and surrounding Vistralou within three days."

"And once the king hears this news, he won't let me leave the castle," Kyr said, cursing his bad luck. "He'll call in the commanders and troops from the surrounding cities, possibly the army he's preparing to throw at Pasdar."

"None of them would reach us in time. The army is near a month out. The closest city is Grosgril, which—while also a three-day march like Heldin—will still take at least six between getting word to them, preparations for marching, and then arriving."

"Good. That should leave plenty of time to take the castle and Vahean."

The captain's eyes tightened slightly.

"What's wrong?" Kyr asked.

"Nothing." Josah shrugged, but his effort to relax was evident. In the time Kyr had known the captain, only one thing ever visibly worried him. "Maksin won't leave, will he?"

"No," Josah said with a frown. "And I've tried every argument I can think of."

Kyr stepped closer. "Did you really expect him to?"

"I had hoped. He could get hurt if there's fighting."

"He'll be fine. You've taught him well how to handle himself."

Josah looked down the hall, his lips pursed. "I hoped you'd side with me on this."

Kyr looked intently at his second. "You love him, right?"

"Of course." Josah turned back, frustration etched in his features. "That's why I want him to leave, to keep him safe."

"Exactly. And that's the same reason he wants to stay." Josah's frown returned as Kyr continued. "He wants to keep *you* safe. You can't fault him for that."

"It's not the same. He's a stableman, I've trained—"

Kyr gripped his captain's shoulders. "Josah. You can either argue with him for the next few days or you can prepare him. You can't do both, so decide now and see to it."

"It's not that easy."

"Important things never are. Now," Kyr said, releasing the man, "I need to get moving. Keep us on target."

Josah nodded sharply. "Yes, sir." He walked off as Kyr sought out the high mage.

Barging into Nikos' rooms, Kyr grumbled when he saw the sitting room empty. Even more books than usual lay scattered about and piled in corners. The mage's chair sat pulled back from the desk, and the patio doors stood open, letting the drapes flutter in the light breeze.

"Where are you, old man?" Kyr called out.

Shuffling sounded in the other room. "I'm coming."

Only slightly appeased, Kyr examined the books the mage studied. As expected, everything appeared magic related. Reading some of the titles, he found topics ranging from transfiguration to thaumaturgy. Due to his dealings with Nikos, Kyr knew more than some people about magic, but considerably less than either the mage or his apprentices. He wondered how much the old man could manage these days.

During the previous regime, magic had been a prestigious profession. Under Vorgal, it was outlawed outside of his court mage and two apprentices. The only reason for the apprentices was if the worst should happen and the high mage needed to be replaced.

Nikos stumbled in with an armload of books.

"Help me out, would you," the mage said.

Most of the room's surfaces were already taken, so Kyr stacked some of the books on the desk to make room for more. "How many of these can you even read?"

"As many as are written, young man, as many as are written." Nikos filled the new space with his armload. "And as many as are brought to me. The lord marshal found a stash of books hidden in an old manor they confiscated from a traitor."

"You mean Hildran Pike?"

"I don't know. Didn't hear and didn't ask." Nikos flipped through the pages in one of the new books. "I'm just grateful for these additions to my collection. Hopefully, I'll find something in them that can help us."

"Speaking of help, I need yours."

"Wait." Nikos closed the book. "Aren't you supposed to be protecting our interests?"

"Yes. That's what I need help with. They escaped." When the high mage didn't even don a concerned expression, Kyr said, "I mean *really* escaped this time. Not just me letting them think they'd escaped with some loose ropes or a distracted guard so I could herd them."

"*By the Protector,* they can't escape! We're too close."

The scene at the campsite flickered through Kyr's mind, making it difficult to keep the anger from his voice. "Well, perhaps if you'd told me their new little traveling companion would throw fire at me, I could have prepared for it."

The high mage frowned. "Perhaps I should have, but with your aversion to fire, I didn't want that to affect your decisions." His face tightened again, and his voice grew gruff. "But you can't depend on me to tell you everything. Despite what you think, I don't know everything."

"I'm beginning to realize that."

The mask of dead, tanned hide seemed to snarl with the mage beneath it. "This isn't how it's supposed to happen." Nikos stepped away from the books and appeared deep in thought while talking to himself. "Something must have happened, something I missed."

"Where are they?" That was the only information that mattered anymore. "How can I find them?"

"Let me think." Nikos was sharp as he waved Kyr off. "Where are they?" he mumbled repeatedly while pacing the room.

Kyr sighed and browsed the books. Not even understanding some of the titles, he tossed one aside and stepped to the balcony. He needed to get back out there and find his quarry. The memory of the fire shooting up his arm made him shiver, but remembering the startled expression on the young man's face soothed his fear. Daalok had seemed as surprised as anyone that his magic had worked. It brought a smile to Kyr.

He peered back through the balcony doors. The high mage sat in a chair by the fireplace, his eyes closed, and his hands flat against his knees.

Since there was nothing Kyr could do but wait, he turned back to the view of the countryside beyond the castle walls. He tried to relax. The rolling hills that surrounded Vahean, with their speckle of evergreen trees, should have been a soothing sight. The swift, dark river that flowed by as it cascaded over boulders should have been a calming presence. The clear blue sky should have given him hope for a good ride once he had his direction. But he had no patience for any of it.

He needed to find the women and their little mage. He worried what might happen without him nearby. They could wander back toward the mountains. Other soldiers could find them and bring them to Vorgal before he could. They could simply wander off where he couldn't find them in time. Cristar needed to deliver in the castle. And he and Vorgal needed to be present.

"I have it," Nikos yelled. He bolted out of the chair as Kyr strode back through the patio doors. "By the Protector's mercy, I know where they are. They're in Klistilin Forest, along the Asperstill, down from Trildin Bridge."

Kyr slapped the high mage on the shoulder. "Good job, old man."

"Now find them, before it's too late."

"It would be easier with you along."

"Yes, but we both know you need to do this alone. Plus, the king ordered the apprentices and I to ride out tomorrow to meet the army marching toward Pasdar. He would never approve my leaving with you."

Kyr's shoulders tensed. "You're leaving?"

"Of course not." The mage scoffed. "I need to be here when you return. By morning I'll have a decent reason to postpone leaving."

"We still have one problem. Lord Marshal Huln."

Nikos snorted. "That man's nearly as slippery as you are, but I have someone in place. He's planted evidence Huln conspired with the Enstrin heir. Tomorrow morning, he'll alert Vorgal to his suspicions, Huln's quarters will be searched, and the lord marshal will be dealt with. Vorgal despises traitors, so he shouldn't give the lord marshal much chance to defend himself."

Kyr imagined the look on Huln's face when confronted with his imaginary treachery. "Good."

They headed out the door.

Hoping Josah had his men ready, Kyr wanted to grab Sherwyn and leave before either the king or lord marshal knew he was about.

He groaned when one of them stalked down the hallway toward them with a deadly glare, his bastard heir in his wake.

"Where is she?" King Vorgal growled. "You both said you'd find her. But I heard my high commander rode in alone. And my high mage? Well, all I have from you are a bunch of promises the infant will be found, that you've seen me with it when it's born. So far, nothing! From either of you!"

The prince flinched behind him but stepped in beside his father.

Kyr and Nikos stopped, bowed their heads in deference and stood straight.

"Yes, sire," Kyr said, donning a serious demeanor. "I captured them briefly, but they escaped." He considered mentioning that a mage had joined them, but that might prompt the king to send a full contingent, or possibly replace him. He couldn't allow that.

"They escaped?" Prince Tryllen sneered. "Again?"

Vorgal's head whipped toward his son. "When I want your thoughts, I'll tell you what they are."

The prince bowed his head with a scowl. Until recently, the king had never spoken to his son so harshly, and certainly not on a regular basis.

King Vorgal turned toward Kyr. "You're supposed to be one of my best warriors." Vorgal's voice grew louder, barely shy of yelling. "But you can't even bring in two women. One of which is *pregnant!*"

"If I may, sire," the high mage said.

Vorgal's voice dropped to a dangerous level. "You may not."

Nikos closed his mouth and dipped his head.

Kyr remained silent. The best thing to do when the king became irate was to let him vent. He'd yell, threaten, and where Kyr was concerned, calm down, relent, and order Kyr to return to his duties. The only other people Vorgal Grox fawned over were Tryllen, the prince; Nikos, his pet mage; and his favorite courtesan, another sort of pet entirely.

Settling in for the duration of King Vorgal's anger, Kyr relaxed his stance enough to ease the tension but not show it.

King Vorgal examined each of them, then stepped before Kyr. "I think it's time I listened to Lord Marshal Huln and removed you from the castle. You're hereby demoted to captain. You'll leave tomorrow with the troops heading to the Pasdar rally point. Get a good night's rest, Captain. You have a long ride ahead."

Kyr stared blankly.

Demoted? Pasdar . . . how . . . what?

It took a moment to realize he had lost the immunity he'd so carefully cultivated. He felt strangely unnerved without it. Thinking quickly while the king strode away, Kyr glanced at the mage. The little bit of Nikos showing below the mask seemed equally stunned. Even the prince stared at his departing father, his face twisted in surprise.

"Your Majesty!" Kyr said, struggling to keep the desperation from his voice. He didn't know what to say, but he couldn't let the king leave without fixing this. "Please, let me explain."

Whirling around, Vorgal glared. "Explain what, exactly? How you failed me? How you've ingratiated yourself in hopes of winning favor? Yes, I've known all along that's what you've been doing, even without Huln endlessly whining about you. But I enjoyed your currying favor, so I allowed it. But it's over. I'll no longer—"

Kyr had never interrupted his king and knew that, with his current mood, Vorgal would likely imprison him for doing so. There was one interruption though, that might keep him on his chosen mission and, at least temporarily, out of the dungeon. It was a dangerous gamble, but he was out of time.

Protector, forgive me.

"One of the women is an Enstrin."

Vorgal stopped mid-sentence. Kyr took the opportunity before the king thought on his own.

"I didn't tell you because at first I wasn't certain, and I didn't want to worry you needlessly. So, I investigated. I only recently discovered she's the middle daughter of the former king. She's Joeselleen Enstrin. I tried to bring her in unharmed, expecting you'd want her intact for questioning, but she's wily. She's been on the road for years working for her brother and knows how to evade notice."

Nikos had moved beside the king and shot Kyr his own threatening glances. As the mage's eyes bored into him from behind the scarred leather mask, Kyr felt the risk was worth it. He had to keep close to the women, bring them in when the time was right. He and Nikos had worked their plan too long to lose now.

"I've tracked them for weeks, learned how they think, how they hide their trail. I *will* find them and bring them to you. I swear it."

King Vorgal eyed Kyr up and down before taking a few slow steps forward. "Do you know where her brother is?"

"Not yet, but I will find her, and once I do, I'll find him."

"Is she the pregnant one the lord marshal claims you let escape?"

Kyr hated to give any more information. "No, Your Majesty. But she's taken the pregnant one under her protection."

"Good. This presents us with an opportunity."

Seeing the pleased smile on the king's face made Kyr's stomach tighten. He clasped his hands behind his back to keep anyone from seeing them clench.

"Sire?" Nikos said, his voice heavy with reluctance.

"She's exactly what we need." Vorgal glanced sidelong at Prince Tryllen with a contemplative expression.

Prince Tryllen finally noticed his father was studying him. He nodded, but obviously struggled to keep up with his father. "To use as a hostage against her brother."

"No," Vorgal snapped. "To add to the legitimacy of our bloodline." His son stared blankly. "Are you really so stupid? She will provide you an heir."

"I don't want to marry an Enstrin." The horror on the prince's face was entirely different than the one stabbing Kyr in his gut, the one he saw mirrored in Nikos' slack jaw.

"I didn't say marry, I said provide an heir. Once you have a son with Enstrin blood from her, no one can question our house."

The prince wore an uncertain expression, and he turned to Kyr. "Is she at least pretty?"

Kyr fought to unclench his jaw enough to speak. "Most would say so, Your Highness."

"Do you?"

Kyr hesitated but gave a curt nod. "Yes."

"Good. Then make sure she's unharmed when you bring her in. I'd hate to take an ugly or damaged woman to bed."

The success Kyr had in unclenching his jaw was undone, but he managed another nod. A quick glance to Nikos found a similar expression in the mage's blazing blue eyes.

"And the pregnant woman?" King Vorgal asked. "Why does the Enstrin protect her? Is this the infant I seek?"

Kyr focused on the conversation again. The topic change was only a partial blessing. "It's uncertain, sire. I believe she protects the woman simply out of friendship, nothing more. But I'll bring the woman in so we can examine the child."

Nikos' lips twitched below his mask. Without a word, only head shakes and discrete hand signals, Nikos warned Kyr against revealing more. But if Kyr didn't, he would be marching a thousand leagues to the west to steal another realm's land. Their plan would be as dead as the women, the baby, and the little mage shortly after Vorgal sent troops after them.

"And when will you bring them in?" Vorgal asked harshly.

Kyr stood straighter, meeting the king's eyes. "Three days." The king once again openly evaluated him, and Kyr dropped his eyes to the man's collar. "If I fail, you can take all my rank and toss me out." The smile that grew before him made it difficult to stand still.

"You have two days, Captain. And I'll toss you, all right, but not out. I'll toss you into The Crypt."

Kyr's stomach lurched. His hands shook behind his back for a whole new reason.

The Crypt was enough to make even Kyr falter, especially after having visited it seven years back. The scenes of torture and mutilation still haunted him. He'd do anything necessary to ensure he never encountered that place again, either as a visitor or a resident.

Only barely able to hold himself in check, he nodded. "Yes, Your Majesty."

The king strode down the hallway, his bastard once again in tow. Kyr turned and tried to keep the screams inside as he regrouped. He'd hoped to keep Eselle out of this. In saving the plan, he had inadvertently made things much worse.

Once the king passed through the door at the end of the hallway, Nikos was at Kyr's side, putting a hand on his shoulder. "Are you all right?"

"I'm fine," Kyr lied, trying to steady his nerves.

"Good. Don't let his threats bother you."

"You heard him. The Crypt. No one comes back from that."

"I know. But remember what I've seen, what the Protector has given us already." Nikos gave a supportive squeeze to Kyr's shoulder. "You don't go to The Crypt. You bring them to the castle."

Kyr peeked back at where the king had departed. "But you didn't know they would escape recently. How do you know something else hasn't changed?"

Nikos dropped his hand. "I don't. We just have to keep to the plan. Adjust when necessary and keep moving forward. We're nearly there."

Things were getting out of hand, things they hadn't planned for emerging.

Kyr took a deep breath to calm his nerves. "You're right."

Despite Nikos' foresight, Kyr couldn't immediately shake his concerns. The Crypt wasn't a threat to take lightly. It was possibly the only thing he feared as much as fire.

More than fire.

CHAPTER TWENTY-EIGHT

As Kyr crossed the courtyard, keeping his distance behind the king and prince, he heard someone call his name.

"Silst!"

Kyr rolled his eyes and turned. The royal pair stopped at the opposite end of the courtyard and watched. Did the approaching lord marshal know Vorgal had planned to reprimand him? About the demotion and threat of The Crypt?

"I'm told the men I sent with you didn't return," Huln snapped. "Where are they?"

Kyr stared him in the eyes, wanting nothing more than to punch the man. If the king wasn't present, the lord marshal would be a good opponent to take his anger out on. Unfortunately, that also presented problems with attacking a superior. Still, he was nearly furious enough to do it.

Instead, he took a deep breath and forced his fists to unclench. His priority was to locate the slippery band of travelers.

"They're dead," Kyr said, keeping his voice neutral.

The lord marshal snarled. "What do you mean, they're—"

"They attacked me. So, I killed them."

Huln's mouth dropped open. He clamped it shut, donning an unconvincingly innocent expression. "And why did they attack you?"

"Because you ordered them to kill me." Though the king watched from a distance, seemingly interested in this exchange between his top men, Kyr doubted he could hear them.

"Why would I do that?"

The urge to antagonize the man was too strong, especially since Kyr couldn't punch him. He gave a taunting smile. "Because you know I'm about to replace you. The king favors me as he never has you. It's only a matter of time before I'm lord marshal."

A flash of confusion crossed Huln's face, but he quickly suppressed it. "How do you propose to do that from a Pasdaran battlefield, Captain?"

So, they had discussed Vorgal's threats ahead of time.

"Ah, yes, *captain*," Kyr mused.

"After years of kissing the king's ass, you're back to captain. You're lucky he stopped there. I tried to convince him to demote you all the way down to recruit, but he still holds a soft spot for you. I can't imagine why." The lord marshal grunted in disgust. "Now that he sees you for what you are, it'll be no time before I convince him to have you mucking out the stalls." Kyr chuckled, which made the lord marshal stop short. "What's so funny?"

"The king changed his mind," Kyr lied, just to infuriate the man. Granted Huln would discover the truth, but not until Kyr was halfway to Klistilin Forest. By the time the lord marshal could cause him problems, Nikos' plan would have been carried out, and Huln's head would be decorating the battlements.

The lord marshal's lips twitched. "What do you mean, he changed his mind?"

"Just that. He changed his mind. He did mention a demotion, but after I explained things, he agreed that wasn't in anyone's best interest. So, I'll still be fulfilling your every order. Well, as much as I ever have." He turned to retrieve Sherwyn.

The lord marshal gripped Kyr's shoulder to haul him around. Moving with the motion, Kyr ducked the punch he knew was coming. He lunged to the side and jabbed toward Huln's gut. The man dodged and countered with a kick to the torso. Kyr caught his leg and shoved it aside, throwing Huln off balance.

Kyr's pulse quickened, and his muscles tensed in anticipation. Huln pulled his dagger and lashed out. Kyr deflected it with one hand as he landed a jab to the lord marshal's ribs. Huln's chainmail pinched his knuckles, but they had long since become accustomed to it. The impact made Huln stumble back, but he simultaneously reversed his swing. The dagger swept within inches of Kyr's face as he leaped out of range.

Huln exchanged his dagger for his sword. His breathing came a little deeper, while his lips pulled back in a faint snarl. "I've had enough of you. This ends now."

"Good." Kyr pulled his own sword. "Would you care to take the first swing?"

"You little shit!" Huln swung.

They were evenly matched as they exchanged attacks. Soldiers who had been scattered around the bailey rushed over and surrounded them, looking uncertain if they should interfere.

Huln was considerably older than Kyr and began to tire first, but he had decades of experience and caught the younger man off guard a couple times. Kyr managed the first strike, a slice across one of the lord marshal's thighs. The man cursed and fought harder. When Kyr delivered the second strike, cutting deep into Huln's left arm, the lord marshal retreated with heaving breaths.

Sweat covered the man's forehead and his cheeks flushed. Kyr pressed his attack while his opponent was winded. The lord marshal swung high the moment Kyr was in range. Realizing too late the man's retreat had been a ploy, Kyr took the blade across his upper arm. The sting in his sword arm made him falter, and he pulled back.

"Stop!"

The lord marshal glanced sideways enough to see where the order came from, but not lose sight of his opponent. Kyr, however, knew Nikos' voice when he heard it. The high mage rushed toward them.

Kyr thrust into the lord marshal's stomach. The man twisted out of the way and landed an off-handed punch. Staggering a step before resetting, Kyr worked his battered jaw a moment.

With a few deep breathes, he ignored the pain shooting through his sword arm. Small runnels of blood dripped down his arm and out of his cuff.

"Both of you, stop this!" The mage was halfway across the bailey when the combatants began another vicious round of attacks.

The group of gathered soldiers doubled.

The lord marshal pulled his dagger again and made a series of attacks that kept Kyr on guard. It was all he could do to prevent being skewered. Despite his extensive training, he had never encountered these maneuvers, and certainly never seen Huln fight like this. The lord marshal used both the dagger and sword to keep Kyr off balance. Kyr pulled his own dagger to evade the lord marshal's blades. It wasn't the double blades that concerned him; he was well-versed in two-handed fighting. It was the way Huln moved, with continuously flowing motions that seamlessly transitioned from one strike to another.

As the blades came faster, Kyr struggled to discern the pattern. His muscles tired with the constant countering; he couldn't fathom how Huln managed so long.

Dodging a high blow, Kyr wasn't entirely certain he could keep from being impaled much longer. Blood seeped from his arm, down to this hand, threatening his sword grip.

"What's the matter?" Huln taunted. He slowed his assault enough to speak. His voice quavered with his growing fatigue, but he was no less dangerous.

Kyr ignored Huln's words. His armor felt stifling, but he was grateful for it since it had taken some of blows.

"Never seen the Jalat fighting style?" the lord marshal asked. "Learned it years ago while traveling. It's not practiced in Likalsta, but I'll show you." With renewed effort, the lord marshal sped up his attack and pressed Kyr back.

The strikes came increasingly closer to hitting.

With no other options, Kyr had to take a risk. He steeled himself, then picked his moment.

Huln's dagger rushed at him.

Kyr let the strike hit.

The blade sliced up across the edge of Kyr's jaw as Kyr's sword drove down through the lord marshal's thigh. Huln roared when Kyr pulled the sword free and prepared to strike again. With the man's momentum broken, he needed to end things.

Kyr flew backward through the air. He slammed down onto the cobblestones.

After a couple of gasps, he found his breath. Sitting upright, he shook away his disorientation, afraid Huln would catch him weakened. Gripping his sword tight, he focused on his surroundings. Huln lay similarly dozens of paces away. They both burst to their feet.

Nikos' hands pointed toward each man. "I said *stop!*" The old mage's lips scowled below his haunting mask. "I don't know what you're fighting about, but you're the top soldiers here, and you're acting like *idiots!*"

"I don't take orders from you, Klaskil." Huln stalked toward Kyr, limping as blood coated his thigh.

Nikos stepped closer. "That's enough!"

Huln's lips rippled in a restrained snarl, but he glanced at the mage's upraised hand, then stood still. He kept his weight off his injured leg as he locked eyes with Kyr.

"You're making a spectacle of yourselves," Nikos said. "What will your soldiers think?"

"You're right," Kyr said reluctantly. There were more important things he needed to handle.

"I don't care what they think," the lord marshal said, his voice grumbling deep. He advanced again.

The man was too angry to let this pass. Short of the king interceding, Huln wouldn't stop. And the king still watched from the side with a broad, dark smile. If Kyr wanted to get back on the road to locate the women and their companion, he needed to go through Huln.

Kyr rolled his shoulders, took a deep breath, and strode forward.

Nikos' gaze snapped back and forth at them as they drew close. He stepped between the soldiers and raised his hands to ward off Kyr. "Stop. There are—"

Huln's pleased expression as he came up behind the mage made Kyr's breath catch.

"*No!*" Kyr cried out.

Nikos went still, and his chest bowed as he gave a startled gasp. He glanced down at himself, but the blade hadn't gone through completely. Kyr reached out to grab him before Huln dropped him on the ground. The lord marshal's dagger came away coated in the mage's blood.

As Kyr lowered Nikos to the ground, Huln stepped back. Nikos' deep blue eyes looked up at him for only a moment before closing. Kyr's jaw quivered. When he realized, he clamped it shut and ground his teeth.

"What did you do?!" Vorgal yelled from the edge of the courtyard. Even an accidental death might earn Huln swift punishment.

Kyr had suspected the lord marshal knew he and the mage were friends; it wasn't difficult to discern they were at least friendly. He'd never suspected, though, that Huln would take things this far. Killing a valuable court mage such as Nikos was a serious offense, and probably why Huln had made it look like an accident. To anyone but Kyr, it had appeared as though Nikos had stepped between the men at an unfortunate moment.

Ignoring everything, Kyr peered into the mage's face, at least what he could see with the mask in place. He considered removing the hideous thing but knew the mage would be mortified if he did. It had been several years since he'd seen the man's entire face, and then only briefly. It was something he'd never forget, something that was indelibly etched into his memory. It was the sort of face that stayed with you even after death.

Not wanting anyone to know how much the old mage meant to him, Kyr kept his mourning brief. Nikos would understand. After he laid the dead man on the cobblestones, Kyr rose. His blood ran cold in his veins. His sight blurred at the edges but held Huln crystal clear ahead of him. He'd ensure Huln paid for killing Nikos.

But now is not the time. Once the plan is complete, not even the Protector will be able to stop me from disemboweling you in the middle of the bailey.

Until then, he needed to leave the castle and secure the last pieces. He needed to give meaning to Nikos' death.

King Vorgal reached them as Lord Marshal Huln wiped his dagger on his pant leg and sheathed his weapons. Kyr held his own tight, his hands clenching around the hilts, unwilling to put them up.

"Lord Marshal!" Vorgal said, his voice irate. "You dispatched an extremely valuable asset of mine. How do you propose to compensate me for it?"

The lord marshal bowed, though his eyes flitted upward toward the king. Josah stood behind Vorgal as he watched the exchange. He shot Kyr a speculative glance, but Kyr only gave a quick head shake before returning his attention to the monarch.

"I'm sorry, sire," Huln said. "It was an accident. High Mage Klaskil stepped into the path of my blade. I will, of course, compensate you in whatever manner you deem appropriate."

"Do you happen to have another mage of Nikos Klaskil's caliber lying around?" the king snapped. Huln lowered his head with a shake of deference. "Unless you do, I don't see how you can compensate me for such a travesty."

"I'm sorry, sire," Huln repeated. "Perhaps one of the mage's apprentices—"

"One of the apprentices could what? Could suddenly leap years ahead in their training and immediately match the high mage you killed?"

"I—"

"Enough! We will discuss this *at length* once this mess is cleaned up."

Lord Marshal Huln looked up, his brow knitted over wide eyes. Kyr suspected though, that the lord marshal had studied him in handling the king. Huln would undoubtedly find a way out of any serious punishment. He wanted to stab the man for that alone. Huln had become too good at the game Kyr had been winning thus far.

The king turned toward Kyr, his face no less aggressive than when he'd spoken to the lord marshal. "Don't you have an assignment and little time in which to complete it?"

"Yes, Your Majesty," Kyr said with a nod. The longer they stood there, the more difficult he found it to hold himself back from Huln. The king didn't seem to notice, but Kyr saw the pleasure in the lord marshal's eyes. He'd enjoyed killing the mage.

King Vorgal stepped away, back toward the keep. Prince Tryllen appeared and looked down at the mage. His mouth twitched in a hint of a smile.

Josah directed a few soldiers in preparation to carry the mage away. As the men obeyed, Kyr pulled him aside, keeping his voice low enough so only Josah heard. "Don't let anyone, not even the king, remove the mage's mask." Josah nodded. "No one."

"He'll be properly honored. I'll see to it myself."

Stepping back, Kyr let the men work.

Huln walked up beside Kyr. "I believe the king said you had somewhere to be. Perhaps you should go there."

Kyr turned away, finally putting up his dagger.

"In the meantime," the lord marshal said, "I'll ensure the mage is properly disposed of on the dung heap out back."

Kyr's sword arm pulled back in the same moment he spun around. He thrust the sword forward. The blade embedded itself in Huln's throat. Kyr watched coldly as the lord marshal stood frozen, his eyes wide, looking back and forth between Kyr and the blade.

"How about instead," Kyr said, "I see you're disposed of on that heap." The lord marshal slid off the sword and hit the cobblestones with a thud.

"What did you do?" Prince Tryllen said, his voice higher than normal as he drew his sword.

Kyr peered back to Nikos as a sudden flurry of activity erupted around him. Soldiers who had now witnessed two murders in the span of minutes rushed forward to prevent anyone else from being killed. If they knew the circumstances, they wouldn't have bothered.

Everyone worth killing is already dead. Well, at least until the end of our . . . my plan.

Not that the plan was possible now.

A pair of armsmen pulled the prince away. As soldiers surrounded him, Kyr remained motionless. No one tried to disarm him, they only blocked his retreat. Instead of interfering, Josah gave him a frustrated glance. With so many witnesses to Huln's murder, the captain could do nothing to help.

Kyr should have known better. This had destroyed his chance of returning to the women and their mage. He shouldn't have let Huln goad him into action. But hearing the man disrespect Nikos so blatantly had pushed him over the edge. Kyr and Nikos had begun their planning long ago, perfected everything when Kyr was rising through the ranks and Nikos was an apprentice. They'd supported each other, commiserated about what it took to advance in Vorgal's service. And now the mage was gone.

"Well done," a nearby voice said.

Kyr looked up from where a handful of soldiers wrapped Nikos in blankets. The king strode toward him again.

"I'd wondered how long it would take you to kill Huln."

"What?" Kyr still held his bloody sword.

"I knew you would one day, but I thought that day was long off. You proved me wrong. And I'm happy for it. I was right about you. You're ruthless. But regardless, we have an arrangement. The women or The Crypt. Once that matter is resolved, Lord Marshal, we'll discuss your future."

"Lord marshal?" Surely, he missed something.

Prince Tryllen stepped up beside Vorgal. "Father, you can't be—"

"Shut up." King Vorgal scowled his son into silence before ignoring him completely. The prince pursed his lips and pouted.

As Kyr watched, the king stepped over to one of the soldiers. He pulled the man's dagger from its sheath, then walked to Huln's corpse. He bent down beside the body and tucked the dagger beneath one of the stripes of the insignia at the lord marshal's collar. That one little stripe was the difference between Huln and Kyr, and the king cut it away. Dropping the dagger by the corpse, Vorgal rose and walked back to Kyr, holding the stripe out to him.

"You dispatched my lord marshal, and you're next in line. Well, were, but we'll forget about that unfortunate business and look forward. So, yes, lord marshal."

Kyr slowly reached for the stripe.

"Of course," Vorgal said, "if you don't deliver those women in two days, it'll be the shortest service in history for any lord marshal. You have the power, and now I know ruthlessness, to prevent that from happening. But only if you get out there and do your job."

Kyr stood dumbfounded. How had things changed so quickly on him?

"You were already tasked with regaining my trust, add earning your new rank to your goals. Bring me those women, Lord Marshal. Now."

"Yes, Your Majesty."

CHAPTER TWENTY-NINE

It was well before sunrise, but Daalok couldn't sleep. He rolled over. No matter how hard he tried to clear his mind, it wandered back to his dilemma. It was safest in this world to hide his abilities, to pretend they didn't exist. If they didn't though, he and his friends would be prisoners right now. They would be heading to the king's castle to be either imprisoned or, in his case, probably executed. And what would they do to Cristar's child?

A slim chance existed that Daalok could be taken in as an apprentice, but only two were allowed at any given time. *I really don't like my chances of outdoing one for their position. Not to mention the high mage. The stories of that man scare me.*

Daalok turned over to his other side. Resigned to his insomnia, he thought about his magic. His body relaxed as he remembered the feel of it when he moved the cup for Eselle and Cristar. Despite the initial struggle, and the embarrassing outcome, it had felt so familiar he ached realizing how much he missed it.

He wasn't skilled with his magic, but then, he rarely used it. He needed to practice.

But where was safe to practice an outlawed art form?

Unable to get comfortable, Daalok rolled over again. The more he thought, the faster his mind raced. He knew what to do, but he worried about doing it.

Grumbling under his breath, he tossed off his blanket and drank from his waterskin, then paced the campsite while debating his next action.

If he did nothing, his friends could be captured, imprisoned, and possibly killed.

If he practiced, his friends could be captured, imprisoned, and possibly killed, because he was horrible at magic and probably couldn't help anyway.

But I have to try, don't I?

While the women slept, Daalok walked over to the stream so he wouldn't disturb them. He couldn't bear it if anything happened to them because he didn't or couldn't help. They'd welcomed him even after discovering his secret.

Finding a comfortable spot on the ground, Daalok sat. The moonlight allowed him to see a short distance. He gathered a few twigs from nearby, broke them into smaller pieces, and set them before him.

He closed his eyes and cleared his mind. Once calm, he focused himself and opened his eyes. In little more than a breath, he uttered his incantation while he concentrated on the broken twigs. When nothing happened, he held his hand out toward the twigs and began again. He whispered under his breath to help him visualize what he wanted.

A long while later, he grew frustrated. It had worked when he'd thrown the fire at the commander, then again the next night, but he couldn't do anything now. That first time he hadn't even really focused. He knew what he wanted, and he'd done it. He saw the commander threatening Eselle, thought about the fire attacking the man, and it had obeyed. It had rushed in and forced the commander to back away. Daalok chuckled at the horrified expression that had flooded Silst's face. He'd only known Commander Silst for a short while but already disliked him. Seeing the commander genuinely terrified at something he'd done was a precious memory.

Daalok saw one of the twigs sliding along the ground toward another one. The moment he realized it, it stopped. The tingling he hadn't even noticed until then evaporated.

He tried again, but nothing happened.

I have to get out of my head, not think too much and just do.

The twigs eventually slid slowly across the ground. Once he got them moving it was easier to keep them going. If he tried too hard, they stopped. When he relaxed, they did what he asked. He soon found the rhythm of it, remembered what it had been like years ago when he practiced regularly.

An hour later, he grew cocky. Instead of twigs, he moved small boulders and rolled logs. He giggled at the renewed flow of magic.

"What are you doing?"

Daalok jolted at the whisper behind him.

Eselle stood smiling at him, glancing occasionally at the various objects he'd been moving.

"Sorry. Did I wake you?" He clasped his hands to his sides.

She shook her head and stepped closer. "No. But I worried when I woke, and you weren't there. What is all this?"

He looked at the mess of rock and wood scattered about the area. "I was practicing. I may have gotten carried away."

Eselle laugh softly. "I can see that. So, it's going well, I take it."

With a nod, Daalok looked over at a small log and focused. After a moment, it rolled toward her, then stopped. He held out his hand. "Care to have a seat?"

Her delicate laughter filled the space between them as she sat. Daalok stood straighter and gave in to the smile he felt.

Over the next few minutes, Daalok showed her some of what he'd been practicing. It felt odd, and incredibly liberating, to share his magic with someone else. Someone who seemed to appreciate it, not fear it.

A soft sound came from across the stream. His body tensed as he searched for the source. Eselle seemed similarly alert. The sun had begun to rise, but the deep forest shadows prevented him from seeing clearly. Instinct told him to rush them back to camp, get back to Cristar, but he forced himself to remain in place. It was better to assess the situation, to learn who was out there, how many and from which direction.

Movement caught his attention directly ahead as two large eyes turned his way. A stag perked its ears up, as tense as Daalok. Laying a careful hand on Eselle's forearm, Daalok discreetly pointed toward the other side of the water. When she saw the stag, she gave a slight nod. When none of them moved, they all relaxed. It was the most peaceful thing Daalok had witnessed in days, and he enjoyed the respite.

Watching the stag, he thought of how to best help his friends. There was one thing he'd always wanted to do, something that could be helpful, but he'd never quite figured it out. Riding the joy of his renewed magic, he thought it worth another try. Even if this particular feat was more theoretical than practical at this point. The simple fact was, he could never learn it if he didn't practice. And he certainly wanted to practice with an animal before a person. Remembering Millie's cat, he hesitated.

But we might need it one day.

He looked over at Eselle and motioned her to remain quiet. She nodded and watched.

After gauging the stag's movements, Daalok shifted his focus to the space before the creature. Holding out one hand, he mumbled, imagining what he wanted. Pressure built in his chest, spreading out through his limbs. The air before the stag rippled once but remained still. Another ripple showed he was close, but it disappeared again. He closed his eyes briefly, cleared his mind, and refocused.

His skin tingled. After opening his eyes, he locked onto the space and tried again. It took another minute, but the space eventually rippled. It flowed out like a hazy, shining pool of water. He heard a soft intake of breath beside him, making him smile. He shifted his vision to another spot a few paces away from the first, farther from the stag still contentedly eating grass on the far bank, unaware of what happened nearby.

Once he had the second portal open, Daalok held his concentration on both. He picked up a small stone and, with discreet controlled motions, tossed it behind the stag.

The stag jerked its head up and bolted forward—right through the first portal.

Daalok's smile brightened his entire face.

It worked!

He waited.

The longer he waited, the more his smile slipped from his face. Horror made his stomach roil.

Come on. Please, come back. Please, please, please.

Eselle's hand found his forearm. He put a hand over hers.

Please.

After a couple of minutes, he couldn't lie to himself anymore. The poor thing had joined Millie's cat.

Daalok took a few moments to collect himself before looking at Eselle. When he did, he hated the sympathetic look on her face. "That wasn't quite what I had hoped for."

"Was that the same spell you did with the cat?"

Daalok nodded. "I thought I had figured it out this time."

"One day, I'm sure you will." She patted his hand.

"I hoped to figure it out now in case we needed to escape the commander or anyone else who might find us."

Eselle leaned over and gave him a hug. "You've already helped us so much. I probably should have said it earlier, but thank you for saving me the other night."

He nodded and looked back at the opposite bank, where the once majestic stag had stood. He'd practiced enough magic for one day.

"We should probably get back," he said. Eselle nodded and rose beside him.

The moment Daalok stood, something came down over his head and his knees were knocked out from under him.

***

Eselle started when Daalok went down beside her. Arms wrapped around her from behind, pinning her own.

"Relax," a familiar voice said in her ear.

Two soldiers pulled Daalok up to his feet, restraining his hands. They had dropped a blindfold over his head. He stumbled repeatedly as they hauled him back toward the campsite.

Cristar!

She was alone at the camp. Eselle tried yanking herself free. She pulled on her arms, swung her feet up, trying to throw him off balance. He held fast.

"If you promise to come along nicely, I'll release you."

Eselle huffed. How had he found them again?

The commander released her long enough to spin her around to face him, then clamped his arms around her again, holding her against him. She froze the moment she met his dark eyes. She tried to worm a hand around, hoping to pull his dagger, but her hands were solidly stuck between them, his mail digging into her knuckles and wrists.

"Good morning," Kyr said, peering down at her. His features were somber, a bit detached even, none of his previous enjoyment of the chase showed in his taut expression. A long, fresh cut decorated the underside of his right jaw.

"What are you doing here?" Eselle asked.

"I'm afraid things have changed. It's time to take everyone to the castle."

After releasing her, he led her back to the campsite a short distance away. Nearly a dozen soldiers milled around. Two stood behind her. Another was behind Cristar, at the side of the clearing, watching the woman as she sat obediently on a fallen log with her bound hands in her lap. Daalok knelt several paces from them, looking much less comfortable with his hands secured behind his back. The blindfold over his eyes would prevent him from doing magic, or at least, from aiming it. If he couldn't see, he couldn't throw more fire at the commander. Another soldier rummaged through their packs, for what, Eselle didn't know. The remaining men stood with the horses.

Eselle glared at Kyr." How did you find us?"

"That's a long story for another day. Suffice to say, I know you better than you think."

Considering how easily he always found her, she reluctantly believed him. The next time she had the opportunity, she needed to reconsider her patterns. Until then, she realized that short of outright attacking, which would risk her friends' lives, there was no easy escape. There were too many soldiers. She couldn't fight them alone, and her friends were bound, one blindfolded. Cristar was far beyond being able to fight anyway; Eselle was surprised the woman hadn't gone into labor already.

A sudden crashing sound made everyone in the camp jump. Every eye jerked toward the river as a stag bolted from the field and into the woods. Several of the soldiers had drawn their swords, including Kyr. With deep breaths, they slowly sheathed them.

Looking back at the commander, Eselle found him studying her again, his jaw tight. Unable to hold his tense gaze this early in the morning, she dropped her eyes slightly and noticed the change to his insignia. There was an additional stripe at his collar. It seemed his schemes had paid off. Shivering at the thought, she wondered what he'd done.

"Gather your belongings, Eselle," he said. "It's time for you to meet the king."

CHAPTER THIRTY

Twelve Years Old

As he watched the blade swipe to the right of the lad's head, the aging man felt his stomach drop.

Why had he thought this was a good idea?

Granted, it was necessary, but that didn't mean he needed to watch.

Ducking to the side, the boy lunged around and thrust his dagger at his opponent's side. The swordmaster didn't fall for the maneuver he'd taught the boy the previous day but jumped backward and grabbed the boy's wrist as it shot past. Utilizing his opponent's momentum, he propelled the boy across the room.

"Better," the swordmaster said as he flipped his dagger in his hand.

"Better?" the boy asked. He heaved heavy breaths. "I missed."

"True. But first, I missed you, allowing you to counterattack."

The boy smiled broadly.

Though his training was taking longer than the boy wanted, the aging man had held more realistic expectations. He continually tried to temper the boy's dreams of rescuing the kingdom by his sixteenth birthday. With each new move and counter move the boy learned, his confidence and expectations grew tenfold. While pleased with the lad's dedication, he worried about the arrogance growing larger than the skill. Then again, despite the boy's recent growth spurt, he was still only a child.

"Now," the swordmaster said, returning his dagger to its sheath, "since we're done with warmup, let's get started." He reached for two training swords, handing one to the boy. After positioning himself, already prepared to strike, he waited while his pupil got settled. "Do you remember what else I taught you?"

The boy positioned himself, his sword raised. "I think so."

The man decided it was time for him to leave. The boy and his swordmaster had progressed to two-handed maneuvers, and the boy improved steadily, quickly even according to the swordmaster. That, however, didn't make it easier to watch the lad take a beating along the way to his own mastery. He knew it was part of learning any form of fighting, but the man cringed every time the swordmaster struck the boy, false blade or no. Better to leave the boy with the swordmaster and worry about his own studies.

By the time the combatants broke for the day, the man was deep into one of his history books. Only when the boy spoke did he realize there was someone else in the room. Jumping around in his seat, he dropped the tome. It landed on his foot.

"Ouch!" He jerked his foot back and slowly wiggled his toes to make sure nothing had broken.

The boy wore a sympathetic expression while retrieving the book. "Sorry. I didn't mean to frighten you."

"That's okay." The man rubbed his foot through the soft leather of his boot. "It's probably almost dinnertime anyway. Are you hungry?"

"Famished," the boy said emphatically, handing over the book.

Rising from his seat, he no longer had to look down to meet the boy's eyes; they stood even with his own. Truly, the years had passed so quickly he hadn't noticed all the changes along the way. Not until this moment did he realize the boy was the same height as him. "When did you get so tall?" he asked, torn between amusement and remorse.

The boy chuckled. "I'm not getting taller," he said with a smirk. "You're just shrinking."

"You know what it is? It's all this eating. Every time I turn around, you're finishing off something or other, and I have to buy more food. Maybe if I stop feeding you, you'll shrink back down, and I'll be taller again."

"Don't count on it, little man."

With a playful knock of the book against the boy's arm, he went to the hearth at the side of the living quarters. "Help me, would you?"

"What are we having?"

"I don't know yet. Let's see what you haven't already eaten."

After they finished off the last of the meat and a few vegetables, the man picked at the remaining fruit.

"What are we working on tomorrow?" the boy asked. "More with the swordmaster, I hope."

"That, but you also have lessons with Gangral."

The boy made a disgruntled face. "Not Gangral. He's so boring."

He couldn't argue with the boy; the schoolmaster was indeed horrendously boring. "I'm sure it won't be that bad. We're past the worst periods and moving into the Horantian Era, when the aristocracy was incredibly cunning and there were almost daily poisonings. You'll love it," he said. It disturbed him that the deadliest times in history were often both entertaining and educational. He hoped his promise proved to be true since he had to endure the lessons too.

"I hope you're right. I nearly fell asleep during his last lesson. Why do I even need to learn about politics? I won't be challenging him to a debate. I'll be fighting him with a sword."

"You have to get to him first, and that means dealing with aristocrats and other bureaucrats so you can get close enough to stab him. Knowing the right people to bribe, blackmail, or possibly even—though I pray not—kill, will help." The boy blanched. "I hope it doesn't come to that," the man said quickly. "But I'd rather you have more skills than you need than not enough. We don't know what you'll face, so I'd rather prepare you for everything."

The boy nodded. "I guess you're right."

"The king is heavily guarded both day and night, so getting to him won't be easy. Trust me, all this preparation, as boring as it is now, will pay off."

"Don't you ever doubt it, though. I mean, what if you're wrong?"

"I'm not wrong," the man said. He put his hand on the boy's shoulder and gave it a gentle squeeze. "However, for argument's sake, what if I am? Who else will do it?" He gave the boy a moment to think. "We know what needs to be done. We're preparing to do it. We're willing to do it. So, why would we stop because of a little doubt whether you're destined or not? The people need saving, after all. So why shouldn't it be you? You, with some help from an old man."

The boy gave an almost bashful smile. "A *little*, old man."

CHAPTER THIRTY-ONE

As they entered Storbers, Kyr led them to three small, well-kept houses near the center of town. They sat beside each other, so keeping everyone close and within reach would be easy. Captain Castare, a nimble looking man who oversaw the city, met them at the cluster of residences.

After Kyr dismounted, he handed the reins to one of his soldiers and ordered everyone down.

Word of Huln's death was still spreading through the ranks, but the captain clearly noticed the new insignia on Kyr's collar. "Greetings, Lord Marshal."

Kyr gave an acknowledging nod, then ignored the captain to watch the prisoners. Eselle climbed down easily enough from her horse, but Cristar had to be assisted from where they had her riding sidesaddle. As for the mage, he was still blindfolded, and the soldiers had no love for him. They manhandled the young man out of the saddle. When he was nearly on the ground, the two armsmen pulling him down lost their grip. He fell the rest of the way and landed solidly on his arm. Kyr winced at the sight, then turned to the captain.

"I was told of your approach," Captain Castare said. "I took the liberty of preparing your usual accommodations." Which was to say, he'd evicted the residents from their home until further notice.

Kyr nodded his thanks, then gave orders for the sleeping arrangements. One house would hold the prisoners, with rotating guards, another would shelter the remaining soldiers, and Kyr would take the last for himself.

As he watched the friends huddle close while they walked between the soldiers, Kyr thought of Nikos. He missed the mage more than he thought possible. Nikos was one of only a few people he cared about. The others, Josah and Maksin, were hopefully enjoying some time together before everything soon changed. The thought made him miss Nikos even more.

He swallowed, blinked his eyes clear, and walked into his temporary residence before anyone spoke to him.

***

With the blindfold still in place, Daalok couldn't see where they took him. They'd only given him a few minutes with Eselle and Cristar before whisking him out of whatever building they'd been in.

Each time Daalok stumbled, the hand holding his arm yanked him up and hauled him along again. The chilly air sent a shiver through his bones. People talked somewhere off in the distance. Daalok's captor slowed, and creaking wood might have been a door opening. Or closing. When they moved again, Daalok's shoulder slammed into something. Pain shot down his arm, the same one he'd fallen on earlier. He cringed, gritting his teeth.

A voice chuckled. "Watch out for those doorways."

The soldier pulled him a short distance, then pushed him down by the shoulder. Daalok felt something beneath him, but when he tried to sit, he missed half of whatever it was and fell to the floor. The resulting jolt hit every joint. It wasn't as bad as falling from the horse, but it hurt. With his hands secured behind his back, he turned away to feel what was behind him, what he had fallen from. It was a wooden chair, the legs and seat smooth and sturdy. He rose, carefully feeling his way up the chair, then sat, grateful to be sitting still finally.

Footsteps moved away from him, then the creak of the door suggested he was alone.

I couldn't be that lucky.

He shifted his head around, tried to catch anything that might indicate where he was. There was no crackle of flame, but the scent of woodsmoke lingered, as though a fire had recently been extinguished. Sounds came from outside, but nothing closer.

The blindfold was snatched from Daalok's head. He jumped and clamped his eyes shut.

After so much time in the darkness, the light bored into his brain and caused an instant headache. Daalok squinted and blinked furiously. He gradually opened his eyes as the pain subsided, though a dull throb remained. A hazy figure stood before him, but he couldn't make out the features. The figure only watched him while Daalok's eyes adjusted. Not long after, the figure transformed into High Commander Silst.

"Are you with me yet?" the commander asked.

Daalok found it easier to focus. "What do you want with us?"

"Well, it's something different for each of you, isn't it?"

The room was large compared to the homes he was accustomed to back in Nist. Daalok sat in a chair that had apparently been pulled from the nearby dinner table. Instead of retrieving another dining chair, the commander pulled over one from the nearby sitting area. After placing it before Daalok, he sat and studied his prisoner closely while remaining silent. As the man's eyes examined him, Daalok shifted in his chair.

"Commander, I don't know—"

"Lord marshal, actually," Silst interrupted without inflection. Daalok blinked. "Recent events have prompted a change of rank."

Daalok nodded slowly. "I see." His tone was flat, and his voice cold when he spoke. "Well then, Lord Marshal, I suppose I should congratulate you."

The lord marshal matched his detached tone. "That's not necessary."

"It's what you wanted though, isn't it? You said you wanted to oust the previous lord marshal."

"Yes, I did. And I have."

Daalok was curious about the man's subdued demeanor. "You don't seem happy about it."

The lord marshal watched him a moment longer, his features faintly strained. "It came at too high a price."

"And what was that?" Daalok could not fathom what a man like Silst would not pay for something he desired.

"Someone special. You remind me of him, actually."

"Me?"

Silst nodded. "He was also a mage. The high mage, to be exact."

Daalok didn't know what to say.

"You're nowhere near his skill level, but even he started somewhere." The man examined Daalok's features again for a moment. "You have his fire in your eyes."

Daalok shifted in the seat, trying to get comfortable. "I don't know what you want from us, but Eselle and Cristar have done nothing. It was all me. So, please, let them go."

The lord marshal rubbed his face vigorously, then rose and paced the room. "It's not like you to make this easy, is it?"

"Sorry," Daalok said out of habit.

The lord marshal stopped in the middle of the room. "How long have you been traveling with the other prisoners?"

"A couple of weeks." There shouldn't be any harm in revealing that little bit.

"And you're a mage."

It wasn't a question, but Daalok answered anyway. "Yes."

"Is that why you're traveling with them? Criminals sticking together?"

"We're not criminals." He knew he should be worried, that he shouldn't antagonize the man, but the comment angered him more than anything else.

"You're a mage, one of the women is pregnant, and the other is a traitor to the realm. Those are all criminal offenses."

Daalok couldn't tell what the lord marshal was after. The man just stood there, expressionless, saying words, but revealing nothing.

"We're not criminals."

Lord Marshal Silst returned to his seat and leaned forward, his elbows on his knees. "Assuming for a moment that you are, what do you think I should do with you?"

Daalok scoffed. "There's nothing to assume. We didn't do anything."

"You tried to set me on fire," the lord marshal reminded him.

"You were about to hurt Eselle."

"I was trying to restrain her."

"Hurt, restrain, was I supposed to let you?"

"Must I remind you about the criminal part of all this?"

"Must I remind you we're not criminals?"

The lord marshal dropped his head. With a sigh, he pushed up off his elbows and sat straight, staring at Daalok. "I assume you know your traveling companion, Eselle, is a member of the Enstrin family."

Daalok hesitated, then nodded.

"And that her brother also lives."

Daalok sat still, trying not to bite his lip.

The lord marshal tilted his head as he stared at Daalok. "And that her brother is conspiring to regain the throne."

Daalok still refused to reply. Silst sat back in his chair.

"Let's assume her brother succeeds, then later discovers there's a spy in his court, trying to undermine his reign. He orders you to capture that spy for sentencing. What would you do?"

"If you're trying to compare that situation to this one, they're worlds apart."

The lord marshal took a long moment to answer. "Perhaps," he said, his voice contemplative.

Silst looked away, then went to the door and spoke to someone outside.

A soldier entered, replaced Daalok's blindfold, then returned him to the house where they were being held. The blindfold was as disorienting as ever, but he made it back without incident. Once he stumbled through the doorway, he flinched as someone new grabbed his arm. The blindfold lifted to reveal Eselle standing before him. The moment he focused on her, the soldier grabbed her arm and hauled her toward the door.

"What are you doing?" she asked.

"Let her go," Daalok and Cristar said together.

The soldier pulled her along. "The lord marshal wants to question you next."

Before anyone could react, Eselle was out of the house. The remaining guard watched the prisoners resentfully.

Cristar walked over to Daalok. Her steps became more laborious each day. "Are you all right?"

"I'm fine."

"What did he want?"

Daalok thought about it a moment. "I don't know."

"What do you mean? What did he ask you?"

"Nothing really. He didn't ask anything I expected him to."

The guards wouldn't allow Daalok's restraints to be removed, so with his hands tied behind his back, sitting was uncomfortable. *At least the blindfold is gone.*

Cristar sat beside him on the couch with a sullen expression. "What do you think he'll ask Eselle? Or me?"

"I have no idea."

CHAPTER THIRTY-TWO

Eselle found herself alone with the new lord marshal.

"Have a seat." Kyr indicated the chairs by the lit fireplace as he poured a drink.

Hesitating, Eselle surveyed the house. There were two rooms off the main and a hallway to one side. A door to the front that—

"If I were you," Kyr said, "I'd sit, talk, and then plan a better escape against the men I have guarding you. Trust me, you won't escape my presence tonight."

Eselle reluctantly believed him. She shook her head and selected the closest seat. How did he always seemed to know her thoughts?

He set the drink beside her, then sat in the chair opposite. "What are your brother's plans for retaking Likalsta?"

"I thought you knew everything about us." Thankfully, there seemed to still be a few secrets.

With a sigh, he closed his eyes. "I have a feeling this will go nowhere." He looked at her and took a sip from a drink he'd already been working on. "At the time, I was angry and wanted to unnerve you. You had, after all, just taken a piece out of me with a sword. I know about you and your brother in general, but not details of his strategy. Any information would be tremendously appreciated."

She couldn't tell if he was being sarcastic, but the congenial attitude disturbed her.

"Why do you think I'd tell you anything?"

"I actually don't think you will, but I have to ask. Otherwise, the king will have my head. Or worse. And if I manage to get information from you, that'll keep me in the king's good graces. We both know how far that can go."

"Yes." She nodded at the insignia on his collar. "He promoted you to lord marshal, apparently."

"He did."

"I'll bet the previous lord marshal was irate. Drus Huln, wasn't it? You'd better watch your back, in case he plans to stick a knife in it."

"It would be amazing if he did, considering he's rotting in a ditch. And, yes, his name was Huln."

A chill ran down her spine at seeing the bland, cold expression on his face. "You killed him, didn't you?"

His smile held no mirth or warmth. Rather, he seemed melancholy.

Eselle shifted in her seat, sat straighter. "Does the king know?"

"He witnessed the entire exchange, saw me kill the man in the bailey in front of at least forty other soldiers."

"Was it just for the position?"

Kyr glanced over to the fire. "No, actually."

"Then, why?"

"He said something I took offense to." He took a long drink from the glass, then set it down.

"So, the king rewards murder with promotion." Eselle feared the world they lived in. "I'd still watch my back," she said, unable to restrain the sarcasm, "in case *the king* decides to put a knife in it."

He waved the comment off. "That's not the king's style, but I take your meaning."

"That's right, the whole losing your head or worse you mentioned. Though I can't imagine anything worse than that."

"Then, I envy you." He looked back from the fire and met her gaze. "To have not witnessed some of the things I've seen in the king's dungeons, or The Crypt in particular. Trust me, he's created things much worse than dying. But I'd rather not think about it, since it's a very real possibility if I don't bring you in."

He said it flatly, as though speaking of someone else, but she saw something in his eyes. She couldn't decipher it, but it brought the slightest tightening to his brow.

Eselle leaned forward. "He's threatened you. Hasn't he?"

Kyr tilted his head as he studied her. "You don't want to discuss your brother, do you? I supposed I wouldn't either in your position. Sooner or later, though, you'll have to."

"No, I won't."

"Other than waiting until we arrive at the castle—where proper interrogation tools can be used instead of homemade tortures—how can I convince you to talk to me?"

After pretending a moment's consideration, Eselle lifted her chin. "You can't." When he continued watching her silently, she asked, "Would you really torture me?"

"Not me personally. But it would be done, yes."

"Don't have the stomach for it?"

"No," he admitted. "It's something I never took to."

"You just enjoy chasing women around the countryside and tormenting us along the way."

"Exactly." The side of his lips slid up into a faint simper. He rose and paced around the room. "Now, back to your brother. What are his plans?"

"How can you work for that man?" Eselle slid to the edge of her seat.

"Stop changing the subject."

"No. I won't tell you about my brother." Her voice grew adamant. "I want to know how you can work for Vorgal."

Kyr stepped in behind the opposite chair and rested his hands along the back of it. "He's the king."

"He murdered my family."

"That's what kings do."

"Not good kings."

"I never said he was a good king. I said he was the king."

"So, you admit he's not a good king?"

"I admit nothing," Kyr said. "He's the king, plain and simple."

"But why do you serve him?"

"I'm a soldier in his military, it's what soldiers do. Plus, I want to reach the top, so I strive to make him happy as a means of achieving that."

"And if my brother regains the throne?"

"Then he'd probably have me executed alongside Vorgal and replace me with one of his own."

"My brother wouldn't do that. He's a good man."

"It's what rulers do when there's a regime change, eliminate the most dangerous opposition of the overthrown house. That includes the nobility and military, even the clergy on occasion."

"Tavith wouldn't do that," Eselle said. "My brother would accept you into his military. Help us defeat Vorgal, and we'll have a place for you."

"But not lord marshal." He said it with certainty.

Eselle hesitated. "That would be up to my brother, but probably not. I'd speak for you, of course."

"If I help you."

"Yes. If you help us."

With a look of consideration, he stepped around the chair and retook his seat. "What are your brother's plans?"

"Will you help us?"

"No. Your brother?"

"Can't you see what Vorgal—"

"Your brother," he spoke over her. "What is he planning?"

Lunging out of her chair, Eselle glared down at him. "Why are you loyal to him?" Her voice grew steadily more insistent. "You say you want power, but it has to be more than that. Yes, you're ruthless, and you're rude. You're arrogant and an actual backstabber, but I've seen how you rule your region, how you took care of Cristar on the road. You can't believe Vorgal is good for this land. It's true, my brother might demote you in preference to his own men, but you can rise back to the top. You're talented enough. I know you would prove yourself and one day be lord marshal again."

"Why would I settle for one day when I already have it?"

"So, to continue being lord marshal, you'd let the lands suffer?"

He didn't answer, only watched her closely. Eselle stepped over to the hearth and gazed down into the flames.

There must be an argument that can convince him to join us.

A hand gripped Eselle's arm, and she spun around toward Kyr.

"Your brother," he reminded her stoically. "What is he up to?"

A chill settled over Eselle. "We're done here. I'd like to return to my prison."

"You'll stay here tonight, so you might want that drink."

"What?" Her voice rose on the word.

"I've decided that for the time being, it's safer to keep you separated from your companions. There's too much risk you'll try to escape, and I don't have time anymore to keep hunting you down. So, you'll spend the night here, where I can keep an eye on you myself. Plus, my men have retired for the night, and I don't feel like heading out into the cold. So, make yourself comfortable."

***

Eselle lay on the bed with her back toward Kyr and stared at the wall, planning to get ready for sleep once he'd gone. Though, the thought of slipping out a window to rescue her friends also crossed her mind. She needed to work out a few more details, but she couldn't let Kyr take them to the castle. Only death and misery awaited them there.

A soft thump drew her attention behind her. Kyr undid a tie on one of his leather vambraces. The other already sat on a table beside him.

"What are you doing!" Eselle sat up and stared at him.

"Getting ready for bed." He didn't look up as he spoke, only continued removing his armor.

"Why?"

"It's what people do around this time of night."

"But why are you doing it here?"

He glanced up briefly. "Where else would I do it?" He set the vambrace down beside the other and started working on one of his spaulders.

"In your own room."

A deep chuckle rumbled out of him. "Did you really think I'd let you out of my sight? That I'd leave you unattended overnight?"

Eselle turned toward the fire. "I guess not, but I hoped."

"Ever the optimist."

She turned a glare on him. "What's wrong with that?"

"Nothing. It's one of the things I admire about you."

Eselle gaped, then rolled back onto the bed and stared at the wall again, putting him behind her.

A short while later, the covers moved, and the bed sank. Eselle jerked around and nearly jumped off the bed. "What are you doing?"

"Didn't we have this conversation?" Down to his trousers and shirt, Kyr slid under the covers and got comfortable.

Eselle stuttered for a moment. "I thought you'd sleep on the floor."

He scoffed. "I'm not gentleman enough to sleep on the floor, or even the couch, for that matter. You're welcome to, of course, but you'll sleep in this room. So, if you choose the couch, you'll have to pull it in here by yourself. I'm too tired for moving furniture tonight." With that, he burrowed into the pillow while lying on his side, facing her. "Also, I'm keeping the blankets. So, wherever you decide to sleep, you'll need to find covers." When she stared at him a while longer, he finally closed his eyes. "Be glad I'm sleeping with my clothes on."

The sudden memory of him lying naked beside her, beneath her, made her pulse quicken; she flipped around with her back to him again. Heat rose to her cheeks when she heard the deep chuckle.

"You've tossed me on my back, climbed on top, and had your way with me. Why are you suddenly timid?"

"Things were different then."

He took a moment to respond. "I suppose they were." The amusement had left his voice. "You might as well get under the covers. It'll be chilly tonight."

She tried to remember if she'd seen any blankets or other items to bundle up in, but couldn't recall anything. With a scowl, she reluctantly pulled off her boots. Wiggling around to crawl beneath the covers, she diligently avoided looking at her sleeping companion. She didn't want to know if he was watching.

"In case you're planning to sneak out in the middle of the night," he said, "I locked the door to the room and hid the key."

Eselle rolled her eyes. She didn't know how to pick a lock, but she knew how to be patient and wait for him to fall asleep so she could discretely ransack the room.

Nearly an hour later, Eselle was finalizing a plan to get around the guards.

The bed jolted.

She jerked upright enough to look around.

Kyr flinched in his sleep. He made a guttural sound she couldn't quite interpret. His eyes clenched. His jaw twitched. His head shifted. His breathing grew heavier.

Eselle wondered what dreams distressed him. If it was anything like her nightmares, she pitied him. Part of her wanted to wake him, to spare him from whatever was happening in his mind. The stronger part decided it was time to move, to slide out of bed while he was distracted.

Worried any large movement might rouse him, she eased back down and rolled to her side. With slow movements, she slid one leg to the edge. Another flinch shook the bed, stronger than the last, accompanied by a soft noise that almost sounded like a word.

The moment she slid halfway over the edge, the bed shifted. An arm wrapped around her, clamped firmly around her chest. It hauled her backward across the mattress until she came up against a large, hard body. Legs curled in behind hers, and one draped across her calves.

"Trouble sleeping, princess?" His voice sounded groggy and strained, but still alert enough she didn't trust testing him.

"I thought I'd take a walk, clear my head to help me sleep." Eselle tried to pull free of his grip. Though not tight, his hand securely held her wrist, and his arm wrapped around her.

"Hmm. I don't think that's a good idea." His breath caressed her neck as his voice relaxed.

She tried again to dislodge him. Failing, she finally conceded. "You can let go. I won't try leaving again."

"I think I'll stay here. You're nice and warm, and the night's getting colder."

She couldn't argue that point. He was nice and warm too. The temperature continued to drop, and the blankets wouldn't help much longer at this rate. Though she could search for more blankets, they could also snuggle together. And he definitely felt good at her back.

Once resigned to the futility of escape with Kyr so close, it didn't take long for her to drift off.

CHAPTER THIRTY-THREE

The distorted face hovered amidst the floating, misty black form.

It surged toward Eselle.

She jumped backward. Something caught her foot, sending her tumbling to the ground on her bottom. A sweet, metallic scent permeated the air. Eyes that had once been a deep blue now appeared dull, sightless, lifeless. Lissil lay on the ground, her limbs twisted. Blood seeped from the tear in her dress and coated her stomach.

Eselle clamped a hand over her mouth and stared at her little sister.

The misty figure surged again. Eselle scuttled across the floor out of reach. The thing maintained no distinct form, only vague undulating shapes; but she knew it was Vorgal.

Three more dark shapes materialized from nothing, spread evenly behind him. They were the same indistinct, inky black form. With a ripple of mist, Vorgal motioned one forward.

Eselle stared. The closer it drew, the more it solidified, slowly growing arms and legs.

She didn't wait to see more. Rolling over, she pushed herself off the ground and ran.

Stone walls flew past as she barreled down the empty hallway. A backward glance showed the form chasing her. It continued to solidify as Vorgal and the others pursued farther back, floating along.

Eselle took a corner that led to the guardhouse. If she could reach the castle guard, they would protect her.

Her breaths came harder, her legs and lungs felt the strain of desperation.

The figure drew close. Footfalls pounded behind her.

Another glance brought a whimper from Eselle. The figure was no longer an inky mist. It possessed a body, with long legs, a clenched jaw, and angry dark eyes.

It was Kyr.

He ran as hard as she did. A snarl marred his features.

She cursed Vorgal. He'd taken too much from her. He couldn't win again. But how could she fight the monster?

Another turn produced a dead end.

No. This isn't right. The guardhouse should be here. I should be safe.

There was no door ahead, only the cold stone walls of a musty-smelling dead end. She didn't stop running.

Kyr slammed into her, wrapping his arms around her waist. She gasped when they fell to the hard floor. He came up on top of her, pinning her wrists as she lay on her back. They stared at each other. His brows bunched together. He released a hand to run his fingers along her jaw while he studied her features. While Eselle's breath came in heavy gasps and her body quivered from exertion, Kyr seemed steady.

He spun around in a crouch. Instead of facing her, he watched the direction they'd come. Eselle tried to speak, but her voice didn't work.

The large black form and its two smaller ones floated around the corner and headed toward them.

Eselle scrambled to her feet.

Kyr peered over his shoulder at her, his face unreadable, then turned toward Vorgal and charged. The dark figure's wavering features had solidified enough that Kyr managed to punch it. His fist, along with half his arm, sank into the blackness. When he pulled back, his arm released slowly, making him fight for every inch. The dark figure reached out a hand, more solid than the rest of it, and caught Kyr around the throat.

Eselle tried to utter a plea, but no sound came. Vorgal lifted Kyr off the ground with one hand. Fear held her in place, as it had with Lissil.

Vorgal's other hand thrust into Kyr's chest. The crunch and squish sounded clear as Vorgal struck. The misty king dropped his victim in a limp pile of limbs. Eselle saw what he'd done, saw Kyr's collapsed chest as he stared vacantly. Her breath shuddered. His body shifted back into the misty form, then dissipated completely. She watched the empty space.

Movement caught her eye, and she looked up. Vorgal advanced, once again a hazy blackness.

A hand gripped her arm.

Eselle jerked around.

Tavith held her. "This way."

Her tension eased at the sight of her brother.

He motioned her into a large hole in the wall that hadn't been there before. She rushed through. They emerged in another hallway.

Two shadowy forms materialized ahead of them. Tavith led Eselle around the nearest corner. The figures appeared again, forcing the siblings to make another turn.

Eselle became lost in all the deviations they were forced into. Things weren't where they should be. They moved even as she watched them.

Vorgal's figure formed before them. Tavith skidded to a halt, and Eselle ran into his back.

Tavith turned and pushed her ahead of him. "Back. Run."

Her heart pounded, and her eyes filled with tears.

"Keep running!"

Tavith's voice sounded farther away. She glanced back.

Vorgal's inky form expanded. It swept up and over Tavith, swallowing him.

Ice ran through Eselle's body, and her legs stopped. Vorgal's wavering form pulled back from where Tavith had been. The space was empty. Wiped from the world like the rest of their family.

Eselle fell to her knees, and her vision blurred.

The inky figure swept within inches of her. She stared up at it. Where could she possibly go that he wouldn't find her?

Vorgal expanded above her and . . .

Jerking upright, Eselle frantically scanned the dark, unfamiliar room.

The image of the floating black form lingered in her mind.

Something around her waist moved. She jumped.

"Lie back down," a sleepy male voice said.

She twisted around. Kyr lay beside her. He tugged her lightly again by the waist. Too afraid to move, she sat there shaking. The dream flashed through her mind in excruciating detail. She couldn't catch her breath. The dreams had haunted her over the years, but they'd been worse this last, since Tavith claimed to be close to marching.

As she tried to relax, tried breathing normally, Kyr sat up.

"What's wrong?" He sounded worried, more awake, and draped an arm across her back. When she didn't answer, couldn't find her words yet, he turned her face toward him. "What's wrong?" He searched her features, reminding her of when he'd done so in her dream.

Eselle shook her head, unable to answer. It was all too much. And they were heading to the man who'd done it all. Her jaw quivered; she didn't want to cry, but it felt so real.

Kyr's arms wrapped around her, and Eselle turned into him, clutching his shirt. She held back the tears, but her breaths came erratically. She couldn't stop shaking.

He held her tighter. "It's all right. It was a dream." He stroked her hair as he tucked her head beneath his chin.

When she spoke, she only had partial control of her breathing. "You . . . you . . ."

"It was just a nightmare." His voice was soft, soothing. "I'm sure whatever horrible thing I did to you in it I would never actually do."

Shaking her head against his chest, Eselle took a moment to collect herself. She wiped a few errant tears off her cheeks.

Kyr pulled her down beside him, wrapped his arms around her, and held her close.

The shivers eased, and she didn't want to leave his embrace. Even as she thought it, she knew it was only a combination of the warm bed, the strong body against her, and her own fatigue and fears, that crippled her reasoning. They made her feel safer with this man than she should.

She held onto him as he pulled the blankets back up. Amidst her fears, she hadn't noticed how cold the night had gotten.

"I'm sure I'll regret asking," he said, "but what did I do in your dream?"

Eselle took a couple of deep breaths. "You died."

He pulled back enough to look at her but didn't let go. "You dreamed I died?"

"Yes."

He blinked and looked away. "Did you kill me?" His voice was devoid of emotion.

"No. Vorgal did." She laid her head against his chest. "He killed you, my brother, one of my sisters who died years ago." She couldn't help but be soothed when Kyr hugged her tighter.

"I'm sorry you dreamed all that. But nothing from your dream can get you here. You're safe."

"But Vorgal is out there. We'll be there tomorrow."

"Don't worry about that right now. Get some sleep."

Eselle pulled away and propped herself up on an elbow. "How can I not worry? You can't take us there." Her breath started to escape her again. "You c-can't."

"Shhh." He gently pulled her back down. "Forget about all that for tonight, we'll deal with it tomorrow."

She focused on his hand slowly rubbing her back. Before long, she felt calmer, in control enough to speak again. It was strange being with him like this. "I wish I had you around like this every time I woke from a nightmare."

Burying his face in her hair, he murmured, "So do I."

Eselle slid an arm around his waist and gazed up into Kyr's dark eyes. In the night, they really did look black. "You could, if you wanted to."

He frowned. "Don't. Don't start that again."

"I don't understand why—"

"It's not something you need to understand." His voice grew firm. "Drop it and don't ask again."

She laid her head back against his chest. His heartbeat pounded against her ear, proof he did have one. Though, despite everything, she'd never really doubted it. "In my dream, Vorgal killed you when you turned on him and defended me."

It was a long while before Kyr finally responded. "I wasn't prepared for you."

Seeing him like this, tender and thoughtful, made her believe there was a whole other side to him. If only she could reach that side, hold onto it and pull it into the light.

***

The next morning, Eselle watched Kyr cross the main room as he dabbed a damp cloth against the slice along his chest. It amazed her knowing she did that to him. In all her training, she'd never actually injured anyone like that. The wound was healing nicely, but still needed regular tending. Looking at the rest of him, Eselle admired his solid build, with its light, even speckling of dark chest hair. She still remembered what his chiseled stomach tasted like.

The man confused her. He'd do something decent—like keep Cristar from falling when a soldier manhandled her—and she'd think they should try recruiting him, then he'd do something despicable—like kill the vagabond—and she'd want to take another slice out of him. Before she'd get the chance, she'd see a flicker of something in his eyes that would make her question everything all over again.

The previous night had been no different. She had her nightmare, felt vulnerable and he soothed her more than she thought him capable of. They laid together for the remainder of the night, wrapped in warmth and comfort. It was the safest she'd felt in months. Which was insane considering she had been lying with the man she'd been running from. Then this morning, he had turned distant, moving through the motions of rising and preparing for the day. Deep down, she still believed something could win him to their side.

Reaching the chair by the fire, Kyr sat while tending the wound.

Seeing the few hairline scars about him, she supposed they were what came of a long, fast climb to the top of the military. He had a fresh cut on his right arm and the one along the underside of his jaw. It was the burns on his elbow and torso though, and the scar across his left shoulder—the one that dipped downward toward the front, running into his bicep— that had her intrigued. She suspected those might be stories worth hearing.

Eselle glanced at the long slice across his chest. "So, you're not invincible."

He raised his head casually. "What makes you think that? I'm still around, after all."

"Those scars." She waved a finger vaguely around his torso.

"Military men tend to collect them," he said, preparing the fresh bandage.

"Where did you get the burns?"

"A fire."

"I guessed that. What happened?"

"A burning building was collapsing, and I shielded my head from falling debris. It caught my arm well enough, though. It was long ago, and I'd rather not discuss it."

"Too personal?" She wondered if she should help him bandage himself, especially considering she gave him the injury. "What about that other scar, the one on your shoulder? Where'd you get that?"

"I did that to myself, actually."

"Slipped while cleaning your sword?" she teased, feeling oddly protective at seeing his scars again.

"I wasn't cleaning it, but yes, it was an accident. An incredibly stupid one." Looking at the old wound, he ran a finger along it, then sighed.

She stepped closer, watching Kyr as he wrapped his chest and shoulder. "I can't imagine you doing anything stupid. Let me help."

He pushed her hands away when she reached out to him. "I've dressed my own wounds for years. I don't need help."

Eselle adjusted the bandage already laid across his chest. "Everyone needs help someti—"

He gripped her hand and squeezed while pulling it away from him. When she tried to pull her hand back, he held fast.

"I don't need your help." His voice was colder than she'd ever heard him.

She tried again to free her hand. "I only wanted to—"

"And I told you no."

When he thrust her hand away, she stepped back while he resumed dressing his wound.

Eselle massaged her hand. "Why is it so difficult for you to accept help?"

"It isn't. I have people help me all the time."

"I'd be willing to bet they're following orders, not helping."

He shrugged without looking up, managing without assistance. Once finished, he leaned back in the chair, and they watched each other silently.

With the lord marshal sleeping so close the night before, there'd been no opportunity to escape. In the light of day, Eselle hated that she'd felt so comfortable with him. After a while, she hadn't wanted to escape, but rather remain in the warm bed with him wrapped around her. It had felt so natural that, aside from the nightmare, she'd had one of the best night's sleep in recent months. She wanted to believe it was the warm bed, but it was also the body beside her.

Likewise, she wanted to believe it would have been the same having *any* body beside her, but it was more than that.

"What now?" she asked.

"We should reach Vahean late tonight. Your pregnant friend will be imprisoned with others like her, but the king will decide what to do with you and your mage."

"And what will he do with us? You know him well enough, I expect you could hazard a pretty accurate guess."

He stared into the fire. "Your mage may be tested for an apprenticeship, especially considering there's an opening. Given his recent traveling companions though, I suspect the king will forgo that and move straight to execution." He turned back to her. "You will be questioned about your brother."

"You mean tortured."

"Yes. But 'questioned' sounds less gruesome." Kyr reached for his shirt and began dressing.

"Did you, by chance, change your mind last night? About joining my brother? About joining me?" She was hesitantly hopeful. Despite his current coolness, he had been his old self the night before, the man she first met.

"No," he said coldly. "I haven't changed my mind."

"If you take us to the castle, Vorgal will hurt or kill us."

"I know what will happen at Vistralou."

"He'll kill Cristar's baby." Eselle hoped to reach the part of him that protected her friend on the road, the part that consoled her the previous night. "He'll kill Daalok. And who knows what he'll do to me."

Kyr remained silent as he donned his hauberk.

"If I tell you my brother's plan," Eselle asked, taking a risk, "would you join us?"

"No. I'd send a hoard of soldiers to decimate the operation and bring your brother and his conspirators to justice."

Eselle stared at him.

He didn't look back as he secured his sword belt. "Your chance to tell me the truth has passed. Even if I wanted to play along and lie to you for information, there's no time. I'll get my answers in Vistralou."

"I thought . . . "

"Thought what? That one night preventing a weeping woman from keeping me awake meant I'd betray the king for her?"

Angry, Eselle started to protest, but he reached out and wrapped a strong hand around her throat. He pushed her backward into the wall, his grip firm, but only holding her in place. The right side of his jaw clenched tight.

"As I said last night, never again ask me to betray the king. Do you understand?" His gaze bored into her, and his voice rumbled deeply.

Instead of answering, Eselle stared uncertainly. He'd changed so quickly, she didn't know how to handle him.

"Whatever you think you see in me, it isn't there. Stop looking for it! You're only making this more difficult for everyone."

"So what was last night about?"

"Last night was a mistake." He ground his teeth before continuing. "I was tired and not thinking clearly. Having a warm woman pressed against me didn't hurt either."

It was harder for Eselle to breathe. Not because he held her tightly, but because she tried to hold back tears.

She'd been wrong about him, and now she and her friends would die.

CHAPTER THIRTY-FOUR

The torch-lit castle looked like a stranger to Eselle. Aside from the deep nighttime shadows, it had been eighteen years since she'd last seen Vistralou Castle. She expected it to seem more familiar. Instead, it was a ghost of what she remembered, a dry, shriveled husk of the vast, lush grounds she and her siblings once explored. The stone seemed darker, the portcullises more intimidating, the ramparts more threatening as they loomed above.

Once past the inner gate, she stared at the keep. It was as depressing as the defenses, larger and more oppressive than she remembered. Heavy clouds hid the moon. In the darkness, the structure stood poised to rise and swallow her. Where was the home she once knew?

The grounds bustled with more activity than she would have expected for this time of night. Several armsmen moved supplies and weapons around, some up to the battlements and others to the ramparts overlooking the zwinger.

"Armsman," Kyr called out to a passing soldier.

The man stopped abruptly and glanced up, then stumbled and nearly dropped his load of arrows. "Lord Marshal."

"What's happening here?" Kyr asked.

"A s-siege."

"The only army I saw riding in was our own. Explain."

"The city guard from Heldin, sir. They're heading this way. Should be here by morning."

Kyr waved the armsman on.

Eselle's heart lightened.

Tavith was coming!

With any luck, she and her friends would be rescued before the king did anything drastic. Under normal circumstances, she wouldn't count on a short siege, but she and her brother knew some of Vistralou's secrets.

Reaching over from his horse, Kyr snatched the blindfold from Daalok's head. "Have you ever seen Vistralou Castle, mage?"

Daalok blinked a few times as he focused on his surroundings. "No."

"Take a look. It'll be your last glimpse at anything other than the dungeon and the gallows."

With that, he and two armsmen led Eselle and her companions across the bailey. They entered the keep through a side entrance. When they reached the dungeon, a dank and moldy odor surrounded them. With no windows, only candles and torches for light, the dark stone pressed in on Eselle.

She worried about Cristar being left in such a place, especially so close to labor.

The lord marshal discussed arrangements with the soldier on duty.

Eselle had played with her siblings down in these lower levels. At the time, they had only been storage rooms. The original dungeon had consisted of a single wing of a dozen cells. The current king had renovated this portion of the castle, adding at least fifty cells divided between three corridors. There were rumors of another secret dungeon, said to contain additional horrors.

One of the soldiers reached out and took Daalok by the arm, leading him down the left corridor. Kyr grabbed Eselle's elbow, and another soldier took hold of Cristar's. They took the women down the right passage.

"Wait? Where are you taking him?" Eselle asked.

"Don't worry about him." Kyr pulled her along even as she peered back for Daalok. "You should be more concerned about yourself."

The cells down the central corridor came into view as they passed through the large main room. Five or six women filled each of them. Many sat against the bars, while others slept on the ground. Each wore a defeated expression. Whether they cried, slept, sat vacant-eyed, or rubbed their flat stomachs, their losses showed in their features. Eselle shuddered. She didn't want Cristar to become like these women, women she assumed had already lost their babies.

"Why are they still here?" she asked.

The lord marshal followed her gaze. "They're waiting to be delivered to overflow prisons in other cities."

"But why are they still imprisoned? If they've already had their babies, why not release them?"

"Because their stories would get out. There's no telling what the populace might do after that. King Vorgal can't risk it."

Using the sight of the women to bolster her courage, Eselle vowed Cristar would leave this castle with her child in her arms.

When they entered the far corridor, the sight appeared considerably different, though no less distressing. Fewer women occupied the room, sometimes only a single resident per cell. Some were nearing birth, others slender, only newly pregnant and sentenced to long months in the dungeon. Several jumped up and bargained for their freedom and that of their unborn children. Eselle stiffened at the desperation in their faces; her teeth ground together. Her fear for Cristar warred with her anger for Vorgal.

The last two cells stood empty, one on either side of the aisle.

"In here," Kyr ordered.

The armsman opened the cell door and tried to push Cristar inside. The woman stood her ground, yanking her arm out of the man's grip. She examined the cell, then the lord marshal, and didn't move.

"In," Kyr said again as they stared at each other.

When Cristar still refused to budge, Eselle expected him to turn angry. Instead, his features softened. The stern brow eased; the jaw unclenched.

"Please." His voice held a conciliatory tone. "There's no reason for this to turn ugly. One way or another, you will enter this cell. And believe it or not, I'd prefer the easy way."

Cristar stood straighter, held her head higher. "Why should I make anything easy for you? You want to kill my child." She wrapped her arms protectively around her stomach and stared down the lord marshal.

"I want no such thing. I have a mission, and I'm completing it. Whatever else happens is simply fate." When Cristar continued her protest, he turned to Eselle. "Would you, please, talk some sense into her? We both know how much better it would be for both her and the child."

Eselle knew he was right. They had little choice, so far into the dungeon as they were. They could only play along until they found another solution, or her brother took the castle.

She turned to Cristar. "He's right, about this at least." Cristar looked horrified, her eyes growing wide. "You're about to give birth, we all know that. You can't very well put up a fight at the moment. We need to get you settled, then we can think of an escape plan."

The armsman who had accompanied them jolted straighter, taking a step forward.

Kyr waved him off. "Let them scheme. Just so long as it gets them in the cell."

"Them?" Eselle asked. "You'll let me stay with her?"

"Why do you think we brought you down here?"

"I thought this wing was for the pregnant women. I'm not pregnant."

His gaze dropped to her stomach briefly before meeting her eyes again. "Are you certain about that?"

It had been long enough that she knew nothing had resulted from their time in Eddington. "Yes," she snapped. "I'm certain."

He nodded, letting out a deep breath. "Better to be cautious. If nothing else, I'll know where to find you. Since I don't want to wake the king at this late hour, you'll stay here tonight. In the morning, we'll see what kind of mood the king is in. Considering your brother's army is bearing down on him, the situation doesn't look promising."

When he looked back at Cristar, she glared at him as she slowly entered the cell.

Eselle started to follow but stopped to grab Kyr's sleeve. "I know you're better than this."

He glanced down at where she had a hold of him, then back up at her. "I've already told you, stop searching for something that isn't there. Instead of worrying about me, worry about your friend when she goes into labor shortly."

All she could do was stare into his intense, dark eyes. Before she knew it, his lips were on hers again, but only briefly before he hauled her into the cell.

Once the door closed behind them, the lord marshal bowed his head. "Ladies." He left, as composed as ever.

Only after he was out of the dungeon did Eselle speak. "How are you doing?"

Cristar stared at her, her eyes tight as she regarded Eselle. "What was that about? Why did he kiss you?" Her voice rose higher. "And what did he mean about you possibly being pregnant? Did he hurt you last night?"

"No. He didn't hurt me," Eselle said. "But . . . it's complicated." She told Cristar about first meeting Kyr, then again in Eddington, a quick mention of seeing him at the inn, and finally their time together the night before when he consoled her after her nightmare.

"You had sex with him willingly?" Cristar's eyes could not have been wider as they blinked several times. Her brows reached nearly to her hairline.

Eselle gave a nodding shrug. "Yes. But in my defense, it was before he arrested you, before all this started."

Cristar only huffed and glanced away.

"Enough about the lord marshal," Eselle said. "How are you, really? I noticed it's getting harder for you to walk these last couple of days."

"I'm fine." Cristar seemed anything but. She slid herself down the wall to sit. "I feel like I have one of my prize-winning melons sitting between my legs."

"What?"

"He's dropped." Cristar rubbed her stomach.

"Who's dropped?"

"The baby."

"He's in your stomach. How can he drop?"

Cristar gave a light chuckle and watched her patiently. "He's dropped into the birth canal. He's getting ready to come out."

Eselle took a deep breath.

Planning for this seemed so easy. Carrying through with it? I'm not sure I'm ready.

"How long?" Eselle leaned against one of the stone walls.

"It's hard to say, but he's been like this for a while. I didn't say anything because I didn't want to worry you. And there was nothing you could do about it anyway. He'll come when he's ready, whether we're ready or not. But I think it'll be soon . . . very soon."

Eselle nodded and paced the small cell. She needed a change in topic. "Prize-winning?"

"Yes." Cristar nodded and examined the ceiling above the far wall. "Every year, some of the townsfolk compete for who can grow the best melons. At the end of the season, we gather in town and have a picnic. I've won twice for largest melons. Never got best tasting, though. I was hoping to this year."

Eselle only half listened while trying to remember if this was the room with the secret door.

If it is, is it in this cell or the one across the aisle?

When she'd played down here with her siblings years ago, the secret passages made hide-and-seek a bit more challenging. The enormous room appeared vastly different, but she was certain the passage was in either this room or the one Daalok had been taken to.

"What are you doing?" Cristar watched her with a skeptical expression.

"I was trying to remember something from when I was a kid."

White speckled gray stone made up two of the walls of their cell. Eselle slid her hands along the sidewall, examined each crevice.

Most of the neighboring prisoners already slept, but Eselle still spoke in soft tones, sharing her memories of the passages. She described the groove the best she remembered.

Cristar eased herself up from the floor. "Let's find this door."

They both felt along the wall, covering each area several times. Please let it be in this cell.

An hour later, they'd found nothing.

Eselle sat against the wall beside Cristar. The limp straw smelled of a year's worth of various human aromas. "I'm sorry. I hoped the passage was here with us."

"Maybe we missed something."

Eselle shook her head. "No. It was well hidden, but not that difficult to find if you knew it was there. It must be in the other room. Or maybe the cell across from us. Either way, we can't reach it."

Cristar took her hand. "We'll figure something out."

Eselle rolled her head sideways toward her friend. "How can you be so positive?"

Rubbing her stomach slowly, Cristar peered out at the bars. "Because if I'm not, I'll curl up and cry. I'd rather use my energy to find a way to keep us all safe."

Eselle saw the twitch in the woman's cheeks as she struggled to hold her features together. She gave a reassuring squeeze to Cristar's hand.

"I'm sorry," Eselle said. Cristar was the first true friend she had that she hadn't grown up with on the farm. "I'm sorry I let us get caught."

"What? No, this isn't your fault. It was that commander . . . or lord marshal, or whatever he is now."

"Thanks."

Holding her stomach, Cristar shifted her position on the floor. "Anyway, you heard them when we were brought in. Your brother is coming. I'm sure he'll save us."

The smile Eselle gave was only for show, to hide the tightening of her throat. "I hope so. But what if Tavith doesn't get here in time? He'll be here at dawn, but so will Vorgal. I don't know which one will reach our cell first. Or Daalok's."

Cristar wrapped an arm around Eselle's shoulders. "We'll think of something. We have to."

CHAPTER THIRTY-FIVE

Eselle began nodding off an hour later. Her head bobbed a couple times, then jerked upright when she heard something. Sitting still in the dim light, she listened for it again. A soft shuffling sound came from down the corridor. She moved closer to the bars and peered out. A stooped figure approached, tiptoeing down the aisle. Though he managed decently, he still had a lot to learn about stealth. In the end, he snuck about as well as he fished.

Nudging Cristar awake, Eselle put a finger to her lips before the young woman spoke. Cristar reached the bars right as Daalok did.

"Are you two okay?" he whispered. They both nodded, broad smiles on their faces.

"How did you get out?" Eselle whispered.

He held up his hand and wiggled his fingers. "Magic. And, luckily, after a long wait, a guard who went to silence a wailing prisoner down another hall. I had barely enough time to sneak in here before he returned. Now, stand back, just in case. Let me see if I can do this again."

After the women moved to the center of the cell, Daalok leaned toward the lock. He placed his fingers on its face, and his features tensed in concentration.

Nothing happened for several moments. Eselle frowned and paced a step or two. The more she watched Daalok appear to do nothing, the more she expected a guard to make rounds. They'd had little luck the past couple of months and, even knowing her brother was on his way, she was losing hope things would change.

Eselle flinched when the click sounded. Though it had barely been audible, she still worried it might wake the entire castle. Her heart raced, and she took three large steps to the door. After Daalok pulled it open, she wrapped her arms around him.

"Thank you," she whispered into his ear.

His beaming smile made him look even younger than his twenty years. "Let's go."

"Wait," Eselle said. Both of her friends appeared confused. She pointed to the cell across from them. "We need to check in here." Cristar nodded and followed, but Daalok hesitated. "Trust me."

The women felt along the rough stone wall. After only a couple of minutes, Eselle's fingers slid into an unnatural groove. With the right pressure and push, a small section of the wall slid inward a hair. Her friends stared as Eselle pushed the wall farther back into itself. It moved into a narrow dark space. Before entering, she studied the tunnel in the limited light, reorienting herself with the passage.

A whimper came from behind her, and Eselle turned. Cristar stared at the ground. A small puddle surrounded the woman's feet. Her trousers were soaked along the insides of her legs.

"What happened?" Daalok asked, looking in concern between Cristar and the puddle.

The women gazed at each other while assessing the situation. As part of their preparations, Cristar had explained this and several other details.

"Her water broke," Eselle said. "The baby's coming."

Cristar stood straighter and took a deep breath. Her jaw trembled when she spoke. "This only makes it more important for us to get out of here. I *won't* let my baby be born in a dungeon!"

After a quick nod, Eselle glanced back at Daalok. "Grab one of the torches in the corridor." While he was gone, Eselle pulled away several spiderwebs from the passage. It appeared as though no one had used it in years. Once the young mage returned, Eselle took the torch from him. "Follow me." She slipped into the tunnel.

Her friends seemed torn between eager and reluctant, with a heavy dose of desperation mixed in.

After everyone was inside and they'd pushed the wall section back into place, Eselle shimmied past her friends. It was a challenge getting around Cristar's stomach in the tight passage, but she managed with only a little jostling. She made her way along while Cristar followed and Daalok brought up the rear.

Hopefully, Vorgal didn't know about the tunnels. And if he did, hadn't renovated them too.

Their little procession moved steadily, allowing Cristar to set the pace. A few times they had to stop as Cristar panted through contractions. The moment she thought she could manage again, she insisted they hurry. The woman's labor was coming on stronger. The panting grew heavier and came more frequently the farther they traveled. The tunnel wasn't long, but traversing it was slow going. Eselle couldn't remember how much farther they had to go, but she wanted to get her friend settled as soon as possible.

Eselle handed the torch back to Cristar when they finally reached the end. She searched for the handle. When she found it, the door wouldn't budge.

She motioned to Daalok. "Help me."

Cristar stood back against one wall as the young man shimmied past her. Together, Eselle and Daalok pulled on the wall section. It creaked and slid a little. With some more effort, they opened it enough that Eselle could peer out. As she remembered, the passage opened into a hallway in the basement where several more storage rooms kept emergency provisions. The area was vacant.

After extinguishing the torch, Eselle led the way down the hall and ushered them into one of the side rooms. From what she could tell, nothing had changed in this part of the castle. "We can stay here for a while."

Daalok examined the room, with rows of crates stacked along the walls. "They could notice we're gone any minute and come looking for us, if they're not already. We have to get out of here."

"Look at her." Eselle motioned to Cristar, who was bent over and breathing in short, shallow breaths. "She can't go anywhere. She's having the baby, now."

Daalok stared at the young mother-to-be. His eyes darted across her quivering form. He started to speak, then took a few deep breathes. "All right. What do you need me to do?"

"See if you can find anything in these crates we can use."

The young man nodded and went to work.

Eselle took Cristar's arm and guided her to the ground. "Sit."

Daalok soon returned with empty sacks and a couple of linens to help make Cristar more comfortable. After that, all they could do was settle in and wait for the newest member of their group to arrive.

***

Sitting in the darkened salon, watching for the sun to rise through the large expanse of windows, Kyr forced himself to be patient. The more the sky continued to lighten, the harder it was to keep seated, to keep his knee from bouncing and his fingers from rapping against the wooden armrest.

A bright spot appeared at the top of the distant mountains. Soon, Nikos' plan would be complete. More than anything, he wanted Nikos beside him for what would happen next.

When the first rays of sunlight broke the horizon, he bolted from the chair and headed to the door. His legs wanted to run, but he held himself to a brisk walk. It was time to show the king he had accomplished his mission. He had found and retrieved both the baby and the Enstrin. The king would be overjoyed.

Kyr suppressed his smile once he neared the council chambers. Even though the king had long since disbanded the council, no one had bothered to change the room's name.

Pushing through the doors, Kyr stepped up to the end of the large table. The king, the prince, several members of the military, and some advisers who were occasionally listened to, poured over drawings and blueprints of both the city's and castle's defenses.

The king peered over. "Where have you been? Heldin betrayed us and sided with the Enstrin you were supposed to find for me. You've disappointed me yet again. I believe you remember the terms of our agreement."

Kyr swallowed. Even though he knew The Crypt was no longer a concern, that didn't lessen the fear of the place. Just the thought rattled him.

"Sire," Kyr said, "may I speak with you privately?"

King Vorgal sneered. "No, I believe I'm done with you, Silst," he said with an offhanded wave. The king nodded to Pytre

Skogsmead, the new high commander now that Kyr had been promoted.

While it pleased Kyr his old friend had advanced, he hated that it currently put them at odds. Skogsmead's loyalty remained with the crown, not friends or former recruits.

Skogsmead wore a frown as he stepped away from the opposite end of the table, but didn't hesitate as he advanced toward Kyr. The barest smile crossed the prince's features as he watched.

Kyr ignored both the commander and prince as he focused on the king. "I've upheld my part of our agreement."

The king raised a hand, and the commander stopped. "You've brought me both?"

"Yes, sire."

Vorgal's brows rose. He stepped around the table toward Kyr. "Where are they?"

Studying those gathered, Kyr found no face he particularly trusted, including Skogsmead. Plus, he needed the king alone. Staring directly at Vorgal, meeting the man's eyes, he asked, "May we speak privately?"

The king studied him, openly judging his worth. Eventually, he turned back to the men at the table. "Leave us."

Everyone at the table looked skeptical, but most filed out of the room. Prince Tryllen held his position across from his father, his eyes bright and smile broad.

King Vorgal glared at him with a disgusted expression. "I said to leave us."

"But, father, I—"

"*Leave!*"

The prince flinched and scurried from the room, his face flushed. Whether it was from embarrassment or anger, Kyr couldn't tell, but he also didn't care.

"What do you need to say that you couldn't say in front of others?" King Vorgal stood straighter, lifting his chin with pursed lips.

"Nothing, sire. But this agreement was between the two of us, and what I've done, I've done for you. If it pleases Your Majesty, I'll take you to them now."

"They're in the dungeon?"

"Yes, awaiting your inspection and interrogation."

"Then take me."

King Vorgal Grox strode purposefully beside his lord marshal. Kyr wondered at the man's enthusiasm, whether it was over yet another birth that might or might not be the one he waited for, or whether it was at getting his clutches on one of the two remaining Enstrins. He was certain Vorgal planned on using Eselle as leverage against her brother, in addition to his other more heinous plans for her.

"Why didn't you wake me the moment you arrived last night?" the king asked.

"It was late, sire. I didn't want to disturb you, and the women would still be here in the morning."

"Unless," the king said snidely, "they pulled off another magic trick and escaped you again."

Instead of responding, Kyr ducked his head in shame he didn't feel but knew the monarch would be pleased with. They walked the rest of the way in silence.

Entering the dungeon's corridor, the men were bombarded with pregnant women jumping up and pleading for the king to spare their children. Vorgal's face twitched in disgust before he ignored them and continued toward the only prisoners he cared about.

The closer they got to the end of the corridor, the more it became apparent the last cell was open. Though it appeared secure from a distance, closer inspection showed the latch hadn't fully caught. The cell stood empty.

Kyr didn't dare look at the king. The man would be furious. Luckily, Kyr knew from Nikos that the women were still in the keep. He even knew where. But he couldn't lead the king directly to them and reveal what Nikos had shared with him alone.

"Where are they!" King Vorgal demanded. "You said you had them!"

"I did, sire."

"Then where are they?" Vorgal yelled, holding his hand out to the empty cell. "How could they have escaped you, *again!* You're the most incompetent imbecile I've ever met! I should never have promoted you past shit shoveler, let alone lord marshal!"

"Sire," Kyr tried interrupting, "I think I know—"

"You don't know your ass from your balls!"

The women in the nearby cells fell silent.

As the king's rant continued, consisting of graphic descriptions of what Kyr could do to himself, Kyr stepped away. He crossed the aisle and entered the cell opposite from the abandoned one.

A damp spot of old straw caught his attention. His pulse quickened. With no one else in the cell for days, it could mean only one thing. Cristar had gone into labor. Not yet ready for the king to know, Kyr discreetly kicked some dry straw over the remnants of the puddle before Vorgal noticed it.

He turned his attention to the wall. Feeling along the stones, he heard the king follow him into the cell. He ignored the yelling monarch as he concentrated on finding the right groove. The moment he did, he pressed it, then the stone beside it and revealed the passage. Silence surrounded him as Kyr stepped back.

King Vorgal stared at the opening, then at Kyr. "How did you know about this?"

"I heard stories when I was a kid, then rumors later. When I was stationed here, I investigated them, in case they'd come in handy one day."

"Why didn't you report this?" the king demanded, though his voice eased as his temper seemed to have given way to curiosity.

Kyr shrugged. "If I told anyone, I'd lose the leverage it gave me."

The king smiled faintly. "You may yet be redeemed, Silst. But how do you know the women went this way? If I didn't know about this passage, how would they?"

"The Enstrin grew up here. Kids wander and investigate things. It's likely she knew about the passage. And," he said, walking out of the cell to grab one of the torches off the wall, "there's a torch missing." With that, he held out his torch to where the missing one's sconce stood empty.

Vorgal's face contorted into a dark grin as he examined the passage. "Lead the way, Lord Marshal."

They worked their way through the passage, noticing footprints ahead of them in the thick dust on the floor. At the end, an extinguished torch lay inside the doorway. After opening the secret panel, Kyr put out his own torch and tossed it aside with the other.

Once in the hallway, the king asked, "Where now, Lord Marshal?"

Before Kyr could reply, a faint noise came from down the hall. They both turned toward it, but it didn't come again. Kyr took a steadying breath. He knew what that sound was. He'd waited for this moment for years, and it had finally arrived. That was why he hadn't put the women in the cell with the secret passage. He didn't want them to escape too quickly and leave the castle before he and the king found them. Nikos promised this would happen, and he'd been right. Everything Kyr waited for, worked toward, sacrificed for, lay right down the hallway.

Vorgal took off down the passage.

Kyr risked grabbing the man's sleeve. As he expected, the king threw him a murderous glare that Kyr had dared touch him.

"Sire. I promised you the women and, more importantly, the child. Let me see this through to the end and deliver the child to you personally. Let me go in after it."

The king glanced skeptically at the door ahead but nodded. "Very well, Lord Marshal. Bring me the child."

CHAPTER THIRTY-SIX

You were right. It's a boy," Eselle said, her voice quivering with joy.

She laid the infant down on Cristar's chest. Cristar ran her fingers down each little limb, smiling as Eselle wiped the baby down. Deep brown eyes gazed back at them, and his arms moved awkwardly as he stretched.

"What now?" Cristar asked a while later when she finished feeding her son. "I won't let them hurt him." She ran her fingers gently across the boy's head, with its light sprinkling of damp, dark hair.

Daalok caressed one of the boy's little feet. "We won't let that happen."

"You have to take him." Cristar peered back and forth between them. "You have to get him out of here." She bundled the newborn in her jerkin, originally Klaasen's. He fussed at the sudden movements, cried out a few times as his mother held him up to Eselle. "I'm too tired to travel quickly. I'd only slow you down. You have to save him."

As exhausted as Cristar was, Eselle had little difficulty pressing the baby back to her chest.

"We'll protect him," Eselle said, "I promise, but we need a plan. I remember a few more passages, but not enough to get us out. And we shouldn't blindly wander the castle in hopes of escaping."

"You wouldn't make it past the door to this room," said a deep voice behind them.

Eselle tensed at his words. She rose to shield her friends. Kyr stood in the doorway with his sword drawn.

"So now you're planning to kill a baby?" Her heart ached that it had come to this, that they were on opposite sides of this confrontation.

"I'll do anything necessary to achieve my goal." He stepped into the room. Despite his words, he seemed distracted. He wore a curious expression as he watched the young mother and her child.

"Take him!" Cristar's voice sounded shrill as she shoved the baby into Daalok's hands. "Get him to safety!"

Daalok gripped the baby tightly, standing while eyeing the doorway behind the lord marshal. The baby made soft noises and flailed his arms. Daalok put a hand on the boy's chest, and he calmed.

"Do you really think you can get past me, little mage?" Kyr regarded the infant for another moment before focusing on his opponent.

"You might be surprised." It would have been more convincing if Daalok's voice hadn't faltered, but Eselle was proud of him for trying.

"How did you find us?" Eselle asked.

"You're not the only one with secrets."

King Vorgal entered the room behind Kyr. "Let me see this baby."

Eselle's hands clenched. Heat spread through her as she recognized the man who had murdered her family. She took a step toward him, for the first time in her life ready to kill. Cristar gave a soft cry behind her, and Eselle stopped. Gazing behind her, she saw her friend's worried brow and teary eyes. Eselle was unarmed and facing two men with swords. Neither of her friends were fighters, and she couldn't take both men on her own.

King Vorgal surveyed the room before his eyes settled on Cristar's infant. "Bring him to me." He waved his man forward.

The moment Kyr moved, Eselle stepped into his path.

With a sharp breath, he clenched his jaw. "Move."

"No. I won't let you hurt them."

"I'll go through you if I have to."

"I don't doubt that." Eselle braced herself. If only she had a weapon. "But you know I can't stand aside and watch you hurt my friends."

"Hurt them?" The lord marshal gave a dark chuckle. He spun his sword in his hand, then gripped it tightly. "I don't plan to hurt them. I plan to kill them."

Hearing him say it, seeing his determined features, Eselle's stomach knotted. She hated that she had ever considered him for an ally.

She prepared to throw herself at him if he advanced again. If she could distract Kyr, Daalok could slip past him and then have only Vorgal to deal with.

The king sneered. "Stop wasting time, Lord Marshal, and bring me the baby!"

"Yes, Your Majesty." Kyr's jaw clenched tighter, and he advanced. A savage expression overtook his rugged features.

Eselle braced herself. When he swung, she ducked the sword and slid sideways, hoping to draw him away from her friends. He turned toward her, and she stepped back. Kyr thrust in the other direction, setting the sword in front of Daalok's face, preventing the young man from slipping past him.

"I don't think so." Kyr pressed the sword against Daalok's chest as the young man backed up.

Eselle rushed Kyr's side. He shifted his attention and swept a dagger before her. The blade flew low, barely shy of her abdomen.

Cristar steadied herself against the wall.

Before Eselle lost Kyr's attention, she charged him, expecting him to block. Instead, he dodged and sliced across her forearm with the dagger. She didn't feel pain, but her sleeve gained a long slice across it. When Daalok made another move around Kyr, the lord marshal drove him off again. He kept the mage penned at the back of the room. Eselle used the distraction to kick the dagger from his hand. It flew behind him and slid toward the king's feet.

"You won't get my son," Cristar snarled, rushing the lord marshal. She launched herself onto his back and wrapped her arms around his neck. Kyr tried twisting out of her grip. The desperate mother was ferocious, yanking back on her opponent's throat.

"Get off," he demanded, already sounding hoarse from Cristar's efforts. He nearly pulled one of her hands free, but she jerked sideways and threw him off balance. "Get her off me! Before I have to do something drastic!"

"Kill her!" King Vorgal yelled. "Or do I have to handle this myself!" He pulled his sword.

Daalok tried to duck around his opponent, but Kyr thrust forward, sending Cristar hurtling over his shoulder and down onto her back. She let out a loud groan.

Eselle dashed in. Kyr dropped down and spun, sweeping her legs out from under her, and thrust her across the room. She slammed into a load of crates. Stabbing pain shot through her shoulder and arm. She crumpled to the floor with a gasping breath. After shaking her head clear, she tightened her hold on the dagger she slipped from Kyr as she flew past him.

Kyr stood over Cristar, his sword tip resting on her shoulder. Daalok had stopped in his tracks, his eyes full of horror.

"Don't move," Kyr said, focused on Daalok. The young man only stared. "Hand him over."

"Don't worry about me," Cristar said fiercely. "Get my son out of here."

Daalok's eyes darted from one person to the next. Catching her breath, Eselle rose on unsteady legs. Despite her growing fatigue, she felt energized, her blood pumped powerfully.

The king stood at the door, appearing simultaneously frustrated and amused.

"I'm not playing, little mage," Kyr said.

Eselle snatched an empty sack from a nearby crate, then hurled it at the lord marshal's head. He instinctively jerked his arm up to protect himself. When the sword moved, Cristar rolled away and scooted back to the wall. Pulling the sack free, Kyr sneered. The mage had once again tried to sneak past. Kyr moved to place himself in Daalok's way.

Daalok glared. "I won't let you hurt him."

"It's time, and I'm out of patience. *Give him to me!*"

"*No!*"

The baby wailed.

Daalok threw out his free hand toward a stack of crates. His lips moved faintly. Several crates rattled. Everyone in the room stopped to watch. The top crate shook and shimmied. It fell off the stack and hit the ground. Several side planks cracked on impact, but the thing remained intact. Daalok cringed.

Kyr chuckled. "Care to try that again?"

The lord marshal's sword flew. It sliced chunks out of Daalok's clothing as he dodged, surprisingly spry.

Kyr could easily kill Daalok. Why is he toying with him?

Maybe he wanted Daalok to give up the baby willingly. Or perhaps Kyr just wanted to torment someone today.

Eselle would love to drive her dagger into the king's eye, but doubted she could manage it. Kyr's back, however, was exposed. Eselle bolted toward him.

Kyr ducked and spun around, kicking her in the stomach. She slammed into Cristar. Both women toppled to the ground. The dagger flew from Eselle's hand and skittered across the stone floor.

"Give me the baby!" the king yelled.

"No!" Cristar tried to extricate herself from Eselle. "Get my son out of here!"

Daalok glanced at his friends. Holding the baby against his chest, he edged along the wall.

Eselle swayed when she tried standing.

"What now, little mage?" Kyr taunted. He made a display of swinging the sword at Daalok, then thrust forward. Daalok leaped sideways and slid farther along the wall. "You can't even save yourself, let alone that little screamer."

Daalok tightened his hold on the wailing baby and rushed to the side. Before he cleared the lord marshal, the sword swept up inches from his face.

"You have *nowhere* to run," Kyr snarled. "Give me the baby!" His jaw muscles quivered, and the veins in his neck protruded.

"Stop playing around, Silst," Vorgal ordered. "Kill him and bring me the whelp."

Eselle found the dagger caught in the crate Daalok toppled. She scrambled around Cristar and dove for it.

Kyr's chainmail would protect his torso, and striking a limb wouldn't stop him. Eselle focused on his throat. With the spaulders, she needed to come in at an angle.

"What are you doing?" Kyr demanded. His eyes grew wider, brighter for a moment, as he stared at Daalok. He raised his sword high. *"You can't escape the past, little mage!"*

Clutching the dagger tight, Eselle charged.

Kyr took a mighty swing at Daalok and the boy.

A shimmering portal opened.

The blade began its downward swing.

Daalok jumped through the portal, taking the boy with him.

But not before Eselle saw Kyr's blade slice completely across the baby's left shoulder, dipping down toward the front as it met his tiny bicep.

***

Sixteen Years Old

The man examined the house one last time, making certain he had everything he needed. While packing the mask he'd stitched together, he asked, "Are you ready?"

"Ready as I'll ever be." The boy pulled his pack across his shoulders as he glanced at the sewn leather. "I still don't understand why you made that hideous thing."

"One day, the king will get a good look at my face. When he does, I don't want him to recognize me and realize what's happening. Trust me, it's important."

"Are you sure about this?" the boy asked, his voice tinged with uncertainty. "Sure this is the only way?"

The man hefted his own pack and met the boy's eyes. "I'm sure."

"But what if I can't do it? What if they ask too much?"

The older man wished he could help the lad. "I won't lie to you. You have countless horrible days ahead, and nightmares aplenty. I've told you everything I know, but it'll still be the toughest thing you'll ever face. There will be times you'll want to quit, want to rush to the end. But you *must* be patient, see it through, finish this."

"But you know what I'll be facing, the things I'll have to do, especially to rise high enough to be there at the end."

"I do. But I also know you. And that's why I know you'll survive this. You're a good man, better than anyone I've ever met," he said, tapping the boy's chest, "especially to sacrifice so much for others."

"What if I'm not me when this is done? What if this changes me too much, so much I won't want to finish this?"

"It won't. I know it won't."

"No, you don't," the young man insisted. "You don't actually know if I'll succeed."

The older man grabbed hold of his companion's arms. "I do know. The Protector wouldn't have given us this opportunity if there wasn't a chance of succeeding." It pained him to see the boy's tragic, unconvinced eyes. "More than anything else, I know *you*. You're stronger than anyone I've ever met, and you have a good heart. You'll have to hide it away for many years, but it will be there when you need it. When the time comes, you'll kill Vorgal. You'll save everyone. But you must be patient, and strong, and wait for the right moment."

The young man sighed and nodded. "I hope you're right. Thanks, Nikos."

"Now off with you. I'll meet you again soon. But remember, we won't know each other then, so pretend we're meeting for the first time." The young man seemed somewhat steadier. "And when next we meet after that, remember that you really won't know me. I'll still be going by Daalok then, so don't slip up."

"I won't."

"And don't forget. I wasn't as capable with my magic back then, so you'll have to push me."

The boy nodded. "I remember. You would cast best when you didn't have time to think, when you were frightened, and your life depended on it."

"Yes. The more you frighten me, the better chance I'll have casting correctly. But the others will try to stop you, try to protect me, and that will give me hope. You can't let them." The young man seemed resolute, focused. "That'll be the hardest part, but you can't let them distract you. We must get through the portal before you go after Vorgal."

The young man nodded. "And you're certain they won't kill him before we're through?"

"We're here aren't we? No matter what they do, don't let them split your focus."

They'd gone over everything countless times over the years, but he suddenly couldn't stop talking. He wanted to keep the boy with him, but it was time. He'd done everything he could to prepare the lad, and the boy had done everything asked of him. He was ready. They were both ready, but it was more difficult to part than Nikos had anticipated. Even knowing they would eventually see each other again.

After closing up the house, they stood at the edge of the lane. The only thing left was to say goodbye.

He couldn't do it. This was his son, the boy he had raised since birth, heading to the most dangerous place in the realm. Instead, he pulled the boy down into a hug. The young man held him firmly before they separated. Having to look up at his younger companion, Nikos was as amazed as always at how tall the boy had grown. His mother had been significantly shorter and would only have reached the young man's shoulders. Nikos was barely past those broad shoulders himself.

"See you," the young man said.

They each headed down a different direction of the path. After a moment, Nikos turned to watch his companion affectionately. "Kyr."

The young man stopped and turned around. "Yeah?"

With a fond smile, Nikos yelled across the distance. "I love you, boy."

Kyr returned the smile. "Love you too, little mage."

***

Seeing Kyr's blade slice through the infant's arm shocked Eselle. She jerked to a halt, nearly stumbling, before she made it halfway across the room. With Daalok and the boy gone, she stared at Kyr, remembering the sight of his own left shoulder. *I did that to myself, actually,* echoed in her head. *. . . . it was an accident. An incredibly stupid one.*

Kyr stood frozen at the end of his swing, one leg braced in its forward position and his blade inches above the floor. His eyes were closed, and sweat glistened across his easing features as he took steady breaths.

"Finally," he muttered.

Eselle's attention was torn between the motionless lord marshal and the hyperventilating woman beside her. Cristar had just witnessed her son sliced with a blade larger than he was and then seemingly disappear from existence. *What did Daalok do with that portal?*

"Where did he go?!"

Eselle jumped at Vorgal's outburst.

Kyr's features twisted into a snarl as his head whipped around toward Vorgal. His body tensed. He pushed off and spun, his arm swinging around in a powerful backhanded arc.

Vorgal's eyes bulged, watching the blade rush at him. He staggered backward enough that the blade only grazed his throat. Blood poured from the slice across his neck and down into his doublet.

Eselle shivered in anticipation.

Kyr stalked the monarch. "He took me to safety in the one place you'd never think to look, and certainly couldn't follow."

With his hand clamped over his throat, the king glared at Kyr. "What are you talking about? This is treason. I'll have you—"

Kyr swung his blade upward toward Vorgal's torso. The king jumped backward again. With a grumble, he readied himself, holding his sword high. He released his throat, now smeared with blood. Eselle regretted that Kyr's blade hadn't struck deeply enough.

Holding her dagger ready, she watched as the lord marshal pulled another dagger from behind him and squared off with the king. His expression was calm, focused. The king's lips curled, and his brow tensed.

With a growl, Vorgal swung. Kyr deflected it and countered. The king shifted away from the wall, immediately blocking another strike, but took a slash across the arm from Kyr's dagger. The king swept to the side, moving into the center of the room. Blood continued slowly dripping down his throat.

From the corner of Eselle's eye, she caught movement.

Cristar stalked toward the fighting pair, her features twisted as she glared at Kyr. *"What did you do to my baby?"*

Before the woman was halfway to him, Eselle grabbed her around the waist, pulling her off her feet and hauling her away from the combatants.

"Stop," Eselle said.

Cristar had never seen Daalok's portal, didn't know about the incident with the stag, how it had reappeared. She also hadn't seen Kyr's shoulder. When they patched him up previously, both Eselle and Daalok agreed it wasn't safe to let the woman near him. Now, she realized, since Kyr had apparently known the truth all along, Cristar was probably the safest of them all where he was concerned.

"Your baby is fine," Eselle said. "Daalok took him to safety. I promise, he's fine."

The woman settled only slightly as she glared at the lord marshal. Tears spilled from her eyes. "Where is he?" A quiver filled her voice. Eselle held her tightly while watching the battle.

The king lunged at Kyr's midsection. Kyr turned and the sword slid across his chainmail while he slashed the king across the ribs. Vorgal, unlike the leader of his army, didn't wear chainmail. The sword tore a long slash through the side of the man's golden doublet. The king stumbled sideways, caught himself, and took a step back.

Both men breathed heavily.

After settling Cristar against the wall, Eselle stood at the edge of the fight. She wanted to help eliminate Vorgal, but Kyr had the man so fully engaged, she worried she'd get in his way.

The king managed a couple of good blows, but took more. Kyr's chainmail protected him significantly, but a cut appeared at the side of his neck. It was small, not much more than he could have managed shaving, but Eselle grimaced seeing it. Though the king dodged the worst of the strikes, blood seeped through multiple tears in his clothes.

King Vorgal ducked a swing, then drove into Kyr. The maneuver caught the lord marshal by surprise and both men fell to the ground. As they hit, Vorgal reached out for Kyr's sword hand. Still gripping the pommel, Kyr punched upward, striking the king across the cheekbone. Vorgal's head snapped back, but he didn't stop.

He slammed the pommel of his sword down into Kyr's shoulder. It hit just below Kyr's spaulder, where Eselle had cut him only a week prior. He jerked, and his features clenched.

Kyr drove his dagger up toward the king's chest. Vorgal had to drop his sword to catch Kyr's wrist before the blade struck.

Stepping behind Vorgal, Eselle plunged the dagger into his back. Vorgal cried out.

The satisfaction that flooded through her was short lived.

Vorgal scrambled away from Kyr and into Eselle. She had to backup to prevent him from knocking her over.

Once clear, Kyr burst up off the ground and kicked the king in the chest.

Vorgal stumbled back, jerked around, and knocked Eselle away with an elbow to the chest. He grabbed for her. She flinched away. Blood seeped from his throat, across his chest, down an arm and a leg. He spat blood.

An arm wrapped around the monarch from behind and plunged a dagger into his throat. It sliced sideways through his neck, cutting deep. Vorgal dropped to the ground, revealing Kyr standing behind him, the bloody dagger in one hand and his sword in the other.

CHAPTER THIRTY-SEVEN

Soldiers rushed into the room, swords in hand. Four appeared to be standard armsmen, but the fifth looked a decade older and wore the armor of the higher ranks.

Eselle snatched up the king's sword. Uncertain which side the lord marshal would take, she prepared for the worst. Being Cristar's son didn't mean his loyalties stood with them. Eselle stepped back, putting more distance between herself and Kyr, while also placing herself between the newcomers and Cristar.

The lead soldier spotted Vorgal's corpse on the floor, blood pooling around him. "They killed the king!" He motioned to the soldiers behind him, and they advanced.

"Stand down!" Kyr ordered, turning around.

The old soldier's eyes grew wide seeing the blood splattered across Kyr's weapons and chainmail. "What have you done, boy?" His expression turned confused before he scowled. "I wondered why you wanted the king alone. Arrest him." He waved the soldiers forward.

None of the armsmen moved. Their eyes darted between their superiors.

"But, Commander Skogsmead," one of them said hesitantly, "he's the lord marshal."

The commander snarled over his shoulder. "And he assassinated the king! Arrest him!"

A couple of the men shifted forward. "Sir," one of them said, keeping his eyes on Kyr's insignia as he spoke, "if you would please come with us."

Kyr set himself. Eselle gripped the sword tighter, glancing between soldiers. Should she help Kyr or get Cristar to safety?

"What are you doing?" The commander shook his head, his exasperation heavy. "Even if those two know how to fight, you're outnumbered. And if they don't, this could get ugly."

"Pytre," Kyr said, "you of all people should know I never back down from a fight."

"I do. And I'm sorry it's come to this. I really did like you, lad."

The four armsmen stood their ground, but one began a slow fidget that quickly spread to the man beside him. Eselle backed up to Cristar's side. Tears glistened on the woman's cheeks. She held one of Kyr's fallen daggers with a white-knuckled grip and glared at his back.

"Take the women too," the commander said. "I'll be securing the prince. Report to me once they're in the dungeon." With a nod to Kyr, Commander Skogsmead left the storeroom.

The first armsman advanced, and the lord marshal threw his dagger. It embedded in the man's throat, sending him to his knees. Kyr spun, grabbed the wrist of a second armsman in an upward movement and plunged his sword through the man's stomach.

Seeing the quick dispatches, Eselle hoped the soldiers could at least detain Kyr while she and Cristar slipped away. She was torn on what fate she wanted for him—between their tormentor of the past couple of months and the person she recently discovered him to be, the man she saw glimpses of occasionally.

Neither armsman paid attention to the women as they focused on detaining their lord marshal. Eselle pulled Cristar to the side. "We need to leave."

Cristar glared at the man she thought hurt her son, but she let Eselle guide her toward the doorway.

As the women hustled, Kyr singlehandedly fought against the remaining soldiers.

Why am I even worried? He can handle them.

One of the soldiers flew against the wall in front of them. Eselle pulled up short, holding Cristar behind her. The man shook himself back to his senses and rushed Kyr. Eselle tugged Cristar along.

But he's Cristar's son.

She'd protected his infant self for two months. It was difficult to stop.

Kyr finished off the last two soldiers—a sword in the back for one and a dagger thrust into the chest for the other.

As he knelt over the final man, Eselle motioned Cristar to stay put. She lifted her sword and stepped up behind Kyr, pressing the point against his back.

"Toss the dagger," she said.

With a sigh, he pulled the dagger from the man's chest and tossed it aside. One of the armsmen had knocked his sword from his hand, so it lay several paces beyond him. Not in easy reach, but Eselle was still uncomfortable with the distance, given the man's skill set.

Kyr began to rise.

Eselle pressed the sword harder against his back. "Stay on your knees, don't turn around."

He knelt back down beside the corpse of the last armsman he killed, raising his hands to show they were empty. "We need to leave. More guards will arrive soon, and I have a plan for taking the castle that—"

"Taking the castle?" Eselle asked. "So now you want to be king?"

"No." His voice grew firmer. "I want your brother to be king. Or you, for that matter. I don't care who takes the crown, as long as it's not Vorgal or his horrendous offspring."

An onslaught of questions filled Eselle's mind. She didn't know which to ask first, but she couldn't trust Kyr yet, not given everything he'd put them through.

"You knew this would happen," she said.

Kyr turned his head to watch her silently, studying her features.

She tapped her left shoulder. "Did that to yourself?"

His features settled, and he turned back around. "Yes. But we need to leave. I have to—"

"How?"

"Nikos told me. We have to—"

"The high mage, Nikos Klaskil?"

"Yes. But you knew him as Daalok Borwin."

"What?"

"What are you talking about?" Cristar asked.

With a heavy breath, the lord marshal turned his head slightly. It wasn't enough to see either woman, but enough for Eselle to see the resolve in his features. "There's too much to explain, and your brother's army is nearly here. Once he arrives, there will be bloodshed, a lot of it. I can hand him this castle without a drop spilled. Or, at least, very little. But if Skogsmead gets too far ahead, we may lose that chance."

"Why should we believe you?" Eselle asked.

"I have no proof to offer. Nothing but my word and recent actions."

"Recent actions?" Cristar growled. She lunged past Eselle. "You attacked my son! My baby! I'll—"

Eselle grabbed her mere inches from her target.

"Let me go!" Fresh tears covered Cristar's cheeks. Eselle pulled her into a half hug. Cristar fumed but allowed it.

Kyr turned toward them, remaining in place on his knees. His face suggested he might have let Cristar take a few swings before defending himself.

"We don't have time for this." Kyr's expression turned desperate. It seemed out of place on him, and a shiver ran down Eselle's spine. "We must leave. Your brother will be here soon, if he isn't already. Please, I knew I'd go after Vorgal and your brother would arrive. I arranged for the castle to be handed over as peacefully as possible, but that won't happen if I don't give orders to certain people. The troops are currently operating on Vorgal's last orders, and Skogsmead is about to hand the crown to Tryllen, who will hold to those orders."

When both women hesitated, Kyr's face hardened, everything else dripping away. He rose with his previous authority. "Stab me if you like, but I'm leaving." He grabbed his fallen daggers and sword, then rushed for the door.

The sudden return to the man he'd been surprised Eselle, enough that she didn't even consider stopping him. Though she should have been more surprised seeing the compliant man he'd been for the past few moments.

Eselle studied the sword in her hand. Other than to thrust, she has no clue how to use it. She dropped it and pulled a dagger from the belt of the nearest corpse. Grabbing Cristar's hand, she pulled the woman along as they ran after the lord marshal.

By the time they reached the hallway, Kyr had disappeared around the far corner. Eselle struggled to keep up, having to hustle Cristar along. The mourning mother kept slowing. Whether from physical or emotional fatigue, Eselle didn't know.

Eselle worried each time she lost sight of Kyr. After turning a corner a level away from the ground floor, they found him not far ahead. Two other soldiers rushed toward him. Eselle recognized Kyr's second by the man's strikingly pale eyes. The other soldier, a corporal, she'd never seen before. While she and Cristar closed the distance, the men reached each other and stopped to speak.

". . . ran by," the captain said as Eselle and Cristar drew within hearing distance. "Since he wasn't part of the plan, I sent some soldiers after him, then came to check on you. What happened?"

"It's a long story." Kyr glanced back at the women briefly. "Is Tryllen secured?"

"Yes. We put him in the guardhouse."

"Good. Get word to the city captain. Springtime is still in effect."

The captain smiled, then nodded once. "It's a beautiful spring day, Lord Marshal." He turned to the man beside him. "You know what to do."

With a nod to each of his superiors, the corporal said, "Yes, sirs," and rushed back the way he'd come.

"In the meantime," the captain, said, "your troops will be ready for inspection in the bailey."

Kyr nodded. "Good. I'm heading there now. What's the situation outside?"

"The Heldin troops arrived a short while ago, being led by Tavith Enstrin. Fighting has commenced outside the city."

Eselle's heart swelled at mention of her brother arriving.

Kyr nodded sharply.

"Unless you need me, sir, I'll help locate and contain Commander Skogsmead before he realizes where the boy is."

"I would appreciate that, Captain. Be careful."

"You too." The blond captain hustled down the hall the corporal had taken.

Eselle stared at Kyr. "It's nearly winter. Why are you talking about spring?"

"I was telling him that I completed my part of the plan, and we're ready for the next phase."

"There are others involved?" Eselle never suspected anyone in the castle might side with them.

"Yes."

"Why springtime?"

"It's a time of rebirth."

"And the next part of the plan is a troop inspection?"

"Not exactly." He walked away, keeping a brisk pace.

Before Eselle caught up, Cristar flew by her, dagger in hand. With a gasp, Eselle rushed behind her. Cristar leaped for Kyr's back. He turned at the last moment and caught her wrist. Spinning her around, he held her securely with her back to him and grabbed the dagger from her hand.

"Let me go!" Cristar hollered. "You hurt my baby!" Cristar tried yanking free from his grip, but he held tight.

"Calm down," Kyr said firmly. "Your baby is fine." Sad eyes gazed down at the woman.

"Give her to me," Eselle said, holding out her arms toward Cristar. "There's something you need to know."

Cristar features twisted in anger. Once she calmed and stopped struggling, Kyr slowly released her. Eselle tried to hug her friend, but Cristar stepped away from them both with a scowl.

Eselle turned to Kyr. "Show her."

He watched the two of them before finally settling on Eselle. "She doesn't need to know."

"Yes, she does. You owe her that much."

"Show me what?" Cristar asked, her voice gravelly.

Kyr ignored her as his gaze intensified, boring into Eselle. "Given everything that's happened the past couple of months, would you want to know?"

Eselle remained silent while considering. Cristar was distraught after losing her baby to the unknown. Would she really want to discover the man who ruthlessly chased them was that same baby? And had known all along what he was doing? Even if he had ultimately saved them?

"At least wait until the rest of this is over," Kyr said, "until things settle down and tempers wane."

Watching him for signs of deceit, Eselle finally relented. "Fine. But you *will* tell her."

He dropped his eyes with a glower. "You would have to pull out my fingernails to make that happen, but I can't stop you from telling her yourself."

"Shut up!" Cristar's face flushed red with an array of emotions. "Both of you, stop talking."

Eselle flinched, having never heard the young woman sound so harsh. All she could do was stare.

"I don't care what either of you do, but I need to find my son." Cristar's limbs shook with raw emotion. "Daalok mentioned experimenting with portals. I need to find out where that one went."

The lump in Eselle's throat became unbearable. She stepped forward and hugged Cristar tight. The woman didn't fight her this time. "We'll find him. Until then, trust that Daalok is taking good care of him."

Cristar spoke into Eselle's shoulder, holding her tight. "It's not the same. I'm his mother, I need to protect him."

Eselle wiped her eyes with one hand while holding Cristar with the other. She peered up at Kyr as she spoke. "We'll get him back for you." His own eyes glistened, but he blinked it away.

"Until then, there's a battle brewing outside, so we need to take care of ourselves."

"What if he's somewhere in the castle?" Cristar asked. "We have to look." She pulled away from Eselle and started to walk off.

Kyr put his arm out to block her.

The glare Cristar turned on him made Eselle cringe. "Out of my way." It was the same glare Eselle had seen from Kyr several times.

The lord marshal continued to block her. "It's too dangerous to go running around the castle. You two need to stay with me, and I need to get to the bailey."

"I'm not going—"

"He's right," Eselle said. "And Daalok wouldn't have been stupid enough to stay in the castle. He would have gotten them out of here."

"But—"

"Trust me," Eselle said. "Please. Trust Daalok. Even if they're still here, he'll take care of your son and find us when he can."

Cristar's strained features, the dark circles under bloodshot eyes, seemed suddenly profound. She nodded.

They resumed their walk in silence, taking a couple hallways, a few turns, ascending a flight of stairs.

It didn't take long for the curiosity to overwhelm Eselle. "How is any of this possible? How are you here?"

The lord marshal gave a quick meaningful nod to Cristar as she walked behind them. "That's a story for another time, but suffice to say, Nikos has been planning for this for the last twenty-eight years. He prepared me well."

Eselle's stomach dropped. "Twenty-eight years? He knew all that time what would happen?"

"Yes." Kyr watched the corridors ahead. They were moving up another flight as several soldiers rounded the corner and passed them, heading down into the lower levels.

Eselle struggled to hold herself in check. Her fists trembled, and she felt hot, despite the coolness of the stone keep. "He knew what would happen when Vorgal took power." She spoke louder than she'd intended. "Why didn't he stop Vorgal sooner, before he slaughtered my family?" She had told Daalok her entire story, in excruciating detail, and he did nothing to stop it.

"He let my family be butchered!" Eselle couldn't stop herself. The fact that the rightful recipient of her anger was long gone only made it worse.

"He couldn't save them. No one could."

"You could," she accused, shoving Kyr's back with both hands.

He stumbled half a step but caught himself, then glared back at her as she stepped up beside him.

"You both knew what would happen, and you let it. You sat back while my family was massacred. You let them die!"

She managed a single punch to his jaw before he grabbed the front of her tunic with both hands and pushed her against the stairwell wall. Cristar lunged forward with her dagger raised. Kyr backhanded the blade from her grip. Eselle tried to pull him loose, but he held her securely.

"We don't have time for this," Kyr said, his jaw tight once again. "But if you must know, it broke Nikos' heart not to intercede. He cried the night it happened. Even though word hadn't spread yet about the massacre, he knew when it was happening. So we lit candles for the fallen, for your family and everyone else who died that night. Believe me, I know how it feels." His voice grew fiercer the more he spoke. "I wanted to save my own father, but Nikos said it was too risky, that we couldn't change anything. So, again, instead of helping, we stood by helplessly and lit a candle the night he died.

"I can't count the number of times I wanted to help, to end this, but I couldn't. Even after Huln killed Nikos to spite me, after he died in my arms, I kept to Nikos' plan because he was right. You have no idea what Nikos—Daalok—what *I,* sacrificed for this to work, to save everyone from the monster."

Eselle stood motionless for a stunned moment while he stormed off up the stairs and turned the corner.

Cristar watched in silence before she rushed across the steps to snatch up her dagger. "What was that about?"

"I'll explain later," Eselle mumbled.

When they reached him, Eselle stepped in alongside Kyr. He looked angry, focused, and more than a little scary.

"I'm sorry." She rubbed her knuckles as he remained silent. "Nikos meant a lot to you, didn't he?" It felt weird calling him by that name, but that's who Daalok had been to Kyr.

"For better or worse, he raised me and made me who I am."

CHAPTER THIRTY-EIGHT

The last of the troops had fallen into place by the time Eselle and her companions reached the bailey. Eyeing the soldiers arranged in units and numbering well into the hundreds, Eselle prayed Kyr's plan was real. If the battle her brother expected occurred, thousands would die.

A loud, deep horn bellowed. It blew repeatedly—one long tone, followed by three quick bursts—growing fainter the more it sounded. Eselle had heard of these horns through her studies, troops used them as signals, but she never learned their meanings. Now she was curious.

Eselle felt confident her brother and his allies, backed by Heldin's troops, could defeat Vahean's city guard. The castle's troops spread out before her though, while fewer in number, were considerably more formidable. With Vistralou's fortifications they could easily hold the castle until Grosgril's guard arrived. Unless, either Kyr told the truth, and he handed over the castle, or Tavith managed to get someone inside to open both portcullises.

She scanned the bailey, the gatehouse, anywhere she thought their allies might conceal themselves, but found nothing. But then, if they were any good, they wouldn't be seen.

The ramparts stood empty. Granted, she could only see a small portion of the walls, but there should have been a good number of men arming the battlements, prepping the hoardings, patrolling. The walls should be abuzz with activity. Instead, it seemed every soldier within the castle stood in the bailey, waiting to be inspected by the lord marshal.

Eselle and Cristar followed Kyr to the far side of the courtyard, stopping near the closed inner portcullis.

Kyr motioned Eselle and Cristar to the side of the stable. "Wait here."

He started to walk off, but a curly-haired young man jogged up to him. A ragged scar ran along the side of the man's face. "Comma—I mean, Lord Marshal, where's Josah?"

"A change in plans."

After a glance at the gathered troops, the young man frowned. "What happened?"

"Don't worry. Skogsmead caused a little ruckus, so Josah is helping secure him. Until he returns, can you do me a favor?"

The young man held his frown, but nodded.

"Can you take care of these ladies for me?" Kyr motioned toward Eselle and Cristar. "Keep them safe?"

The young man nodded again, appearing no less dire.

"Stop worrying," Kyr said. "He'll be fine. Until then, this is Eselle and Cristar." He guided the man toward them. "Ladies, this is Maksin. I'd say you can trust him as you'd trust me, but I don't think that would be in his favor. So, trust him as you'd trust each other. He's one of the most honorable people in the castle."

As they said their greetings, Kyr walked off.

Before he was out of earshot, two armsmen approached, herding a pair of commoners ahead of them. The men were mussed and dressed like stable hands.

"Lord Marshal," one of the armsmen said. "We found these two in the gatehouse, trying to open the gates."

Kyr studied them briefly, then waved them away. "Secure them for now. I'll deal with them later."

Eselle's blood chilled as the soldiers escorted the men toward the keep. If Kyr was lying, and he didn't open the castle, Tavith's plan had just had a horrible setback. Grosgril's reinforcements couldn't be more than a few days off. If her brother's men couldn't breach for a quick victory, their troops would have to take Vistralou the most difficult way possible. And fast.

Her more immediate concern, however, had reached his destination. Kyr took his position, his eyes bright as he stood straight. He clasped his hands behind his back while examining his troops. Eselle hoped her trust was well-placed, and they hadn't traded one monster for another.

Kyr's voice filled the bailey. "I'm sure everyone has heard by now that there's an army approaching. Right now, they're engaged with Vahean's city guard." None of the soldiers seemed surprised. "What I'm certain none of you know yet is that the king was assassinated." That garnered gasps from more than half the troops and wide eyes from everyone. Kyr held up his hand. "Attention!" he bellowed above the clamor. "It shouldn't be all that surprising, given our late king's demeanor. We all knew it would happen eventually.

"As many of you know, before Vorgal Grox another house ruled Likalsta. The Enstrins. With Vorgal Grox gone, the throne will return to them. From this moment forward, we serve the new king, without question, without hesitation. Is that understood?" He scanned the troops as they digested his news.

Striding to the gates, Kyr drew his sword but kept it lowered at his side. Once there, he turned back to the soldiers.

"King Tavith Enstrin will enter the castle shortly," the lord marshal said. "Look sharp!" Every soldier stood straighter, more alert, despite any misgivings they might suffer.

Hearing his acknowledgment of her brother's claim, a weight lessened inside Eselle. It didn't entirely diminish, and wouldn't until Tavith and his troops arrived safely inside the castle, but it eased enough to feel true hope.

Turning to the soldiers at the wall, Kyr called out, "Open the gates!" The soldiers manning the gatehouse looked leery, but after a glare from the highest-ranking soldier in Likalsta, rushed into the gatehouse to follow orders.

Eselle watched as the portcullis slowly rose. Each inch opening beneath it made her heart lighten.

Kyr stood immediately before the iron gate. When it reached his knees, it stopped. Flashing a glare at the gatehouse, Kyr jerked sideways. An arrow suddenly protruded from one of his leather spaulders. Eselle gasped, along with two other voices on either side of her.

"That'll be enough orders from you, boy," a loud, grumbling voice yelled.

The soldiers standing in formation shifted, some grabbing their swords, others bracing themselves and glancing around. Kyr stared up at the ramparts while pulling the arrow from his armor.

"You know me well enough to know that's where I meant to hit you." The voice came from somewhere above where Eselle and her companions stood. "This next shot is aimed at your head. So, you'd do well to listen to what the new king has to say."

Examining the wall, Eselle found the armored soldier who had confronted Kyr in the storage room. His uniform had blood splashed across parts of it, but he moved as if it wasn't his own. Beside him stood a dark-haired young man who appeared to be in his late teens. She assumed he was Tryllen Grox.

"Josah," Maksin whispered.

"That's Josah?" Eselle asked.

Maksin's eyes took on a pained expression. "No. That's who he went after. That's the new high commander, Pytre Skogsmead. And that's Prince Tryllen with him. Josah wouldn't have let Skogsmead out of his sight unless something bad happened."

The prince stepped forward. "Hear me, my new subjects. This man," he pointed to Kyr, "murdered my father. That makes me your king."

Maksin took a few steps toward a set of stairs that led to the top of the wall, a short distance down from the commander and Tryllen Grox.

Eselle grabbed his arm. "Where are you going?"

Maksin's eyes blazed. His face flushed, and his lips clenched tight. The puckered scar made him look fierce. "I won't let them get away with this."

"You can't—"

Pulling his arm free, Maksin stalked to the stairs. Eselle turned toward Cristar, who watched the man with sad eyes.

She didn't want to leave Cristar alone, but Maksin shouldn't go off by himself. Why she cared, she couldn't say. She didn't even know him.

Still, she pushed Cristar toward the stable door. "Stay in here. Don't come out."

"What are you doing?" Cristar asked.

"Stay here, please. I'm going to make certain he doesn't get into trouble."

"And who's going to make sure you don't get—"

"Please," Eselle said. "You just gave ... you're exhausted and in no condition to help. Please, keep safe so I don't have to worry about anything else while I help Maksin."

With a frown, Cristar stepped into the stable. "You can't save everybody. But fine, I'll stay put."

"Thank you."

Eselle rushed after Maksin. By the time she reached him, he was halfway up the stairs, slowly stalking the last few steps.

The prince continued yelling down to the troops, while Kyr argued against him. The soldiers looked back and forth between them.

"—my family. That makes me—"

"The Enstrins are the ruling family of Likalsta," Kyr yelled.

"They're all dead!" the prince said. "They died years ago."

"Two survived." Kyr turned back to the soldiers. "One of them is currently in this castle, and the other is riding here as we speak."

A rustling rippled through the soldiers.

Eselle blocked it out as she and Maksin reached the top of the wall. The old soldier and young man stood only a few paces away. Hiding at the corner where the stairs met the wall, without a plan, she and Maksin nodded to each other.

Maksin darted from cover and rushed the commander. Catching Skogsmead off guard, Maksin tackled the soldier, who lost his grip on the nocked arrow. It flew off. Hopefully, it wasn't still aimed at Kyr. Or anyone else.

Tryllen Grox stood watching the fight, shifting his sword as though wanting to stab something. Taking advantage of his distraction, Eselle rushed him.

When he noticed Eselle, he swung at her. She dodged sideways, ducking the swing, and punched his jaw. He staggered and tried to swing again, but she caught his arm and yanked the sword from his grip. She threw it over the battlements, out of the castle completely.

"What the fuck? That was my sword!" Grox glanced at the wall where his blade had flown, then glared at her. He lunged forward, swinging.

Eselle ducked and jabbed his ribs. With a spin, he threw a backhanded blow and caught her across the cheek. Her vision blurred as she stumbled. Eselle gathered her senses. She fell forward when her opponent plowed into her back, sending her onto her stomach. Pain radiated through her chest.

Grox gripped her hair, making her cry out. He spun her around onto her back and punched. Blocking it, she wrestled Grox for control.

Grunting and gasping came from nearby, but Eselle couldn't spare the attention for Maksin. She hoped he was all right, that he had some fighting skills beyond his burly size. From farther away, metal rang, and voices yelled.

Little by little, Eselle outmaneuvered Grox's limbs to her advantage until she secured him in a headlock. She wrapped her legs around his torso, pinning his arms to his sides. He struggled, thrashed his legs, but she pulled tight against his throat. His fighting eased as he began losing consciousness.

Ahead of her, Maksin roared and slammed Skogsmead's head into the stone walkway. Maksin's sleeve was torn and his brown jerkin askew. His hair was disheveled, and his lip and eyebrow bled. Fire flared in his eyes as he punched Skogsmead's face repeatedly.

"Maksin!" Eselle yelled, seeing the commander's bloodied features. She didn't want Maksin to do something he would regret, but she couldn't release Grox either.

"Maksin!" another, deeper voice called out.

Kyr's light-eyed captain ran onto the wall from the staircase and gripped Maksin's arm before he threw the next punch. Blood ran down the side of the captain's head, coating his blond hair and running down his neck.

With one last failed attempt to punch Skogsmead, Maksin growled and glanced behind him. He lunged off Skogsmead and plowed into the captain so hard he knocked the man back a couple steps. "Josah!"

Kyr's captain is Josah?

Wrapping his arms around the captain, Maksin buried his face in the man's bloody neck. Though Josah was a big man by any standards, Maksin's frame engulfed him. Josah held tight.

Grox gave another twitch in Eselle's grip. She yanked tighter on his throat.

Maksin pulled back from Josah. "I was so worried. What happened? Are you all right?" Before he got halfway through his words, he wrapped his arms around Josah again.

"I'm fine," the captain said. "How—"

Maksin cut him off with a kiss. "Don't ever scare me again."

The laugh Josah gave sounded more relieved than amused. "Only if you promise me the same." He kissed Maksin and grabbed him in another strong hug.

"Um," Eselle said, "can someone help me?"

Both men looked over at her. Startled expressions crossed their faces. Josah hustled around Maksin. "Your Highness. I'm sorry, I didn't even notice."

Eselle tensed, her stomach clenched tight. She'd thought he was loyal to Kyr, and that Kyr was loyal to Tavith. But . . .

Josah turned toward Maksin. "Find something to tie up Skogsmead and Tryllen." He motioned toward the gatehouse. "And tell them to get the gates up." Maksin, with Josah's blood smeared across his face, nodded and ran off toward the gatehouse.

The captain reached down to Eselle. "I have him now, Your Highness."

Hearing the address again, realizing it was indeed for her, took Eselle by surprise. She couldn't remember the last time anyone called her that. But then, if the captain truly was part of Kyr's plan, it stood to reason Kyr would have told him.

The sounds of swords and fighting surrounded them. Eselle handed over her opponent to Josah and rose to look down into the bailey. The soldiers were fighting each other. Did some of them really prefer a Grox ruler? She couldn't tell who sided with who since they all wore the same uniform. A few wore armor, but most wore the standard red arming doublet. She couldn't find Kyr among the mix.

The portcullis began to rise again. Moments later, several men ducked beneath to enter the castle. They spread out to the side while more of their allies entered behind them. Some wore gray arming doublets with white trim, the Enstrin colors, while others wore red with silver trim. They were her brother's troops and the Heldin city guard. Tavith was close. Instead of engaging, they formed up along the outer wall. Many had nicks and tears in their clothing, several bore blood.

Maksin ran back down the rampart toward them, rope in hand. While he tied up the two unconscious men, Josah stood watch. Eselle descended the stairs to find Cristar.

Her feet hit the ground when a pounding began nearby. She turned as horses erupted from the zwinger below the now open portcullis. They raced into the bailey, two abreast, and surrounded the fighting soldiers, many who stopped and repositioned for this new threat. Tavith's mounted soldiers, a few dozen, had their swords drawn. A loud horn blew, catching the attention of the last few fighting hold outs. The troops who had formed at the wall surrounded their mounted comrades. Once

Vistralou's soldiers settled, Tavith's foot soldiers eased through the horses and took over guarding the prisoners. The mounted soldiers pulled back, and two rode off to the side.

When someone grabbed her arm, Eselle spun around, pulling the dagger from her belt.

Cristar jerked back, her eyes and mouth wide. "Sorry."

Eselle reached for her friend's arms and pulled her in for a hug. "No, I'm sorry. I'm just extremely jumpy."

"Aren't we all," Cristar said.

Josah and Maksin descended the stairs to stand beside them. The captain studied the situation with the soldiers. "Maksin, watch the ladies, please."

"You can't go out there," Maksin said.

"I'll be fine."

Maksin scowled. "There's nothing you can do that Kyr can't do himself. Plus, how do you propose to get through that hoard of soldiers?"

Josah looked at the hundreds of bodies between him and his lord marshal, then he scowled too. "You may be right."

His features easing, Maksin stepped closer and held onto Josah's arm.

One of the mounted men who had pulled back removed his helmet. It was Tavith. His brunette hair, the same shade as Eselle's, was short, and his gray eyes reminded her of their father's. Over his gray and white doublet, he wore a leather hauberk dyed with their house colors. Like the other soldiers, nicks and blood splatters decorated him.

Tavith spoke to the man beside him, who also removed his helmet. Eselle recognized her brother's lord marshal.

Holding onto enough common sense not to run across a bailey of tense soldiers, Eselle walked toward Tavith. Her pace was quicker than she intended, but she kept from running.

When she drew close, Tavith peered over. His smile was profound, and he jumped down from his horse and hugged her. "You had me so worried. Where have you been?"

She melted into her brother's arms. He always eased her fears. "I'm fine. I had some things to take care of."

"Why didn't you get word to me? I was beginning to think you'd been captured. Or killed." He finally stepped away and studied her. "A little worse for wear, but you look good."

Her smile was broad. "So do you."

"How did you wind up here?"

"That's a long story."

Turning to Cristar, Eselle motioned her over. Josah said something to Maksin, who frowned, then hustled to Cristar's side and walked with her. Maksin watched with a grimace from his place by the stairs.

Once the pair reached them, Josah nodded to everyone and spoke before anyone else could. "Your Majesty, the former high commander and prince are tied up at the top of those stairs." He nodded to the stairway behind him. "Someone should take them into custody before they have a chance to escape or be released."

Tavith and his lord marshal gave surprised looks, but the lord marshal called over some soldiers and sent them to investigate. He also tasked a couple armsmen with escorting Josah to the other detained castle soldiers. Eselle frowned, but trusted things would work themselves out in time.

Until then, she made introductions. "Cristar, this is my brother, Tavith Enstrin. Our new king." Tavith smiled at Cristar as she curtsied. She did it surprisingly well considering she probably hadn't had much practice in Eddington. "And this is my friend Cristar Maesret."

Tavith nodded a greeting. "A pleasure to meet you."

Two of Tavith's armsmen walked forward with Kyr between them. His sword had been confiscated, as had his primary dagger. Eselle was willing to bet all of his other daggers were still scattered about his body.

Tavith's lord marshal dismounted and stood beside his king, his hand on his hilt.

The soldiers stopped with their prisoner several paces short of Tavith.

"What is all this?" Tavith asked sternly. "What have I walked into here?"

"Vorgal Grox is dead." Kyr stood straight as he explained, meeting the new king's gaze. "The castle and troops are yours, Your Majesty. As is all of Likalsta."

Tavith's expression grew intense as he stared at Kyr. "What do you mean, he's dead?"

Eselle stepped closer to her brother, taking his arm to get his attention. She worried how the next few minutes might go. "Lord Marshal Silst assassinated Vorgal Grox to help you reclaim the throne."

With a furrowed brow, Tavith looked back at Kyr, eyeing him skeptically. "Is this true?"

"Yes, Your Majesty. I admit to recent regicide and surrender myself to your judgment."

"Why would you submit so easily?"

She heard the distrust in Tavith's voice and wanted to alleviate it, for both his and Kyr's sakes.

"Now, Silst. Kill him now!"

Eselle whipped around at the yelling voice behind them. Four armsmen were escorting Skogsmead and Tryllen Grox down the stairs. The former prince tugged at the grip on his arms while yelling.

"You promised to make me king! Kill him like you vowed!" The armsmen yanked Grox along while he continued spouting orders.

A shiver spread down Eselle's spine as she turned back to Kyr. He watched Tryllen Grox with a grimace, then turned toward everyone staring at him. When his eyes settled on her, Eselle's throat tightened. Surely Grox was lying.

Wasn't he?

Tavith's expression had gone cold. "Take him to the dungeon."

CHAPTER THIRTY-NINE

Eselle opened her eyes the next morning to a mass of dark hair lying on the pillow beside her. A faint snore reverberated. She slipped out of bed, careful not to wake Cristar. Grabbing a shawl against the chill, she started a fire to warm the room.

While Tavith had managed the realm the previous day, she and Cristar, along with various staff, tended to the women in the dungeon. By late night, everyone had been moved to higher levels and quartered in proper, if cramped, accommodations. Utilizing the abundance of soldiers as escorts and drivers, women who had already given birth or were fit to travel were being sent home. Others were being cared for until their babies arrived.

Helping the women gave Cristar something to focus on aside from her own troubles. Eselle hadn't figured out yet how to explain Kyr to her friend. She was still trying to figure that out for herself.

The dungeon's political and falsely imprisoned inhabitants received their freedom. Those in The Crypt—Vorgal's hideous combination of prison and torture chamber—had either been put out of their misery or treated in the infirmary. Of the dozen prisoners it held, only a few were expected to recover, though all would be disabled in some fashion.

Some genuine criminals remained, along with Tryllen Grox, Pytre Skogsmead, and Kyr. Until their exact involvement in recent matters could be determined, they would be detained.

Eselle headed for the dungeon.

"I'm here to see the prisoner Kyr Silst."

"On whose authority?" the guard asked, standing straight and examining her objectively.

"On my own. I'm the king's sister, Joeselleen Enstrin."

Judging by his red and silver uniform, he'd previously served Vorgal. There hadn't been enough time yet to reoutfit every soldier into the gray and white of her family's house.

"How do I know you're the king's sister?" He stood alert, but he was still adjusting to the castle's changing conditions. Part of the old regime, this man was accustomed to being ordered around by spoiled, arrogant officers and nobility. The easiest tactic would be to bully the man. Not her preferred method, but she could manage when needed.

Stepping closer, Eselle glared. "I said, I'm here to see Kyr Silst."

The guard seemed to consider things, but his service in Vorgal's demanding army won out. After another quick perusal, taking in her stern features, he nodded. "I'm sorry, Your Highness. I didn't recognize you." He turned toward the corridor. "He's down here."

Eselle followed the armsman along the short passage that made up the original twelve prison cells. Instead of the metal cages Vorgal installed in the other rooms, these were individual stone cells, each closed off from the others. Eselle scrunched her nose at the lingering smells of waste that permeated the air, blending with the general mustiness of the lower levels.

When they reached the last few heavy, wooden doors, the guard unlocked one. He glanced inside. "You have a visitor."

Eselle stepped up to the door. Kyr sat against the wall of the empty cell. He'd been stripped down to his simple linen shirt, brown trousers, and leather boots. His brow creased as he looked up at her in confusion, then slowly released as realization dawned, before turning into exasperation.

"I don't want visitors."

Eselle stepped forward to enter, but the guard put out a hand to block her. "No one's allowed inside, Your Highness."

"Need I remind you of who I am?" She kept her voice firm, but he didn't relent. "If you don't let me speak with this prisoner privately, I'll have you occupying the cell beside him."

The guard flinched, then pulled back. "Yes, Your Highness. Call when you're ready."

The armsman closed the door behind her but didn't lock it. She imagined him standing on the other side, ready to burst in if she cried out. She couldn't help but feel grateful, though she didn't expect she'd need the assistance. Now that Kyr appeared to have accomplished his plan, she was pretty certain he was harmless, for the most part. Stepping farther into the small cell, she studied him.

He gazed up and huffed in amusement. "I never suspected you'd turn into an overbearing, arrogant princess."

She adjusted her shawl, crossing her arms. "I figured it was the fastest way to make him let me see you. Did you really conspire with Tryllen Grox to kill my brother?" Though Eselle had her suspicions, she needed to hear him say it, needed to see his face when he did.

Kyr's features tightened. "You don't waste time, do you? No."

"Why did he yell orders like he expected you'd follow them?"

"Only he can answer that." Kyr frowned as he watched the opposite wall. "My guess is he's angry I killed his father and tried to give the crown to someone else."

"He's framing you out of revenge?"

"Yes."

"Why should I believe you?"

His gaze remained steady. "You probably shouldn't."

She stepped in front of him, examining his somber features. "I actually do, though."

Kyr's eyes narrowed and turned up to her. "Why?"

She shrugged. "Faith, I guess. Explain everything to Tavith and he'll release you. Then you can—"

"I don't want to be released."

Eselle froze. "What do you mean?"

"Just what I said."

"But you weren't trying to kill Tavith."

"But I killed plenty of other people."

Eselle shifted, adjusting her shawl, searching for an argument. Kyr focused on his clasped hands. "I'm not looking for mercy."

"But Cristar—"

"Doesn't need to know about this." His face was resolute, his voice stern.

"Kyr, she's your mother. This is your chance to really meet her and spend time with her. You can't do that if you're locked up."

He leaned his head against the wall and watched her. "Looking back, she'd wish she'd never known. This is the last thing I can protect her from. She doesn't need to know what her son became."

"To never know you sacrificed having your own life to gain access to the man who killed tens of thousands over the years? And who would have killed tens of thousands more if allowed to live?"

"It doesn't matter. Every horrible thing I did along the way negated every good thing I ever did. Not that there were many of those."

"I don't believe that." Eselle squatted in front of him. "I never could figure you out, how you'd be gentle one minute and heartless the next. But you were playing a part, pretending to be the ruthless, power-hungry man you presented to everyone."

"You can only pretend to be someone like that for so long before it takes hold, and you actually become someone like that. Believe me, I'm closer to heartless than gentle, so stop trying to save me."

"No, you're not." She saw his frustration as she spoke the truth. "Deep down, you're more like your mother than you know. She would do anything for you, and now you're doing the same to protect her from more pain. You love your mother."

Jumping to his feet, he snapped, "Who doesn't love their mother?"

"Vorgal."

"Even he loved his mother. He also hated her for cursing him, but he still loved her." With a sigh, he walked to the back of the cell and paced. "Let me do what I think is right. Please. It'll be easier for everyone if I'm out of the way."

It was awful seeing him surrender, but Eselle didn't know how to fight for him if he wouldn't fight for himself. Until she could think of a way, she didn't want to argue.

"All right," she said.

Kyr stopped pacing and gazed down at her. "Really?"

"Really. I do, however, need answers."

"I'd expect no less. Would you care for a seat?" He held his hand out to the ground.

Seeing the matted and molded, half decayed, unidentifiable substances, she frowned. The cell was even more horrendous than the one she and Cristar had occupied. "No, thank you."

"Suit yourself." With that, he returned to his spot on the floor. "I have to admit, I feel sorry for the poor souls I sent down here. This place is truly disgusting."

When he peered at her, she considered her first question. "How are you even here?"

"The portal," he said. "Nikos had to act quickly—"

"Wait." Eselle held up her hand. "You said yesterday that Daalok was Nikos, or Nikos was Daalok. What does that mean?"

"I'll get there." He crossed his arms over his knees. "Until a few weeks ago I only ever knew him as Nikos. But for clarity, Daalok had to act quickly. That portal he opened wasn't just to travel to another location, but another time. He didn't intend that particular little feat, but he wasn't very good with his magic back then. He meant to take us to his home village—which he did, but twenty-eight years in the past. For months, he tried returning us here, but never could repeat the process, at least not well enough that he trusted our lives with it. He eventually realized we'd been given a unique opportunity to stop Vorgal, one Vorgal would never suspect. Knowing that eventually he'd be in this world twice at the same time, he changed his name to Nikos Klaskil, trained me, and we infiltrated the castle."

"So, all along, you were the baby Vorgal hunted?"

Kyr shrugged. "I don't know. But Nikos believed I was, so he raised me to be."

"His name is Daalok," Eselle said firmly. "How did he know who you were? He saw the scar that night he patched your wound, but there had to be more."

"How did you know?" Kyr asked instead.

"When I saw you get the scar yesterday, I remembered you mentioning giving it to yourself. I thought you meant a sword or knife slipped, or something like that, but you were being literal, weren't you?" He nodded. "I also saw Daalok practice that portal once. A stag went through, then reappeared awhile later. I thought it was a different stag, but now I wonder." Kyr gave a faint smile, but she wasn't done. "Most of all, I remembered all those times you watched Cristar. It wasn't the interest I accused you of. You were watching your mother. She was so close, but you couldn't tell her anything."

The corner of his mouth twitched into a quick bittersweet smile. "I doubt Nikos picked up on that last bit."

"Daalok."

"But he saw the scar, like you said. When he discovered we'd gone back in time about the same number of years as my age here, he remembered a conversation we had a couple of days ago, the night you had your nightmare. I told him he reminded me of the high mage. He put those pieces together and came to the conclusion about my identity, and who he must have been here, High Mage Nikos Klaskil."

"His name is Daalok Borwin. And he would never serve Vorgal, even for this crazy plan." Crazy or not, it worked. "Why didn't he come to us, tell us what was happening? Or have you tell us?" Despite her efforts, her voice grew harsh.

"We couldn't risk changing things."

"But you had hundreds of chances to kill Vorgal. Why didn't you?" She clenched her fists. "Why didn't you stop him before he killed my family? Knowing everything he did, why didn't Daalok kill Vorgal when he was a child?"

Kyr gave a frustrated huff. "It's not that simple. Believe me, I wanted to kill Vorgal every opportunity I had, but Nikos wouldn't let me. I hated him for it for years, but he was right. It had to be this way, after we were safely through the portal. If we had done anything differently, we would have risked failing, of negating everything we'd done to that point."

"What do you mean?"

"When Nikos—"

"Daalok."

"Daalok," he said with a groan, "realized who I was and the plan we must have been working, he raised me to infiltrate Vorgal's military, while positioning himself inside the castle. I couldn't kill Vorgal before yesterday because if I did, none of this would have happened. Yes, I would have been born, but you never would have fled with Cristar, met Daalok, Daalok never would have taken me through the portal, so I never would have killed Vorgal, making everything reset itself. Vorgal would have once again become king, killed everyone, but I wouldn't have gone through to the past, so I never would have killed him." He shook his head. "It doesn't make sense, I know. I get lost trying to understand it sometimes. Nikos explains it better."

"Daalok," Eselle said absently. "Why should I believe you? Especially about Daalok becoming High Mage Nikos Klaskil. Do you know how ridiculous that sounds? He could barely move a cup of water with his magic. I've heard stories about the high mage destroying entire cities with fireballs."

Kyr chuckled lightly as he watched the far wall. "He trained. While I learned how to wield a sword, he practiced magic. He was so determined to stop Vorgal, to gain the high mage position and be close to the enemy, I swear some nights he didn't sleep. Just practiced for days until he collapsed into an exhausted heap."

He finally looked up at her. "As for proof, it doesn't matter if you believe me or not. I've done what I set out to do. It's over."

The truth of his words frustrated her, but she was determined to get more answers from him.

Seeing her frustration, Kyr sighed. "But if you must have it, my only proof is the scar and knowledge Nikos relayed to me. It's how I knew where to find you all those times. Nikos knew where you'd be because he'd been with you or you'd told him about your previous travels. Cristar told him she lived in Eddington, where you two met, so I made certain to become regional commander for that area. When I knew you two were about to meet, I headed for Eddington to await your arrival.

"Nikos told me about your necklace, a knot for every member of your family, so I realized who you were the moment I saw it. Though I'll admit, you had me fooled for a while. I knew to expect someone of your description near Eddington, but not Grimswold. Still, when I saw you, I wondered. Then you said your name was Tarania, and I didn't question it again. Nikos never heard that alias, never knew we met before Eddington, so he never told me about it. I actually believed you were Tarania. Though I knew Florial was a lie."

"And if you'd known who I was then?"

"I would have begun the next phase of our plan, to get you two away from anyone who might harm you."

"Would you still have seduced me at the inn?" Eselle wasn't certain what answer she wanted.

"Probably not. The plan was too important. Which is why I'm glad I didn't know." The corner of his mouth turned upward.

"But you knew the second time."

"Yes." His half-smile grew into a real one, and Eselle couldn't help but return it.

His request to remember their time at the inn suddenly made sense. He'd known what was about to happen, how things would change, and she would soon hate him.

"If Daalok told you where Cristar was, why didn't you take her somewhere safe until you were born? Find Daalok in his hometown or on the road and have him take you through the portal?"

"Do you really think anyone would have believed me? And, you said it yourself, Daalok could barely do magic back then . . ."

His brows scrunched as he tilted his head. "Or, yesterday, I suppose. He wouldn't have had the confidence or skill to manage it. The only reason he succeeded was because he was terrified. He knew he worked his spells better when the stakes were highest. When we devised our plan, he insisted I promise to scare him to death to help him cast correctly. But, even if I told everyone, and his spell worked, no mother would send their newborn through an unknown portal with a stranger. On the word of another stranger."

"But you could have—"

"*No!*" he roared, making Eselle jump.

Kyr trembled with anger, and the door burst open. The guard rushed in with his sword drawn. Eselle waved him back, but he didn't leave, only stood ready while watching the prisoner.

"Whatever you're about to say, no!" Every muscle in Kyr tightened. "We couldn't have succeeded any other way. If we could, then I've given up everything and committed countless atrocities for nothing! Killed for nothing! I can live with most of what I've done, but there's too much blood on my hands to make it all meaningless by dissecting this entire scenario and finding there was something different that would have worked. So, please, leave it alone."

His grief was palpable as he gazed at his hands, slowly rubbing them. After a frozen moment, Eselle nodded and folded her arms across her chest. She had to do something with them so she wouldn't sit beside him and wrap her arms around him. To distract herself, she turned to the guard and nodded that she was all right. He looked between them, then stepped out and closed the door. Once again, it didn't lock.

"I'm sorry," Eselle said softly. "You're right. I should simply be grateful for what you've done. And I am. Thank you. You're a better man than I would have thought, given the last few weeks.

And knowing her as I do, I believe Cristar would be proud of you." Seeing his sudden concern as he lifted his eyes to her, she added, "But, I'll honor your wishes and not tell her until you're ready."

"Thank you."

Overcome, Eselle sat down beside him, trying to ignore the grime as she made certain she only braced herself with the wall and didn't touch the floor with anything that wasn't covered.

"Daalok . . . I mean . . . Nikos, raised you?"

"Yes."

"And he told you all along what was coming?"

"At first it was bedtime stories. The tale of the young mother and her friends protecting her baby. You were the main character, by the way." He gave her a sideways glance.

"Me?"

"Yes. I think Nikos was a bit in awe of you. He always told me stories of your heroism. And, I'll admit those stories put me in awe of you too. You were my hero growing up. I looked forward to meeting you as much as meeting my mother." Eselle was speechless. "He told such incredible stories of how you protected them while I chased you."

"Well, it's less impressive knowing you weren't actually trying to capture or kill us."

"You didn't know that. And toward the end I actually was trying to capture you."

"Was any of it real? Any of the times we escaped you?"

"When you wounded me with that sword, and Nikos threw fire at me, that was real."

"But not any of the other times?"

"Does it matter? Nikos was right; you're a hero. You're *my* hero."

Eselle shook her head in denial.

"You protected my mother when you didn't have to. You could have left her with me to meet her fate, but you rescued her. Then you could have left her in some town or forest, but you stayed beside her. When you met Daalok, you could have handed her over, but you remained. You stayed until the end, no matter what I threw at you. So, thank you for saving my mother. For saving me before I was even born."

Eselle swallowed down the tightness in her throat. She rubbed Kyr's arm and rested her head on his shoulder. "When did he tell you?"

"I was around seven. I didn't know what to think, but I followed his training. Vorgal wasn't in power yet, so after a while we forgot what we were training for. Eventually, we stopped, grew comfortable living in a land with an honorable ruler. He'd forgotten about Vorgal's terrors, and I'd never known them. Then Vorgal seized the throne. Still, we were far from the capital and thought we had time. Eventually, Vorgal sent troops to our settlement." He rubbed his elbow with the burns. Eselle peeked over, wondering how he acquired them. "That day I lost the two closest friends I've ever had."

Shuddering, he snapped himself out of it and looked down at her. "After that, we resumed training with a vengeance, eventually making our way to Vahean and infiltrating."

Eselle wrapped her arm around his. "You miss him, don't you? Nikos?"

"Of course." He leaned his head against hers. "He was the only parent I've ever known."

CHAPTER FORTY

Leaving the dungeon, Eselle sought out Tavith. She found him in the council chambers. Looming outside the door, she listened while he and his advisers discussed distributing Vorgal's food stockpile to surrounding villages.

"You sounded great," she said when Tavith waved her inside an hour later. "Father would have been proud hearing you say you won't take 'no' about feeding your people."

He stepped around the table to her. "I hope so. But I wish he or Brassil were here instead of me."

"You'll be fine. You ran the farm well, and you'll do the same here."

Tavith snorted. "This is a lot more complicated than a farm." He waved a hand as if brushing away his concerns. "Enough of that. How are you? I've been so busy I've barely spoken to you."

"I'm fine," Eselle said with a shrug.

"And your friend?"

"She's fine too. Or, at least, she will be."

"Yes, you mentioned helping her, but not what happened."

Eselle paced around the room. "It's a long story, and frankly, not mine to tell."

Tavith nodded. "Well, if there's anything I can do, let me know. I'd like to put her in the rooms beside yours."

"Thank you. For now, I think she's lost too many people and doesn't want to be alone. She's fine with me a while longer."

When Eselle stopped pacing, her brother stood straighter, clasping his hands before him. "And now we get to it."

"What?"

"The reason you've come here. I knew something was bothering you when you walked in."

"What will happen to Kyr Silst?" Even if Kyr didn't want mercy, she planned to find it for him. Whether for him or for Cristar, she couldn't leave him in a dungeon.

"Silst? He'll be put on trial."

"When?"

"When there's time. Right now, more important matters take precedence."

Eselle grimaced and straightened her shoulders. "He's innocent and needs to be released."

Tavith's eyes widened. "He was about to kill me."

Shaking her head, Eselle stepped closer. "No, he wasn't. Grox lied so we'd think Kyr sided with him."

"Kyr? You're on a first name basis with Vorgal's lord marshal?" His brow creased.

"Yes, actually. What Grox said yesterday—"

"Do you know what he said later when questioned by Lord Marshal Frithen?"

Eselle shook her head, not knowing Tavith's lord marshal had questioned Grox.

"Young Grox explained how he, Pytre Skogsmead, and Silst all planned his father's assassination. That after letting me enter the castle, they planned to kill me *and you* so the little shit could eliminate his rivals." Eselle's mouth gaped slightly. "According to him, Silst initiated everything months ago when Vorgal wouldn't promote him into Drus Huln's position."

It took Eselle a few tries to speak. "Grox lied."

She wanted to tell Tavith everything, but it sounded too outrageous, and she wasn't certain he would believe her.

One of her brother's brows drew upward. "You're certain? Because Grox sounded convincing."

"I'm sure he did, but I know what I saw. Kyr killed Vorgal Grox to put you on the throne, not Vorgal's son."

Tavith sighed, sitting at the table. "Even if he did, I can't take the risk, not without evidence."

"Talk to Kyr." Eselle stepped beside the table, meeting her brother's gaze. "Hear him out."

"There's still the issue of him being Vorgal's lord marshal."

"For three days."

"Yes, but he was high commander for years before that, perpetrating all sorts of crimes." Tavith shook his head and grumbled. "Why are you even concerned about him?"

Eselle sat opposite Tavith. "It's complicated, but I've gotten to know him. Please, trust me."

He watched her for a moment, seeming to consider. "I do trust you, but I also can't ignore the facts." He watched her in silence for a moment before speaking again. "But I'll talk with him. Depending on his answers, I *might* release him."

Eselle beamed.

"Don't look so pleased. I seriously doubt he'll say anything that will change my mind."

"Perhaps, but at least he has a chance. When?"

Tavith rolled his eyes. "When I have time."

"Why wait? Have him brought up and get this over with. That way I won't pester you for the rest of the day."

"Fine. If it'll make you happy and let me return to running things, let's get this done."

While waiting for Kyr to be brought from the dungeon, Eselle described meeting Cristar and Daalok, the basics of how Daalok had taken Cristar's son to safety, but none of the details relating to Kyr. In return, Tavith explained everything that had transpired while marching to Vistralou, about the unexpected allies they acquired along the way.

"How did you get through Vahean?" Eselle asked.

"The city guard stood down." Tavith leaned back in his chair. "After marching from Heldin, we attacked. With evenly matched forces, both sides lost a lot of men. Then horns blew, and Vahean's troops stopped fighting. They formed up outside the city, and the captain handed them over to me."

Eselle wasn't surprised, but it was still incredible to hear.

"I thought it was a trick," Tavith said, "but the captain claimed we were expected at the castle, so I brought some men, and you know the rest."

Kyr arrived, with his hands bound and surrounded by three guards. Eselle scowled seeing one of the armsmen wearing Vorgal's red and silver. They couldn't reoutfit everyone fast enough. The soldier walking behind Kyr, Hanoth, she knew from her brother's farm. He'd lived there the past several years. She was pleased to see him wearing the Enstrin colors.

Tavith stood and stepped around the table. "I reluctantly agreed to speak with you because my sister thinks you should be released. What do you have to say in your defense?"

"Nothing, Your Majesty." Kyr stood stoically.

The king looked over at Eselle. "Even our prisoner agrees with me."

"Kyr," Eselle said, stepping in beside her brother, "this is your chance to tell your side, to show Tavith you should be released."

When Kyr remained silent, Eselle frowned. Even though he claimed to not want mercy, she hadn't expected him to dismiss an opportunity for it.

"Kyr Silst," Tavith said, "you're accused of too many charges for me to list from memory, the worst of which are regicide and various murders throughout the years. That's not counting, of course, possibly planning to kill my sister and me. Why should I release you?"

"You shouldn't."

The resigned expression on the former lord marshal's face concerned Eselle. The moment she approached Kyr, the two front guards stepped up to block her.

"Move," she snapped. When they didn't, she glanced over her shoulder at Tavith. He nodded, and they retreated. Stepping in front of Kyr, Eselle gazed into his dark eyes.

"What are you doing?" she whispered. It wasn't soft enough that anyone else in the room wouldn't hear, but she wanted to get through to him, and bullying wouldn't work. "You don't deserve this."

"Your Majesty," Kyr said, turning to Tavith, "as you said, I'm responsible for countless crimes, both ones you know about and many more you don't. I've murdered, tortured, extorted, bribed, falsely accused, and worse. I've also allowed, and sometimes sanctioned, many of these crimes to be perpetrated by others. Whatever sentence you deem appropriate, I will accept as penance for the pain I've caused over the years. I waive my right to a trial."

Eselle's chest constricted, as though Kyr had stomped on it. How does one come back from an admission like that? Kyr looked her brother in the eye and awaited the king's judgment.

Tavith pursed his lips. He pulled Eselle back and took her place. "Before you waive anything, I must remind you of the penalty for the crimes you're accused of."

"Death by hanging," Kyr said without inflection.

Tavith nodded solemnly. "Is it still your wish to—"

"Yes." Kyr stood motionless, meeting the king's gaze.

Tavith straightened his shoulders and watched Kyr for a few moments before stepping back and leaning against the table. "Then we'll schedule a hanging. I can't believe I'm saying this, but thank you for your honesty." He looked at one of the escorts. "You may return him to his cell."

Eselle stood dumbfounded.

Before they left, another soldier in Enstrin colors hustled into the room. His cheeks were as red as his hair. "You're Majesty, I have urgent news."

Tavith pushed off the table and stepped forward. "What is it?"

"The Grox heir and Commander Skogsmead have escaped."

"What?" Tavith's shocked features matched others in the room.

"Stop him!" Kyr yelled.

The red-haired soldier, now within a few paces of the king, pulled his sword and thrust.

One of the guards pulled his own weapon and stepped in the dissident's path. The red head struck the guard instead of Tavith, running him through, then pushed him aside.

He tried another attack. The second front guard, wearing Vorgal's colors, drew his sword and shoved Tavith behind him. Kyr tried rushing toward the assault, but the remaining guard, Hanoth, restrained him.

Eselle bolted forward to help. The dissident lunged around the king's protector, but the guard blocked, keeping himself between the king and danger.

"Stop him!" Kyr yelled, growing ferocious, yanking on the arms wrapped around him.

Before Eselle reached the dissident, he repositioned and saw her. He jumped sideways and punched her in the gut. She gasped and doubled over. Hauling her upright, he wrapped an arm around her chest and set his dagger to her throat. She froze, as did her brother and the guard protecting him.

"No one call out," the dissident said, "or the princess dies."

Tavith tried circumventing the guard, but the man kept blocking him.

"No, Your Majesty," the guard said, "it's too dangerous."

"He has my sister," Tavith growled. "Out of my way!"

"I'm sorry, Your Majesty, I can't do that." While holding Tavith back with one hand, the guard kept his sword toward the dissident.

"What do you want?" Tavith asked.

"I want you." The dissident shifted, keeping everyone in sight.

Hanoth struggled to restrain Kyr, his arms looped through Kyr's bound ones.

"Fine. I'll trade for my sister."

The moment the dissident turned toward Tavith, the sounds of Kyr's struggle increased.

Eselle flew forward, the dissident with her. Two bound hands dropped before her face. They gripped the dissident's wrist, thrusting it and the dagger, away from her throat. Eselle slipped from the man's grasp and tumbled to the floor. Boots stomped around her. She rolled to the side and back to her feet.

Kyr clutched the dissident from behind, enveloping him, trapping his arms in place and securing the man's weapon hand. The dissident flipped the knife to his free hand, then thrust it down into Kyr's left thigh. Kyr grunted in pain, but his grip didn't loosen.

Tavith's guard overpowered him and rushed him from the room, calling for reinforcements.

"Get her out of here!" Kyr ordered, struggling to restrain their attacker.

Hanoth hauled Eselle toward the door. Nearly there, she twisted out of his grip.

"Help him." She didn't wait to see if Hanoth followed as she rushed back to the ongoing struggle.

The dissident stabbed Kyr's leg several times. Kyr shifted out of striking range, but their tie-up gave him limited options. The attacker thrust an elbow into Kyr's stomach, then twisted around, changing back to his dominant hand, and drove the knife into the side of Kyr's abdomen. Kyr tried pulling his arms free. The dissident grabbed hold of them before they cleared his shoulders and continued stabbing.

Hanoth ran past Eselle, reaching the fight first and grabbing the dissident's arm. The dissident thrust his elbow into Hanoth's chest, making him stumble backward. Eselle snatched her dagger and rammed it into the dissident's ribs. He yelled and released Kyr's arms. Kyr cinched his arms around the dissident. He lifted the man and slammed them both to the ground.

Eselle pulled Kyr's bound arms over the dissident and hauled him back, while Hanoth tossed the assailant onto his stomach and ripped the dagger away.

She dropped beside Kyr. He bled from his thigh and abdomen. She pulled off her tunic, wadded it up, and pressed it to his stomach, while placing her hand to his thigh.

"Get help," she ordered, as Hanoth pulled the attacker to his feet.

"I can't leave the prisoner," Hanoth said.

"He needs help!" Eselle's voice turned shrill.

Hanoth looked confused. "He was just sentenced to execution. If this hadn't happened, he'd be dead soon anyway."

Soldiers rushed into the room, Captain Ilkin among them. Two secured the dissident, while others tried hauling Eselle to safety. She snapped at them and slapped their hands away.

"I'm not leaving. Get the healer. Now!"

Seeing Kyr on the ground, Josah grabbed the nearest armsman. "You heard her. Get the healer." He shoved the young man toward the door before kneeling beside Eselle. "How bad is it?" He pulled his dagger and cut away Kyr's bonds.

"We need to stop the bleeding."

Kyr watched them calmly, but his features were tight and his breathing unsteady.

After shouting orders, Josah retrieved bits of cloth for makeshift bandages. He wrapped Kyr's leg first.

Eselle's hands shook as she held the tunic over Kyr's abdomen.

"Let me." Josah nudged her hands aside and dressed the wound as best he could.

Eselle leaned back, taking a shaky breath.

"You should get out of here." Kyr's voice was soft and ragged. He spoke slowly, struggling for every word.

She shook her head, taking one of his hands between hers. It felt colder than she remembered and contained little strength.

"That armsman was right, about a hanging coming. Leave this alone."

"No." She'd been fighting tears, but one finally escaped. "I would have talked both of you out of it."

"I've no doubt of that." He gave her hand a light squeeze. "Eselle, it's over."

"No."

"Vorgal is dead." He paused to take a few breaths. "Let it be over."

Eselle wanted to argue but couldn't form the words. Instead of answering, she shook her head and blinked away more tears.

He was right, it was over. But she finally knew the truth. He couldn't die now.

Would it be kinder to let Kyr pass away without Cristar knowing, or kinder to give Cristar the chance to say goodbye?

Looking into his strained eyes, Eselle made her decision. Regardless of what Cristar suffered, she was strong and could cope with anything given time and friends. This could be Kyr's only chance to have his mother at his side. Though Daalok had been a caring father figure, Kyr had never known his mother's love or support.

Once Josah had Kyr bandaged enough to transport, the soldiers carried him away. "We can't wait for the healer anymore."

Eselle nodded and ran in the opposite direction.

She found Cristar sorting through papers at the desk in her room. She still appeared slightly puffy from crying through the night. Eselle had hated withholding the truth from Cristar. Now she agonized knowing that to make things better she first had to make them worse.

"I need you to come with me," Eselle said.

"I can't, I'm trying to decide how many escorts to send with the next group of—"

"Now." Eselle rushed over, and Cristar finally glanced up.

"What happened?" Cristar leaped from her seat at the sight of the blood across Eselle's clothes. "Are you all right?"

"It's not mine." Eselle's voice was strong, but shaky. "It's Kyr's."

"Oh, thank goodness." Cristar took a relieved breath. "I thought—"

Eselle grabbed Cristar's hands. "There's something I didn't tell you. I wanted to, but Kyr convinced me not to. But you need to know."

"What is it?" Cristar's eyes grew serious.

Eselle paused to collect herself. "When Kyr sliced the baby's shoulder," she said, and Cristar's jaw clenched, "I realized something. I've seen that exact scar before. Kyr has the same scar on his shoulder. I've seen it. Daalok saw it when we patched Kyr up in the woods."

"Lots of people have scars on their shoulders."

"True, but these two are identical—the same location, same length, same angle." She took a deep breath. "He's your son, Cristar." Eselle grew more frantic as she went. "I've spoken with him about it. Daalok's portal took them back twenty-eight years. It's an incredibly long story, and we don't have time. But I promise you, on my brother's life, Kyr is your son grown. And he needs you."

Cristar shook her head, tears welling. "Why would you say such a thing?"

"If I had time, I'd explain everything easier than this." Eselle's tone grew harsher. This was taking too long. "There was an attack on Tavith, and Kyr saved us. But he was injured. I don't know if he'll survive."

Cristar shook her head more vigorously, her face flushing as the tears fell. "It's not possible. Why would you say this? My baby—"

Eselle gripped Cristar's shoulders with a rough shake. "This may be your only chance to see him, to speak with him. And he needs you." Eselle lost the battle to her own tears.

"No, no, the Protector wouldn't do this to me." Cristar's voice cracked. "My son is barely two days old. He can't be here. It isn't possible."

"Somehow, it is." Eselle collected herself enough to guide Cristar to the door. "Please, trust that I would never lie to you about something this important."

Instead of giving Cristar time to think, Eselle pulled her through the halls. Cristar's features grew more strained the farther they traveled.

Two guards posted at the infirmary stopped them when they approached the door.

"I'm sorry, Your Highness, no one is allowed inside."

"Move aside armsman," Eselle said firmly.

"I sorry, but we have a prisoner in there and—"

"I'm fully aware of who is in there. He was injured saving my life. I *will* go in to check on him. And I've brought the only family he has. Stand aside."

The armsman gave a curt nod. Eselle pulled Cristar behind her.

The court healer stood over a table where Kyr lay unconscious. One of the midwives had been recruited to assist. She stitched Kyr's leg closed while the healer had his hands buried in the side of Kyr's abdomen. Blood covered the man to this elbows, and more seeped down Kyr's side, pooling onto the table before dripping down to the floor. Eselle's stomach clenched, and her heart pounded in her ears. Wiping her eyes, she stepped closer.

Cristar pulled on her arm. The young mother looked distraught, her brows bunched and lips quivering. Eselle nodded but couldn't speak the words. After everything Cristar had been through to protect her child, she couldn't lose him twice in as many days.

Eselle wouldn't allow it.

She walked to the table, standing across from the healer. "How is he?"

The man's eyes were focused as he stitched something together inside Kyr. "He'll probably be dead before supper. I'm surprised he's not dead already." His voice was rough.

A quick choked sound came from behind Eselle, but she ignored it. "You can't let him die. Do anything you must to save him. Anything."

"I know," the healer grumbled. "The new king already demanded I save him. Though how, I have no clue." His eyes flicked upward before resuming their determined fierceness. "There's too much damage. Just when I think I've sewn up everything that's bleeding, I find something else."

Considering how many times Kyr had been stabbed, Eselle wasn't surprised.

Cristar approached the table, studying Kyr's features. As she watched him, her eyes watered again.

"You shouldn't be in here," the healer said. "I'll send word when I know more."

Eselle watched Cristar. "We're staying."

Cristar stared into Kyr's features as she ran her fingers lightly along his jaw. "I don't know how I missed it, but he has Klaasen's sharp jawline . . . and those eyes," she said while closing her own. "They struck me the first time I saw them back in Eddington; there was something familiar about them. Klaasen had those same dark eyes. The ones that could swallow you if you gazed into them too long. They ran in his family." She looked down at Kyr again. "We used to joke about it, how you could always spot a Maesret by their eyes." Cristar's breathing quickened. "He can't be . . . he just can't."

Uncertain she was doing the right thing, Eselle pulled the torn shirt back from Kyr's shoulder. Once Cristar saw the scar, she broke. Eselle caught her in her arms and pulled her away from the table, hugging her tight.

"Leave," the healer snapped, raising his voice to be heard above the sobbing. "I must concentrate if I have any hope of saving this man! Leave!"

Eselle led Cristar away, wishing she'd kept silent, heeded Kyr's request.

If Cristar lost her son again, she would never survive her devastation.

CHAPTER FORTY-ONE

Fire raged through his gut. Throbbing pain radiated through more of his body than not. His only comfort was a soft warmth that surrounded one of his hands. He focused on it, not yet ready to open his eyes. Whether alive or dead, nothing good could be awaiting him.

Life couldn't be avoided for long though—or death, for that matter. Eventually, they both catch up to you.

When Kyr opened his eyes, the mismatched stonework on the ceiling looked familiar. He'd woken to it every morning he slept in Vistralou, ever since being assigned the room five years back.

Was this an argument for life or death? If death, at least he was dead in his own bed.

Curious what else he would find, he peeked to the side. Cristar sat propped in a chair beside him. Her head lay on the covers, and her eyes were closed. Both of her hands wrapped around one of his. Kyr's chest tightened. His breathing stuttered, and he closed his eyes once more.

There'd only been a few other instances when he'd touched his mother, and most of them involved him issuing empty threats or otherwise fighting her. This was the first pleasant instance. Feeling her warm hands, he no longer cared if he was alive, so long as this moment didn't end.

When he felt in control, he looked back at her.

Movement caught his eye, and he glanced beyond Cristar. Eselle sat scrunched up in a chair against the wall. It wasn't his chair, so they must have brought it in. She stared off toward the crackling fireplace. The light turned her soft features golden. She'd pulled her feet up beneath her and was wrapped in a blue wool blanket. Her soft brown hair had fallen halfway out of her braid. It lay against her slender throat as her head tilted to one side, leaning against her arm.

He watched her, studying each detail. Gazing between the two women, he couldn't remember feeling this content, despite his entire body aching. He savored the moment and prayed the Protector didn't take this from him as He had Nikos.

Eselle shifted in her seat and turned toward him.

Noticing him awake, she leaped from the chair and hurried over. She began reaching out to wake Cristar, but he shook his head. He wasn't ready to face his mother. That required emotional control he couldn't manage yet.

Eselle pulled her hand back, glanced between him and Cristar, then nodded. She walked around to the other side of the bed and sat on the edge.

"I'm glad you're awake," she whispered. "We were worried." She grasped his other hand, gave it a squeeze, and didn't let go.

His voice sounded hoarse but eased as he spoke. "It's cruel to save a man only to hang him."

She gave a faint smile. He wasn't sure if in relief or amusement, but it was what he had hoped for.

"You're not going to hang." They kept their voices low to prevent waking Cristar.

"Considering how I feel right now, I'm not sure that's a good thing."

Eselle frowned. "It's a very good thing. Don't joke about it."

"Sorry. But I am curious why I'm here. Why save someone scheduled for execution?"

"It's difficult to hang someone after they saved your life. I don't know what Tavith plans to do, he won't talk to me about it, but I know your hanging has been canceled."

"Beheading then?"

"Stop," Eselle whispered harshly, scowling at him. "It's not funny. We were really scared."

"Sorry."

Without warning, she leaned close, grasped the sides of his head, and stared him in the eyes. "I forbid you from dying."

The sentiment surprised him. Only Nikos had ever shown such concern for him before; he wasn't certain how to respond. Normally, he would toss out a joke about the consequences of disobeying, one involving execution, but he pushed the thought away. He should probably work on keeping his tongue in check. "Yes, Your Highness."

Her features relaxed as she released him and sat back.

Some part of him felt relieved to be alive, but another part was concerned. He'd fully expected to be dead by this point, that he'd be killed by either Vorgal, soldiers who learned he assassinated the king, or the incoming ruler. Both he and Nikos had known the odds of survival, so there'd never been plans for afterward. With what that dagger had done though, he should probably continue holding off on making plans awhile longer.

Cristar stirred, moving her head against the covers. After an unintelligible murmur, she settled and continued sleeping.

"I assume you told her," Kyr said.

"I know you didn't want me to, but you both needed it. You need her support and, if the worst had happened, she needed to be able to say goodbye."

Eselle was probably right.

Cristar shifted again in her sleep. He wanted to reach out and soothe her, but he didn't want to lose her hands around his. And he was still working up the courage to speak to her. After what he'd done, he dreaded their first conversation. He'd never been so afraid of anything as he was of hearing he had disappointed her.

Kyr blinked the tears away before his emotions got the better of him. "Thank you," he said. "I don't think I could have told her."

"You're welcome."

"How did you get her to believe it?"

"Apparently, you have your father's eyes."

For a long moment, Kyr gazed at her absently, unsure how to respond. Eselle's eyes grew troubled. His surprise must be showing.

"What's wrong?" she asked.

He shook his head. "Nothing. I just never knew that." He watched his mother again. "Other than what Nikos told me, I never knew what either of them looked like, not until earlier this year when I saw them in Eddington. I didn't dare get close though."

"Why not?"

He shrugged. "I was afraid knowing too much—knowing *them* too much—would make it more difficult to keep to the plan."

"Well," Eselle said, inching closer, "apparently you also have your father's build, and jaw, and temperament—the real one, not the one you put on for show. She's been going on endlessly about it these last couple of days."

He gave a deep, relieved chuckle. Shooting pain tore through his abdomen. With a cringe, he tried to collect himself, taking deep, steady breaths.

"Are you all right?"

"I'm fine," he lied, trying to push the pain from his mind.

Whether from his flinch or their conversation, and whether he was ready or not, Cristar woke.

As her eyes opened, she glanced around. She jerked upright and gripped his hand tighter. "You're awake. How are you feeling? Can I get you anything? How about some water?"

She started to rise, but Kyr tightened his grip on her hand. "I'm fine."

"Are you sure?" Cristar settled in again and stared at him. He only nodded.

"I'll leave you two alone," Eselle said. "I'll let Tavith know you're awake."

After Eselle left, Kyr wondered what to say. He had never anticipated this moment. While planning, it had seemed too much to hope for, so he hadn't. He'd focused on the mission instead of the aftermath.

"I'm not sure what to say," Cristar admitted.

A deep breath escaped Kyr as his tension eased. Her eyes flitted around the room for a moment, before settling on him.

"I thought I would know," she said, "had hoped I'd have the right motherly words to make this easier, but I don't know what I'm doing."

"Neither of us do." Kyr gave her hand a squeeze. A tightness had filled his chest since she woke up. "I'm sorry for what I put you through."

She waved if off with a faint smile, then turned solemn. "Don't be sorry. Eselle explained everything. I hate that things happened this way, but I understand."

"Can you ever forgive me?" He'd never spoken that question before, not even to Nikos. He held his breath while waiting for an answer.

Cristar's face softened. "You never have to ask me that. You're my son. Of course, I forgive you."

The tightness eased.

"But promise me," she said, "nothing like this will ever happen again, that you'll be honest with me from now on, no matter what."

He nodded. "I promise." He couldn't help the catch in his voice.

For as long as he could remember, Kyr had had a purpose, a task to prepare for. This new sensation of being unencumbered felt odd. "What now?"

His mother leaned over to hug him, careful of his injuries. "Now, we move forward."

Kyr closed his eyes and held her tight.

***

"You're certain?" Cristar asked, her eyes shining as her lips twitched in a suppressed smile.

Eselle's stomach had been tied in a knot since the healer entered the room.

"Yes," the man replied, tying off the fresh bandage around Kyr's torso. He turned his attention to his patient. "Keep treating the wounds as you have. It'll take a couple months to fully recover, and you'll probably always have trouble with that leg, but despite what I thought when I first saw you, I think you'll be fine."

"Thank you," Kyr said, sitting against the headboard.

"Thank you," Cristar echoed.

She'd spent the last week moving between doting on Kyr and repeatedly cleaning the few things he possessed. Eselle had tried taking her out for walks or introducing her around the castle, but the new mother was always too distracted for it to do any good.

"If anything changes, let me know," the healer said before leaving.

Once the door closed, Tavith took a few steps forward from his place against the wall. "Now that the healer has cleared you, it's time we talk."

Kyr nodded but remained silent. Wringing her hands, Cristar wore her concern openly as she sat at the end of his bed. Eselle kept her seat across the small room, wondering how involved she should get.

Shortly after the attack, Eselle had spoken with her brother about the full events that had transpired. She explained in detail everything she had glossed over previously, including the relationship between Cristar and Kyr, that though she was actually younger than Kyr, Cristar was his mother. It had taken some convincing, and she still wondered if Tavith thought they were all crazy, but he claimed to believe her. To everyone else, to explain Cristar's excessive doting, they claimed the two were siblings. It was easier that way.

Afterward, Tavith had irritated Eselle with his silence concerning recent events. At first, she thought he'd been too occupied ruling Likalsta. And that had been part of it. Knowing him, however, it became evident he'd been avoiding her, fearing talking to her might allow her to influence him. Eventually, she'd left him to his musings.

Standing straight, Tavith clasped his hands behind his back and studied Kyr. "As everyone here is aware, we need to discuss your death sentence. I'll admit, I briefly considered leaving you to your injuries as an alternative to your sentence."

Kyr nodded, but Cristar gasped and rose. Eselle kept silent and forced herself to remain seated. She controlled her breathing while waiting to see where Tavith went with this.

"But, to be perfectly honest, I was never comfortable with that sentence." Tavith took a deep breath as he peered down at Kyr. "I only agreed because you seemed determined. Now that my sister has explained things in greater detail, I have decided to pardon you for past crimes."

Cristar's face brightened, while Kyr gaped before clamping his mouth shut. Eselle smiled and leaned back into her chair, feeling lighthearted for the first time in months. Now that things were improving for the realm, this issue had been the last remaining uncertainty.

"You saved more than my sister last week. I am, of course, eternally grateful to you for that." Tavith glanced over at Eselle briefly. "If that traitor had succeeded, he could have gone on to hurt others. He could have thrown the realm into even more chaos, giving Tryllen Grox an opportunity to take the throne if we had both died. For preventing that, as well, I thank you."

Kyr nodded. "You're welcome, Your Majesty."

"So, instead of execution, I'm putting you to work." Tavith peered at Kyr serious enough to make Eselle squirm and rise from her seat. "Lord Marshal Frithen discovered that the man who attacked me and stabbed you was following orders from Pytre Skogsmead, who in turn received them from Tryllen Grox. It appears the young man thinks the crown should be his. He's attempting to gather support to retake it. I can't have that. Likalsta wouldn't survive that child trying to rule it."

"Agreed," Kyr said. "What does this have to do with me?"

Tavith crossed his arms over his chest. "You're still part of my military."

Kyr frowned, and Cristar looked a little less certain than she had. Eselle stepped closer. What did Tavith have planned?

"I've returned some authority to the nobles, but I also decided that the use of regional commanders has a certain law enforcement benefit. From here forward, the nobles and commanders will work together, balancing each other, to run the regions. So with decidedly less authority, I'm keeping the regional commanders around, though restaffing all but one position. You will stay on as high commander, but without a region, since I have another task for you.

"No one has been able to locate Skogsmead and Grox. I'm all but certain Skogsmead will be handling their daily logistics, and from what I understand, you trained under him. Hopefully, having some knowledge of him will give you an advantage. Once the healer clears you for travel, assuming we haven't apprehended them already, your mission is to locate and arrest Tryllen Grox and Pytre Skogsmead. Can you do that?"

With a reluctant nod, Kyr agreed. "Yes. But why?"

"It should be obvious. For starters, they killed their guards while escaping, and tried to kill me and my sister."

"I mean, why me? Why are you being so lenient?"

"After all the recent chaos and my sister's claims, I asked around about you. The soldiers, your men in particular, speak highly of you, claim you weren't like the other commanders or Huln. While you allowed some pillaging, you prohibited much more. Somehow, amid Vorgal Grox's horrendous world, you retained some degree of honor."

Eselle looked between the two men, trying to keep her smile in check.

Kyr still appeared skeptical. "Why would you keep me as high commander though?"

"Every other commander position had been given to my men. Giving you high commander will keep someone familiar in place for Grox's former soldiers, something to lessen the blow of change. But mainly, despite your past, you appear to be one of the few ranking soldiers from Grox's army that I wouldn't mind having in my own."

Kyr gave a single nod. "Thank you, Your Majesty. I'll bring you your prisoners as soon as I'm able."

Eselle stepped to the end of the bed. "Does anyone know even vaguely where they are?"

Tavith shook his head. "Unfortunately, not. That's why I'm hoping our high commander here can help."

"Have someone look into Skogsmead's family in Halmbridge," Kyr said. "If he's not there, they might still be able to give some information."

Tavith nodded. "I'll have someone get on it. Anything else?"

"Not at the moment, but if I think of anything, I'll let you know."

"Thank you." Tavith stepped toward the door. "I'll leave you be with your company. And get some rest. I need you out there as soon as you're able to travel."

"Thank you, sire."

Cristar sat on the edge of the bed. "Things didn't turn out exactly as I expected, but the Protector has blessed us with this chance."

"Yes, He has." Kyr pulled himself straighter up against the headboard. Eselle had expected him to be happier, but his expression appeared downcast.

"Still," Cristar said, "I'm not sure I like you staying in the military." She nodded toward Kyr's torso. "I'm not sure I can handle more of things like this."

He smiled lightly and reached for her hand. "I'll be fine. Hopefully things are settled for a long time now."

His mother seemed unconvinced. "It's almost supper time." She turned to Eselle. "Will you be joining us this evening?"

"I've spent the last several nights eating with you. I should probably let you two spend some time alone, especially after Tavith's news."

"Nonsense," Cristar said. "You're family."

Eselle glanced toward Kyr.

He nodded. "Stay."

"All right," she said.

Cristar bounced to her feet. "I'll go get us some food from the kitchen. Be right back." She left with a broad smile.

Eselle walked over to the bed and sat beside Kyr, still shirtless due to the healer's examination. The slice across his chest was nearly healed. Without thinking, she ran her fingers along its edge. "I'm sorry your collection of scars is growing because of me."

"They're worth it."

The warmth in his voice made her realize what she was doing. She jerked her hand away, feeling her cheeks warm. "Sorry."

"Don't be. Your touch is always welcome."

Ever the flirt.

That was something she felt certain she would never tire of.

"I'm glad Tavith is letting you stay in the military, but I'm sorry to see you heading back out into the field. I know you looked forward to spending time with your mother."

"You're right," Kyr said, "I'd like to stay, but it's better this way." His features turned somber. "There's too much history, too many people who will be angry he didn't execute me, whether they know exactly what happened or not. He doesn't need that kind of distraction. Neither do you. And I certainly don't want to deal with it."

Eselle brushed her fingers against his, not quite taking his hand. "I'll miss you."

A bittersweet smile crossed his features. "And that's the other reason I need to leave." He slid his fingers through hers. "The longer I'm here, the harder it is to remember you're out of my reach."

Eselle's pulse quickened at the admission. She squeezed his hand, and he returned it.

Though wonderful to hear he cared, she hated acknowledging the truth. When she and Tavith had discussed overthrowing Vorgal and helping the realm, she'd known that if they succeeded, she'd once again be a princess. What she had not considered was the restrictions that came with that title. Whatever marriage she ended up in, it would be one with a purpose.

"I'll never have the noble birth needed to court a princess, much less marry her."

She blinked a couple of times and sat a little straighter. "Is that something you want?"

"I may have jumped ahead of myself." Kyr released her hand. A frown flashed across his features, but disappeared as he shifted his position on the bed. "But I wouldn't have thought all this through if it hadn't crossed my mind at some point."

Eselle dropped her gaze and brushed a wrinkle out of her trousers before looking up again. "Do you think we could convince Tavith that since you were born in a castle, that counts as a noble birth?"

"No," he said with a chuckle. "But I like your thinking."

She scooted closer. "I'm not ready to let you go."

He reached out and caressed her cheek. "Me either. But as soon as I find Skogsmead and Tryllen, I'll be back."

"Let me rephrase that," Eselle said, scooting closer yet again. "I'm not ready to let go of you."

His eyes narrowed as his lips twitched upward. "I sense trouble for your brother in the near future."

Eselle smirked. "You really do know me. It dawned on me that there's another way to consider your remaining time in Likalsta."

"How?"

She moved up the bed enough that their hips touched and put a hand on his bare chest. "The healer said it should take you a couple months to recover, so, we could simply enjoy the time we have left."

The devilish smile she hadn't seen in too long returned, and her stomach fluttered. She ran her fingers along the lines of his muscles, taking it slow and deliberate.

"This goes against trying to remember we can never be," Kyr said, but he didn't stop her fingers from exploring him.

"Perhaps." She readjusted her position and stretched out alongside him as he wrapped an arm around her. His shoulder was warm against her cheek. "Have you ever wondered what would have happened if we'd met in Grimswold, and then in Eddington, and none of the rest of it had happened? Where we'd be right now?"

When he didn't respond, she looked up him. He cupped her face in his hand, then leaned down and kissed her.

CHAPTER FORTY-TWO

Standing across the table from Kyr in the council chambers, Earl Holgood addressed the king. "The last of the supplies Vorgal Grox sent to the Pasdaran border for his invasion have returned home. They'll be sorted and dispersed to those most in need."

"Good," King Tavith said. "And the soldiers?"

Lord Marshal Frithen leaned forward, his arms crossed in front of him on the table. "Those you deemed excess have been released and sent home. I still think we should have retained more, at least until everything is stable."

"We still have twice as many as when my father was king, which was more than sufficient. With peace ahead, we should be fine."

The lord marshal frowned and leaned back in his seat.

King Tavith turned to Kyr. "Where does your assignment stand, Commander?"

"After failing with local lords, Grox and Skogsmead have moved into Pasdar. They hope to gain favor with nobles and to convince King Sulsta to send troops to assist Grox in retaking the throne."

A few muffled laughs emanated from around the table. Kyr tried to ignore the soft, breathy chuckle beside him and instead focus on the conversation.

The king smiled. "It's amusing the young man believes they'll fight for him when his father planned to invade their country less than three months ago."

More chuckles rumbled.

"Once they fail with the Pasdarans," the king said, serious once again, "is there anyone of concern who would aid him?"

"Unlikely," Kyr said. "The only Riandori realms close enough to pose a threat are Ristaria and the Jalat city-state of Scalcier. We only have minor relations with the Ristarians, and no cause for them to dislike us enough to invade. Also, they're loyal to the Pasdarans, so if the Pasdarans won't support Grox, the Ristarian's likely won't either. For the Jalat, until recently they've been excessively reclusive, so we have no relationship with them. It's unlikely they'd care enough to venture this far."

"Good," Tavith said. "Regular armies I'm not overly concerned about. I have faith in our people to defend us. But I don't want to imagine them fighting Jalat soldiers."

"Agreed," Earl Holgood said. Several others around the table echoed his sentiment. The lord marshal nodded, his frown still in place.

Kyr remembered his difficulty fighting Drus Huln when the man used the Jalat style against him. And Huln hadn't been properly trained in the technique. What would a true Jalat fighter be like in a fight?

Returning his attention to the king, Kyr cleared his throat. "Grox and Skogsmead are heading to the Pasdaran capital of Borthal. I plan to leave tomorrow morning to track them down."

The king nodded with an appreciative smile, but a small gasp sounded beside Kyr. He probably should have told Eselle first.

King Tavith stood. "Take as many men with you as you need."

"Thank you, sire." Kyr rose, as did everyone else at the table.

Restored nobles and soldiers ventured from the room. Kyr and the princess remained. How mad would she be?

He turned slowly to find a glowering Eselle.

"You're leaving!"

"We knew I would once the healer released me."

She huffed and crossed her arms. "That was this morning. You shouldn't jump into a cross-continent journey so soon."

"Now that I've figured out where they're heading, I can't miss this opportunity."

Eselle pursed her lips. "I know, but that doesn't make it easier hearing for the first time in the middle of a crowded room."

"I'm sorry." Kyr stepped close and put his hands on her hips.

Since returning to life in the castle, she'd taken to wearing dresses on occasion. Today's was a particularly pleasing one, offering enough hint of cleavage for him to admire, but not worry about others admiring too much.

"With any luck," Kyr said, "I'll only be gone for a few months, four or five at most."

"That's almost half a year."

"Almost."

She ran her hands along his arms, up the sleeves of his gray arming doublet. "I hoped something would have changed. That someone would have found them already, and you wouldn't have to leave."

"Me too," he admitted. "But even without two fugitives to apprehend, this is probably for the best."

Eselle's face twisted in a perfect blending of confusion and anger.

"Neither of us is doing very well with keeping our distance." He reluctantly released her and stepped back. "This will help with that."

Clasping her hands before her, Eselle appeared thoughtful. A hint of frustration flashed across her features, but her eyes softened quickly. "On the bright side, figuring out a way around all the royal courting and marriage laws will give me something to do in my downtime."

He chuckled deeply. "I can't tell if you're more optimistic or relentless."

A brow rose. "Both."

Kyr stepped closer. "If it weren't so inappropriate, I'd suggest you come with me."

When he reached her, Eselle slipped her arms around his waist. "Even being inappropriate, I'm tempted."

Leaning in, he rested his forehead against hers. "May the Protector help me, I'm not ready to give you up either."

***

Standing near the stables, Eselle and Cristar watched Kyr secure a pack on his large black warhorse.

Once done, he stepped to the side to speak with Josah and Maksin. Both men had visited Kyr several times during his recovery. The three stood out of earshot. Though Eselle didn't know Josah Ilkin well, she was pleased he'd been kept on as a captain.

Josah and Maksin said their goodbyes, then left the courtyard with somber expressions.

"Are you ready?" Eselle asked as Kyr approached.

"As I'll ever be."

Cristar leaned in and pulled him down for a hug. He held tight and closed his eyes, not letting her go for a long moment.

"I'll miss you." Kyr gave one last squeeze and released Cristar. He kissed her cheek before she stepped back.

"I'll miss you too." She patted his cheek, then put her hand over his chest. "Take care of yourself out there. I know you're a big, tough soldier and all, and it's ridiculous to worry, but I do. So be careful."

He gave her a fond smile. "I hate that you'll worry, but I also love that you do."

She nodded and stepped back.

Not for the first time since they'd arrived at the stable, Kyr took in Eselle's dress. It was a simple cut in blue silk, but the white sash at her waist added shape. His eyes lingered on the curves it created, exactly as Eselle had hoped they would. Still, she blushed, but didn't cover herself with the shawl around her elbows.

She reached up and put her hand along his jaw. "Take care of yourself, especially in Borthal. I've heard Pasdar's capital can be a rough place. And don't be gone too long." She leaned up and kissed him.

Eselle planned for it to be simple and quick, but when their lips touched, he reached a hand into her hair and held her close as he deepened the kiss. She made no complaint and eased into him, a warm tingle spreading through her at the feel of him pressed close. When he broke after a moment, she mourned the loss but stepped back. There were people watching, after all, including his mother, who averted her gaze with a faint smile.

Despite her best efforts, Eselle blushed. Kyr gave the playful smile she'd always loved. She wished things were different so she could see more of it.

Kyr kissed each of the women's foreheads, then walked to his horse. His limp had improved, but Eselle suspected he would never be completely rid of it. There'd been too much damage.

She watched as he put his foot in the stirrup, took a deep breath, then hauled himself onto his horse. She winced at the sight of his pained expression. Once in the saddle, he massaged his scarred thigh. His tight features slowly eased. With a final wave, he maneuvered his stallion toward the gate, where three other soldiers fell in line behind him.

Cristar stepped closer and put her arm around Eselle, whether for comfort or seeking it, Eselle wasn't sure, but she leaned into it. Wrapping her own arm around Cristar's waist, she rested her head on her friend's shoulder. What Cristar planned for the future, whether she went back to Eddington or remained to await her son's return, was undecided. Eselle hoped she would stay, but whatever the choice, she was grateful for any time they had left.

Eselle and Cristar watched until Kyr took the final turn at the end of the zwinger and passed out of sight, and out of Vistralou Castle.

EPILOGUE

Rietser mounted the waiting horse and headed to the cavern opening. He gazed around the city one last time. It would be a long time before he returned to Scalcier. Though he'd grown up here and it really wasn't necessary, he scanned everything, memorizing it before he left. The cavern walls that rose to the opening where the roof collapsed centuries ago, revealing the clear blue sky above. The artfully crafted wooden buildings that always made him feel welcomed. The waterfall cascading over the northern cliff as it flowed down from the mountains.

He hated to leave. But it was time.

After crossing through the cavern entrance, he navigated the rock field that stretched hundreds of paces out from the city. He followed the rough trail until he reached the end and found his traveling companion waiting for him.

Gilstin Harvil had been selected to represent the Ristarians.

Out of long habit, when Rietser saw a Ristarian soldier mounted beside Harvil, he put a hand on one of the twin crescent blades strapped to his thighs. He immediately forced himself to release it. The war was over, had been for nearly a year now. But a lifetime of war was difficult to put aside.

"Good morning," Harvil said.

Rietser gave a nod. "Good morning."

Harvil indicated the man beside him. "This is Stols. He'll be joining us, assigned for administrative duties. And this is Captain Rietser Viscet of the Jalat military. He's here to represent the Jalat in our negotiations with the Pasdarans."

Stols and Rietser exchanged pleasantries.

"Ready to go?" Harvil asked, glancing between his companions.

Rietser gazed out at the ocean. Its soft blue near shore warmed his soul. Its deeper blue farther out made him smile. It would be many long months inland, and he would miss the ocean nearly as much as his family. Luckily, Pasdar's capital sat on the ocean on the opposite side of Riandor, so he would be able to see an entirely new ocean once they arrived. The thought excited him.

His eyes drifted down the coastline. Beyond the southern hill ahead, out of sight, sat Alya's manor.

Rietser cleared his throat and looked away quickly before memories surfaced.

"I'm long past ready to put this place behind me. Let's see what kind of trouble we can find in Borthal."

Thank you for reading my book!
I hope you enjoyed it. Please add a review on any of
the websites where this book is sold or other book
review sites and let everyone know what you
thought.

Special Thanks

Thank you to everyone who believed in me and helped me along my writing journey, from family and friends to those who helped me fine tune (or entirely rewrite) my book.

Special thanks to my editor, Corrine Nicholson, a real-life Wonder Woman; my cover artist MarcoLax DZ, who captured Eselle so perfectly; all of my beta readers for their honesty; and all of my Scribophile critters for sharing their talent. Without you, this book would still be trapped inside my head.

About the Author

Stephanie Briarton has been weaving fantasy and paranormal stories of adventure and romance for decades. The Riandori Realms series is a culmination of all that daydreaming. Behind a keyboard and walking through the woods are her favorite places to be, especially with her son, Caleb, by her side. Based outside of Atlanta, she dreams about moving into the North Georgia mountains one day. She received a Bachelor of Arts degree in English, with a concentration in Writing and Rhetoric, from Georgia Gwinnett College.

Come say hello and connect with Stephanie on her website or social media.

www.stephaniebriarton.com

www.facebook.com/stephanie.briarton.3

www.instagram.com/stephaniebriarton/

CPSIA information can be obtained
at www.ICGtesting.com
Printed in the USA
LVHW090656120520
PP15873600001B/5